was born in Sydney in 1902. She tra... left Australia for Europe, where ... working from 1930–35 as a secretary in a Paris bank. She went to live in Spain, but left on the outbreak of war and with her husband, the novelist and political economist William Blake, she settled in the USA. From 1943–44 she was an instructor at the Workshop in the Novel at New York University and in 1943 she was Senior Writer for MGM in Hollywood.

Acknowledged as one of the greatest novelists writing in the English language today, Christina Stead's first work of fiction, a collection of stories, *The Salzburg Tales*, was published in 1934. Since then she has published eleven novels: *Seven Poor Men of Sydney* (1934), *The Beauties and Furies* (1936), *House of All Nations* (1938), *The Man Who Loved Children* (1940), *For Love Alone* (1944), *Letty Fox: Her Luck* (1946), *A Little Tea, A Little Chat* (1948), *The People with the Dogs* (1952), *Cotters' England* (1966), *The Little Hotel* (1974) and her most recent novel, *Miss Herbert* (1976). She has also published another collection of stories, *The Puzzleheaded Girl* (1967). In 1947 Christina Stead left America for Europe, settling in England in 1953. She now lives in Australia.

Virago publish *For Love Alone, Letty Fox: Her Luck, A Little Tea, A Little Chat, The People with the Dogs, Cotters' England, Miss Herbert* and a selection from all her great works, *A Christina Stead Reader*. *The Beauties and Furies* and *The Puzzleheaded Girl* will be published in 1982.

CHRISTINA STEAD

The People
With the Dogs

*With a new Introduction
by Judith Kegan Gardiner*

Virago

First British publication
by VIRAGO PRESS Limited 1981
Ely House, 37 Dover Street
London W1X 4HS

First publication USA, 1952
by Little, Brown & Co. Boston

Copyright © Christina Stead 1952

Introduction Copyright © 1981
Judith Kegan Gardiner

Printed in Hong Kong by Colorcraft

British Library Cataloguing in Publication Data
Stead, Christina
  The People with the Dogs. – (Virago modern classic)
  I. Title
  823[F]   PR6919.3.S75
  ISBN 0-86068-177-7

Introduction

The People with the Dogs is Christina Stead's most amiable novel and one of her least appreciated. Based on her experiences in the United States, where she lived with her American husband, the banker and writer William Blake, from 1937 to 1946, it was published in 1952 and completed her series of four novels analysing American mores and sexual politics. Her next novel, *Cotters' England* or *The Dark Places of the Heart*, appeared in 1966. *The People with the Dogs*, then, marks a turning point and a pause in Stead's evolution as a writer.

Stead began her study of the United States with her masterpiece, *The Man who Loved Children* (1940), an autobiographical fiction about her Australian childhood reset in a carefully researched Maryland and Washington, D.C. In the transplantation, she inscribes some insights about the nation into which she married. Sam's egotism, sexism, and personal fascism masquerading as socialism might be found anywhere, yet it is particularly appropriate that he become the "softsoaping", hypocritical Voice of America as the "Uncle Sam" of a radio children's hour. Then, through the heroine of *Letty Fox: Her Luck* (1946), Stead satirised the middle class America of World War II as a restless, faddish nation filled with Freudian nonsense, a sexual "liberation" that allowed both men and women to dominate each other, and a generous, sometimes genuine, political radicalism. However, her guarded optimism in *Letty Fox* boiled away in *A Little Tea, A Little Chat* (1948), Stead's bitter denunciation of American capitalism thriving on war-devastated Europe. Safely back on the continent, away from American Cold War hysteria and anti-communism, Stead sought a more positive note for her next novel. "With *The People with the Dogs* I decided, 'I can't go on criticising'," Stead told an interviewer in 1975. (John B. Beston, "An Interview with Christina Stead", *World Literature Written in English*, 15.1 [April 1976], p.91).

The novel opens like a movie – Stead had worked briefly in Hollywood in 1943 – with a "pan" of lower New York and a narrator who introduces the scene and then disappears. In the opening vignette, a "dumb waiter" stabs his wife in an argument about crowded housing, revealing a tense New York of potentially violent sexual relationships. Against this background we meet the novel's kind, confused hero, Edward Massine, around whom odd people gather like lint on an old suit.

Perhaps Stead's most attractive male character, Edward is the perfect nephew and friend. Home from the war without parents or a profession, unmarried and in his thirties, Edward owns two buildings and listlessly does favours for others while seeking direction for himself. He defines his condition as a state of "undefined hesitant anticipation". Through Edward, the novel explores several types of community. People thrown together by class and chance form one kind of community that was exploited by the "Grand Hotel" movies of the 30s and developed in Stead's *House of All Nations* and *The Little Hotel*. Edward's buildings house an attractive counter-culture of men and women who are actors, artists, emigrés, and political radicals. Often Stead contrasts such "houses" with "home", the catastrophic, claustrophobic life of the nuclear family. "The things people say in families!" Edward marvels. However, in this novel the intensities of the nuclear family are calmed and dissipated into the communal life of the extended family. Edward's rented houses thus recreate the tolerant plenitude of the Massine family summer farm called Whitehouse. Here flourish Edward's aunts and their husbands, children, and dogs, on whom the women lavish their overflowing affection. The chief of these nurturing older women is Edward's Aunt Oneida, and Whitehouse thus echoes the Utopian strain in American socialism, recalling the Oneida community of "Perfectionists" founded in 1848 by John Humphrey Noyes and practising communal property, communal childcare, and "complex marriage".

The country retreat from the striving city, Whitehouse embodies both the negative and the positive aspects of pastoral. It heals the "modern restless nervous man" "in the deep sweet summer cold, sluggish and healthy, like a pool that never stagnates under pinewoods . . ." With its entangling hopvine and uncultivated gardens, it symbolises sloth and oblivion. Yet it is also a place of classical retreat, classical music, and democratic rejuvenation. Edward's grandfather left it to the family, undivided, "under certain conditions; peace, liberty, a roof for everyone, all claims equal". One of his friends tells Edward, "You need abundant multiple life around you like Whitehouse, like the Massines; the perfect still life . . . Fruitfulness with grapes and rabbits . . . and many dogs and dishes and many children and many days". Food and love represent one another throughout Stead's work: this novel simmers with happy eating, with midnight snacks from the Russian delicatessen and filling stews at Whitehouse.

The dogs that romp through the book have more complex narrative functions. Daybreak brings a marvellous, lyric overture to life at Whitehouse as pets and humans awake and call to one another, a scene comparable to the morning of "Sunday a funday" in *The Man who Loved Children*. In another mood, Stead borrows the techniques of 1930s "screwball" film comedies to pile the whole Massine family into a veterinarian's tiny office where they hover over one small sick dog. Sometimes Stead takes a literal, affectionate outsider's look at the mad devotion of pet owners, yet she also uses the dogs to reflect her characters' ideas and human attachments. Oneida's credo is that "a love of dogs makes you understand human beings . . . You *realise* people have their weaknesses and faults but they have their wants too . . ." Yet she knows her "cult of dogs" is a distortion. After one of her favourites dies, she laments, "To live in a community is the way to live . . . I lived for dogs and dogs can die! We must live for others . . ." Soon she has another dog on her lap.

A haven of generosity and decency parallel to Whitehouse but at a lower level in the social scale is a poor boarding house run by two old anarchists. Their lives reflect the same altruistic values as Whitehouse does, but without the lucky Massine concatenation of modest wealth, professional talent, and strong mutual support, their community founders in a hostile society. Music, dogs, food, all fail. The drunken anarchist brother dies saving his dog from a trolley. Then his lonely sister resolves to stop speaking and to starve herself to death. Man to dog, sister to brother, their touching but misguided loyalties parallel their dedication to an outmoded political cause. They had grown up in a time when "the hope and belief in American destiny . . . had resulted . . . in the establishment of these idealists' communities where, it was hoped, purity of principle, absolute equality, freedom and free land, would abolish, reduce or sterilise human weakness and state iniquity". Edward's sympathies, like Stead's, are always with the exploited over the exploiters. He joins a May Day parade by chance and swells with mob emotion, but "it wasn't like the glorious or bloody May Days" of before the war. The Left is splintered into fragments, and Edward can't expect "causes and wretched suffering peoples to save his soul".

By the end of the novel, Edward has emerged from the Oedipal lethargies of Whitehouse and taken the dark voyage into sexual commitment. He ends his long, vague affair with a woman who hurts him and spends a sunlit day with the singer Madame Sarine. She complains that men do not understand the woman artist and only want "a pretty little woman, a trophy". Many of the women in the novel are artists; most of the women work, from the casually promiscuous "Nan-Mann", a department store accountant, to the actress Lydia, who looks like Edward's double and becomes his wife. However, when Edward finally chooses a wife who is an equal, and independence from the warm sleep of Whitehouse, he doesn't lose his family community; rather he earns the right to rejoin it. At his wedding reception, his family harmoniously surrounds the new couple. "In this moment, as in all others, their long habit and innocent, unquestioning and strong, binding, family love, the rule of their family, made all things natural and sociable with them".

Both nostalgic and satiric, *The People with the Dogs* looks back at lost American ideals. As Edward says, Whitehouse celebrates "creative sloth: what life ought to give but it doesn't . . . Why there with a little good will and mutual aid and sensible mild nonchalance, with live and let live, we take vacations from the epoch of wars and revolutions". By this time, Stead had clearly lost her own confidence in the possibility of sterilising "human weakness and state iniquity". This novel takes us on a charming "vacation from the epoch of wars and revolutions" to which Stead returns with bitter force, fourteen years and another country later, in *Cotters' England*.

Judith Kegan Gardiner, Chicago 1980

Part One

EDWARD IN TOWN

IN lower Manhattan, between 17th and 15th Streets, Second Avenue, running north and south, cuts through Stuyvesant Park; and at this point Second Avenue enters upon the old Lower East Side. The island here is broad between the two rivers and heavily trafficked, north-south, east-west. Here, Third Avenue up to 18th Street is still the Old Bowery, with small rented bedrooms and apartments like ratholes, cheap overnight hotels, flophouses, ginmills, fish places, bowling alleys, instant shoe repairers, moneylenders, secondhand clothing stores, struggling cleaning and tailors' places, barber schools, cellars where some old man or woman sells flowers and ice in summer, coal in winter, dance academies up crumbling stairs, accordion and saxophone schools and such businesses as are carried on for very poor people by very poor people and so occupy a very small space in a very old building. It is the last of gaslight New York. If the great iron structure of the "L" were torn down, people would gape at a tottering double line of two-story buildings, of frame and brick, unpainted, defaced with weathered advertisements and dusty windows. Third Avenue sweeps far uptown: it is never grand and never handsome, always the address of the poor. However, a lot of people have got used to it, they like it, just because there is no longer any other place like it in the city. But no one ever gets used to the crashing roar of the trains, especially at rush hours, and people living or working on the Avenue or even two doors from it on either side have a haunted, agonized air, or else they doze too much or drink too much bad beer. They say that there are any number of suicides, broken homes and nervous ailments on Third Avenue. Anyone who has lived thereabouts is accustomed to the sobbing, howling, shouting at night of the men and women turned out by the liquor places. The liquor is bad and the people are poor. Sometimes the unfortunates sound as if they are dying, at other times they argue grandiloquently with things and persons in the streets of two A.M. where no one is. On the east at 20th Street and below is a district of hospitals: injured and sick people, and their relatives or eventual mourners, pass to and fro. There are plenty of old people, male and female, roaming round with bent backs and bad skins. There are desperate or suspicious-looking people wandering about the sidewalks at any hour.

At the same time, it is a home district and, especially through 14th Street and 23rd Street, which bound this district, pass, at five and six, thousands and thousands of young workers hurrying home, and school children. A few streets below is New York University and nearby are clinics, gasworks, heavy traffic and lofts. There are a number of big squares, where girls sit at their lunches and mothers with babies come in the morning and afternoon. Thousands of white-collar employees pour out from the only tower skyscraper in this area, the Consolidated Edison Building, and fill little lunchrooms and the parks at midday. This skyscraper's huge stone pinnacle, with its clocks, lantern, painted top and mesh of dazzling windows at night, is a solitary spire standing between the herded peaks of the Wall Street range and the uptown massif. It dominates a mile of two- to four-story buildings of this area, slums, brownstone houses, shacks from Civil War days. It hangs its lantern high over living quarters, now mostly converted to lodginghouses and the like.

In this quarter, almost at the foot of this man-created peak which has its own winds and icefalls, Edward Massine, a young New Yorker, owned two adjoining brownstone houses in a street just off Stuyvesant Park, spent his first years in a house on 19th Street East,

[4]

lived then in one of those two houses on 18th Street which he inherited from his parents. He had been to school at the Stuyvesant High School on 16th Street and spent a great deal of his time at the homes of relatives living on 14th Street East and nearby. He disliked taking the subway, bus or trolley car and he never left Manhattan Island if he could help it. He walked everywhere for miles and sometimes arrived a little late and weary but when he walked, the district he reached seemed to be an extension of the few streets in which he had been born, lived, and in which, for the present, he intended to die. He had a joke, that he would probably be killed crossing Second Avenue, between 16th and 15th Streets on his way to visit someone at Beth Israel Hospital.

On Easter Saturday morning, just after the war, Miss Waldmeyer, an estate agent, friend of Edward's, was walking slowly round this district under Consolidated Edison's huge stone pinnacle. Her office was in 9th Street. The plate-glass window was dusty and inside it on a bench were two rubber plants. There were modern glass partitions, wash drawings of houses, prints of Old New York, attractive furniture; but all this had become grimy and stood about in disorder. In the window there had been for several years a homemade notice:

> PLEASE *do not ask us for apartments. We have none. If there were any we would know of them. We have been here for forty years. Inscribe yourself on our waiting list. This is the best we can do. Sorry.* WALDMEYER AND LAMBKIN.

Miss Waldmeyer did not expect her friend Edward to be up before eleven and she had started out at nine-thirty to take a walk. She was excessively fat, a stub tub. Her waist stood in line with her plump shoulders and bosom. She wore a new Easter dress of flowered silk with a narrow belt. Miss Waldmeyer was rosy-faced, short-nosed and wore a new flowered hat and new red shoes. She never took a step without business in view, and she could not stop eating. She said to herself, puffing as she ate, I am nearly fifty; eating is my only pleasure. My dressmaker can easily let out my belt: why should I

[5]

make myself miserable for the fashion? However, a few years before when there had been apartments to let, Miss Waldmeyer had been a gay, chubby woman. There were few elevators in this area. She had run up and down staircases, inspecting and letting studios, apartments, penthouses, basements. Now the only way to get a new apartment was to walk round looking over the houses. Once she had discovered a place to let by noticing that a woman was taking down rather clean curtains. She walked now, quickly, looking over the small buildings and apartment houses. She knew very many of the houses in every detail from basement to roof, and the family situation of many of the tenants.

Moving day, for example, she was always out on the streets: but there was little moving now. Gone were the old New York days when everybody thought it his duty to himself to seek a new apartment in the beginning of October each year. Population of dreamers. At that time a man rising in business paid a little more each year for apartments for his own family and for his mother and father: families were deeply ashamed if forced to seek lower rents. Women said in stores, casually, "Where are you moving to this year?"

On the last of September and the first of October, before the war, the streets of New York and adjacent counties were choked with immense moving vans, and the sidewalks choked with the inner life of apartments, their bedding, rickety bookshelves, gate-leg tables, lame floor lamps. The beautiful apartments which had shed light on the night air and looked so dignified with lamps, curtains, pastel-shaded walls, small pictures, suddenly showed their seamy side — laundry-baskets, baby cots, pots and pans. And while the goods of one family about to quit, abandon and insult this apartment stood on the sidewalk and slowly were eaten up by the van, the goods of the next family, eager, anxious, in love with this apartment, would arrive and the moving van would slowly disgorge onto the sidewalk goods which seemed almost the same; these would gradually go up

[6]

the stairs and once more the lamps would go on and one would see the same pictures, lamps and curtains.

But what difference did that make? The principal thing was to move: that showed one had money to move, and taste too; one was not satisfied with conditions. However, since the war and the housing crisis, the chief thing was to have an apartment at all, and the worst and darkest holes were now prizes . . . and no one moved except for death, or going to Mishawaka, Indiana, for a good job, or to Hollywood. The best one can say of a New Yorker nowadays, is he has somewhere to lay his head. This is why Miss Waldmeyer was so fat and why she took this walk on Easter Saturday and why she was going to see Edward Massine.

Just before eleven Miss Waldmeyer turned towards the short street in which were her client's two houses and she presently was walking through the western half of Stuyvesant Park. She did not see the children, the old men, the Third Avenue strays, the sandpit, nor look at the fat, greasy buds on the trees: she did not see the pale green leaves on the Ginkgos on that street. She was thinking, Edward had had exceptional luck, you might say. After his mother died, his father, who did not seem to bother about life after his wife's death, and so died, left two houses to Edward. A small amount in the estate had been applied to reconditioning the houses. Having no ambition, when his parents died Edward had left college and had no extra expenses. The two houses which came to Edward from his parents are his own. Edward inherited his father's vote in the Massine family council which controls the Massine family estate; and his father's share in all their property, cash, house or land, when and where divided. Edward inherited the houses in good condition. There were second mortgages on both. At a time when money was cheap, the father, Dr. Edward Massine had been paying as much as 6 per cent on that one house, 5½ per cent on the other. One first mortgage was due in two years and there were only the rents, almost no cash in the bank at all. I induced Edward to reconvert the mortgages on the first house at the bank. The other fell due later. By that time the war had come, and Edward, after receiving good money as a mechanic on precision instruments, was called to the army and soon worked his way up to top sergeant's pay. He saved it, nearly all. Miss Waldmeyer surveyed windows and continued to meditate: the tenants he has are people chosen through the years by me, an artistic kind of people, with incomes or big paying jobs, people who can look after themselves, are glad to be left alone, never complain and always pay; and are friends into the bargain. That is Edward's own stipulation, "The people in my houses must be friends." During the war, Edward, on my advice, sold that farm upstate and with this and other things, one house is now clear and the other one has a long-term first mortgage at 3½ per cent. He can improve the first house at any time, put in a fire escape; by getting a new mortgage, even fix up the partition wall. But no need for that yet. . . . I had an offer for the first house this week, at thirty-three thousand dollars, a bit above its real value, and for both, sixty thousand. He probably made a mistake in turning it down. Still he might sell one. In any case there are two possibilities for apartments in his houses. In the other house, on the top floor there is Dr. Pilsener's laboratory for cats and dogs. In Edward's house there is the unoccupied front basement. Dr. Pilsener knows he has a great bargain there, prewar rents. Edward, personally, is a very tractable landlord. He has no need to occupy so much space for himself. If we could get Dr. Pilsener to move, get the basement ready, have Edward move to smaller quarters elsewhere, I could fit in from three to four new tenants and get a bonus from each. But to move into any roomy apartment, suitable for himself, Edward would have to pay a premium of at least five hundred dollars. Skip it, for the moment. There remains the basement in the second house where Edward himself lives. Now the fourth floor is interesting. It has a separate room at the head of the stairs which could easily be let as a separate hall bedroom except that the person using it would have to use either the bathroom in the apartment, or that on the next floor. The ground floor is satisfactory. The former two principal rooms with consulting room or library in the center have been converted into a fine apartment, with bathroom and kitchen in the middle. Since the war we have put in a new staircase leading into the garden and put grilles over the basement entrance at the back. It is by far the best apartment in the two houses and one of the best I have on my list. Several separate rooms for rent could be made out of that, perhaps . . . Well, let us come to the basement rooms.

There the cat's room is the front room. It's a room with a washbasin and toilet in a closet. This can be entered through French doors from the street. Then the basement, reached by the stairs. The back room has steps, now cut off, to the garden, and so has the kitchen. In short, the basement can be cut up any way, there are entrances everywhere. At the moment, we have two living rooms, full kitchen and washroom. We could install a bath in the kitchen, make a kitchenette.

The house is paying for itself and Edward has his roof over his head as he says, but the house could bring in more. Would it pay him to put in a fire escape? That is the stumbling block. We'll talk it over.

Miss Waldmeyer, walking slow and solid, had been for some time behind a quarreling couple in the park, the man about forty, thin and with the careful shuffle of an old waiter. The girl walked a little in front of and aside from him. She was perhaps about twenty-eight, with black hair loose on her shoulders, a worn dark blue suit and high heels. Miss Waldmeyer suddenly heard the words:

"I have a place for you to live."

"I'm not going to live behind a curtain in the same room as your old people. I don't want you coming after me, trying to see me. I'm making my own living. Leave me alone."

"You told me to do something about it, I did something about it."

"Finally, no. Leave off bothering me."

"Where are you living?"

The girl walked rapidly away through the park gates across the street and onto the sidewalk that led to Edward's house. Miss Waldmeyer crossed the street. The man came out of the park gate, shouted, started to run and caught up with the girl. She turned and shook off his hand and Miss Waldmeyer could see a pale girl, with orange-red lips, blazing with anger. The man clutched her arm, argued and she shook her head without answering, pulled away from him. The man, bent, pulled something from his coat, struck at her chest. The girl yelled and fell to the asphalt and almost at once the blood started from her breast and flowed over her side. The orange lips, the falling and the flowing were the only things that Miss Waldmeyer saw clearly. Halfway up the street a woman shaking a mop leaned out of the window, the mop stiff. A man ran round the corner of the street and people ran out of the park. The waiter, in his shuffling run, had gone round another corner and already people were crowding out the victim. The blood ran between their feet and they drew apart. Miss Waldmeyer saw Edward's house and a man hurrying past her said:

"There's a doctor up the street there. Dr. Massine."

"Oh, he's dead. Go and tell the druggist at the corner," Miss Waldmeyer advised. She called after him to tell him that there were three doctors in the parallel street when she heard the ambulance bell. She had reached Edward's house in the middle of the street.

The front door, just painted green, stood open and Nate the Croat, the family house painter for all the Massines for many years, stood beside the medical nameplate urging two carriers not to scratch the paint. He himself owned a house on that street. In front of the house was a truck, half full of folding chairs and light scaffoldings and stagings. The front hall was choked with folding chairs; heavy planks stood on end against a chiffonier behind the front door. A white wall with doors, all newly painted, ran along the corridor and from it rose a long flight of stairs against a dingy high wall with niches for statuary. The stairs were carpeted, turned neatly at the top and were lighted from a skylight on the top floor. The door at the back was open and in it stood a tall, strong young woman, who was now in a brusque contralto voice urging the carriers to take some things upstairs. No, they would not. They were only allowed to deliver to the hall, they said. At the foot of the stairs was a small heavy press. Miss Waldmeyer said:

"Hello, Miss Holland, how do I navigate?"

"What was all that shouting, Waldie?"

"A man stabbed his wife, I guess it was his wife."

"Why?"

"No place to go, it seemed like. No apartment."

"Poor devils."

"How do you like that?" said one of the men.

"Are you giving a show?" Miss Waldmeyer asked Miss Holland.

"Yes, my Easter show, upstairs, in the studio, tomorrow. Come."

"Thanks, but I won't. I'll lie in bed. Is Edward about?"

"He's still in bed, I think."

There was some skirmishing while the men got out more of the chairs and Miss Waldmeyer tried to squeeze herself behind the door to let them pass. Nate the Croat prevented them from scratching the door. Miss Waldmeyer was pressed over a small Japanese table decorated with a bead plant in a china pot. Just above her in the niche in the rising wall were a bronze slave boy holding up a lamp, and a large Chinese vase.

"Are you painting the whole house, Nate?"

"The Doc is going to tell me today."

"Are you doing the basement?"

"He didn't mention it."

"What's this thing?"

Miss Holland answered, "That's a silk-screen press, the men wouldn't carry upstairs. I shall have to take it up myself."

One of the carriers, who was bringing in chairs, said, "You better watch your step, Missus. It weighs two hundred pounds. I had my side strapped up the whole summer last year, four months."

Miss Holland looked at him and it calmly. She was tall, very stout and strong, with bobbed hair, a thick white neck. She went into the back room. Through the doorway showed a blue carpet and clear sunlight coming through the French windows at the back. White silk curtains puffed into the room. On the carpet were a ginger buck rabbit with a stuffed-out shirt front, a long smoky cat. On one side was a small organ and a painted blanket chest. The lid of this chest was open showing a quantity of colored stuffs rolled up in bolts inside and a piece of rose cotton which boiled out into the room.

Miss Waldmeyer said to Nate the Croat, "Mrs. Annichini has two naval lieutenants with their families waiting for that long room with the sleeping alcove, you know, the one with the mirror? It's a shame to have Edward's front basement room occupied by a cat."

Nate the Croat looked at the stairs down which was crawling an uncommonly large black and white tomcat. His large green eyes were apparently outlined with kohl. This was Westfourth, Edward's cat. On his neck was a decayed leather collar with a silver plate; and on this was engraved *Massine, West 4th Street*.

"Hello, Westfourth."

The cat stopped, stared and meowed.

Nate the Croat said, "He's had three breakfasts upstairs and now he's coming down for a bit of my lunch."

"I never get over how beautiful Westfourth is, and I don't like cats," said Miss Waldmeyer.

"There's an army of cats round this district look a lot like Westfourth; that one in the Rectory garden."

The cat was sneaking through the chairs and they heard him bounce down the basement stairs. The phone rang at the head of the stairs. A dog barked.

"There's Musty. Edward must be awake."

Miss Waldmeyer edged between the silk-screen press and the wall and craned her neck. There could just be seen a line of half-glazed partition and folding doors. It was dark inside.

"I'll wait a bit. Do you want to come down to the basement with me, Nate? You're going to paint for Mrs. Annichini next week?"

"Yep, I'm painting for Mrs. Annie. I'll be down."

At a quarter to twelve, Miss Waldmeyer went out and called upstairs, "Edward! Edward! Hey, Doc!"

There was no answer. Nate said to Miss Holland, "I'll give you a hand with these chairs and get them out of the way."

"Come and see the Witch, Nate," said Miss Holland.

They went into the front room and minutely admired three puppets of about thirty-four inches in height. The three puppets represented the Witch Macka Shayfer; the first was merely a gray and flame-colored puff of gauze with a nose in the center, the second was a head and arms without body, in a flimsy dress, and the third was the witch entire, not yet dressed. The body was made of a head with a rolling, lantern eye, limbs and a very mobile body composed of wood, rubber sponge and cork, an original design by Miss Holland. Edward had arranged the trick lantern eye and wired it. He had also done the wiring, lights and control board for the stage. It was now past twelve o'clock.

"I'll go up and knock," said Miss Waldmeyer.

"I'll take the press up and then we can clear the passageway," said Miss Holland.

The old painter waded to the partition door at the head of the stairs, opened it gently and put his head inside. It was quite dark. He could see nothing. Suddenly he felt a little dog dancing at his legs.

"Musty, old boy. Hey, Doc!"

The little dog barked. On the bed was a young man's dark head.

"Shut up, Musty! O.K., Nate, let the poor bastard go out."

"Edward, there's a lady to see you, Miss Waldmeyer."

[13]

"Tell her to come up."

A big van went past the house, which shook. Edward's room was protected by the thick walls of old houses round him but he could hear the roar of the rush-hour expresses.

"She's been here an hour already. She wants you to paint the basement."

"O.K."

There was a very heavy slow tread on the stairs; and from the studio opposite on the same floor, a sound of hammering. The voice of a puppeteer cried out, "The puppet must never leave the floor."

"O.K., Nate, thanks."

Nate the Croat closed the door.

Edward was a good sleeper. He had come to the surface several times during the morning and heard the house sounding with heavy weights, thumps, men's voices and on the same floor, backstage sounds; he heard Musty's snuffling and scratching. The curtains, long, blue, with soiled white linings, swayed into the room with a walking motion and let in warm air and sun, exclamations and whistling. Westfourth meowed. The partition moved faintly. The unlocked door shuffled and Musty whined. He heard Nate the Croat and the men at the front door. Doors and windows were open all over the house. His tenants lived on five floors in a sort of free communal spirit, there were no cantankerous or suspicious souls among them. Rarely the telephone rang. His own phone stood on the bedside table but the receiver was off the hook all night. Occasionally, faint scratches and clicks came through it. Edward slept. At some time in the late morning Nate the Croat opened the door and stuck his head in. "Take the poor bastard out," droned Edward. Someone was bringing a monstrous weight upstairs.

Edward lay on his back with his cheek poked into the pillow and tried to doze again. He had an effective method for getting to sleep. It was to piece together names, faces, backgrounds, times of day, temperatures and seasons, tones of voice, things that had been said to him that had caused him emotion. He tried to form an idea of any given person's character, temperament. Edward was very short-sighted and had for some years developed his memory for sounds and other nonvisual sensations. If wrong, he became a little sour or angry. He would then say:

"I'll be a testy old gentleman of forty!"

He was now thirty-three.

Edward had just taken a fresh plunge into the gulf when he heard *Edward, Edward,* in Miss Waldmeyer's voice and again *Edward, Edward,* in Miss Allison's voice upstairs. Something extraordinary was coming upstairs, a heavy foot put down on one step and then, a long time after, another stump on the next step. Someone groaned. At this moment Miss Allison ran downstairs and knocked at his door.

"Come in!"

She put her head and shoulders round the door; light haloed her fair hair and he saw the glint of her glasses.

"Your aunt Mrs. Solway rang to say she couldn't get you on the phone and not to forget the appointment with the veterinary this afternoon."

"O.K."

He put his head back on the pillow.

"Mr. Edward?"

"Come in, Miss Allison."

This time she stood about a yard away from the man in the dark on the bed. "Miss Waldmeyer is here to see you about the basement room."

"Yell out to her to come upstairs, will you?"

"Miss Rossi rang me to say she couldn't get you on the phone. She wants to know if you're going over there today."

"H'm."

Miss Allison laughed and went out, leaving the door half open.

The heavy tread reached the landing and there was a great bump with a creak of timbers.

"What's that?"

He raised his head and peered. Miss Holland was leaning against the press breathing heavily.

"Jesus! You didn't bring that press upstairs yourself?"

The strong woman looked over the stairs and said in a muffled voice, "Come on, you can come up now."

Edward said, "Leave it there a minute. I'll put something on. Say, you're crazy, you'll break something."

"The men wouldn't do it."

Miss Waldmeyer appeared at the door, moved in, stood by his bedside. "Are you getting up? I want to talk to you about the basement room. I went down with Nate. He says he can do up the whole place now if you want it done. He's going to Mrs. Annichini next week and your uncle Jonathan the week after."

"Sling me that bathrobe. What's the time, anyhow?"

"After twelve."

"I thought I was getting hungry."

There was an immense whistling, a sighing as of cordage and they saw Miss Holland, with the press, slowly stagger past. He put his feet into his slippers and went out to help her, saying sorrowfully, "Jesus, Holland, you'll kill yourself."

They lowered the press into a corner.

"It weighs two hundred pounds and I weigh a bit over two hundred, I have the advantage."

"A-ah, Holland, a-ah, no, no — you shouldn't do it. You're a woman."

"I'm a sort of a woman," she said, smiling slightly. She sat down in one of the carved Gothic seats on the landing and panted. She drew some deep breaths. "You never saw me wrestle, I've wrestled against men."

She had a broad full forehead, blue eyes in deep sockets with full lids. Her skin held the light. She was very blond with thick hair which flung itself round her face and neck as she moved, in skeins. She was faintly flushed now; her fine eyes shone with exertion, but they were bloodshot, dark-circled; and the nose folds were pinched with fatigue.

The floor on which they were was high-ceilinged and was one vast drawing room divided into three parts, by means of two glazed partitions with folding doors. The steep, graceful staircase lighted by the *œil-de-bœuf* in the roof rose against another high-niched wall.

He returned to his room. A strange young girl with an intense empty face came and held both sides of the doorway while she looked into the room and asked for a tieback, a light chain, a rope.

"Have you got one, Edward? We need one to tie the chandelier back. It hangs right over the stage."

He looked round, yawned, shook a slipper from his foot. "There is a chain somewhere — yes — over there. And a rope upstairs under the mantel."

The young woman took a few steps into the room. He asked over his shoulder, "Are you a puppeteer?"

"I help along. Everyone calls you Edward. I hope you don't mind."

He pointed with his foot to a corner of the room. The young woman went towards it, picking her way, asking, "Here?"

Edward pulled the curtains wide apart. High bookcases stood along the walls and a large double desk crossed one corner. There was a white marble mantelpiece. A secretary, armchairs, a settee, small tables. Books, papers, letters, files covered all the flat surfaces. The mantelpiece and tops of the bookcases were crowded with family relics, vases, medicine bottles, jars by the hundred, of all sizes, shapes and colors, containing fluids, powders; and there were pillboxes and a stethoscope case. On the mantelpiece in the midst of all this stood two beautiful twisted candlesticks in silver holding three candles each. Six or seven of Edward's suits hung about a bookcase on wire hangers. His shoes and a number of socks were in one corner on the carpet and two socks hung from the chandelier where a friend had thrown them one day for a joke "to complete the picture." On the floor were parts of Edward's clothing and a great number of newspapers, dated over several months, as well as some piles of old radiology journals, and several sets of bound works. Some old clothes ready for the wash were stuffed in the unused grate and in front of the grate was a set of large ornamental firedogs, with an old valise in between. Edward's divan bed stood towards the door. On the floor could be partly seen a fine old rose carpet, very dusty. Between the bed and the door was a dog's box, dome-shaped, with a little wicket.

Edward came over and poked about with his foot in a pile of things near the hearth, saying, "Somewhere here."

He murmured, "I must have done something with it. Here, this is strong."

He took the girdle off his bathrobe and handed it to the girl. She laughed. He took a pin out of a piece of flannel on the mantelpiece and fastened his gown and went to the window, looked out. In the yard opposite was a baby boy in a baby carriage. He was a magnificent black-eyed child, now lying on his back with his fists raised above his head. Occasionally he tried to grasp, with uncommon determination, the shadows of the new shoots on the Chinese plantain which grew up the wall. A flight of steps led from Miss Holland's rooms into the yard and there sat Westfourth washing his whiskers after eating some of Nate's lunch. Nate was painting a bit of lattice green. On one side of the steps was Musty sniffing and barking through the basement grating at the basement dog, Charlie. Charlie was a large black old man of mixed breeds but mostly Newfoundland. He whined through the roof bars of his prison.

The yard was not more than forty feet long and twenty wide. It was paved with cobbles and flags, with a stone urn in the middle. A few flags had been taken up at the end of the yard, for the cats and dogs. A cat was treading the fences toward Westfourth. The house on the left occupied the same space and was built in the same way. Facing him were the backs of five or six old buildings used as flophouses and rooming houses. The view was ornamented by light iron balconies, fire escapes, old trees, a privet hedge, some bushes, a kitten, a child running out of a laundry, a washtub, some grass plots, a flowering vine. The whole scene was that of an unpretentious suburb and had an air of sunny quiet and no struggle, even though the trains ground and shrieked a few yards away, and in the high sky Consolidated Edison's tower rose immediately to the right. Edward's room was low in the mass of buildings; but it trembled with the rattling girders and wheels. He heard birds singing, the scratching of the plantain twigs of tremendous growth, the baby's unintelligible remarks. In the stone urn the girls downstairs had planted a fir top with cones, from last Christmas, gilded and silvered. Edward's newspapers fluttered and he closed the slit of window. The sun and shadow of the tree fell on the dusty windowpanes. He put the receiver back on the cradle. Immediately, the telephone rang. Edward threw himself across the bed, took up the receiver and supported his arm with the pillow. It was his girl, Margot Rossi. He talked lazily into the phone, yawned, was dryly, impertinently, drolly caressing. She had been up early, gone to confession, taken a walk, done her shopping. She expected him for dinner that evening. She scolded him for yesterday's neglect. She asked him to come right over.

"I have to go with Oneida to the vet. He's operating on Madame X today."

Madame X was his aunt's French bull terrier bitch, one of the oldest dogs in the family; nearly thirteen. He continued, "You know what it means to Oneida."

He ended by saying that he would telephone her after the visit to the vet's and if the dog was all right he'd come over for supper. If the dog died, he could not see her at all that night; or at least until early morning.

Edward, still in the same attitude, telephoned several people. The door blew gently open. The light from the window lay on a broad beam of dust. The pleasant smell of the familiar dust and his naked-ness in a dressing gown so old it felt like silk, made him dreamy. A bottle of London gin and one of rye whiskey with two unwashed and dusty glasses stood on the middle table and the sun shone through. His mouth was scorched with too much smoking. Edward put down the telephone and tried to recall the exact words of the conversations. He said to himself, "I would make such a damned good witness that they would take me for the murderer. What hap-pened on the night of June seventeenth? That would make a good play."

He was hungry. He had a slight headache. Behind him stretched the perfect life of sleep; and now he had various irritating little things to do. He felt disgusted and bored. He was a very kind man, and had a hundred things to do for friends, but no interesting project for himself. He put out his hand, caught hold of his drawers which were lying on the bed and was pulling them on, when someone called him from the lower hall.

"Dr. Massine! Herbert's. Herbert's Market!"

Someone looked down the stairs. The butcher said:

"Two chickens for the doctor."

Edward plunged off the bed, ran to the stairs and looked down, "Hey, Chubb! Give them to Miss Holland."

"O.K., Doc."

Chubb was a tall strong man with black mustaches and bright brown eyes. He wore a long white apron and had a stiff gray hat on. He always wore this, even into the icebox. Edward grinned.

"Been to the numbers yet, Chubb?"

"Sure have, Doc. I made forty-five bucks. Car loadings came out seven-four-three. That made you seven bucks."

"Come up and have a quick one."

"Thanks, Doc."

At this moment Miss Waldmeyer called up from the basement stairs.

"Jesus Christ! Forgot about you, Waldmeyer. Can you wait one minute? Come up and have a drink with Chubb."

"No thanks. Make it snappy, Edward. I've got to get back."

Mr. Chubb came into Edward's room, took a look round and asked:

"Are you moving?"

"No, I like it this way."

"Is it always like this?"

"I have a girl comes in once a week."

"You want to get married, Edward."

"Maybe you're right. I'll try it some day."

"You do that. Well, chin-chin. When are you coming to see the wife and me?"

"I've never been in the Bronx in my life."

Mr. Chubb clapped him on the back, tossed off his whiskey and went. Edward put on his dressing gown and went downstairs. Miss Waldmeyer, looking up from the basement hallway, saw Edward's bare feet, bare legs and his woolly chest bare as he came down.

"You have nice legs."

Edward kept on down, nonchalantly. He remarked, "I bought an old suit from my cousin, Rex. He put on weight since he left the army. Result of getting married. I'm still the same."

"Was it the gray check you had on the other day?"

"Where was I?"

"Crossing Union Square."

"Where was I going? To Oneida's or to Margot's?"

"To Miss Rossi's."

He thought for a moment, then, "Yes, about half-past two. It was a cold day. That's a warm material. Why? Didn't you like it?"

"It's not your style so much. That's what surprised me. I thought you were maybe going to get married, with a new suit."

[21]

He went into the room with her, saying, "Well, I thought of getting married when I went to Italy, but I didn't know what to do about the houses; and I used my pay for the houses. I'll never be without regular work again if I can help it. The army taught me the pleasures of payday. Maybe you know a regular job with work about two or three hours a day paying about a hundred a week?"

"I'll keep it in mind. It's a shame to let a cat occupy this room."

"I have a friend, Al Burrows, who comes here nights, when he works late. He lives in Far Rockaway. He's a pharmacist and the union meets after the stores close. They go on till four in the morning. Then he has to open the store at eight. He flops here."

There was not much light in the room which was entirely below street level.

"He uses the downstairs door?"

"No, it's locked. He comes in the front door. I don't think the people on the top floor use that spare room. Perhaps I can arrange for him to flop there. Otherwise, he has to go to a Turkish bath. The room is a junk room for the rest of the house."

"Some people might be afraid of that basement entrance: but we can't block up the French windows. We can have a safety lock put on the basement hall door. You will have two exits to the garden. Here are two rooms with kitchens and washbasins and I have hundreds of people on my waiting list."

"I don't mind picking up some loose change, but I'm not a scarcity-hog. I told Mrs. Annichini to stay in the back until her new houses get fixed up. If I can fix it for my pharmacist friend to flop upstairs, O.K., for this one. We'll clean it up anyway."

"Put bars outside this French door and you're all right."

"I don't like the look of bars."

"But you're just off Third Avenue. Put in a couple of floor lamps and some curtains. People would take it now, just as it is, but you don't want a flophouse."

"Things that might have been said otherwise."

They laughed. Then Edward looked round and said, "I don't know why I'm stalling. It's true people need homes, too."

"Yes."

"If Miss Holland takes two whole floors, and I'm upstairs, we could fix up here and give the fire-escape angle a miss. Maybe."

"Mull it over. That missionary wants to put those Formosans here."

"Yeah, I'll mull. But don't let's do anything before fall."

"There's a chance of the two houses next to Mrs. Annichini's new ones being on the market and she wants you to buy next to her.

"I can sell these any time. I've got buyers every week. They can't get apartments: everyone's going in for houses. People are afraid of the boom. A lot of them are going back to real estate. Come over to my office next week."

"I'll do that, Waldie."

They stood looking for a long moment at the bed in the corner. It was an iron bedstead, with a thin mattress and Edward's army blankets on it. Across these had been thrown a strip of thin blanket on which was a large round black smudge. When the pharmacist came he lifted this off the bed and when he went he put it back on the bed. Westfourth slept in the neighbor's coalhole or on coal sacks next to the boiler. When he got too hot, he retired to his own bed here. Edward ended by saying:

"I can fix Al up anywhere. He can sleep in a cot in my room if he's stuck. No one will notice the difference. Yeah, I'll tell Nate to paint."

"Good."

Miss Waldmeyer was pleased. Before she went out, she took the book which she had been carrying under her arm all morning and, showing it to Edward, said, "Why don't you write a book like that? This man Taylor Caldwell makes money, and he does good too. He turns out one best seller after another."

"He's a lady," said Edward dreamily.

She seemed disconcerted. "No, no."

"Sure! Why don't you write one, Waldie?"

He laughed.

"You're full of ideas, Edward, and you have the same ideas as this author."

"O.K. I'll call in my secretary and dash one off tomorrow."

"You ought to do something serious in life, Edward."

"What's *Life,* ten cents," he said.

"Well, so long."

"I'll be seeing you."

Edward looked at various things, the two ironing boards, the sleeveboard, a broken bicycle, some gallon jars in which he made wine, with the help of Nate the Croat.

Mrs. Annichini saw him through the glass panels. She quickly opened the door.

"Edward, my dear boy! Come and have a cup of coffee. I know you haven't had breakfast yet."

"Miss Waldmeyer wants me to let the front room."

He sauntered through the boiler room, the kitchen, and so into her room. The room was filled by a double divan bed, a bookcase, a large oval dining table. On a ledge stood some geraniums. The noon sun no longer fell in here, but through iron bars out on the steps, where the old dog still lay. A thin flowered curtain drawn aside showed night clothes. On the wall on a nail hung a little carved shrine containing a crucifix and an inch-long wax candle. On the wall was a chalk sketch of Edward himself at the age of three or four. He had then looked like a pretty little girl with long blond curls, plump red cheeks. He wore lace, buckled shoes and gloves. Mrs. Annichini spread a small cloth on the table. Edward plumped into a chair.

"The difficulty of finding something to do, Annichke!"

"Yes, you need clothes, poor man," said Mrs. Annichini with a laugh, looking at his bare legs.

"I have enough to eat and women are keeping me," said Edward, referring to his tenants. He went on to explain that he had his army savings, his separation pay, and he felt sure there would be another bonus with so many fellows coming back and finding nothing to do. They were all signing up for gas stations under the big companies, or were going into modern businesses, frozen foods, radio, things they knew nothing about and for which they hadn't enough cash, sure to be overcrowded in a short time.

"Then they'll just throw them up and wish they'd taken the wife out for a good time or bought their mother a piano."

The government would be sure to grant the bonus, just to stop the grousing.

"And to fill in the gap till the next war, or the draft. It'll be inflation and they'll inflate. There'll be a boom for a while and my tenants will keep their jobs. They've all got soft jobs, charity jobs, art jobs, and they won't get the boot for their political opinions. They don't have 'em, to speak of. Some of them have property and they'll be safe. The value of my houses will go up for the time being. I won't be able to raise my rents, but I'm not that kind of roughneck anyhow. As long as I've got a roof over my head, I don't think of my houses that way. The question is for me to get something to do that I want to do. I'm actually in a position to wait and see. My father and mother were much worse off than I am now. Communism is a great mistake; when one fellow has the property, he's ever so much better off."

He talked through the open door to Mrs. Annichini, while she worked at the stove. She came back with a plate of ham and other things, listening to him and answering. She interrupted:

"It is a shame my dog poor Turco cannot go into the yard: but he always sits here on the steps and lays his head on the steps. It makes me feel sorry. If you have people here, dear boy, you must take the grille away."

Through the ceiling they could hear Miss Holland's weighty footsteps, furniture being moved.

"When I went to Italy for a trip with my husband, we had such fun, such goings-on. They danced and sang for three days at Easter and feasted all day. And such blue skies, such lights, laughing and joking all day and everything made Gino tell an anecdote: he had a story for everything." She laughed.

He commiserated with her. "Ah, Annichke, mm-mm, eh, Annichke."

"And romance, romance too! You must get married, my boy! When will you stop being my boy?"

"When I get a little older; and then you will say I am only a boy still and then I will get a little older and you will say I am just a boy; and a bit after that, you will say I am not much more than a boy. And lastly, you will say I am a boy at heart. There is only one step more — you will say it's hard to believe that I used to be such a pretty little boy."

"*Carissimo mio!* By that time you will be married and have a pretty little boy. You will not have to worry about a fire escape. You will use half the house yourself."

"Well, I hope so, Annichke." He laughed pleasantly and sprawled on the table looking at the paper, with his back turned to Laura Annichini, who looked at the Christmas bough in the yard and remarked:

"Christmas in July."

"Miss Holland carried the new press upstairs by herself. The powerful Katinka."

"Beer's very fattening."

"It's muscle, not fat. She worked all night for three nights, do you know? Did you hear her?"

"No wonder she can't sleep. She does too much. You, too little."

She put down in front of him a plate of hot buttered toast and two eggs fried with Bologna, in margarine.

"Sixty-eight cents a pound; a quarter of ham, half a dollar," said Edward. He began to eat. Laura put several plates of food on the

[26]

table and a pot of coffee. He finished them all. Laura sat at one end of the table looking at him and chatting with him. She was about sixty and strong, but very stout. She straddled on the small kitchen chair, threw her back against it. Edward thrust a finger into his ear, pushed back his chair, tweaked his nose, crossed his legs, and picked his teeth leisurely. He said through his fingers, "The trouble is to find something to do."

"You could have gone on with your languages. I have that photo of you taken in Italy. I could hardly believe my eyes when I saw your letter written in Italian."

"I could have gone to the university with the G.I. Bill of Rights, but I had enough of that at Georgetown. I'm too old to be boiling down textbooks. Why should I take up a subject like geology or German just to waste three years of my time and government money? There are about 275,000 of those G.I.'s and not enough seats for them; a lot of those fellows will have to whistle for their chance, and they need the holiday or they need the diploma. It's only unemployment or some bum job when they come out. I don't blame them."

"You have a language gift. It is a shame though."

"Look, Annie, I was in Germany, France, Italy, England, I was in Cairo, Palestine. Everywhere I went, in England too, I only heard people talking New York. Going along the road near Alexandria I hear a Brooklyn brogue. It made me homesick for 14th Street at 6 P.M. In Cairo I heard a beansprout making a black-eyed Susan in deep Dallas. They're still talking American in Europe. Especially if you want to change dollars."

"Remember when you were on a machine with Annichini, making parts for precision instruments. You were good at that."

"Ah, that was to keep out of the army. My only war wound. Contracted on the Chelsea battle front."

He pulled up a sleeve to show a scar from elbow to wrist.

"I'll never forget the poor doc. He seemed only to have industrial accidents. His waiting room was so seedy and I was his only patient. He actually looked hungry, I never got him out of my head."

"Your poor mother would have been very pleased if you had become a doctor like your father and her father."

"Oh-ho! I only like to look at good-looking women, Annichke. Like you. I'm impatient with the sick. I suppose Mama told you I was wasting my time? She complained that at my age I still went out in the rain without a hat? No, I tink I'll ber-rowse," he said in a New York dialect and quoting from one of his own jokes. As he said this, a shadow crossed his face. The joke in question had been one of his best-known but it was about caskets and he did not tell it now.

"You said you would buy another farm when you came back from the war."

"Ah, Annichke, what would I do with a farm? I'd do just what we all do, keep a couple of dogs on it. Invite people up. I like to go and shop for string beans and salad. Why should you go to the trouble of growing them when other people make a living at it? They do it better. Why should I keep chickens? I wouldn't know how to delouse the little yellow bastards. Mrs. Mustbrook, up at the farm, grows them all for us. She's got wire-netted floors and iron mufflers on their beaks and no roosters. Yolk without yoking. No like. I don't get it. Then look at the characters of people on the land. We've got a mile of a Tobacco Road around the farm. They work like madmen and sweat their very bones. You work like a lunatic to produce a crop and that's the year no one can buy. The Egg, not I. And if it were good soil what would I know to do with it? Soil should be heated, all kinds improvements. You can't do nothin' with the Home Farm."

The old woman said thoughtfully, "You have the land and the time but not the drive. I would be looking after those chickens like little ladies from morning to night and I haven't the land or the time. That's funny, isn't it?"

"Ya-hum!"

"If you keep the lights on at night, they don't know the difference

and they lay extra. You have to be very gentle with them: they do
better. You have to let them run about a bit freer than Mrs. Mustbrook does. You mustn't shock them. I'd have a big barn with two
floors, heating and lighting and running water and plenty of feed.
I'd knock at the door; I'd call out, Little ladies, let me in, ladies;
they come running, they like to be treated with respect. When I open
the door, they're clustered round and you go in walking gently, you
say, Hello, ladies, hello, ladies, pretty ladies, let us have some eggs,
have you got some new eggs, ladies? You have some good cats to
keep the rats out and mice away from the feed, some orchard and
flower garden to peck in. A bit of natural life is no harm. Let them
roost in the trees at night, but watch them if you do, and watch the
ones that lay in the woods. You can always tell them, for they
cackle, but some are very clever, they pick their way out so neatly
and wait till they're in the open before they cackle. They're such
little things; and if you treat them properly, you do well. But it's
constant watching."

Edward said, "It's all in the hands of the black marketeers now.
You've got to have a tommy gun to keep off thieves. They come in
the middle of the night, with a truck and guns. And you've got to
have an organization with outlets in the city. And then you're
ruined. Look at the chicken-parts fellow down the block. For weeks,
he's hardly moved a gizzard. Price too high. I tell you we're nearing
the top. We're going over the ridge, in a couple of months."

"Life is sad, don't you think, Edward? Eh, listen, Edward, don't
you think life is unfair?"

"Sure, it's unfair."

"What can you do about it, eh, Edward? There's nothing you can
do about it, is there?"

After a pause, she continued, "My brother said he would give you
a job in the furniture factory, Edward. You learned French polishing. You did this table up nice."

He sighed, "I have almost decided to take the first thing that offers, that's true. Why not? I dread the thought of going to White-house this summer. I haven't been near it since 1943."

"What about your novel? You came first in writing at school."

"Ah — for that I need an idea," cried Edward, suddenly irritated. He stamped out his cigarette and looked gloomily at the woman. He took out another cigarette. She offered him a light. He said, "It's only because there's full employment I know that I'm so worried about working. Flora and Mark want me to go into a radio show with them. Why? Every cluck in New York is in some little show business now. Al Burrows who comes here to flop wants to save his feet, get out of pharmacy and get into the black market! Electric goods for South America. Comes the crack-up, everyone flat on his back and can't get up, like a black beetle. Have I got to be one of them?"

"In the furniture business, you wouldn't have to worry. My brother has been doing very good and he will for years. It's very hard to get furniture."

Edward got up and looked out of the window, his brown eyes turning reddish with irritation. He grumbled, "If I'd needed a job I could have stayed in the army. In Cairo we had so many servants, three or four to an officer, there wasn't room to turn around and they had to close the barracks and send the officers away: they were turning to hog-fat. I was one of those noncom officers. I rang up a pal of mine used to be an actor in the Art Theater, and he got out to Hollywood and got to be a sitz-major, a desk-colonel. That guy thought the world of me. One day I rang him up and said, 'I want to see you, Joe.' He said, 'Is it for the war effort, Sergeant?' 'No, Joe, I was passing through,' and, 'I haven't a minute I can spare, good day,' says my desk-colonel and he slams down the receiver. He never did leave the U.S.A. but he got to Washington. In Washington he was a bit more relaxed. I got to see him. He was in Intelligence. They had it there on the door as large as life, 'U.S. Intelligence Divi-sion.' And believe it or not, the intelligence was right behind the door too; at least Joe was. 'Do you want to see what I can do?' he asks me. He rings a bell and a man comes in in uniform. 'Get me that blue A/C file, Major.' Major salutes. He is a real shooting major. Ha-ha. Very funny.

"What happens else? An officer with the army of occupation, say, a major, gets about five thousand a year, lives with his wife, has cheap German servant girls, outside Frankfurt or Karlsruhe, for example, and if he's smart, he saves three thousand. If he's smarter than that, he can save ten thousand a year. His wife, some *Woman's Home Companion* post-deb with a hair-do, a little voice and a cigarette, some cutout kid, this kid who wouldn't be anyone here in New York, but would be stuck away in a dark little hole with central heating, now she's got three or four sturdy German girls to complain of, she finds the prices too high in any country where she travels, because in Germany she's in conquered territory and living off the fat of the land: and oh, boy, would she hate to see the U.S.A. again. She wouldn't know what had struck her; and the desk-major wouldn't either. They'd feel there was injustice in the world. That desk-major may be a good guy, a businessman who got into the army and found out it's as good as any other line: he probably was a good guy in civilian life and his wife was just a sweet little nobody making excuses for everybody. But now!

"Well, Annie, that would be me. I wouldn't be an American, I wouldn't be a New Yorker, I wouldn't be a Massine, I'd be a heel. It's a quiet life but I couldn't take it, Annichke, I'd get corrupted. Everyone does and why not your little Willy? As for business, Laura, why go into business? Why? Name one good reason? Every heel thinks he's a business brain now. If I sell the house, where will I be? One house isn't enough for me to live on. Unless I start papering and painting and holding families up for every pigeonhole. Then, I don't wear out any clothes here at home. Going to work, I'd have laundry bills, tailor's bills, I'd wear out the shoe leather, there's transportation and lunches; you're so fagged out at night

[31]

you go to the movies or to the shows; you spend your time in cafés, just to see a human face. Eventually, you have to get yourself a home, a wife. I take an apartment I now get rent for. That's the result of going into business. And not a creative moment to yourself. No integrity, no freedom. You begin to sit around with the *schmoosers* and *schnorrers* and drink too much, mulling over the headlines, just to prove to yourself you've got a heart left. You tell funny stories; you get two hundred best friends; you go into debt. If I get a wife, I need a proper setup. Rent is about one quarter if not more of the expenses of every New Yorker. As it is, I don't pay no rent."

He grinned lazily. "You haven't got another cup of coffee, Laura?"

"Of course, my dear boy. But Edward, this is not a normal life."

"Staying at home this way I save a lot of money. Pay is handy but for a man like me with a rents background, I'd be ruined. I'd regard my pay as a sort of windfall, a weekly numbers game I always won. Work for me would be a waste of time and money and from the point of view of my character, ruination. As for getting married, Annichke, my girl doesn't want to get married: or at least she says she wouldn't marry me and take me to live in her own furniture. That's what she says. She says what would people think? She thinks, they think! An idealist. That means a lot of expense then for me. She's a bit of an interior decorator. That means a three- or four-room apartment. She has stacks of stuff there, silver, curtain lengths, and so on. She's old-fashioned and she's been buying it for years. I don't know what I wouldn't have to find room for. All put away with lavender and mothballs. She shakes it out every so often and lets the air at it. Her silver is all wrapped up in shammy leather and black paper. She even has pictures. They're awful, incidentally, for my money. She has a lot of hand-painted china, real china from China. But she doesn't like her furniture. We'd have to get more. And what for? For the same situation as we have now, without all that trouble. She's a fine girl, but there's no sense to our

[32]

setting up housekeeping. . . . So there it is, what am I to do with my life? At least it's all before me. Troubles! I want to do something worth while but I don't want to get balled up. Maybe I should close the First Lesson on Doubt and Worry and just start trying."

He laughed good-naturedly, cut a piece of dry bread and ate it.

Mrs. Annichini looked at him with amusement, got up and started to clear the table, meanwhile asking him whether he wanted anything else to eat. She continued, "Your poor aunt Big Jenny! Her cat Zero is too timid. She cries too much. If I don't let her sleep with her whiskers next to my face, she cries all night. Annichini don't like a cat on the bed and he tells me to throw her off. Then she sits there on the carpet and cries. He didn't get any proper sleep the last five nights. I think I'll have to give her back to Big Jenny; but I hate to. Jenny's dogs are too rough for her."

"She's timid because those dogs beat her up at Whitehouse. Then she was dropped off a fire escape, when she was a kitten, by those Croat kids," said Edward.

"She's feverish, too. I gave her some medicine. I gave her some oil. I thought she had eaten her fur. Then I tried to comb out her fur. She was so patient, poor little thing. Her fur is full of knots. That's the trouble with those Angoras. Then I had to cut some of them out and do you know what I found? In each knot was a big dog flea. That was what made her feverish."

"Not from Musty," said Edward, thrusting his hand into his dog's untidy coat, which was weighted under the belly with winter-long clinkers. In the coat were many gray hairs.

"What will you do with yourself then, this summer, dear boy?"

"I guess I'll get the two houses done up. Maybe I'll help with yours."

"Yes."

They sat thoughtfully.

"Musty! Where is the little dope?"

"The front door's open."

"For Chris' sake! One of the pups is in heat. He's probably running over to 20th Street. He's not so dumb when it's spring. Goddamn little Romeo."

Edward gathered his dressing gown round him and ran upstairs, slippers flopping. He stood on the asphalt sidewalk whistling in both directions. Musty toddled round the corner from Third Avenue. Edward shouted:

"Come home, you little bastard. You'll get under a trolley."

The doorman in the apartment house at the corner begged Musty to go home. The mailman approached and Miss Holland came to the hedge.

"Anything for me?"

"Not a thing."

"What's noo," said Edward.

"Are you kidding?"

"Ain't it murder," said Edward.

"Looks like we'll have to go underground. Looks like the Russians got atoms too."

They all burst out laughing.

Miss Holland said, "I can't go underground. I'll have to pull a mountain over me here."

The mailman said, "It was in this street you had the murder, wasn't it? I see the stain."

"What murder?" said Edward.

They told him. The mailman continued, "They caught the guy hiding in a dumb-waiter. Do you know what he was?"

"No."

"Just a dumb waiter. From a Greek fish place on Second Avenue."

The dog turning into the house turned back, sniffed the mailman and danced at him barking. Edward cried, "See him do a double-take? He's getting old, his eyes are dim. I got to get him washed."

"Do you wash him in spring?" said the mailman.

"Sure. Come on, got to get you manicured, Musty," said Edward, taking in his letter. He went upstairs to telephone a firm who called themselves *Canine Shampooing and Tonsorial Artists*. He found Lola, the Negro maid, in his room, making the bed. She had opened the window a little and was keeping an eye on the papers in case they fluttered.

"Do you want me to pick up the papers, Edward?"

"No. I haven't made my cuttings yet."

He sat down on the bed and pulled on his trousers, dropped his dressing gown on the floor and padded out to the front room where the puppet stage had now been erected. The chandelier had been tied aside to a curtain bracket and was partly reflected in a tall mirror which hung between the two windows. The Venetian blinds were down but high-lights fell from them, the ceiling and the chandelier to the floor. The stage divided the room into two unequal parts. The stage curtains of light fuchsia velvet were being opened and closed.

A girl swung a wooden cloud awkwardly about the stage. Edward sat on a milking stool in front and gave advice. A puppeteer with a peacock voice now climbed up the ladder and showed off the antics of a pink doll-puppet who teetered out of tissue paper in a cardboard box. The play had been written for them by Edward, *The Magic Door*.

The mirror, about ten feet high, was attached to the wall. Its gilt frame was carved in fruits and flowers. It was dusty and tarnished. Reflections and shadows from the cloud-peopled afternoon sky, glints from the traffic wheeling underneath, passed through the bars of the light on the ceiling and in the mirror. Edward studying himself in the mirror saw himself framed in the little stage, and passed his hand over his jaw. "What a face! Not even beauty," said he. When someone said "Two-ten," Edward got up and said that he must ring up the Turkish bath for Musty. Lola was still in his room with a duster.

"I've got to get the hell out of here. You better scram. You can come back tomorrow."

"You ought to do those cuttings, every day, Edward. That news will be stale when you get to it."

"My idea is not the news but to get a political orientation, an education. My cousin Rex says I'm a political illiterate. I don't lose anything by leaving them laying around, Lola. I can't see the plays in day-to-day reading. I never understood a campaign till it was finished. . . . The older these cuttings get the more you can see of the game."

"Why don't you put these in the incinerator and start again tomorrow?"

"Look, I'll start on them tomorrow."

"O.K., Edward."

She closed the door. He picked up a shirt from the chair, started to put it on, changed his mind, threw it on the floor, picked it up and pushed it behind a writing desk in the corner. A cuff stuck out. He took a drink of whiskey and sat down to telephone for Musty's appointment. While waiting, he reached down and picked up one of the older papers from the floor. Underneath it was Miss Allison's rent check from some other month. At some time or other, the wind had blown it to the floor. Edward leaned over to glance at it, left it lying there while he telephoned. Then he rummaged under a pile of files and papers on the center table for a pair of editor's shears and pulling the nearest newspaper towards him on the floor, squatted down to inspect it. He cut out three items. Then he crumpled the paper and threw it in the wastepaper basket. He picked up the check and put it in with the cuttings on a small space that he cleared on the coffee table. He studied another newspaper, made a cutting. By this time, his eyes were tired, so he put the shears on top of the cuttings and went to the writing desk to get a clean shirt. Before he left, he prepared the room for the night by closing the curtains. He picked up Musty's dish, took it upstairs to Miss

Allison's room. He knocked, went in, and had a few minutes' chat with her about country students coming in for summer courses during July and August. She was a college teacher. She and the top-floor tenants might sublet their apartments to them. Miss Allison gave him her check for the rent and Edward said in a hurt voice, "You don't really think I came for that, do you, Gertrude?"

He went into her bathroom to get fresh water for Musty and went downstairs. At three-forty, he went down to Mrs. Annichini, neatly dressed and in a tie he hoped she would admire. He pointed it out to her. "My girl gave it to me: she has much better taste than I have. It's handmade and it has a heavy silk lining." Musty whinnied and shivered with impatience. Edward said, "The cute little bastard knows we're going over to Oneida's. Wherever I go, I'm wading through a mess of little animals."

Mrs. Annichini, in her hat and jacket, with a big handbag on her arm, came running to him with a wet comb.

"Your hair's every which way. I kept lunch for you. It's in the icebox: eat it tonight."

The telephone rang upstairs. Edward said in a bored voice, "That's Oneida's hurry-up call. She's jittery; I don't blame her. Madame X is thirteen at least, although Oneida never admits to more than ten or eleven. Let's hustle."

It was a bright afternoon. A lively damp breeze blew softly elsewhere and howled under the stiff precipice of the Consolidated Edison tower. A few old men stood in front of the Automat on 14th Street and in front of cafés, getting the sun and catching puffs of hot air from revolving doors. Some men had gathered in Union Square; and were huddled together, getting warm. They were mulling things over in low tones, one man talking very earnestly in the center and all craning towards him.

"Do you get a queer sensation from that? My girl does: she says it's the bull herd," said Edward.

"I wouldn't sit on any seat in that park," said Mrs. Annichini.

"For fear of zoology," Edward laughed.

Just as they crossed the head of University Place, a girl planted herself in front of them and said in a rough voice, "Broadway."

Edward pointed across the square, gave directions, jerking his head. He thrust his hand in his pocket, watching her for a moment as she strode off without a word. Mrs. Annichini sneezed while she was looking for her handkerchief and her top set of teeth in plastics fell to the pavement but did not break. A little girl going past in a ski-suit stopped and opened her mouth. Edward shook out his handkerchief, stooped and gave the teeth to Mrs. Annichini who quickly fitted them in behind her big hands, "No one was looking, Annichke."

When they reached the long low brick building in which the Solways had their apartment, Edward said he would go up and get the family. Mrs. Annichini sat down at a polished lobby table bearing a big lobby lamp and talked to the Italian porter and handyman, Anthony. He was a bright-eyed fallen-in old workman who was interested in the making of jams, fruit juices and jellies. He had an invention for sealing cans. He said to Edward:

"Going to have the old dog put away?"

"No: she had an X ray; today she gets carved."

"That's bad. Mrs. Solway feels bad."

"Like hell," said Edward.

"Hell-an', hell-an', Helen I love you," said Anthony politely to Mrs. Annichini. The two sat and admired a picture of Anthony's boy who had got into the army at sixteen by lying about his age. Edward, going up a back staircase, heard Anthony telling one of his jokes: "The happiest days of my life, I spent in the arms of another man's wife. Nothing wrong. My mother."

Presently Edward reappeared at the back of the lobby, at the head of a group. He was carrying a dog's traveling box. Inside the door could be seen the muzzle of the bull terrier, Madame X, like the head of a giant grizzled and dew-lapped mouse. Behind him came a short high-colored woman in a fuchsia silk dress with a gold-embroidered purple bolero over it, a fur coat, and a peaked velvet hood from which the inky tendrils of her hair escaped. She had handsome eyes and, at the moment, a girlishly resentful expression unsettled her features. This was Oneida Solway, born Massine, Edward's aunt. Behind her was her husband Lou Solway, the pianist, a tall man, with a powerful neck and shoulders, who wore a black fedora, velvet-collared coat and a white silk muffler. Beside him were two members of the family, Leander Massine, short and quick with blue eyes and a shock of white hair, and his wife, always called Lady, a pale-skinned stooping pretty woman, wearing blue, thin lace and gray fur.

"Ah, sweety-pie," said Oneida and began to weep. Lou wore a quiet air. Lady and Leander said nothing. Mrs. Annichini rose quickly, went to Oneida and kissed her. Oneida threw her arms high in the air to catch Mrs. Annichini's neck.

"Laura! My poor doggie is so sick, oh darling, oh my poor sugar, your mummy is here."

"How you are suffering," said Laura.

"They think I make too much fuss, Annichke." She flashed round to her brother Leander and cried imperiously, "You don't hate my dogs but me."

Madame X growled in her box.

"Watch it, Oneida," said Edward.

"You're exciting the poor thing. She hears your voice. Let her lie still," said Lou, kindly.

"You mustn't let her feel you're upset, she loves you so much," said Lady.

"Oh yes, I know, I know, I mustn't. She's such a sensitive — " She began a deep strong crooning, a humming like a cello. Her voice changed suddenly and she cried in a stirring voice, "Oh, isn't it awful, they have to suffer, and they can't tell us?"

"Can it," said Edward.

"Oh, but I feel such agony, I feel it there. If they could do it to me, I would let them, I would suffer for her," cried Oneida, her voice changing once more to a dominant ringing.

They reached the sidewalk, with Anthony holding open the doors. Here a discussion took place about who should walk and who should ride in Leander's car; and whether Madame X should be carried or should ride. Eventually, Leander said he would drive with caution and, as it was only a few minutes away, they all packed in. The first part of the journey passed in silence. The second part was enlivened by the sight of Oneida's eldest brother, Jonathan, and his wife, Little Jenny, who were waiting outside the railings of the veterinary's house. It was a narrow three-story house with a dark basement. Oneida cried out that it was lovely, how lovely of them to come, how thoughtful and that surely so much love would help her darling, it must help, such things must help or what was love for?

Oneida's brother Jonathan took the dog box carefully out of the car.

Little Jenny was in her early fifties. Over her slight body still floated shreds of that kind of gauze an enchanting girl carries round her in adolescence. She fondled, coaxed. She pronounced her words in a liquid, sugary way, melting down every consonant so that she had a set of consonants of her own. She turned and scraped delightfully like a figurine on a clock and repeated with a crashing of thin china, "Oh djear, oh, djarling, oh poo' heuhny, what you musst be seuffering! Oh, be brave."

Oneida kissed Little Jenny. Little Jenny flung her arms round Oneida. She gave a message from her daughter in the same peculiar tone and accent:

"My darlings Flora sent all their love and says we must telephone them after the results are known. I do think it very very kind of them, don't you, Oneida darling? Flora could not come only because they are doing final rehearsals for the new show. You know that now they are featuring her dance? She is such a beautiful girl."

Oneida said mechanically, "Oh Flora is a beauty."

Jonathan Massine was a broad, gnarled man with snow-white hair and brilliant blue eyes. He was seventy-three and wore a dreamy expression. He now bent down slowly, scrutinized the dog, picked up the box and carried it to the door with a solemn air. He announced:

"Your dog is breathing normally. I think she'll come through as good as new. She's not at all nervous. A brave dog."

Oneida exclaimed. The others twittered, rustled. Oneida said, "She is giving me a lesson; I must be brave."

She straightened up, gave a hard bright look all round and took command. "Come on, we can't mill round here weeping and complaining about a dog. Let's go in and get it over."

"Djarling! Think how very funny, djarling! Ollie is inside waiting, heuhny! We saw her through the window but we didn't want to go in. Isn't it sweet of her, djear?" Little Jenny giggled.

Ollie was one of Oneida's sisters, and lived in Albany. Oneida cried:

"Ollie! What's she doing here? Oh, I do think that's kind."

She laughed, said crossly, "Ollie never has anything to do when she comes to New York. She has time on her hands and she runs anywhere we go. It's a wonder everyone isn't here. All for a dog!"

"Oneida, it's very kind of Ollie," said Lou, in his slow voice.

"Five hundred of us all for a dog."

Jonathan rang the bell. Oneida said, "What are you all pushing in for? He'll think we've all got sick dawgs with us."

Lou grinned, "Just say it's all of the people with some of the dog."

Edward said in his grating, contemptuous way, "Philip Christy, the optometrist, calls me that young man with the cat."

"Kit for Kat," said Lou thoughtfully.

No one laughed. A slight pause ensued, however, during which the family jostled orderly through the passage.

The waiting room was a small dark front room whitewashed and furnished with upholstered benches and a small table littered with dog annuals and monthlies, a few cat books. On one of the benches sat Ollie Massine Benson. She was a dumpy elderly woman, with large dark eyes. Her hair was pulled straight back and fixed in a knob under her plain felt hat. She rose quickly, established her weight on her small feet and rotated forward, spreading her hands. She embraced several of her relatives and muttered shamefacedly, "I've been waiting and waiting. I saw you there but I thought you were coming in any minute. They asked me what I wanted. I pointed to you through the window. I told them the dog was coming."

She laughed, wiped away her tears of emotion. She was one of the smallest of these small women. When she had finished kissing and lifting her arms, her hat had fallen to the back of her head. The family began taking seats but Ollie remained standing. She felt she had to explain herself and she continued more cheerfully, "I don't see you except in summer at Whitehouse and I can hardly ever get up there. It's so far from Albany and Ben-son doesn't like me to be away so long."

"I don't see what it's all about: you never help him in the business," said Oneida. "A woman your age afraid of your mother-in-law."

"Ben-son says he feels uncomfortable if he does not know I am at home. And Mother may die any time."

She had an agreeable way of teetering slightly as if to keep her balance. She burst out laughing suddenly, "The doctor looked at me but couldn't see a dog the matter with me."

They all sat down. Ollie said, "Do you remember last summer when we were at Dan's? Old Sister Mary drank four brandies like a wooden Indian. I laughed all the winter. I told Ben-son. I told Ben-son he must get me some brandy."

Lou said, "And Ollie couldn't remember her husband's first name. We asked her, What does E. stand for? E. Benson?"

Ollie colored. "Edmond."

"Of course she knew," said Oneida.

"Of course djear Ollie knew."

"It's because you call him Benson," said Lady.

"It's because Daddy insisted on her marrying a man he knew called Benson. He thought we didn't know anything. He wanted to pick nice men. He wanted me to marry Victor-Alexander. Because I fell asleep on Victor-Alexander's porch and slept there the whole night in the sling, the swing — the sailor's — the awning," said Oneida.

"Oneida, Oneida, the hammock."

"The hammock. And next morning I was furious and Daddy said, What a fine man, he never touched me. That showed what Daddy knew about life. But he thought he could pick men for us because he knew more about men than we did. Anyhow I chose Lou. It was my own doing. Victor-Alexander was away in California visiting some astrologer. Cagliostro? I forget. I was so furious I sent him a telegram: Engaged to Lou. That was that. *Fini!* Ha-ha-ha! and Daddy let Victor-Alexander build a house on our land, so he could marry me! That was a poser for him."

"Oneida! We've heard it," said Edward.

"Daddy thought if he whistled we would all dance the tune."

"Daddy was lovely to you, Oneida," said Ollie.

"Oh, I loved djear old Daddy! He called me Little Jenny first."

"Daddy saw a little girl round the place and he gave me quarters and candies. I don't think he knew who I was most of the time. Someone visiting."

"Oneida!" Ollie said, and continued; "One night, Dan took us to Wurzburger's in the village, for a beer. You remember the children dancing to the jukebox? I don't go out at all in Albany. Remember Dan phoned for a taxi? The taxi was drunk. But Dan thought it was a good time."

"He never thinks. I don't call him good. He made Big Jenny walk all that way," said Oneida.

"He called a taxi."

"It's Big Jenny's fault. He never thinks and she, instead of saying something, just pats his arm and gives in to him on everything. She would do it again for Dan."

"Yes, Big Jenny walked with us all that way. I was behind with Lady. Remember! What a night! Do you remember how the stars shone that night?" said Leander to Lady.

"Big Jenny was pale and out of breath when she got to Wurzburger's and she walked back," said Ollie. "With her hips."

"We-el, she took a beer to please him. Dan's such a good-time Charlie! He's a nitwit. Anything for a laugh. He's a boob. Ye-es, honeybuch, he's a ni-itwi-it!" said Oneida. She turned to them and began again, "Dan seems lively but he's selfish; he has no heart. He excites all the dogs. He calls them nitwits. I call him a nitwit. He makes Darly jump at the moths and he knows it's bad for her heart. He hopes she'll fly to pieces one night."

"Oneida, don't say those terrible things," said Lou, laughing.

Leander commented, "Dan has a new moron in his business. The other day, the moron stayed on after, to clean up. Dan likes to have morons and they like him. They come early and they stay late. They have nowhere else to go. They stay there any hour just to be with Dan. Two or three of them live in the hall bedroom. Dan sends out for sandwiches for them. This day Dan saw some pink ribbon coming out of the moron's pocket. He recognized the ribbon. He had just got it in. It was on a lady's bra."

"It wasn't a gentleman's bra?" murmured Lou.

Edward said, "I know, it was Teddy, his new moron."

"Oh, do tell it, Edward. Leander, let Edward tell it: he has such an accent."

"Dan pulled on the ribbon and said, 'What gives, Teddy?' and a net bra came out of the pocket. Then he said, 'What have you got in the other pocket, Teddy?' The moron looked sheepish and pulled out a pair of step-ins."

"Oh, that's dead, they don't call them step-ins any more, Edward."

"Then Dan put his hand inside the moron's coat and said, 'Have you got some more here maybe, Teddy?' The moron laughed and pulled out a pink rayon slip. He pulled out five or six things from the moron's pockets and he said, 'What do you want to steal all that from me for, Teddy?' The moron said, 'I want them for my girl.' Dan said, 'Here, take them, Teddy. And put them on your girl yourself. And don't let her wear anything you can't wear yourself.'"

"I don't understand that," said Oneida.

"And Teddy said, 'She's a moron too, Mr. Barnes. She's in the Home, but she gets out Saturdays. I have a few moron friends and they have girls in the moron Home.' So Dan said, 'Why don't you bring her up with her friends to Whitehouse? There's a place there called Big Jenny's where they give planked steak, French fries and beer, all free. One Saturday I'll hire you a truck and we'll all go to Big Jenny's and have a good time.'"

"I call it stupidity to deceive those morons," said Oneida.

"Who mentioned deceive," said Lou in a vaudeville accent.

The family laughed musingly.

"The moron said he would. Then Dan told him to promise he would come to him for anything he wanted like drawers for his girl. When the moron started to go home, he called Dan and said bashfully, 'Here's one you missed, Mr. Barnes'; and he pulled a bra from inside his shirt. And when he was putting on his overcoat, Dan saw another pink thing hanging out of the pocket."

"He wanted her to have more-on," said Lou.

A pause followed; then Oneida said angrily, "I don't understand why he employs those morons in his business."

"He has a kind heart and a sense of humor and then he's an Englishman. You forget he was born in Liverpool, England," said Ollie.

"That's a hell of an explanation," said Edward.

"Those morons work all the time, but I don't think it pays him," said Leander.

"But he gets a big kick out of it," said Lady.

"Those morons worship Dan and they ought to, who else would have them?" said Oneida. Then she leaped to the wire grille of the dog box and imitated herself impudently, in a baby voice, "Those morons worship Dan because he is a moron."

"Dan is very kindhearted," said Ollie.

"Dan would do anything for a laugh."

The doctor, hearing so many voices, looked in, in his shirt sleeves, and was surprised to see his waiting room full of clients. Oneida and Jonathan rose at once.

"Doctor Parks, this is the sick doggie."

He inquired about the dog and looked round the room questioningly. Oneida laughed.

"Oh, these are just friends of Madame X."

"We're all just one dog," said Lou.

"We're just her family," said Lady.

The veterinary surgeon smiled in a puzzled way. He said, "Just a moment."

Oneida cried angrily, "Why say the family? Annichke isn't the family. Perhaps Mrs. Annichini doesn't like to be called the family of a dog."

They laughed hesitantly. Lou said, "I'm not the dog's family either."

"Do you remember the butcher at Whitehouse always called Annichke Mrs. Annie Massine? He doesn't know any better," said Ollie, stuffing her handkerchief into her mouth.

Oneida said, "At the post office they call me Miss Massine though I've been married for twenty years. They probably think Lou is still visiting us."

"IB," said Lou.

"But djarling, more than twenty surely, you were married, angel, in . . ."

"Twenty years and they don't know the difference."

"You'd better send them a wedding announcement to the post office," said Ollie. "Tell them you're sorry you omitted them."

"It's because I'm the youngest and they always think of me as a girl. Ollie still makes my clothes and Big Jenny braids my hair."

"We all know that," said Lou.

The veterinary now came out of the office in his long white coat and lifted the box. Oneida started to go with him but was repulsed at the curtain which divided the lobby from his consulting room. She made an outcry at this and explained to the doctor how much her presence would help the animal even under ether, but presently she allowed Lou and Jonathan to bring her back to the waiting room. She sat there with her hands folded and a look of anxiety. She had found out that the operating room was in the basement and she had seen the doctor's assistant, a young man with waving dark hair, in a long blue coat. She kept exclaiming that it was a funny thing they wouldn't allow her to be present, for if she had any germs to give Madame X she had given them long ago and vice versa; and that she knew strange young men could have foreign germs and why should they try to be kind to her old dog. Meanwhile, the family, to divert her, kept up family conversation.

Leander said, "Do you remember how Mother used to sit in that footstool chair with the Siamese cats on the armrests? They were smoky cats, Smoky and Sultry."

"Mother was an old woman to me, just an old woman in the house. When I went down to Whitehouse Village with her, people asked her how was her grandchild. I told people she was my grandmother," said Oneida.

"Even as an old woman, she was beautiful! You can see from the painting at Whitehouse," said Lady.

Oneida said, "They were just barn cats, the same as Westfourth.

[47]

I remember those cats. That smoky color is just the way Doctor Edward painted them to look de-co-ra-tive — yes, ye-es! Why is he so long? One was smoky, one tiger-striped. Smoky and Tiger they were called. Tiger was the barn cat and killed mice. The farmers used to borrow her. They came for miles."

"Oh-ho-ho, do you remember when Mr. van Kill borrowed Tiger for the kitchen and she stole the roast chicken and fell asleep on the hearth? The mice ran in and out of the hearth all around her playing peek-a-boo," said Ollie.

"Mutt and Jeff were the black cockers."

"No, djarling, that was Boloney and Salami. Jonathan gave them to your djarling mother when we were married. Cockers are so friendly."

"They're a darn sight too friendly. We thought Salami was going to have puppies for months and months. They both died of over-eating. They went round the whole town begging. People must have thought we didn't feed them."

"Not when they looked at them," said Lou.

"It's stupid to call a pedigree dog Mutt," said Oneida.

"I pedagree."

Ollie became animated. "Oh, do you remember the black and white Gordon setter, Jeff? He used to run away whenever he had to visit a girl, that lovely white setter down the road? Alice was her name."

"Oh don't you remember sweet Alice, Jeff Bolt?" Lou commented.

"He never left home! Our dogs never ran after other dogs. They don't feel like that. And Jeff was so sensitive. When Lou wouldn't let him sleep with us, once, he ran away, for three days."

"That was when he went to see Alice," Ollie reasoned with her.

"What Alice? I don't remember any Alice. Jeff was devoted to us. Do you remember when he dug up a whole warren of little rabbits and brought them all as a present. That morning the whole slope was literally covered with bunnies. He was a very loving dog."

"Ugh!" said Lady.

"Why? Those rabbits only try to decoy the dogs down the hole so that they'll suffocate to death. I hate them. They're little devils," said Oneida.

The family, very animated, went on babbling.

"Do you remember the morning Jeff got the black and white bird and Oneida kept shrieking, 'Oh, Lou! Oh, Lou!' "

"Jeff never did any such a thing. Cats do that, not dogs. You don't know what you're saying! What are you gossiping for? You're just a pack of village gossips," cried Oneida getting up and wringing her hands. "What is he doing? I hear something just under our feet. That's the basement. What is he doing? It's very strange he wouldn't let me go along. I knew a woman who only lived through a danger-ous operation because her husband stood beside her and spoke to her and whenever she had a few moments of consciousness, he was there saying, 'Stay with me, stay with me.' Oh, why can't I go? She would know what I was saying. Why is it a male nurse, when she is used to a woman?"

"Oh, think of the poor heuhny, oh djarling, control yourself and do what the djear doctor says: he is so very kind."

"It's a major operation; she needs absolute calm," said Jonathan. Oneida sat down saying, Yes, it was a major operation; she must be calm. Ollie said, "Oh, all our dogs! All Massines have to have dogs."

"Do you remember Red Wing, Oneida's favorite dog?"

The whole family laughed and some said, Shh! Shh! while others said, Oh Red! Red Wing!

Ollie cried breathlessly, "When Red Wing died, Oneida cried for days and wanted another red dog and Dan said he had bred a real red dog in Long Island; so he got a Dalmatian and painted it red with a pot of paint he got at the painter's and decorator's, Mr. Sienkiewicz. He said he wanted it to cover some spots. Then he brought it up to the Home Farm for Oneida's birthday. Oneida was eleven."

"I was eight, or I should have known. I believed it was red at first, and then the paint started to wear off."

"Except on the wings," said Leander.

"Then he was black and white and everyone said, Why do you call him Red?"

"I always hated Dalmatians after that; they seemed to me such cheats."

"I wonder how young Sienkiewicz is getting on now Roosevelt is dead?"

"He's fixed; he's a lawyer for the Pennsylvania Railroad," Edward said. "Like Lincoln for the Illinois Central."

Oneida laughed. "Edward! Lincoln never was a lawyer."

"He was every kind of a bush lawyer, believe me."

Lou added, "He was Herndon his living, at least partly, that way."

Oneida said, "Of course he wasn't a lawyer. And on a railroad!"

Lou said, "That ties it."

Oneida said angrily, "How can you say he was a lawyer?"

Edward smiled. "Yes he was, Oneida."

"I know. He was saved by a dog," said Oneida suddenly.

"He often barked his shins," said Lou.

"When he was eleven years old he fell in a hole and a stone fell in front of the cave and his dawg went and barked till someone came. They saved him. Without that dawg you wouldn't have had any Abe Lincoln."

"What paw-sight! They should have made the dog President."

Oneida said, "How can you say he was a bush lawyer?"

Edward moved over beside Leander and told him that Miss Waldmeyer wanted him to sell the two houses.

Leander asked, "Are you going into business?"

"No. I don't want to get into a cold sweat over the week end, wondering if the government's going to open the safety-deposit boxes on Monday."

"Well, you'd better come up to Whitehouse this summer and let's see about fixing up the Home Farm."

"I'm fighting shy of the idea at present."

When the operation was over, about five-thirty, Madame X was brought to the car again by Jonathan. They all headed for the Solways'. At home, Oneida, very weary-looking with her sleepless nights, nevertheless hustled about, set a table, prepared a light meal. They had chicken fat on radish slices, egg, fried onion mixed with fried potato, sardines on toast. Edward went for a drink with Lou and returned with herrings in cream, smoked oysters, sweet pickles, potato salad, a pound of ham and bottles of beer. Oneida opened a bottle of port wine kept from some previous event and half a bottle of white wine which was very old and had perhaps been left over from last summer.

There were two high ceilinged rooms with paneled sliding doors, magnificently furnished. In the front room Oneida's and Lou's grand pianos stood side by side. It was a rather dark apartment. There were oriental rugs and pillows, a long mirror, old handsome lamps and a few books; translations of authors known about seventy-five years ago. The large bathroom contained a sort of pantry without a door stuffed with old clothes in all kinds of materials, old satin pyjamas in Chinese style, Japanese dressing gowns, evening gowns and cloaks, gardening pants, *huaraches,* scarves, ropes, leashes. On the wall at one side was hung as a tapestry a handmade linen tablecloth, embroidered in Madeira work, and dyed a peculiar dull blue; and in the middle of it hung a large blue medallion, a replica of a Rembrandt painting but in enamel. On the wall was a plate representing the seven deadly sins. In a corner cabinet were pieces of cut glass and a set of glasses won in a Bingo game. At the back was a dummy piano and a green velvet reclining chair covered with a rug, on which the dogs reposed. Madame X was in the bathroom, away from harm. Another dog of Oneida's, Madame Butterfly, a toy Boston, was skipping round people, flying at them and kissing them.

The family and Mrs. Annichini talked of family matters. Edward presently said, "I've got to go and see Sam Innings about my eyes. I'll take Musty uptown with me, poor little dope."

Lou said he was going uptown that evening, to Madame Sarine's concert at Town Hall, and he would walk up with Edward. Oneida said she could not leave Madame X, but would send something to Madame Sarine to apologize for her absence, and after routing about in a carved chest for some time she brought out a silk-lined wooden box in which were various pieces of jewelry. She selected a handsome old Chinese bracelet in gold filigree, wrapped in an old Chinese silk handkerchief and gave it to Lou for Madame Sarine, telling him to explain that the little pin which fastened the bracelet was loose and she must have it repaired; it had been her mother's. Lou put on his black fedora, his black coat with the velvet collar, his white silk muffler, and stuffed the little present in his pocket. Edward put on his leather windbreaker and his army cap on his head and prescriptions for Madame X in his pocket. They walked first in the direction of Edward's house.

"Are Sam Innings and Vera Sarine still on the outs?"

"I should know if they don't know themselves."

"Crazy! How old is Musty now?"

"Jonathan gave Musty to my mother on her wedding anniversary, which one I don't know. Musty's about eleven. We didn't know his age when he came."

"That makes him nearly thirteen, though."

They passed through 16th Street between Fifth Avenue and Broadway. Edward said, "It's a bitterly cold street in winter."

He pointed out a tall, overhung doorway to a loft building. It was above three steps, on a platform, and was screened by the next wall.

"The wind cut my breath so short one night, I thought my lungs had stopped working. I dodged in there. There was a fellow there,

without a coat, before me. When I got home, I had all those rooms!
It was after Father's death and I hadn't rented Miss Holland's apartment. I would have taken a cat or a dog home. When I look at it,
I can't believe it. The whole thing, I mean, about society. The next
day I read of several people who were found dead in doorways, some
without shoes."

Lou said tranquilly, "Why don't you come over three times a week
and take up your music again?"

"Yeah, I'm looking for someone to study with. Walt gave me *The
Eighteenth Brumaire* and I didn't get a word. He said if I tried, I
would. It's ABC he said. I need someone as dumb as I am. I got to
join in somewhere."

"What would you want to do that for, Ned?"

"Get the social angle. You've got to have it even for Broadway.
I have no idea . . . I've got a couple of good ideas for plays. Open
with a taxi crash at the corner. I can think up plenty of openings.
A crossroads, it's 3:10 A.M., no one around. What are you doing out
so late? Cop's irritated. Characters come out of the side streets.
They disperse. Just then there's information there's a murder in one
of two houses you can see. Everyone saw everyone. Where do you
go from there? Name and address, monkeys? Naturally everyone
has something wrong, is a phony or living with the wrong woman
or tries to escape. Why? Social meaning: we're all second-class citi-
zens nowadays. Or here's another one. A murder is committed.
They pick up a handful of suspects. One of the men has total recall.
His alibi's good but he knows too much. It's all confirmed by a
good-natured muttonhead who makes so many mistakes everyone
laughs. Of course, he's the murderer. Mr. Memory is condemned:
there's a last-minute rescue. For the victim, I thought of a good
angle. Papa is murdered, he's ninety-two. He won't die. Every year
he issues bulletins to the newspapers and he says he has an infallible
recipe for old age. He's incredibly wealthy, dies suddenly; it's murder. His son, seventy, grandson, fifty, great-grandson, thirty-one,

[53]

great-great, seven; and others to match. He's at his third wife, they were all rich. Everyone's going crazy. He's a nasty old man, too, says he's a hundred and one. Everyone buttering him up, watching the other. What chance have they got? Everyone's guilty. Turns out he's the murderer, killed former wives, this time made a mistake . . . Eh? It's full of possibilities. Take some of the suspects above: one's a fellow who goes round saying he doesn't care if he kills millions; he wants to be known as a killer. Another says killing is his business, he's a professional. A third bird's a wholesaler too. The first is Napoleon, the second a butcher, the third a munitions-maker — too gruesome, eh? Never mind, forget that angle. People believe in the enemy in our midst. They're uneasy. Then the amateur solver. He's the stool pigeon. Love the stool pigeon and the informer. They make life safe for the uneasy millions."

"Edward! What views!"

"I guess I'm fed up. We people of the brownstone age are out of it."

"Let's get tickets for the new show with Lou Holtz."

"What do you say to Saturday?"

Edward got Musty and all three walked rapidly uptown. Lou was ahead of time and said he'd have a glass of milk later at the bar next to the Hall: he'd go along to Sam Innings's place with Edward.

Dr. Innings had his office on upper Madison Avenue. He put Edward into the chair and during the eye examination talked about Vera Sarine. He was a blond with a curling reddish beard. He said plaintively, "She never wrote to me all the time she was on tour and she has not received me since she came back. I am in the doghouse. And I got an apartment for her, paid a thousand-dollar premium. I had insomnia every night. Do you know I thought that door was alive; I thought someone would knock on it and bring me a letter, a telegram. I telegraphed to every address in her tour but received no reply. Why should I go to her concert? But I will. You will see me there." He sighed. "I suppose she told you all kinds of things about me."

The men protested that they had heard nothing from her for months. Dr. Innings said, "Yes, but I am sure she told Edward plenty about me."

He sighed and did not believe their denials. He gave Edward a prescription and said, "You take it to Philip Christy, don't you?"

"I'm coming to the concert with you, Lou. Let's go over to the apartment and get a drink: I need one. I'll try to see her tonight, surrounded with a hundred other people and then I'll toss all night."

"Why don't you resign yourself to the idea that she's a concert artist?" said Lou, smiling.

"No, no, I won't see my wife on the stage with everyone staring at her and all the journalists writing about her beauty," he said testily. "She won't live for you; you live for her." Edward laughed. Lou went home with Dr. Innings, but Edward left them.

"I have to go to Al Burrows to get my prescriptions filled, for the dog and me."

He took Musty with him and walked on uptown, crossing the park over to Broadway. He loved New York, especially at this time of night. It was rich and tender with neon. There was a faint shine with big gobs of light in the duckpond at the end of Central Park. Edward loved all the town, even the broken parts of Sixth Avenue. He walked from block to block, store to store, recognizing all the names, signs, kinds of wares: he was quite at home. He and Lou walked everywhere. The crowds of people were still pushing homewards, by bus and on foot, but the crowds were thinner now. Edward stopped for a sandwich and tomato juice. After a long trudge he got into the uptown district where again the stores improved in appearance and there were more restaurants with attractive entrances and lavish lights. He was in one of the Manhattan dormitory districts, among the wealthy apartment skyscrapers, near Riverside Drive. Al Burrows was manager of a large prosperous drugstore with candy, fountain and cigar concessions, on Broadway near 78th. Al Burrows came out from the compounding section settling his coat and looking dignified. When he saw Edward, he held out his large hand and said, "What can I get for you? Is anyone sick?"

"It's only my lamps and a sick pup."

Al looked over the prescriptions.

"I'll get you the eyewash right away: the other will take a bit of time. When do you want it? Sit down! Hey, Ben, give my pal a cup o' coffee. Or what do you want? Name it."

"Coffee."

Al Burrows came round to the soda fountain for a moment to lean over and ask why Edward was not at Madame Sarine's concert, said, "How's her boy friend? Are they still on the outs?"

"I guess so: he's weeping and wailing."

Burrows laughed slightly, "Why should a girl with her name in lights cook eggs for an eye-doctor? He's maritally illiterate. He's a male chauvinist."

He came round presently with the eyewash and told Edward to come back at closing time, if he could, for the other. They were rushed and he couldn't make it up before then. Edward said, "O.K. I'll be seein' you."

"So long, Doc."

"So long, Doc."

Edward sauntered off. In 104th Street, in a little wooden building, in a loft over a small, poor, Jewish congregation, Edward was working in a show. He was a Yale-trained man; had had jobs on Broadway. The glamour of stage and success surrounded Edward in his family and this only increased the stiffness of his walk, his seedy way of talking through his teeth, the number of dry tags in his speech, the number of vaudeville dialects, the weariness of his skin and the deadly ennui he felt. At the same time, he was proud of the present business. A group of successful little theater people, like himself, actors, stagehands, and all categories, self-organized, were putting on a poetic drama written by a young actor-dramatist called Roselli. The words, rhythm, background and characters belonged to the U.S.A. but the poetic conception and dramatic shadows were children of classic Italy. The poet Roselli, a tall fellow whose father had been born in an ancient village near Rome, had come out of New Mexico mines, come to New York and, with some friends, without any money, organized this unit, the Little Stage, chiefly for the production of his own works. All the work was free, offered by the artists and technicians who saw no outlets for their talents as in the days of the WPA.

Rehearsals began late in the evening, since several of the workers had to come from offices and factories at a distance. The play was called *Big Ditch* (*Acequia Madre*). *Big Ditch* had six weeks to go to the opening — "We hope," said Edward. Formerly, the readings had been held at houses round the Village, in Edward's house and once in the apartment of Edward's girl, Margot Rossi. The present room was a shabby meeting room with a stage and a refreshment bar in one corner. They had rigged up black rehearsal curtains. They had walked the play twice, and were just beginning to act it.

Edward with Musty walked up the broad dusty staircase of the tottering building. When he stepped onto the floor of the meeting hall, he felt the tremor of the old timbers.

"One day, we'll come crashing through on the heads of the True Believers of Bialystok," he said, as he came down the aisle. Musty trotted forward with his ears up. Edward referred to him as "that well-known dog-actor" because he had once appeared in summer stock in Long Island. He had been trained to run along a balcony at the back of the set, led by an actress, Mrs. Wharton.

On the black curtain was pinned a notice, "Episode 21." The working script with plans and designs lay on the stage, opened at Episode 21. Edward sat down at the piano and began to play a five-finger exercise. Musty paddled up and down, sniffing, and found himself a seat by the director. They had the top center floodlight on.

On the stage were three chairs and a pine-wood table and behind was
the back inset of a play then playing, a fallen log, a tree with a pale
green drop suggesting evening and against it, a dangling rope; a
swamp-water drama.

At this moment, Harry, an accountant, arrived panting. He was
the hero. He had a lank face, a dramatic voice and was restive and
docile, through self-discipline. Some girls from the swamp-water
play who did not know where they were to rehearse, meanwhile
waited in the wings and looked out, ignoring those who belonged
to the play in rehearsal. There were several handsome buxom girls
in slacks, some of the covergirl type in light dresses, a bony, rough-
skinned fiery woman in sweater and skirt, a hilarious, racketing, de-
mented little blonde with her hair in a topknot and tendrils of
hair on her neck; and a plain, flat blonde, the ambitious sternness
of whose face was concealed still by her seventeen years and her
sensual movement: she was a born actress. Sitting on the stage by the
wooden table was John, a prissy intellectual blond in a heather tweed
coat and tailored slacks. One evening, with his Princeton accent,
he had filled in as a cab driver. Since then he had been the only cab
driver in the outfit. Previously, they had cast him for intellectuals:
it had always been too flat. He was proud of his cab-driver role.

"Let's go," said Bob, the director.

Edward swung onto the stage in a big hop, was cheered, then
made an excuse to come down and go more soberly up. The girls
went up, swung round, showed their plump oily haunches, their
neat waists, their professional good nature. Only the crazy little
topknot kept showing off: she had a lover in the audience, a tall
grocer's assistant, a young man from upstate who was stage-struck.
He was understudying one of the parts in *Big Ditch*. He was large,
big-nosed, thick-haired, with a fighter's hands and a clean skin.
He had learned his part by heart at once and from then on waited
tranquilly for his cue, delivered his lines like a message and waited
ceremoniously for the next cue. He never missed his cue or showed

anxiety. When corrected, he politely attempted to adapt his manner or tone. His legs were like tree trunks. When told to walk in a natural way, these great legs shook like wires, his trunk crumpled. If left alone, he took long steps or tottered about with a peculiar roll in which he seemed to have confidence. When not on the stage, he read a sports paper in the back seats, or watched his girl. She could never get enough of his admiration and was always out and about to attract it. He loved fighting and was in a fight scene: however he was afraid of his fists and had to have many directions about what to do. When they showed him how it should be done, he laughed. He had never fought with anyone like anyone he saw on the stage; that was the trouble. He realized he must not hurt anyone, it was only a sham; and so he pulled his punches. Right at the end of the rehearsals of the fight scene, however, after he had patiently gone through the actions a number of times, some thin shadow of a real fight would appear on the boards and on these occasions he would stroll off the stage, smiling slightly, licking his lips; and he would go back to his sports page.

Edward was in the fight scene. He now spoke between his teeth, in a way which was intended to be weary, humorous, and to placate: it was the tone of voice in which he told most of his jokes. He said:

"Now come on fellows, now let's quit kidding around, now let's give it all we've got, we can throw that on the manure-pile, let's get this scene out of the ash can where we left it yesterday," and other commonplace expressions, somewhat snarling. Mrs. Wharton watched him persistently and smiled at him.

People got to feel they had known him a very long time; and he was one of those everyone called by his first name. Strangers talked about Edward long before they met him, and would even retell his tales and recount what he had said, without ever having met him. What he said got round town, in some circles. It was almost as if people were his friends for years and at last managed to meet him. Edward had spent about ten years in the theater for one thing.

It was his workshop; and here he felt at home, both ordinary and active. He had a pleasant importance, he was useful and he made essential decisions. He said, "Maybe I'm not an artist, but I am an utilitarian artisan."

He placed his right hand on the lap of the stage as a good-luck gesture. He stood now, for a moment and looked upwards into the raised scenery, into the light and the same sort of thought came to him as always when he first came to, or onto the stage, where a piece was in the making, before it was cast: This is the most ancient of the arts, some day, somewhere, some time, some fellow, perhaps like Mike there, the grocer's boy reading the form sheet, a big-handed, big-voiced fellow, stood up on a red rock, the sun striking hard, and said something, he laughed, he got excited and he cried, he failed altogether in his simple way and a real actor came up beside him, some little nervous thin-skinned man who needed grease paint to cover up his feelings; and so the stage began. Edward had a super-stition that the stage itself would teach him to write: he would produce a play out of and for the boards only.

At half time they went to the back room where someone had made coffee. Coming across the stage from behind, in his khaki sweater, spectacles glinting, lounging amiably, belly out, with his neat, crisp, brown hair, its thick brush going back over his ears, grinning, he moved among the actors, dropped to his haunches by a covey of stooping and squatting, rising and settling girls, all beautiful and vain, and put his arms round two of them, kissed both, said, "I'm a lonely heart, I want to get me a mistress."

"I'll be a mistress but never a wife," said, instantly, one of them in a scarlet dress who, at the same moment, withdrew her soft plump bosom from the comradely hands of a rakish young actor and moved back and up in one single voluptuous motion, as if startled. She laughed, took a step back. Suddenly her face clouded, became proud and she went and stood against the black curtain, arms akimbo. No one took any notice. At the end of the rehearsal, a number of the girls were standing near the curtains, a lovely frieze. Edward passed them without a look and they did not look at him. But a few moments later, he was talking to Mrs. Wharton with a satisfied look.

After the rehearsal, they nearly all went to a nearby cafeteria; but Edward had to get Madame X's medicines before the store closed and he set off at once with Musty, the well-known dog-actor, for Al Burrows's drugstore at 78th Street. Musty fluttered along, excited by his customary night walk, by the figures which appeared in and out of the dark — he would start, snuff, give an excited bark — by people talking in doorways. They were coming down Amsterdam Avenue. About 90th Street, a Negro taking a stroll appeared suddenly in the darkness. Musty jumped nearly out of his skin and began to bark nervously. The Negro, a tall, angular man, made a bogey gesture at the dog as if to pick him up: bent down, he splayed his fingers at him. Yelping hopelessly, Musty took to his heels and fled down the side street. Edward was startled, somewhat frightened, for the man took after Musty, running fast. Edward gave chase. Edward knew this part of town very well, but the man might have been a newcomer, a dope-taker, might simply hate dogs. The dog fled before them, yelping, scrambling, running for his life. At the corner, the Negro caught him and held him struggling against his coat. When Edward arrived, so breathless that he could not speak, the man handed him the dog, saying, "You don't want him to bark at folks, brother."

He went off into the dark. Edward, holding Musty, came back up the side street, so winded it seemed like a steep hill to him. He could feel the dog's heart pounding too. Presently he dropped the dog on the sidewalk.

"Dumb little mutt!"

Musty barked and sailed ahead. Edward was tired. He had been still full of his workshop, the effect of the little cavern of whispers and silences, the team that worked with him, the strange, poetic, ribald play, the appearance of the author Roselli, a tall, half-bald, lamp-eyed man, with his curious stage suggestions, a man who felt the stage more than anyone he knew. He was excited by two drinks he had taken at a ginmill on the way down Amsterdam Avenue. Some plays were written, for example, for the stage furniture. Example: *Arsenic and Old Lace*. Theme — the gruesome humorous. A (flat) closet and staircase play. Some plays were written in this way: Act One, closet farce; Act Two, substitution of costumes, or mask farce; Act Three, Belvedere or many exits farce. The author Roselli had written a play about a set of three chairs. Edward concentrated on the present play, *Big Ditch*. They planned to turn the back of the bar to the audience. Perhaps this gave the whole thing an indecorous undressed look and doubled up on the effect of the tumbled bed and the girls in their dressing gowns? The stage was decidedly *négligé* at that moment. He tried to think of precedents. What about Roselli's interludes, done with black curtains and black cubes at different levels, terrifying brass masks and black cowls? For Edward it had a great poetic sweep: the director was plainer minded. New York had decided on its kind of poetry, psychoanalysis; "and so that's that," said the director.

I'll strike out into something new if I can, thought Edward and reverted to his search for Ideas. How about Episode 21? Nowadays, he thought, they have gone in for the cosmic mystery story, What is Life? What is in the Subconscious if you fish? What is Time? What is Destiny? What is anything? All a means of shouldering off the present, but they like it. A man walks through a door, he's in yesterday or tomorrow or his own mind or what have you? That's the cosmic closet form. A man's himself, then a murderer, then God, and so on; the cosmic change of costume form. Dumb though. Then there is the social heartache. People don't like. As for me, I like the character sketch. There's my accountant: when he went with me to the income-tax people he trembled like a leaf all the morning, yet everything was aboveboard. Take a lawyer, say a corporation lawyer. For the first time in his life, he has to defend a criminal. He's sick. He hasn't a ghost of a show and he sees his client in horizontal tailoring. "To think I should have jailbirds among my clients!" He's sure to lose. D.A. has a water-tight case. Some intervention and he wins brilliantly. No zebras in his zoo. But it's been too much for him. He faints in court. Then what? Too thin, though, for a play. Maybe all right if — Episode 21. The way they play it's the play.

He had arrived at the drugstore. It was half-past eleven and Burrows was ready to close. He was talking to three pickup girls who were finishing Coca-Colas at the fountain. They were from the quiet houses around the corner. They came to Al for their troubles. Al stood, his tufted hair right under the light showing thinner, his sleeves up, rolling up a package in white paper.

"Hello, Doc."

"Hello, Doc, here's your medicine."

The pharmacist took a nylon toothbrush in a plastic tube down from the stand and said, "Try it: see if you like it, just came in. Are you going over to your aunt's? I'll drive you down. Just sit down while I close up."

An old man came in and stood at the side counter between boxes of goods. When the pharmacist came down the alley he whispered to him. The pharmacist presently handed him a little packet. The old man, neatly dressed, well cared for, about sixty, went carefully out and as he passed the girls smiled sweetly and bowed slightly.

Said one of the girls, "Do you know that refugee?"

"Sure," said Al; then, "Come behind with me, Eddie."

They went behind the shelves piled high which hid the dispensing section. The pharmacist began to clean up. He smiled, fixing things with his big nimble fingers.

"The law says you must have a square yard of table clear for mixing prescriptions."

"Did you get your mother home, Al?"

"Yes," he said, showing the edge of his teeth, faintly, as if smiling.

"How is she?"

"She's got about two months to live. If anyone comes within a foot of her she says, Don't hurt me, don't touch me. You'd think she could actually feel a foot away."

"Must she live two months more of this?"

"Yes," he said, under his breath, showing his teeth again as if smiling. Someone entered the store. Burrows looked through the spy hole which was just behind the cash register in the rear of the shelves and went out.

"My old pal!"

He returned after a while wearily grinning and went to the sink to wash a measuring glass. He had some coffee on a burner and offered Edward a measuring glass full. He jerked his head towards the store.

"He calls me the Fixer. He's a magician. He lived round here in an attic for years when he was a down-and-outer and he says I'm responsible for his good luck. He got a turn on the vaudeville stage and since then he's done well." Al leaned forward confidentially and smiled. "He calls himself Bolo: the team of Nello and Bolo." He swabbed down the counter, sighed and grinned again. "He has faith in me. He wants me to go fishin' on Sunday out from Sheepshead Bay. You pay a couple of bucks and you catch enough fish, maybe, for a few days. Would you like to go?"

"Never crossed the sea but in a Constellation," said Edward.

"No good for fishing."

"I was frightened when I looked at the map and saw those couple of pin points we had to land on, the Azores. But I sat up front the whole time and swapped stories with the flight officers, both New York boys, and I forgot about it."

"Doesn't your girl like the water?"

"I don't know. We never go out. We just go from one apartment to the other and sometimes to the theater. Once, about ten years ago, when we first met, we went to Staten Island to see what it was like."

[64]

Another man came in through the doors, now standing ajar, and asked for a cigar. The stand was closed. Al gave him one of his own, after the man had demurred for some time. Al had a box full of some unbranded cigars that he got from a store near Astor Place. They had a talk. Al let the customer out and came back. Passing Edward to hang up the dish towel, the pharmacist murmured with a boyish grin, "He says he has a bit of ground up over on the Palisades and I can go there with my girl if I want to."

He had a great joyous melodious laugh that made the glassware jingle. Al locked the drug cabinet, emptied out the cash register, shut a double cabinet which had stood open all the evening, finished up chuckling, "Thieves were in the other night; they pried open that double cabinet and they never found the dangerous drugs right in front of their noses."

They stepped out. Edward said, "Aren't you afraid coming out with your cashbox at night like that?"

Al strode along towards his paintless jalopy, parked round the corner. The old man was just stepping out of a grocery store with a middle-aged girl with long blonde hair. He was carrying a large bag of groceries and looked mortified. Burrows glanced, said, "I started selling drugs in Harlem, the big brown boys used to come in and get Jamaica ginger, it's a stomachic and stimulant, you know. They took a lot, got quite drunk on it, that was during prohibition. They got to know me. I got to be quite popular with those guys. They'd come in all the time, they got over trying anything rough on me. Are you going home?"

"To my aunt's, then to my girl's."

They started to ride.

"I've got to get off my feet. I spent a lot of money on special shoes the last couple of years and none of them works. The doctor said it might be the smoking," said Al.

"Are you going to flop at my place tonight?"

"No, tonight I'm going home. Got to see if the old lady is cheatin'."

"She rang up the other day to find out if you really slept at my place. I said sure, because you'd eaten the ham sandwich and two cold pancakes."

"Was she convinced?"

"I don't know."

Al gave a ringing laugh. After a while, he said, as he maneuvered a corner carefully, "Did I tell you about the time we had a drugstore in 125th street." He paused to laugh thoughtfully. "One day, a girl comes into the drugstore and tells me she has three black hairs between her breasts; she can't get them out herself because it hurts too much; she wants me to take them out with a pair of tweezers. 'It's very embarrassing,' she says. So I got into the big storeroom with her — "

He gave his tranquil, deep laugh. "I got excited and I couldn't stop there."

"Did she have the three hairs?" inquired Edward.

"Eh? I suppose so; I don't remember now."

His voice cleared, he continued, "Eh, you saw that fellow with the hat on hanging round the back tonight? That was Truex, the boss. He's a friend of mine. He believes in me. He wants me in a store of my own."

"Why don't you do it?"

"He'd put up a couple of thousand, but I need more. Then I want to get off my feet. Also, you see, I'd be a boss, I'd have to quit the union. Truex wants to come along and put up the shelves; that's the whole story: he loves carpentering. The only kind of store I could buy would need a lot of carpentry. I've been round lookin' but I can't make up my mind. I suppose I'll be here this way till I'm an old man with clean-shaven whiskers. Every now and then I get smacked down with the thought that I'm joggin' 'long in the shafts like a good old nag and one day I'll slip on the ice. Maybe I'm in the dumps. The hell with it — I'd like to make a bag of money before everything caves in. I'd be doing fine finagling if I were free. I'd know how to pick my time, I could see when things were beginning to tempo down so that I could jump before the big crash. But to go into the shortage business I need a partner. It has two advantages: I'm my own master and I'm off my feet; and I can really make money. I've been looking the field over for a place to strike root and I'm willing, strong and able enough to stand up to the New York drive for another coupla years — and then I'd like to lay off, go somewhere. If I could figure out where. I'm only held back by the thought, would I make friends as good as I made in New York? What do you think?"

"I met our guys everywhere I was: you can't get away from them," said Edward.

Every time they passed a drugstore, Al told him about the man who ran it and the style of business done, as well as the cost of the installation. When they passed 20th Street he pointed west and said, "Louise lives there now." He mentioned a name Edward had heard before from men, well-known Village name. Al said with pride, "Four children and wouldn't marry their fathers. She's living with the Swedish janitor now," he ended doubtfully. "Well, here's the house, Doc!"

"So long, Al."

"So long, Eddie."

The old car tottered respectably round the corner.

In the apartment he found only Oneida and Lou Solway with Madame Butterfly, the toy Boston, who was still up. Lou was reclining in a chaise longue, holding Camels, a very old tiger-striped cat, spread-eagled on his chest and purring harshly. The pinkish ceiling lights dazed them all. Lou said, "Let's eat: I haven't had any dinner yet."

"Would you like a bacon sandwich, Edward?"

"O.K."

"Where were you all evening, Edward?"

"Taking a walk."

"You weren't at Margot's."

"H'm."

"At Mrs. Wharton's?"

They sat round till it was nearly two o'clock. Time dragged on. They said little. Lou told one of his funny tales, the point of which was that he had missed the point. Edward told a Willie Howard story. There were long silences broken by the buzz-saw sound of the cat and the apparent irrelevancies of people who have known each other a lifetime. Edward related a recent experience.

Musty was nervous lately with the coming of spring. A few nights ago, he had darted off, in the direction of the Solway apartment; perhaps to see Madame Butterfly. Edward had run after him whistling, calling. It was about three in the morning. Musty had stopped dead under a lamp and there Edward saw another dog, a black-backed old Alsatian with a broken front paw, which he knew at once; and with it its master, whom he knew by sight, a straw-blond, hunchbacked dwarfish Pole with a thin face, in age probably nearer thirty than forty, but looking old. There was a Polish house somewhere in the district, an old brownstone house taken over and used by a "White Polish Society." They had a restaurant there, a piano always going, a stunted tree, a cat with kittens in all colors, that played along the sidewalk like fleas. Often one heard Chopin played there in a fiery style. Coming towards it, going from it, one met Polish types, the men distinguished at once by their hats aslant, a jaunty air, peculiar dandyism and their conventionally fierce looks at every other male, conventionally romantic looks at every woman: old-style exile Poles, doing some exile job. Edward had first seen the hunchback one evening a few years back, leaning from an open window upstairs, in summer, while others sang in the room, this one, with his gaunt looks, big eyes, and lank hair, being the image of the European movie nationalist revolutionary of old days, something out of a 1906 romance anyhow, thought Edward. Later he

[68]

found out the man was deformed and the janitor or porter of the place.

The Pole stopped and took Musty by the collar. He too knew Edward and his dog quite well by sight. "Thanks," said Edward, panting. "I know you're the man with the Scottie," said the Pole. He fastened the leash to Musty's collar. The hunchback made a gesture towards his forehead as if to raise his hat. He never wore a hat, that Edward had seen. The Pole nodded, smiled, hesitated, said "Good night," whistled to his dog and went deliberately away. As he plodded past Edward, "at the last moment," Edward said, he flushed and Edward was sure that he had wanted to make friends with him and had not the courage. Edward went on with Musty, forgetting to scold him and himself aching because he had not spoken to the lonely man. In the afternoons, when he went out, he would see the Pole walking with his big black Alsatian, in the streets, just before sundown, or coming through the park, and always following one path. But Edward had seen him once in Washington Square, in the early morning, when he had been returning from Margot's. He was lying face down in the grass and his dog sitting beside him.

"Two men and two dogs," said Edward. Musty yapped.

"Yah! Don't make believe you understand me," said Edward. He continued, "A play about a hunchback? Two men struggling together to knock each other over the cliff. He's your political enemy or a panhandler you're sick of, someone you met in an elevator or a hotel that you just can't stand, an impulse, a bore, a map of the streets you must avoid, the world a prison and then two men on a cliff, struggling to get free, that's friendship or love most of the time, so why not two men brought together by two dogs, the Pole and me? And then there was one."

Oneida suddenly said, "Edward, are you going to take that brass plate Dr. Edward Massine off your door?"

"I'm known as the Doc as far down as 5th Street and east and west from First Avenue to Broadway."

Oneida was putting on a black satin Chinese lounge suit, which she sometimes also wore to the stores, under a coat.

"First Avenue. Margot and I got a salad there the other day. It's the place where we get the grapes for wine. We got two whole bags full. The Italian said, 'It'll sprout out of your ears, Doc.'"

"I thought you were going over to Margot's, Ned."

"No hurry. Are you going to bed?"

"Soon. It's half past two."

"I suppose I should take down that brass plate. Someone ran near the house asking for the doctor, today. There was that murder down the street."

"Oh-oh, did you see it, Edward?"

"Naw, was in bed." He laughed. "They used to have dicks on my line during the war, you know, on account of my work. One day, I had the phone off and when I picked it up, I heard one man say to the other, 'I'm going off to lunch, will you watch the doctor's line?' They must have been sorry for me, a doctor with no patients. If I take it down, it seems to me as if I agreed to my father's death. The room's just as it was when we first bundled everything in, to let their apartment."

Edward wiped his glasses. There was another silence, which Oneida broke by saying crossly, "Edward and I were brought up by the old."

Lou got up, fetched his pyjama suit, and started to undress, yawned.

Oneida said, "I remember you were such a pretty baby. I cried when they cut off your curls. It was Ollie did that!" She colored.

Edward said, "Now I look like one of those little guys with a baize apron you find in the back corridors of hotels with a dustpan in their hands. Or the Sad Sack."

Oneida said, "You do not, Edward."

Lou laughed.

[70]

Oneida said, "I don't believe in self-analysis. Let sleeping dogs lie!" They all burst out laughing.

Edward said, "Well, got to go and see my girl. Will you keep Musty? She can't bear him."

Oneida said angrily, "What a shame. It shows up a person."

"It shows up what? Margot says dogs show greed, sloth and venom in us."

"She has a wicked nature."

"I told her, what about working-class dogs, shepherds, war dogs, the Belgian dogs that drag the carts about: it would break your heart."

They said nothing for a while, but went on with what they were doing, with tired, peaceful looks. Edward got on his gear, took his soldier's cap out of his pocket and remarked, "I'll get Musty about eleven tomorrow. The girls' lunch is at three. Miss Holland was peeved that you invited Margot before she did."

"She seemed crusty to me this morning when I telephoned."

"Sourdough, like," said Lou.

There was another pause. Edward patted Musty and handed his leash which was trailing to Oneida. He slouched towards the door and said, yawning, "See you about eleven tomorrow."

"Yes."

"If Margot doesn't shoot me."

"Edward! It's nearly three. You'd better go home at this hour."

"One of these days she'll get real mad and look for another fellow," said Lou, seriously.

"She'll never leave me."

"Whom could she get?" said Oneida.

"Thanks," said Edward.

The telephone rang.

"There she blows," said Lou.

But at the other end of the line was Pat Hornsby, top-floor tenant in Edward's house. He told Edward that he had telephoned all round town for him. There was trouble next door in Edward's other house; the fire engine was there and someone was breaking in the door with an ax. Edward retailed this strange bit of news to his relatives and rushed out, begging them to telephone Margot and tell her this had happened, just as he was leaving for her place.

Oneida went to the phone and broke into a grand cooing. After a considerable chat, she put down the phone and turned to Lou.

"She was waiting up for Edward. She said even the fire department comes to Edward's aid. You heard me. I asked her why she made the man go over there at this hour. She told me to stop dripping poison. I told her her honey was on a thorn bush."

"Mee-ow!"

"It would be a tragedy if Edward married her; it would finish him."

"Something will finish him, unless he dies before. Give me a cup of black coffee, Oneida. It's too late to go to bed. I'll go over and see if I can do anything for Edward. I'll just put my coat on over these pyjamas."

"Oh, I can't leave Madame X."

"I'll go," said Lou.

Edward ran as far as Third Avenue where his wind gave out. There were a few people walking up and down Third Avenue leisurely, and a brawl going on at the corner of 16th Street, between two men. One man was rolling the other in the gutter with his foot. Edward saw this same couple brawling most nights. He hurried on up the avenue, turned down his street and found the fire engine just turning away. He hailed the firemen and asked about the fire.

"No fire, false alarm, someone in the basement had a bad dream," said one of them. Edward went on with a heavy heart. The basement apartment next door had recently been taken by an intellectual couple recommended by Miss Waldmeyer. Miss Waldmeyer had made few mistakes; and they had conformed to Edward's conditions, that is, a couple on good terms, intellectuals, with a regular job, no problems. From the beginning, these had been quarrelsome and had already got up five or six petitions about things in the house, petitions signed by one or two of the other tenants, perhaps just to have peace and quiet. The Barbours were persistent, regular gadflies. The petitions were about dust in the front hall, the peeling front door, the age of the boilers, the dampness of the back kitchen, the presence of dogs in the garden, the piano practice of the young man above them. They pretended to the sole use of the garden, while the tenants on the first floor back wanted it too, and Dr. Pilsener wanted it for his dogs: likewise his laboratory was in the garden. The fact of the matter was that there was scarcely any garden: three people in it made standing room only, said Edward.

The front room and back room on the first floor were occupied by different tenants. In the front room was a pale young man with a small income who played the piano from eight-fifteen in the morning till twelve and from one-thirty till a quarter to six. Sometimes, he tinkled a little at night, but not beyond nine-thirty. The trouble was that for four and a half months, since his arrival, he had played the same ten bars from a Mozart concerto. In the Barbours' bathroom you could hear his boot thumping out the time. If he made an error he stopped at once and began to play that bar over and over, and then began the whole thing again. He had some motor defect which caused him to make mistakes in nearly every bar, and to make mistakes as often after one month as after one day. He went away each week end. When he came back, he had lost all his skill and would begin from the beginning.

The Barbours had sent round a petition. The tenant on the first floor back was slightly deaf. He declared that he liked music and he thought it wrong to hinder an artist's practice. The man above said he heard nothing. Edward said he did not see what he could do, as the young man kept to such reasonable hours. The Barbours then said that Edward had hired the young man to get them out and get a higher rent for their apartment. As nothing whatever was done, they began to keep a book of observations about what went on in the apartment upstairs. "We must have evidence, it must not be a matter of assumptions," said Professor Barbour. They kept showing their diary to Edward. The pianist's name was Drinkwine, obviously an assumed name. There were two doors to his apartment: one was kept locked with a huge rusty bolt and chain; the other he locked whenever he went in or out. He did not seem to eat anything. Sometimes, he put a very small tin which had contained sardines or pâté de foie on the floor outside his door. He had no one in to clean: Heaven only knew what the place must be like. He was unnaturally pale with bright eyes and straggling hair. He never said good-day, nor did they. One never heard a sound from nine-thirty till eight-fifteen in the morning; there were no visitors. He received no mail: they had examined all the mail, each morning, on the table in the front hall. On the other hand, mail did come for a person not tenanting the house, a Mr. Bassett: therefore Drinkwine was Bassett. "Or Drinkwine is a corporation and Bassett the managing director," said Edward. Before a thunderstorm, he played the piano more than usual and once up to ten-thirty at night. During every thunderstorm, he took a bath. If he happened to see them on the stairs, or in the hall, when he was coming out of his door, he gently retired and shut his door, only emerging when they had gone. Mrs. Barbour was afraid to stay in the house with him.

The other petition had concerned the couple who lived on the second floor of the house. They were playwrights and had a boy of eleven. Edward was very fond of them and intended, if he ever got an Idea, to ask them to fix up his play for Broadway. The Barbours read their plays avidly, tore them to pieces, stopped Edward on the street to discuss them. The little boy made marks on the stairs, bounced his ball against the front door and whistled in the yard. They had spoken to him and no question but that he did it with a vengeance. He gave the whole house the appearance of a tenement.

Edward's heart was jumping away and he was flushed with indignation when he came to the house. The lights were on in the windows under the basement steps, the door stood open, and fragments of glass and wood lay about. It was true, the door had been smashed. Edward took off his glasses and rushed in.

At the middle door which entered the boiler room stood Professor Barbour dictating to a policeman. He wore his pyjamas, shoes and spectacles. He was saying:

"The partition wall is only one brick thick as you can see, and so contravenes buildings regulations A, B7c, and Y2 and tenement laws subsections K99 and P–IIa, and is a violation and actionable as set forth in the prosecution's case in Smudge *v*. Browne. I have had my lawyer look into all this and my information is correct. I am going to bring suit against the landlord. There is no superintendent in the building and persons not tenants are allowed to occupy vacant rooms in the house next door. No one knows what they may do and they are not responsible. The landlord no doubt receives rent from these persons but pretends that they are friends in order not to install a fire escape which he would be obliged to under the law. The ceiling of the basement is so thin that bad smells pass from the first floor down to the basement, and persons upstairs can be heard coughing."

"What the hell is going on? Where's the fire? I'm the landlord," said Edward, stepping forward, peering, sniffing and putting on his glasses again.

Professor Barbour turned and pointed at Edward:

"This is the responsible person. His buildings are standing in defiance of the law and should be condemned. We suffer from one hundred per cent negligence and overcrowding in defiance of the tenement code. He should have installed two fire escapes at least two years ago, when he permitted a number of tenants, including Koreans, the missionary's converts, in the basement. The garbage is not appropriately provided for, as a tenant in this house puts his garbage in the corridor, thus attracting vermin and making obstacles,

[75]

which might prove dangerous to life in case of a fire. The tenants on the top floor next door, Mr. and Mrs. Patrick Hornsby, violated the building regulations last Christmas Day in having a curtain drawn across part of the hall, in front of the single room at the top of the stairs. It was a flimsy curtain of red crepe paper and highly inflammable. We swear to this because we were there at the party. No one has ever been inside the apartment upstairs in this building and it is likely that the tenant has vermin there as we observed some vermin in his garbage."

"Say, Barbour, where is the fire?" asked Edward and pushed past the professor into the kitchen. Mrs. Barbour was there making a cup of Postum. She was a strong middle-aged woman, with wiry hair, powerful eyes and hawk nose. On the table were cups and saucers, and the proofs in galleys of her latest book.

"Hello, Mabel," said Edward.

"Hello, Edward! I'm glad you're there."

"I'm glad too! What's all this? You could have telephoned me."

"Oh, he's so nervous, Edward, and you know he's always had a grudge against you."

"Against me, why?" Edward looked into her face.

"No reason why, against you, specially." She laughed. "It doesn't seem natural to Joe a man younger than him taking rent from him."

"A perfesser, sure," said Edward.

Mrs. Barbour laughed. "He's really O.K.," she said.

"I know he's O.K.," said Edward.

"But he does too much: he's nervous," said Mrs. Barbour.

"Yeah, I know," said Edward.

"Were you at that meeting in 34th Street? He got fifteen hundred for the School for Freedom," said Mrs. Barbour. "Only a small audience too, of middle-class intellectuals, not organized."

"Did he? Well, I would have gone: but I can give you ten bucks," said Edward.

"That'll be swell," said Mrs. Barbour.

Edward handed her a ten-dollar bill, drank a cup of Postum and sidled out of the kitchen.

Mrs. Barbour was an energetic professional body-snatcher. She wrote passionate biographies of the fashionable extinct, such as Henry James, Tchaikovsky, Chopin, Freud, Baudelaire and Tolstoy, and dealt with popular resurrections at the rate of not less than one every year. She was a well-known liberal publicist and had the admiration of certain groups among the intelligentsia and of course of her husband, Professor Barbour. He was a well-known cerebrator who gave courses on a number of subjects in the Modern School of Sociology and Philosophy; and had well-attended week end and summer courses. He was a nuisance as a tenant only because he imported his judicial, impartial, logical outlook into affairs in the basement. He did it consciously.

Said he, "If you have the neophilosophical approach you can virtually understand and interpret anything without specific knowledge: for the ideological approach is correct."

His theory about Edward's two houses can be summed up as follows: Edward was a landlord, hence an oppressor of his tenants, whether he willed it or not, and anything that happened to his profit, whether instituted, managed, shaped or brought to a head and otherwise procured by or for him, voluntarily or involuntarily, was for the oppression of his tenants and the expression of a profit. Where the tenants' need and Edward's instinct failed, society itself, shaped by and for landlords, secured the desired results for him by its laws, conventions, silent compacts, hindrances, laxities and licences and by necessity alone. This was all expressed all the time in Edward's two houses. "The part is as perfect as the whole in that without it the whole cannot function: there are no permissible exceptions," said Professor Barbour in this connection. "There is the old story of the bum who picked a louse off his shirt and put it back, saying, That isn't the son-of-a-bitch that bit me. It is no use our saying we need not concern ourselves with Edward Massine because he seems inattentive to the business of extracting profit." Edward was, because he was theirs, the most perfect expression of landlord society at that address in time and in that frontage of space they occupied. As the rest of the tenants were a distracted sort of people, unaware of what was going on about them, the Barbours declared them to be "politically illiterate" and tried to educate them in the forms of freedom. This they did by visits, by getting up petitions, and by sending round typed circulars. Mrs. Barbour did the typing.

In the present instance, they had found out that a fire had been started in the old fireplace in the basement next door: they had felt the heat and feared a fire, because of the one-brick wall. They had determined to call the fire department and the building inspectors in the middle of the night because there was no other way to get their attention. While the building inspector was there (they had called him at his private address and asserted that the house was coming down on their heads that minute) they drew his attention to a large crack in one wall and to the way the rafters trembled.

The fire department had now gone, the inspector had gone with an unpleasant expression, but upset in his mind, and the policeman on the block was left; he was taking down the professor's notes. Mrs. Barbour explained all this to Edward.

"Well, you can quit as soon as you like; I won't hold you to your lease," said Edward.

"You can't put us out in this housing crisis, we have our lease; and we will see that you put no one else into it. We would rather have the place condemned."

At this point Lou Solway arrived, with his pants pulled over his pyjamas, his black hat and overcoat on. He was still wearing his slippers. At the same time, Mrs. Annichini and the Hornsbys came on the scene. They were in night-gear. Mrs. Hornsby was a fascinating ugly woman about thirty-three with such a stoop that her backbone was the shape of a question mark. She was long and thin with a bony nose and her scarce straight hair was done in a topknot from which sprouted mouse-colored strands. This was held in place by a bandanna handkerchief and a Spanish comb. She had a reporter's notebook and was smoking a cigarette. She wore a flannel nightgown and a man's windbreaker. "I quite agree, honey, it's fantastic," she said to everybody. Mr. Hornsby was blond, forty, had a red face and was six feet tall. He wore blue silk pyjamas, a camel's-hair overcoat and horn-rimmed spectacles. He peered closely at everything and gave opinions while his wife leaned her backbone politely against the walls. Miss Holland was in her working overalls and Mrs. Annichini had an overcoat over some dark-blue satin pyjamas given to her at one time by Oneida. There were long explanations and Professor Barbour objected to all these people invading his quarters. "I quite agree, honey, it's fantastic," said Mrs. Hornsby, making very neat and pretty notes. She was a free-lance reporter.

Presently, everyone left and Professor Barbour tacked up over the broken door a bit of coarse cloth he usually wrapped round his typewriter when he was traveling.

The policeman had finished taking notes but still listened to the professor's remarks. The professor peppered him with mentions of the Board of Health.

"This man is not Doctor Massine, I am Doctor Barbour."

"O.K., Doc," said the cop to Edward.

"Tough luck, Barbour," said Mrs. Hornsby.

When the patrolman left, he found Edward on the sidewalk. Edward said, "You look punch-drunk, officer. The screwiest things happen on this beat at this time of night."

"You're telling me, brother."

"The professor's not a bad guy."

"That guy ain't a professor, he's a dentist: he's got some line of laughing gas I don't get."

"Yeah, a hell of a note. Look, officer, grab yourself a sandwich and a cup of coffee. It's tough, the graveyard shift. Since this rumpus took place in my house, I feel I owe you this couple of bucks."

"Thanks, Doc."

"So long. I'll be seein' you."

The officer saluted and walked off towards Third Avenue.

Mr. Hornsby went back to bed but Mrs. Hornsby went into Mrs. Annichini's kitchen with everyone else. Edward burst out laughing. They all sat down at the kitchen table and drank some rum offered by Mrs. Annichini.

"Edward, why don't you go over and see your girl? She telephoned while you were at the fire," said Miss Holland.

"I will: I'll give her particulars of the great fire," said Edward.

Edward walked towards Margot's house. As he was going through Washington Square, a small, hatless man came up to him and, holding up three fingers successively, remarked breathlessly, "Adyin, dva, tree, adyin, dva, tree, toid avenya, sixty-eight, toid."

"Do you want to go to 86th Street? Take the Third Avenue trolley." Edward pointed. The man shook his head and repeated what he had said, added "*Neetchevo*" and shook his pocket. Edward laughed, pulled out the first coin in his pocket, a half-dollar. The man held it up in the faint light of morning, and suddenly ran off, weeping aloud and saying in pure American, "Now I can get one — oooh, now I can get one."

Edward went on. At the other end of the park a lamp was shining on the tough shining network of twigs, now sharply uplifted, strong with the running sap. The buds were fat, heavy and glossy as beetles. There was a slight mist about. Edward stopped and scrutinized the tree. Margot usually said things to him like this:

"Do you ever stop and look at trees and shadows, Edward, or do you only think of your family all the time? Have you any of the mystic in you?" He had at first been puzzled by this because Margot was not a mystic. Once, she had said, "You, I am sure, would only write works of imagination, that is all you have in you I prefer

[80]

books of analysis where the writer explains a people's motives. You never understand anyone that I can see. That is the weakness of living all your life in one setting. You get shortsighted."

She knew Edward was shortsighted. She said on one occasion, "On the benches in this park, what do you see?"

"I see a sort of . . . huddled masses, blocked-out shapes."

"While I see every detail, what they are wearing, and even their characters from this distance."

She had a bitter idea of people. What she meant by a work of imagination was an adventure story. Whatever she said about him was not to his advantage, but was a contemplative foreboding for his future, and yet a desperate hope, like a widowed mother with a good-natured son. He felt at ease with her stony unbending nature, he was afraid of the storms of passion, ignorance of life, vengeance, recrimination that boiled in her. They had been with each other a long time, eleven years, and she had the dramatic attraction, the power of the unsuitable mate. She was the only person besides his mother who had ever made him unhappy. He was very sorry for her, of course. Walking towards her, he thought a little about her. He expected to be scolded, even hated today. She gave him periods of rest, out of consideration. He was like an old husband. She was going to tell him to marry her, for this was what she had threatened over the telephone. He had no reason not to marry, but it hardly paid him and he felt that he would have been closing the door on someone else who had not come into his life yet. He often felt the stirring of a passionate attachment, of genuine love, of self-sacrifice. He kept waiting.

He said to a taxi driver who was waiting at the corner of the street, "What's the time, bud?"

"Later than it was before."

"Come on, a lady's waiting for me."

"What the hell kind of a lady?"

"My wife."

[81]

"Tough! A quarter after six."

"So long, brother."

At this hour, Margot was waiting for him, in her clothes for the day, with a pretty blue smock over them. She was wearing horn-rimmed glasses. Her work, a piece of white satin, on which she was painting a design, lay under a daylight lamp on a trestle table of heavy wood. She was cool, dry, when he let himself in. Edward took off his jacket and settled himself in a chair with an irritated air. He yawned. She turned the light off, covered the work and went into the kitchen, returning almost at once with an apron on and food, with a linen napkin, on a tray.

"Coffee or a drink?"

"Everything you can lay before me."

Edward kicked off his shoes and lounged showily in his chair; he loosened his coat and belt to show a small pot belly which had been growing on him since his return. She stood for a moment in the door looking at him, then went back to the kitchen. Edward kept looking down with a sullen knowing expression and twiddling his toes. When she went out, he looked round the apartment, which was composed of two main rooms with kitchen and bathroom. It was handsome, furnished in a heavy style of the twenties. There was hand-painted china in a dresser, books behind glass, a crackle-glaze bowl full of potpourri on top of the book-cupboard. Each room had a single intention. There was no breakfast nook in the kitchen, no sofa in the dining room and no bookcase in the bedroom. Margot, however, was forced to have her worktable in the dining room; and had put a big leather chair for Edward opposite her own chair in front of the fireplace. The kitchen and the bathroom were uncommonly neat, and the clothes closet and shelves in the entry had all the trimmings, boxes, moth-proof bags pictured in women's magazines. The walls were pleasantly done in mauve and gray with long dust-yellow curtains, made of an old fabric. Through the half-open door, Edward could see the neat bedroom with walnut furniture, cut and beveled glass, a tiger rug across the bed, ceramic pots of face cream, flower prints. The tiger on the bed was the one strange thing, and Edward admired it.

Edward rose and looked at Margot's work, drinking but holding his drink away from the table. She had asked his help with the design. She had taught him various things about what was needed for women's clothes. Birds were unlucky: you could not have an allover pattern of dogs. She had designed a scarf with a single word scrawled over it in various beautiful scripts. Edward had got a friend of his to design a couple of special scripts for it. The word used was: Love.

Margot stood beside him, discussed the present design, told him what was going on uptown. He told her news of the theater. All this was in subdued usual tones.

"I only need to write one," said Edward, pouring himself another drink, "if it goes. I have a Broadway success, Hollywood, radio, and all kinds of rights follow. You can live for years on one success."

"You're not strong enough to leave me straight; you're always looking for something to take you away from me, like Hollywood."

"Don't you want me to do something in life?"

"I'd like you better if you had the courage to do anything on your own, even go to the dogs."

"You leave my family out of this."

"I know you think our marriage wouldn't be very successful."

"You make me unhappy: I don't want to take up with you permanently."

"Isn't it a bit late to think of that?"

"We've been sustained by a long series of mistakes and misfits. It's like a rack-and-pinion railway — we must be going somewhere, you think. We're not going to trouble, we've always been there."

"Everything you say is so strained. You're nervous. You live upside-down. You don't realize you'd be a different man if you led a natural life. I don't want you to be bored, just a happy medium."

[83]

"Bruised ectoplasm: or, the man who struck a happy medium."

"You think yourself very funny."

"I don't think anything very funny."

"I mean what I said on the phone."

"Which of many things you said on the phone lately?"

"About getting married. It's a pure sadistic pleasure for you to hear me say it over and over."

"A Sad Sackish pleasure. It's not a pleasure. You don't really desire me. You only wait to pick at me. You're getting neurotic."

"That's the remark of a hardhearted man."

He drank the coffee she had now given to him, lapping it up noisily. She said sadly, "You're wasting your life and mine too."

"Why suddenly now, Margot? Why out of nothing?"

"Six years ago we went to Florida to get married. When we got there, you said nothing about it, and I was ashamed to. We hung around and came back just the same."

"I don't want to get married yet. I have my reasons, and they're good."

"Name just one."

He passed his cup. She started to fill it, but abruptly put the cup down. Coffee spilled on the cloth. She cried:

"Look, look!"

He was sorry. Her face turned haggard.

"You don't want to be bothered with anyone. You're self-sufficient."

"I'm very fond of a lot of people. I have hundreds of friends, people who love me, even. I'm not very energetic but I'm useful, I do no harm. There's nothing sacred in eight o'clock rising."

"Yes, but your object in not marrying, not getting an ordinary job like other men, is that you're afraid to measure yourself with anything and find out you're just another one of eleven million."

"There's a lot of truth in what you say, Margot."

"But you've kept me hanging around. Every time I wanted to

go you said to wait awhile: you were too young yet. You played on the fact that I'm so much older than you are. You said, you'd do it when it worked out with your family. One broken promise after another. It's so hopeless."

"I wanted to keep you, Margot."

"Then why don't you marry me?"

"I don't know, so help me."

"I want you to find out now, this morning, then, before you go off again without telling me something definite, even when I'm going to see you again; before you go off to doctor some dog. You can't let a dog suffer, dear good Edward, but you can twist the soul of a human being. You've turned me into a disagreeable woman."

"You're a shrew, my dear," said Edward, smiling.

"Will you do something for me?"

"What?"

"Promise me first."

"No."

"I want you to ring up your friend Lou and get him here. Let me tell him the whole story as you told it to me."

"No, no, no, no, no. Lou's working on his composition. He has no time for such things."

"Very well. Get your cousin Walt."

"What do you want a referee for?"

"That's just what I want. You're afraid for anyone to know the real story. They know your speech. If they heard mine, their verdict might surprise you. Say something."

"Haven't I heard your story? I'm in a fighting mood against myself. Here's my advice: Get rid of that guy Edward and get a real man."

"You think that's very funny."

"You told me to say something. I'm handing you solid advice."

"If anyone could have heard you just then! I'm tired of hearing about the good, the kindhearted, the wonderful Edward and knowing what I know about you: that you're selfish to the core, monstrously selfish, that nothing disturbs you. You're very pleasant on the surface, until one gets to know you. I'm sick of hearing strangers rave about you. Someone said to me, Oh, is that Edward: it seems to me I've heard all my life about the wonderful Edward. Everything's been done for you. Everyone's loved you. You've never had to love anyone. I don't say you couldn't, at one time, but now you're past cure."

"Don't you think it's peculiar that I was able to put it over on the human race so long?"

"No, everyone loves an extra man in New York."

"That's the hard word," said Edward, looking sour.

"You're the thief of time: I've given you the best years of my life," cried Margot, miserably.

"You've had the best years of mine."

"Perhaps it's true. Oh, what have we been doing all these years, Edward?"

"I don't leave you and you don't leave me, Margot, because we think, perhaps, it's always like this: perhaps our case is just the ordinary human life: that's it."

"You don't think that, though. You have hope still."

"Yes: so have you."

"I am not sure."

Walt was a short plump frog-faced middle-aged man with large brown eyes and thin hair. He was a ready speaker, full of fun, and disliked any kind of scene. He tried to pacify them at first by putting his squat hands on both, by talking all the time about politics, by telling jokes and even by pulling faces; he imitated Quasimodo, a salmon, a frog and a dog scurrying off with a shoe. Edward chimed in. He spittled his jokes from the side of his mouth in the accepted American way. Walt vomited volumes of sound. Margot watched them both drearily. Walt said he had to go at one-thirty and kept watching the clock. Every time there was a silence he burst out laughing and started on something fresh. Even while he was talking, he allowed no pauses but filled them in with laughing, or with repeating what he had just said, or with "Eh-eh-eh?" His hands trembled slightly; he said he would just take a glass of milk and go. However, Edward went out shopping to add to what they had and they had an early lunch, which consisted of delicacies which tickled Edward's palate and which Margot had come to like, for example, pickled salmon in oil and capers, liver-sausage, Virginia ham, sweet Spanish red peppers, a blue cheese from a 56th Street cheese store, a hickory-smoked cheese from a place near the Elevated on Third Avenue which Edward himself had brought, two breads of the pretzel type (*bagels* and *salzstengels*), German black bread (pumpernickel), sour and sweet cream, bacon and eggs and an immense bowl of salad with green stuffs of all kinds, artichoke hearts and early avocado pears, homemade potato salad with hard-boiled eggs, and chives. They also had potato chips out of packets and frankfurters, boiled, split and fried.

Said Walt, "Call this brunch? Give it its proper name. I call it a banquet." His face glowed, he chumped and chewed and undid his belt.

"We always have this on Sundays," said Edward with pride.

"It's a wedding breakfast," said Margot, suddenly. And with this she began to tell Walt her story, without weeping, but she would stop to catch breath, and her body would stiffen and tremble.

"But I want you to know him as he is. He thinks you're his friend. He's proud of you. He says, My family always had men of talent in it and round it."

Edward frowned. "That's true and I'm proud of it. Whitehouse has been open to anyone since my grandfather's day. He left his house and land to the family undistributed under certain conditions: Peace, liberty, a roof for everyone, all claims equal. If it is all coming down to us two, Oneida and me, two persons suffocated with *dolce far niente,* as Margot says, and even if the land is dying of sloth, if the dogs growl at every stranger, still it is a piece of land left for communal living and it is so used. My grandfather said that no one could buy it, no one own it absolutely and we and our friends, those that we accepted as friends, must have the hospitality of Whitehouse without question. You see he was a button manufacturer and he wanted halfway a community like that at Oneida. Has anyone ever been questioned who came to Whitehouse? We have had all sorts of people. I wait for the property and I'll do what he wanted."

"Can you imagine a man who marries what his grandfather's ghost dictates? If you loved a woman and she said, dump the whole impractical idea in the sea and come with me, if you loved her, you would say yes. The trouble is you cannot love. So old aunts and such come first. And ideas of a roof over everyone's head."

"What's wrong with it? What's wrong?" said Edward, flushing.

"He thinks a lot of you, Walt. It's always Walt this and Lou that. I'd like to paint a picture of Edward the good; that's not the real man. I want to show you this morning the real man, Edward, the side-stepper, the double-crosser, the fourflusher, the cruel dull hard persistent profit-taking type underneath. I've always heard, Edward is such a friend."

"Well?" said Walt.

"Then why is he my enemy? My torturer? My devil?"

"Sticks and stones can break my bones; but words can never hurt me," said Edward. She burst into tears. He looked upwards through his lowered lids. His clear blue and white eyes glinted curiously through his bronzed closed face. His lips parted, he licked his lips; his skin softened in the open neck of his clean shirt.

She stared at him and said, in scalding words, "Another wisecrack from the prince of side-steppers, I can't even get an answer out of him; he isn't even ashamed. It isn't on paper and so it isn't dangerous. He's hardly ever written me a letter. He'll never do anything the law doesn't force him to. Yet he's been ashamed to appear

[88]

shabby in front of you or Lou and that's why he's never told you my story."

"What can they say or do if I can't do it?" he asked.

"Nothing!" and she gave a cry. She controlled herself, and said to Walt, "Tell him to marry me; he'll do anything you say."

"If he won't do it for love of you, Margot, he won't do it for respect of me. I'm sorry."

"I have no friends. All right. But I want you to know him as he really is. He isn't Edward the good. That's a wonderful act he puts on to fool everyone. You ask him for something if you're dying and you'll find out what he's like."

Edward watched her and said nothing. His face had grown quite small and dark. Walt said he must go. Edward said, "We must let Walt go now. If he's not convinced now, you can't convince him. What she has said is true, Walt. Now Margot, let him go."

"The man you describe, Margot, is barbaric. I don't recognize Edward in him. I don't know what to say."

She stood up.

"Ah, there it is, say it again, Walt, say it before you go."

"Say what?"

"Tell him again that he's barbaric. I want him to hear you use those words again. They are words I want him to hear from your mouth. Do you know what he says about you? 'He is my cousin, but that isn't important: what is important is that he's my best friend.' I want his best friend that he admires to tell him that he's barbaric, and lives like a savage, not fit for the New York he's so proud of and loves to live in. Say, say the word! You're not a New Yorker, Edward, fit for civilized society, Edward, you hear, you are a savage."

Walt got up and seized his Sunday paper. She went up and held him gently by the sleeve.

"Walt, you are a kindhearted man, they say. Look him in the face and say it once again."

[89]

"Margot you know and he knows what I think about such things. I do not like human suffering, but I don't know what's to be done about a situation like this. Would marriage solve it? I'm not comfortable. I can't do anything. When two people want to marry, they both know it. But not to cause suffering is surely a settled question for civilized men."

"But he is a savage, barbaric, you said so yourself. Say he's uncivilized again, say it to his face, Walt. Let him hear it."

Edward cried, "It's said, Margot: leave him alone; let him go."

"Say it, Walt."

"Well, if he has done this, as you say it, then he is uncivilized, it's barbaric."

Margot cried in a loud voice, full of suffering and joy:

"You heard it Edward, it's said. Now you know what Walt thinks of you. You've no right in decent society, you're not a man like other Americans. Now you can't forget it. He has made a picture of you. It's not a pleasant picture. Only a sadist would make me suffer so."

"Good-by, Margot, now," said Walt.

"Good-by. I'm glad you came and found out at last."

"I'm coming too, Walt. I have to pick up Musty at Lou's."

"Then I'm coming too, wait for me," said Margot.

She came back to them in a few minutes, neatly dressed, with a fur-piece round her neck. She was a very pretty woman with soft dark hair and a white skin. She was many years older than Edward and weary with staying up all night but she had the dark and cheery look of a girl, while his skin, with fatigue, held no light, and his eyes were bloodshot. They started to walk. Margot wished to take the subway. The men insisted upon walking. They walked her to the nearest station, put in the nickel, and remounted the steps into the sunshine. Walt said, "You're meeting Margot at the Easter luncheon this afternoon?"

"Yes."

Walt took a penciled envelope out of his pocket and ran his eye over it.

Edward smiled. "Do you know the latest line of story? What's noo? The sea burned up. Well, a lot of fried fish. What's noo? They found out the earth is just a hole in a big cheese. Well, hereafter Welsh rarebit. What's noo? Empire State Building fell down. Well, I sold omelets short. What's noo? Wind froze over New Jersey. Let's cut out a hunk and make noodle soup. What's noo? Man can't whistle. Ate no baked beans. East River fell through a crack in the earth. Maybe one day I'll roller-skate to Brooklyn. What's noo? Tornado chased a man in a Ford all the way to Kankakee. Wet his dog."

Walt chuckled despondently.

"I'm not good at that. Don't see it. Do they have that Confucius line any more? You know all these jokes are in Greek and Hebrew too?"

Edward said, "But who the hell digs them out of Greek and Hebrew? You know the formula, the unlucky commentator? My house burned down. Too bad. No, my wife burned it for the insurance. Well, that's smart. No, they're starting criminal action. Not so good. Very good, because my brother-in-law is their lawyer and getting five thousand dollars a day. Lucky break. No, because when he's rich he kills people. That's tough. No, because we got him to promise to rub out our butcher; we owe him twelve hundred dollars and can't pay. Lucky to owe the butcher so much. No, because we gave it to the dog and he got so he tackled a horse. The dog won the contest, eh? No, the horse fell on top of him and killed him. Too bad, you lost your pet. No, we sued the truck driver and collected and bought a bigger dog. You get all the breaks. It isn't as good as that: this dog peed on the landlord's wife thinking she was a lamppost. Ho, ho, that was bad. No, she thought she was a lamppost too."

Walt said, "I don't suppose that's in the *Arabian Nights*. Did you ever hear the story about the difference between champagne and beer?"

"Sure, I told you that."

"No, it came from Bart."

"I think you're right. Your best story was the one about the caskets," said Walt.

Edward paused, then murmured, "I sold the Pennsylvania but if I'd sold when you told me, I would have been six hundred and sixty ahead. As it was I dropped two thousand on everything."

"What about the Standard Oil?"

"I'm counting that loss in. That week I was running round with Leander looking at houses. He's always against selling. He took his own advice and he lost money. He thinks the boom will have another crest."

"He'll miss the top. You can't afford that."

"No, like the rest of the family, I live on margins."

"How's your novel going?"

"So-so as the tailor said. I need an idea."

"I thought it was about yourself, your own life."

"Well, I sit down and I ask myself, what happened to me, I can't remember anything. I was born. I'm still alive."

Walt burst out laughing. There was a pause. Edward knew that Walt wanted to get away.

"Do you think I should go into business then?"

Walt said hastily, "You'll feel you've lost everything you've ever struggled for as a soul, all your life, Edward. You love liberty, independence, the arts, you want to love, you're a friend of man. Feeling that way, if you go into business you'll feel like a scarab rolling up a dung-pile: you'll start wondering why you lived the first part of your life in leisure and later you'll wonder why you're living the second part. Take advantage of the freak existence you enjoy."

"They're all trying to find me something to do: Margot is not alone in that."

"Let them thank God for once there is a young man who doesn't have to wear out his youth earning the rent for his father, sick aunt, disabled grandmother, wife, children, the landlord and himself. Tell us about it. You might convert people. Work is to get something to eat: but you have something to eat. Other people work because they have a message for mankind. Have you? All right, God bless you. You haven't? Then don't annoy the world. If I had enough to live on, I'd maybe sit round in cafés talking to people."

"Maybe I should let the Government support me," said Edward.

Walt threw back his head and gave a long golden chuckle, a heu-heu-heu-heu with the sound in it of some Negro boy he had played with as a child.

"It seems to me something is gnawing to get out," said Edward.

"Let it. What has despair to do with a young man with his life before him, and plenty of friends, an adoring family?"

"I ought to go fight for somebody." Edward lit a cigarette.

Walt went on, "Distant fields are bloodier, my boy. Maybe if you bide your time, you'll end in a pool of blood here. Fighting for freedom is not a matter of sentiment but necessity. Anyone who expects causes and wretched suffering peoples to save his soul ends up a traitor. Living the way you are you can't possibly betray anyone. A man isn't a sister of charity."

"I think the way to solve a lot of things these days would be to turn Anarchist. How else can you stop the slaughter? I believe in terror."

"Why?"

"A secret band of terrorists could stop atom destruction: they would have to be saints and martyrs. I believe there are such people about."

"Do you think you're a terrorist at heart?" said Walt, looking at him and smiling faintly. Then he added, "No one used more of it than Hitler. That's café-revolution, it's laziness."

Edward raised his nose in the air and kept an obstinate expression. However, he said, "The trouble is, I don't know enough."

"That's simple. Study something. Come to the library with me right now, pick a subject, look in the card catalogue and begin from the ABC."

"Too much trouble. What sloth!" Edward said cheerfully.

"Be lazy then. Good-by, I've got to go. The library's been open half an hour." He took a step away and then came back and took Edward by the arm. He said hastily, "Ned why put it that way? You only understand the communal life, that's why you don't want to marry, isn't it? You don't see the reason for crawling into a corner with one woman and having one child. You need abundant multiple life around you like Whitehouse, like the Massines; the perfect still life, eh? Ha-ha. Fruitfulness with grapes and rabbits dropping over the edges of an oak table on a woven cloth — and many dogs and dishes and many children and many days? Isn't that you fundamentally? You run a lodginghouse, you run a community. You're married to many! Ha-ha-ha. Lucky man. You're all right, Ned. And all without any theory, Anarchist, Socialist, what-have-you, just the Massine Bill of Rights. You're born in the Golden Age just because old Dad Massine established the Fiftieth State of the Union, the Massine Enclave, with the following sweet words: 'I leave Whitehouse to furnish a roof for you all, rich, poor, working, idle. All will be free on the Home Farm to do as they like.' What has happened, Edward? You are all the friends of Man. In God's name, what more do you want out of life than to be such a man? Forget the New York passion for knowing the score and heading the procession to your own grave. The conditions at Whitehouse make you an exceptionally good man, whether your heart is big or small. Whether it is, we shall probably never know. That's an untold blessing. What does it matter what your individual weaknesses are? You are the result of land and liberty. You must try to convert Margot, that's all."

Edward said, "So, not a savage? Not barbaric? If I had been born a Frenchman, I would kiss you, Walt, but it's too late now to be

[94]

born. Why are you going to the library? Come to Miss Holland's Easter Sunday dinner."

"No, I don't enjoy company when my wife's away. I'm a much married man."

As they separated, Edward smiled and said, "Do you know, I am not as lost as I make out. My state of mind can be called undefined hesitant anticipation."

In Edward's house, in the downstairs back room, tables were dressed with white cloths and a profusion of things in yellow: daffodils, toy chickens, satin ribbons, china designed in yellow. Edward's candlesticks stood along the table, with yellow candles in them. Arranged about were all kinds of Easter eggs, decorated hard-boiled ones and candy eggs. There were place cards and menus showing an imposing variety of dishes all made of eggs. This was Miss Holland's Swedish family tradition.

All the tenants and many of the other guests had arrived. On one side a group of marionettists were seated in a big circle, gravely hairsplitting.

"The question is, how far is it legitimate to go to create the illusion? Where are we to draw the line between amusing the public and cheating the public?"

"That can't be the criterion. The public knows nothing about marionettes, they don't care what you do so long as they laugh. They want to be hoaxed if it's amusing."

The sculptor of the troupe, a handsome young man with a dark beard said severely, "You know that in the Dorian group ballet, *Swan Lake,* they used two glass turntables, and the puppets didn't move. That's not puppeteering, that's engineering. It belongs to the Hall of Inventions."

The young girl with the dark hair who had spoken to Edward about the rope said, in a craven manner, for she wanted to be considered a professional too, "I was shocked when I saw the Dorian group using rods for the tap dance. They were advertised as string puppets but they were actually rod-and-string puppets."

The woman with the peacock voice shrieked, "I saw the strings lying on the stage as clearly as anything. A child would have noticed them: at least three inches of string on the stage." She gave a terrible laugh, coarse and sharp.

Then the third speaker, a man of about thirty, who was one of their "voices," remarked again, "At the same time, the public doesn't care what we do: they are not being tricked."

Some others of the guests sat apart feeling confused, small and dull. They thought puppeteering weak and foolish and yet they knew they were ignorant. To keep themselves in conversation they murmured about politics. Edward sat down near the organ where Oneida was reading music. Margot was sitting beside her as if resting, one pretty hand on Oneida's strong arm.

Edward remarked, "There's a pile of plates in that antique store on Irving Place that I'd like to get. The china has an oxblood border and a spray in the center. It's a beautiful thing. I'd like to get it for you, Margot, but I think you do that sort of thing better."

"If you think so much of me and my work and my opinion, why don't you marry me?"

They fell silent. Oneida went on sight-reading and playing.

"Look at that suit Leander bought for Lady for an Easter present. He waits on her hand and foot," said Oneida.

"Edward bought me nothing for Easter. And he turned me down again. Why don't you let him marry me, Oneida? It isn't religion. You have no religion. If you had any legitimate excuse, I would respect it. If Edward had another passion, I would love him for it. But inside he has only a hard sharp stone and even his skin is getting thick."

"Hath yet a precious jewel in his head," murmured Edward.

"Ah, it's miserable to love someone who can't find a kind word for me when I'm in anguish."

Oneida was wearing a black skirt and a beautiful blouse of black chiffon, with colored flowers hand-worked in silk. Edward examined it.

"That's your blouse from Florence. I haven't seen it for years."

"That's the one Victor-Alexander brought me from Florence when he went there to study. I wore it to his recital. His-first-and-only-recital!" Oneida showed off the blouse, sat down, and said in a firm voice, "Edward is unemployed. He is in no position to keep a family."

"I don't want a family. I'm too old. You've kept me waiting eleven years."

Oneida continued sagely, "Edward is a kind boy and he will do anything for you if you are sick or in trouble, but you can't make him do anything against his will, Margot. He was always as stubborn as a mule. Ollie always said, What Edward wants he will get and I am sorry for anyone who tries to make him do differently. Edward has a quiet exterior and he does not like to let you see what is going on, but he thinks deeply. You see, we were brought up together. He just doesn't want to be bothered and he disappears from view. Ye-es, from human sight. Or he goes to sleep. He sleeps it off. Ha-ha-ha. You have to watch and wait till he's ready. In his own-go-od-time, oh yes! Oh, did you ever see anything so sweet as that curtain upstairs? And Miss Holland did it all by herself! And she-ne-ver-sleeps! Why is that, do you think, Margot?"

All the time Oneida continued her playing. Margot said:

"She works too much, and she hasn't found happiness, like me."

"O-o-oh, ye-es, she is always in a state of tension and she accepts more than she can deal with and then I think she seems rather sad and restless. You yourself are like that, Margot. But don't you sleep? Lou these last few nights has not slept until 4 A.M. because of the ventilator next do-or and then I wake up at 4 A.M. thinking of the poor doggie; and so between us both you see we do get a go-od night's sleep. But with Miss Holland, I think it's too much activity and alertness and responsibility, and discontent, and you're in the same boat yourself."

"You are just rephrasing everything I say, you always do that when you want to get round the point at issue."

Oneida remained silent for a moment and then went on chatting fast.

"Oh, I am just an echo when my thoughts are elsewhere and I'm interested in what's before me, superficially for my ideas are wandering; but my eyes take in what's in the flesh and I remember what I hear, for what is present is the sharpest, acutest to me; material things, present things come first and so I say them again to myself. Aren't we all children in that? You too, you just try to paint or model what you see. Aren't we all lit-tle-chil-dren-ye-es-lit-tle-children," she said dreamily. She laughed merrily. "Why do I do that? You see, I repeat myself too. Why, yes, I was thinking of the little rabbit Leander bought for that sick child at the school. How wonderfully sweet it was. But it began the first night by eating bits out of the carpet, a wo-onderful Delft blue carpet. Why is that do you think? And it ate the burlap off my father's Tolstoy. Ha-ha! It's unnatural to have a rabbit shut up and so it develops perverted tastes. It needs air and sun. I hate rabbits though. Dr. Parks told me he would never treat a rabbit, they get diseased and they are not natural diseases, they can communicate their maladies to man. He says they should all be shot. He would never touch one. They are full of brass and impudence: they would even defy a dog and they try to get the dogs to chase them down burrows to stifle them to death. The dog gets his jaw caught, the earth falls in, and the dog dies. Then the dogs run too much, they get excited and it is bad for their heart, their blood-pressure. When I saw Lady in that lovely blue blouse, Margot, I thought of it, the blue carpet. Why do I wander off and think of a Chinese carpet, when my eyes are here looking at you? Yes — it is — you put it so well — you are so direct in your expressions; it is because my mind is not fixed, I am thinking of the dear doggies, how I love them, I stare blankly at people and I become mesmerized. It is all. You have thuch a clear wonderfully direct forthful way of exprething yourthelf, as Edward thays."

"Look out, crime is on the way, Oneida is lisping," said Lou laughing.

"I suppose Edward really did say that? When? This morning?" asked Margot.

"Oh, I don't know when. Often. Always. Not this morning though. Oh, Eleanor darling, the curtain is perfect, just ravishing. But it's not at all too brilliant, oh, it fades into the surroundings because of the perfection and the beauty and because it attracts the eye when the drop curtain is down: the audience has something to think about and doesn't get restless."

"I still think it's too bright; and look at the color of that fuchsia when the lights are on it," said Miss Holland.

"I have no chance against you," said Margot. She looked down at the seated family, Lou, Oneida, Edward, and behind them Lady and Leander who had their backs turned and were examining the prints hung along the wall. She spoke again with bitterness, "The family is an army surrounding this house and this house is filled with allies and all is a fortress to keep Edward safe from me."

Oneida laughed heartily. "You are always attacking from the outside and we surround Edward like a regiment."

Lou said, "O-ne-i-da!"

"Well, I gave him an ultimatum, he must decide today."

Oneida straightened up, and she laughed in a different way. "What sort of an ultimatum? Surrender, or I retreat?"

Edward said, "Shut up, Oneida! I've inspected the lights and Holland doesn't need me. I'm going to Al Burrows's to get the other medicine. Be seein' you."

"When it comes to getting a dressing for a dog, Edward's a good boy," said Margot.

"Yes, when it's a matter of obtaining plasters or bandages for the

[99]

dogs, you can rely on Edward. Edward has been so much with dogs: he spent his whole life with dogs, he understands them and feels for them. Dogs need understanding like other creatures. Why do people hate the helpless creatures? That shows conflict in a person. If you have a dog you are unselfish: you think of it all the time. During the war, Lou and I gave up all our meat to the dogs, because they couldn't understand why they must go without and we can. So why shouldn't Edward go and get things for the poor sick animal? She cannot understand why she must suffer: but you can understand, Margot."

"Yes, you can't bear a dog howling, but you can bear a soul howling."

"Oh, one night, Edward went out in his pyjamas, not even slippers, to get something for Musty. He can't see a dumb animal in pain. It shows his tender feelings. But if we have something the matter with us, he pretends not to notice." She stopped and said impatiently, "I don't know. I don't know that they think of anything. They are bores, yes, Musty you are a bore. Oh, why must we spend our lives with dogs! Isn't it hideous. I have never had a life of my own."

Edward had gone.

"I shall never beat her," said Margot to Leander and Lady in a low voice.

Oneida laughed and fondled Musty's ears. "No one shall ever beat us, no one will ever get the better of us because we don't want anything, do we, we only want each other. Ah, we must be good to dogs, Margot, because we have ruined them, dithtorted them, thwarted them . . ."

"Done what?"

"Oneida is lisping again."

"I call it hissing," said Margot.

"And made them the cruel ungrateful creatures they are," said Oneida. She then added with pain, "If someone else were to feed

[100   ]

them tomorrow, Musty and Madame X would forget Edward and me. You see! You're not like that. You are loyal and faithful no matter what happens. So they need our care more. Otherwise, they will turn against us. They hear some other person tapping on a plate and they run to them. Just like a baby. And we love such creatures! Lost love, lost love! For they don't feel it. Yes, and there are men like that. You can love them all your life and they feel very little, especially young men, young men who have lived too long in the house with the old."

She hugged the dog and tweaked its ear.

"Lost love, lost love!"

"You curse me and you curse Edward separately," said Margot.

She got up with an expression of painful contempt and went to the window; next door the baby was crowing in the sun. She looked at it too with contempt and went towards the kitchen.

After Easter the Solways and other Massines began to rearrange their furniture, their clothes and to telephone each other about their plans for going to Whitehouse. The Solways with Edward usually stayed at the Home Farm at Whitehouse all the summer from the middle of May to the beginning of October. The Massines, Leander and Lady, had their own house there. All the others would soon prepare to go. The big stretch of land was dotted with their cottages and farms. But Edward now wanted to stay in town.

He did not want to go back to the idle gossip of family life. He did not see Margot for three weeks more. *Big Ditch* had run only fourteen nights and he now spent his time in a delightful way, by himself, without Margot and without Musty, calling on friends, dining out. One of his cousins, a dancer, was starred in a successful musical on Broadway: he spent a good deal of time at the theater. Her sister, Elvie, who used to come to Oneida's to make ragouts for family parties, had injured her backbone doing exercises: he visited her in a hospital. A married woman, Mira, who had been his girl

during a summer at Whitehouse, was redecorating to match the blue
bedspread on the Solways' wall and the rose of one of Edward's
vases. He dined out about once a week with a sprightly sentimental
woman scientist aged eighty-three, who had been a friend of his
father. He visited a poor middle-aged woman who was a Greek
scholar and playwright; who was trying to revive the Greek style
of writing drama and had not yet had anything performed: he took
her plays to agents. He visited two puppeteers who lived in a loft
in 20th Street and whose names he never mentioned at home: they
were refugees from Fascism. They ate at three in the afternoon, a
time very agreeable to Edward. Sometimes when they went out in
their station wagon to country dates, he went with them and helped
them erect the heavy staging and fix the lights. He sat in with members of the Little Stage, now getting up an election libretto to be
staged at street corners on a big truck. He met young men, girls,
all busy, all inventive and he fitted in with all of them. He meditated politics while listening to Walt's orations, human values while
listening to the radio in one of those big evening sessions which are
characteristic of New York, pictures at the latest exhibition at the
Museum of Modern Art (he had studied painting with his father
once), music at the weekly Town Hall concerts where Lou and
Oneida were always to be found (he had studied the violin and the
piano during five years). He worked, jokingly, seriously, with Miss
Holland in her upstairs room now a studio, working a puppet and
inventing backchat: at this he was very quick and had a challenging
dry style with the puppet which brought Miss Holland's plays to life.
At Whitehouse he could stroll about, play baseball with campers,
water Oneida's plants when she managed to catch him, gossip with
van Kill the tenant farmer, hear the same old family talk and yawn,
yawn, yawn; be greeted in all the stores, say the right thing in a low
intimate voice to new summer girls and yawn, yawn, yawn; perhaps
not even go for a swim the whole summer, though there was a fine
pool which caught hill water on the Home Farm. And the sisters,

[102]

the brothers would be there, and they would recall all that had ever happened to them, days fifty years before (Jonathan was seventy-three), and laugh because "in every corner of the house someone had sat who was now dead." They would recall all those dead, their characteristics, and they would still be alive, for those present were their contemporaries. And in the many window seats and blanket chests, cupboards, dressers never opened, were books, letters, photographs from those old days. Yawn, yawn, the whole summer.

"If you don't go up there, I shan't go this summer," said Edward to Walt. "If I could study economics or something with you, I'd go."

"Not interested," said Walt; "I'm not a schoolteacher! My wife doesn't know where she is going this summer."

Oneida had invited Madame Sarine to Whitehouse for two months to prepare her November concerts.

Edward dined with the Solways almost every night, at midnight or two or three in the morning. "Come, do come to Whitehouse with us, Edward," Oneida would beg. "Your heroine Vera Sarine will miss you."

"Yes, do come Ned," Lou would say stroking his cat and looking thoughtfully towards the window.

"Elvie saw you in the Russian tearoom with your eighty-three-year-old sweetheart," Oneida said one evening or other.

Edward looked indifferent; he was always seen by someone.

"You were telling her all about Dr. Evatt! You said you knew him! And you said he wore his shirt sleeves rolled up!"

"When I saw him he had his shirt sleeves rolled up," said Edward.

"Oh, Edward, you don't know him!"

"I've been at a party with him," said Edward.

"Oh, Edward, is there anyone you haven't been at a party with?"

"I've even been at a party with the Angel of Death," said Edward in a forbidding tone.

Lou laughed. "That's the Host of Hosts."

Oneida did not like this. "I should have invited Dr. Sam, but it was one or the other and Lou wants to practice with Vera," she said brightly.

Lou asked, "Edward, have you been studying Gluck?"

Edward said, "Yes, I practice every day but I don't like Gluck." Lou laughed and stroked his cat.

"Well, you will come up some time, Edward," persisted Oneida as always. "Your first summer home, since the war! They'll all be looking for Edward!"

Edward looked down at his feet. He had only socks on and his socks had holes in them. He looked at the carpet. "Perhaps I'll stay here and let Nate the Croat paint my place."

"And in the fall, Edward?"

"In the fall maybe I'll take Whitworth's place: it's smaller. Or maybe I'll shake the dust of New York from my feet."

"Where could you go?" said Oneida anxiously.

"A man offered me a job the other day in Cleveland, Ohio," said Edward looking at them impishly.

They all burst out laughing. "Oh, Edward, how ridiculous!"

About four or five in the morning he would go home, and after smoking a few cigarettes and reading the *New Yorker* or the *Nation,* would fall asleep, sometimes half-dressed.

"Here's a gray hair on your sleeve, Edward," said Oneida picking it off.

"One of your ancient belles," said Lou laughing. He had got up and was brushing the cat fur off his coat.

Edward turned to one after the other, with resentment in his eyes.

"Is it R. L. Stevenson? Or E. A. Poe? The shortsighted man? First she took off her wig, then her teeth, then her eyebrows, then her cheaters? Ha-ha-ha!" said Lou.

Edward flushed and looked angrily at them both.

"He won't marry an old woman," said Oneida. "Let him go with old women: there won't be marrying or giving in marriage! Ha-ha!"

"It's like heaven," said Lou cheerfully.

"There's a taboo on the marriage of an old woman with a young man," said Oneida willfully. "It's a law of society! And old women all have such foul tempers too: and they have developed prejudices and are sour and can't co-operate. You don't see Margot's faults: you're too kind."

"I see more than you see, but I'm fond of her too," said Edward at last. "I forgive them: what does it matter?"

"But what's the attraction? Does she even love you?"

Edward hesitated: he said unwillingly, "She needs me."

"We need you!" cried Oneida.

"No you don't, Oneida," said Edward quietly.

"Yes, I do: if you left us the whole old life would dissolve. Where would I be?"

"Only with me," said Lou.

Oneida came close to Edward with her hair hanging loose, making her more girlish.

Edward telephoned Margot most days but had grown cold towards her. On May the first he had spent part of the day with Roselli, the author of *Big Ditch,* who was now working on another poetic play, in which again there was a question of personages duplicated by masks. About five, Roselli said he had an appointment at 37th Street and Eighth Avenue and asked Edward to walk along with him. Some way uptown, they saw a procession with banners. Edward exclaimed, "Golly, I forgot it was May Day. They haven't had it since before the war."

From different side streets, masses of people in line, chunks of a living matter, turned into the main avenue and joined the procession, which was organized in lines of eight, ten and twelve individuals. These influxes caused long halts. The procession moved slowly and Edward and Roselli easily passed various units. At 37th Street between Eighth and Ninth Avenues, they found people waiting who had waited from two in the afternoon. They were mostly youths and girls carrying small pennants which announced that they belonged to radio, dance and theater groups. There were a few journalists, playwrights, poets and other writers and it was these that Roselli had come to meet. A broad banner stood against the buildings, and indicated that the band represented writers, artists and intellectual workers. As there was little organization for this group, except among the radio artists and dancers, there was a good deal of strolling up and down of artists and teachers looking for a group to join. The banner was picked up, abandoned, picked up, moved and picked up again.

About six-fifteen, the suspended mass suddenly crystallized, without anyone having heard an order, and they began to move out of the street. Roselli took the pole at one end of the large banner which indeed stretched right across the street and called to Edward to take the other. Edward had been pleasantly, amicably, spending the time meeting many old acquaintances among these people, and by accident he now found himself marching ahead of them, announcing them. He thought it droll and laughed heartily, turning round to signal to his friends. At the same time, his breast swelled, his breath came deeper: he felt proud. Manly pride seemed to slap at his face, as he turned into the main avenue. He had never marched in New York, his own city. The banner was heavy and numerous halts made the march painful. Workers from the loft districts and midtown stores were marching disorderly along the sidewalks on both sides, going to Pennsylvania Station or the subways, but few stopped to look long at the procession. There were some sympathizers lined up and some of those were either languid, or timid. Down about 28th Street, on an otherwise apathetic sidewalk, two drunks under an awning, just thrown out from a low-class saloon, jeered, cocked a snoot. Opposite Pennsylvania Station, someone had started to sing the "International," but only two lines were piped by a few reedy, bashful voices, and it died away. Their only refrain, "Solidarity

Forever," came round and round. There was no band. After a while, Edward and Roselli made signs to the ranks behind them and two others came forward to carry the banner. Edward and Roselli fell back to the ranks.

Edward found himself beside Mrs. Wharton. He looked behind and distinguished, some way back among the dancers, an old acquaintance, Rosalinda, with her orange lipstick, her black and white dress, a little black fur coat. They exchanged a smile. Edward felt better. He was with many friends. Nevertheless, the trip was dull and it was very clear that even these irreducibles, who, as Roselli said, "had been in foxholes, some real, some silk-lined" during the war, were both determined and disappointed. They had been official patriots during the war, many of them, and now had to begin all from the beginning. It wasn't like the glorious or bloody May Days of years before. Edward trudged although he was bored and would have liked to have dropped out. But his friends were there. The procession turned left at 17th Street, to reach Union Square. His group halted just after the turn. Here, the sympathetic had gathered at last and stood rów upon row, on the sidewalks and on the steps of the houses, ranged like vegetables and flowers on market day. A faint cheering was going on. Edward, last man on the line, turned and scanned the faces. He could only see the nearest and among them he found another friend.

"Didn't expect to see you there," said the friend.

"Why?" asked Edward and began to talk to the friend, telling what he had been doing with the dancers, with the theater, with Roselli.

"What is it," he said to his friend, "that stands on the roof at midnight, flaps its wings and crows: not a rooster?"

"Not a herring, I suppose," said the friend.

The procession moved off rapidly. The halt was caused by the turn into Union Square, but once the turn was made, the marchers walked fast to cover the open space and catch up with their predecessors.

At this moment, a woman, tired of carrying a cardboard notice on a stick, planted it in Edward's hands and he hotfooted it off to join his line, holding the placard without noticing what was on it. He turned and shouted something back to his friend.

"Maybe a crazy man."

"Wha-at? What the hell's that?"

Edward grinned in a self-satisfied way and went on. They were a long way up the street. Now Edward noticed the rounds of cheering that were pouring down the street like machine-gun bullets, circulating, falling upon them, flailing at them. It increased in volume as they walked, and made this drab street seem rosy, compared with the avenue they had left. The cheering increasing, Edward's heart rose, his mind swam and it was as if the evening sky cleared, the air floated with lilies. He said to himself between his teeth, "It was roses, roses all the way, what's that? And never a sprig of yew. I've forgotten that. They threw to me roses, roses, and never a sprig of yew." His thoughts floated away. The cheering at the entrance to the square was intense and rose strangely from the banked crowd. Edward did not notice his feet nor the placard he was holding high, nor those alongside him. He was carried away by an emotion such as he had never known. A single thread of thought floated past him, "Is this mob emotion?" He forgot this idea, and felt overcome by a great passion. The world was glorious; choirs of blessed spirits were around him. He had never experienced an emotion like this one, that his own city was cheering for him, that unknown faces he could hardly distinguish were blazing away at him with happiness, pride in him, for this is what he felt from the radiant smiles and the shouts delivered in his direction. At the turn into Union Square, his enthusiasm changed, became colder and airier, and a most curious emotion swept them all: they were taut, vigilant. They had to traverse the immense open square which is the highest point north of the Lower East Side, the old slums, the traditional forum of the old working-class city, and in some of the side streets, corps of mounted

[108]

police were stationed. There had been no incidents and there were none, but it was as if they emerged from youthful glory into the real world. The crowd at the saluting base was considerable.

They were now stacking the banners and notices. Edward heard a hail and Al Burrows, ducking under the barricade, ran hobbling across and joined the line. Said the other people in the line to Edward, "Do you know Al Burrows?"

"Why not?" said Edward.

He was a little hurt and they too seemed surprised, if not hurt, at these separate worlds. The giant pharmacist hobbled along between them, took the notice from Edward and stacked it with the others.

"I was watching for someone I knew, I didn't see many. I got to go uptown and they wouldn't let me into the square, but I walked round till I got to this exit, where everyone is walking round, and got in."

They all went to have a beer and Edward did not beg off. He said to Al and his wife Edie, flushed, smiling and happy with the procession, "I have to go and see my girl but I'm so damn late now that nothing can make any difference. She either throws me out for keeps, or she forgives me, one of the two."

"You don't want her to throw you out, you'd better get going," said Al.

"I don't know. What will be will be."

"You don't seem to like women much," said Edie, moving along the bench to touch Edward's arm.

"I love women," said Edward.

"I love men, too," said Edie, suddenly sitting up and expanding her voice. She put her arm round Edward's waist. Edward moved away.

"I don't love men too."

She sat softly, looking full at Edward with a hazy smile, her soft colored cheeks drawn down a little by her thoughts. "Why don't you come to Karefree this summer?" she asked, giggling suddenly.

"No more camps," said Edward.

Edie said naïvely, "Don't you think my sister's naïve? She got together with a guy at camp last year, and she's going there this year to look for the same guy!"

Al cleared his throat. "Are you going up to your folks soon?"

"No. I hope I never see the place again!"

Al grinned questioningly. "What are you sore at? I wouldn't mind spending the summer on my back where green grow the rushes, oh."

"You wouldn't like to do it for thirty years."

"What do you bet?"

Edward spent the night hanging round with them and did not see Margot.

About the middle of May, the heat struck New York, just as if a furnace door had been opened; but the nights were fairly cool. Edward visited friends and relatives, helped one man hang water colors for his exhibition, worked for a couple of days with another on his musical comedy (he was so good at gagging and joking) and, at home, began to translate a novel about modern Italy, which had been sent to him. He saw Margot rarely. As the weather grew hotter, he spent every evening away from home, in restaurants or with friends in the Village, or with the family drinking Collinses and iced tea and iced coffee; and he was often accompanied, towards the end of May and in the beginning of June by a Mrs. Barron, a blonde rowdy woman taller than himself, who had already been married twice and wished to get a divorce from her present husband, a printer who worked at night. She herself worked in a publisher's office in Madison Avenue. Edward got up about twelve or one o'clock, and met her after her work or after dinner. She was about forty and of an extraordinary egotism. She told Edward she intended to marry as soon as she was divorced but whom she yet did not know. She had induced her husband to marry her and now had no feelings about throwing him out. Edward listened to her shouting, watched her awkward strong antics with pleasure: she was a wonderful character, to him.

His uncle Leander came to town every two weeks and about the middle of June, began to remind Edward that he was expected at Whitehouse for the wedding. Two young people, Mark and Marian, younger than Edward but once Edward's playmates at Whitehouse, were to marry at the Big Farm in mid-July. Edward had once been taken with the girl and had flirted with her during a whole summer. She was extremely pretty, lively, dark, gifted in music. At one time she had been attracted to the stage and Edward had taken her around town to his theatrical haunts. But he had never yet sincerely cared for a young girl.

"You can't miss Marian's wedding, Ned."

"O.K. But it's a nuisance. I didn't want to see Whitehouse this year."

"I'm going to fix the pergola and clear out the terrace," said Leander: "you could help me."

"No, I won't help you." Edward yawned and grumbled. "I lose my poor soul, Whitehouse, there with thee. Margot calls us the Lotus-eaters."

"When we sell the Little Farm, we'll overhaul the Big Farm and make a real place out of it, plow under those neglected fields and lawns, one time lawns."

"The soil is poor, Leander. Let us stick to holy shiftlessness! Let it rot: let it rot. Admirable humane sloth, as Walt says: he likes it all right. The right to be happy. The right to leisure. Tell me what harm we do."

Leander smiled. "He doesn't come up there though."

"He has admirable humane sloth in the Public Library at 42nd Street."

"O.K., O.K., I'll be there the day before the wedding. You can count on me to bring the fatted blintzes. I'll get Margot to paint a wedding present for the bride."

By the middle of June the heat was intolerable and in July had begun those sweltering, sweating days and nights, which turn New Yorkers pale and damp and call out their remarkable nervous diseases, their remarkable nervous courage. Thunderstorms groaned, with fireballs, roaring trees, plunging awnings, darkness black as night at three, torrents of rain; and passed, leaving the day and night, bright and hot as before.

"What are you staying there for?" asked the Solways, ringing him every day.

"Basic Training for the hereafter," said Edward.

In the second week of July, Edward went to Whitehouse by the bus. He saw Margot just before he left and said that nothing would hold him up there in the Catskills more than three days. But he showed a photograph of the Big Farm to Mrs. Barron, and said, "It's been my family's for seventy years," and she saw a large, low house with several solid pitched roofs, rising in shelves against a steep near mountain range. Below the house, the hill dropped away in uncropped lawns and deep fields to orchard trees.

"That's our Home Farm," said he and as he looked at the photograph he began to stare. His eyes, when he lifted them, were shining.

"Do come! You'll like it," he said. "Change your mind! This is the second summer my Aunt Oneida's expected you!"

"Oh, I'll write to you."

"You won't come," he said laughing. "You're afraid it's old-fashioned. Well, I'll be back in three days."

Part Two

WHITEHOUSE

IT WAS midsummer. Their nights were long and cold on the mountainside. They went to bed early and slept without waking. All through the night in the sky were reefs of stars and shoals of cloud. In the early morning, the old trees rounding the gardens stood nearer to the house, looming in land-cloud. Towards sunrise, this land-cloud began to pour down the valley which widened away to the east. Cloud reeked out of all the mountain wall, poured towards the sun. In the garden, in each corner of the house, old pear trees choked by a great vine stood like bronze, with their rare leaves and pears in the first light. No one slept indoors, but on sleeping balconies, inclosed or open, which projected from all parts of the old house, upstairs and down. On the higher hill the farmer and his family woke first and drank their black coffee, the cows lowed mournfully, the old horses stamped and the dogs woke in the big house.

About five, the Abbot, a young Manchester terrier, began chirruping. He stood on the body of his owner, Flora, with his forepaws on the sill of the balcony, stared through the green rattan blind and trembled. He could see the farmer in the field, and Edward asleep on the next balcony. Musty, invisible on a third balcony, barked in reply. Massines began whispering to their dogs. At a quarter to six, the first trumpet, with a sweet airy tune, came from the watchtower of a summer camp in the neighborhood. Dingy, a Skye, was already out and flopping through the long grass. His mistress Norah was scouring pots in the kitchen. In the silence came the sound of a heavy car approaching. The car panted up the slope to the front of the house, doors slammed, all the dogs barked. The van skipped away, over the ruts, tussocks and stones. Flora got up, dressed, and they heard the Abbot scampering down the wooden stairs. He rushed through the screen door with a shout of triumph. He was silent for a time and then ran wolfishly through the long grass. There was now a noise of pails, a jingling of harness, shouting and swearing on the hill as van Kill the young farmer got ready to take his milk down to the high-road where it would be picked up. The thirsty cows lowed plaintively. The wife called from the cottage on the hill. The farmer kicked a can, jingled the harness, cursed: his two little boys imitated him and it came out quaint and harmless in their fresh, ragged voices. Flora could be heard mixing in a bowl, Norah was scrubbing.

The Abbot started to bark near the barn, saying that he had found a rat. The other dogs answered him from all parts. There was the sound of a station wagon approaching out of the silent valley. It labored up the slope, stopped. The Abbot left the barn post at which he was digging and, rushing round the house, attacked the car. A man quickly unloaded a lawn mower, jumped in the car. Its doors slammed, it rushed through the grass and made its way tossing and leaping through the great stone archway, which stood, without fences or gates, at the front of the gardens; it took the difficult turn at top speed, fell into the deep concealed gutter. At this turn was a wooden box wired to receive quart milk bottles, and full of empty bottles. The car skirted this by an inch, swayed down the farm road, jumping high into the air, where the damp flowing earth had been banked over stones to protect water and gas pipes. When the car had run away, the Abbot investigated the Massine garbage cans along the road, strewed rubbish around them and at last ran home carrying with him a sheep's head. Norah, sweeping the veranda, called out, "Big Jenny got her sheep's head, isn't that funny?" The other dogs had gradually become silent or uttered a few querulous remarks to their yet sleeping owners. All became still.

Another bugle sang out. The Abbot, worrying and caressing his sheep's head in the grass, began his warning barks again. A cart and horse had turned from the high road and rattled fast now up the farm road. It rushed past the stone gate, reached the bend of the barn road and there besieged by the Abbot and Dingy, turned tail, with the horse rearing and jibbing, and tore through the low branches, leaped the ruts, escaping the two dogs who were aided by a great roar of sound from the upper windows of the Big House. It was the milk-man's cart. It rattled, crashed, skimmed and flew. At one jump, it landed straight upon the crate of milk bottles at the front gate and smashed them; but without dislodging the driver, a blond big-faced lad of fourteen, a van Kill cousin, who still managed to stand up in his seat, whipping the horse, yelling with fright and looking be-hind at his pursuers. Over the ruts they all leaped, the horse with ears turned back, eyes roving, and jaws dripping foam, the wild-haired blond boy screaming with fury now, his red open mouth dripping. The Abbot, a thin black racer, like a swallow, skimmed after them; Dingy, the fat Skye flopped up the road. The milk cart assaulted the two garbage cans left out at Dan's and Big Jenny's, rose at the gas pipes, flew into the ditch, reached the high road in safety but at the sharp turn overset the two milk cans which had been put there by the farmer. Suddenly, no more was heard. The Abbot ran softly back, sniffing at things. Now he sauntered, now he lagged, now he stopped at the sheep's head lost in the grass by the gateway, now he sneaked and wove round the house. He became silent. Dingy pot-tered up the road towards the Adamses.' The only thing to be heard was the sound of birds stripping fibers from the vine that strangled the pear trees, their remarks to each other and the water dripping into the empty trough by the barn.

A little dog barking woke Edward a little later. He tried to recog-nize it. Was it Darly, Big Jenny's toy Boston? It was three hundred yards from here to Big Jenny's cottage down the hill; the air was calm and still. He could hear a paper rustling somewhere on the road and a dog pulling at its chain. The little dog went on harping.

"Arp, arp, arp."

"Suppose something happened to Big Jenny?" he called, lifting his head. The Solways were on the next balcony.

"Arp, arp, arp."

It was Darly. At this moment, the Abbot broke out into a furious barking by the barn. He was, as Edward knew, although his face was buried in his pillow, digging up a clayey stone from a damp hole. The other dogs answered. The little harping dog stopped to listen. Edward turned over, pulled the weather-beaten blankets and dog-torn quilts to his chin and closed his eyes. Another bugle spoke, the sunrise flushed the whole sky. Edward thought for some time. People had recognized him at the stops in the valley. With him in the bus yesterday was a factory girl coming to Haines Falls for three weeks. She was a strong broad-toothed bronze-haired young animal, ferocious but good, and she was exhausted by work. He had drawled out the names, Haines Falls, Saugerties, pointed out the things to her and said with pride, "I lived here all my life; this is my home." In France, in Cairo, in Rome, he had hated Whitehouse and thought of it as stifling his talents. In the deep sweet summer cold, sluggish and healthy, like a pool that never stagnates under pinewoods, healing, with this cloud on the orchard, the open air and the bear they said was still on the mountain, and the strong black-eyed women of the family up at dawn and active, people of a gaiety and love he had not met elsewhere, he thought; I am wrong, a modern restless nervous man: this is right, and what is wrong? I am wrong. He fell asleep again.

About six-thirty, Oneida woke on the large sleeping balcony facing north. Through the broken rattan blinds to the north she saw the sky mild and fair. Facing her, there was no blind nor sky, only the rising hill on which she saw, as in a painting, the horses, farmer's cottage, the hill beyond and to the right, the corner of an old plantation of pines, elms, birches. She heard the noises of the dogs outside with interest. They indicated to her how far the rising and house-keeping had proceeded. Some noisy birds in the pear tree behind her head troubled her. And then she knew what had been insistent in her last dreams, far off, continuous, a little dog barking, a nervous female dog quivering, wearing herself out. She knew it was Big Jenny's favorite dog. And why? She pondered, no, she can't be in heat, a danger to the dogs. Perhaps it is only Charlie, that poor Spitz tied up all his life at the Adamses' shack. She murmured to Lou asleep at her side, "That Spitz . . ."

"H'm, h'm?"

"That Charlie of the Adamses' is so neurotic with being tied up, he has no more sense than to bark at our dogs. If Madame X attacked him, the Adamses would be angry." She gently pulled the ears of the old French bull snorting away into her breasts and neck. She observed the farmers, without raising her head from the pillow, saw young van Kill the farmer coming down the slope, down the kitchen steps. He dropped out of sight and knocked at the kitchen door. Oneida remarked, "Lou, the farmers want to leave today. There is no water for the cows again. They are going to the Morgans' after all."

"Why doesn't he see Leander?"

"Leander saw the reservoir man. He went up and turned on the water, but the pipes are too small and those summer camps take all the water for the showers and kitchens."

Madame X barked sternly into Oneida's face, telling her to get up, while Musty teetered anxiously upon Oneida's legs, unwilling in his old age to leap to the floor for nothing. Lou stretched his broad white throat from his blue shirt and said, "Keep those dogs away from me. I dreamed I was reading a book written in a beautiful unknown language. I read a page and then turned it over. I read it all and I understood it too, page after page. When I waked up, I could almost remember it."

Madame X who had jumped to the floor, put her paws on the bed

[119]

and sent her iron knelling in Lou's direction. Lou looked slyly at the dog, "LO K9 OBCT," said he.

Madame X barked angrily. Lou leaned over and kissed the smooth top of her head, "Hello sweetheart."

"Lou, get up, it's the wedding day."

Oneida, puffing, was now tying on a pair of rope-soled sandals. She wore her sleeping gear, faded blue cotton overalls, something the dogs could not harm. Her breasts stood out in this, full and heavy, but with her tousled hair, brown arms, freckles, small stature, with her pants torn and flapping at her ankles and the spoiled, clever grin on her face, she suggested a boy. When the dogs saw her sandals on, they stopped barking and ran to the door.

"Come on, poor babies," she shouted, tearing out a ribbon she had been trying impatiently to braid into her hair, "Mama will do iss way," and she suddenly raised her voice and repeated it babyishly, naughtily, "Mama . . ." with a laugh to herself, she opened the door and left it open. They scampered on the dusty worn wooden floor of the corridors and stairway.

All the way she talked to them. Old grass-covered ruts led down between the laurels and lilac to the stone gateway. Outside, the crashed crate of milk bottles lay in the ditch. Oneida looked at it indifferently, saying, "That moron!" The little procession went downwards and was at once lost to sight under trees, bushes, between hedges and plucked out woods. In this little voyage, Oneida each morning passed Big Jenny's house, Leander's house, three summer cottages rented out by the Massines, and came to the high road which, at that point, passed through Massine lands. She saw the milk cans turned over, the spilled garbage, "Oh that moron," she said, laughed, turned back, and after noticing that all were still sleeping in the four or five houses, came within view again of the attic windows of the Big Farm. Through the long dewy grass the little blue figure toiled up the slope puffing and her stout dogs puffing with her. At the veranda-post she stopped to tie up a climbing rose; and then she noticed an old black spaniel and an old lady in curling-pins looking through the screened window of an upstairs room. The old lady complacently unrolling a curling-pin remarked, "That butcher came at five this morning and threw the meat on the porch. Perhaps the dogs worried it."

"Why didn't you come down and stop them?"

"It's not my home. Not my dog. I don't interfere," said the old lady.

"You could have shouted to him to leave it in the kitchen."

"I don't interfere, that's my rule. Poor Sambo is obliged to stay locked up here all day. Other dogs roam about at liberty."

"You wouldn't save our bacon. You'd rather be prissy."

The old lady peered through the screen at Oneida, with gay interest. Oneida was ducking and scanning the porch and the garden round it. She found one packet of meat under a seat and one had been pulled into the clumps of Funkia round the steps.

"Sambo is so spoiled," she called. The old lady was Mrs. Walker, mother-in-law of her dead brother Henry.

The old lady at once replied, "It is unfair that poor Sambo should be shut up all day while the other dogs roam about at liberty."

Oneida struggled into the house with the packets of meat, the dogs crying and leaping at her.

"Greedy pigs — get away! Flora! The Abbot ate our meat!"

Lou, in the second movement of his Beethoven sonata, stopped the piano and listened. The catbird was in the pear tree outside the studio window. Every day, the bird, which began the morning by singing would listen for a while to Lou's practice, then would run over two or three times some little theme that interested him and, inspired by art and jealousy, would burst out with full throat and try to outstrip, outsing the music. At certain brilliant trilled passages he would stop again, listen; and once more song would pour out of him. He sat on a naked twig. Sometimes, overcome with effort, after nearly bursting his throat, he would fly off to a distant birch, sing there on the top branch and fly back, fly off to the dying top of the poplar by the barn door, give a splendid solo and fly back. Each year, this superb musician came back from his winterings, to the same pear tree, chased away all other birds from it. There were a few catbirds in this part of the hill, attracted by the overgrown slopes, water-courses, groves and thickets of laurel, but for singing and mocking, not one like this one. Lou played a bar over several times: the catbird, in the middle of a repetition, began to imitate it. Lou paused and listened, smiling, played it again for the bird.

Meanwhile, he heard skirmishing in the kitchen, which was distant the breadth of two sitting rooms and the length of a hall. He heard his wife's childishly severe, "Musty, Musty, stop it!" He sat back on the piano stool smiling faintly in a reverie. After the first bird awakened him, about three-thirty, he had fallen asleep for a while and awakened to hear the cedar waxwings stripping the fibers from the vine on the pear tree. Then the bugles, the cows, the clanking of the enamel coffeepot on the stove in the farmer's house, the empty milk cans, the mewing of Westfourth, the cat he loved, miserably mewing to be let in for breakfast; and Darly, that spry little dog, that jumped like a butterfly, singing for a mate. Surprising that after that he had not heard Big Jenny's loving contralto. Lou heard Oneida clattering and the answers of her sisters, Norah and Ollie. Far off up the slope from the long disused bowling green he heard the first notes of Vera Sarine's morning scales. The clock had not struck. Oneida was angry but not worried. Then nothing had happened to Big Jenny in the night. He heard Flora, full of love, say to her dog, "Abbot! Bad dog!"

Then came the mad race of the Abbot through the downstairs rooms. He knew everything that was happening. He had lived with this family since his childhood, been loved by Oneida's parents, known all her friends. Lou was hungry and thought, "Yes, but I must wait, of course, till the dogs have got through their breakfast." He started playing again. There was old Vines now, the piano-tuner, in the studio upstairs working away on one of his own compositions, also waiting for breakfast; and Irene, an old friend of the family, a young war-widow, practicing in another part of the house. Overcome by hunger, or some other passion, Lou stopped and looked through the window past the pear tree and the climbing rose. Down the slope he saw Dan Barnes, clean, spare, handsome. Dan went into the kitchen and kissed and embraced every one. He refused to have breakfast because he was going to Hunter village, said he, to order twenty pounds of minute steaks and thirty pounds of potatoes for French fries. And ten dozen of beer from Wimpelstein's. All for the wedding of Lou's two pupils, but he wouldn't tell them more than that the celebration would be at suppertime: they must all come and no one must breathe a word. Oneida cried, "Oh, I don't believe it: it's a hoax."

"And bring Madame Sarine with her serenades!"

"I'm not going to ask her to a hoax! I know you Dan!"

"Come and see: I'll give you a glass of brandy anyway. I have cherry brandy, akvavit, rye whiskey, bourbon, London gin, benedictine. I have twenty bottles, there," he said with enthusiasm. He made them all promise to come and to bring Old Sister Mary, the bride and bridegroom and anyone else there. There was room for all, he said.

"I hope it's only for a drink you're asking us. Big Jenny can't take care of all that," said Norah, anxiously, looking into his merry lank brown face. The lively fellow shook his head and assured her that it was only for a drink, and as for the glasses, they could all pitch in and wash them: his wife, Big Jenny, would have nothing to do. Not the slightest exertion.

When he left, Lou looked among the pots and pans, cook books, bags of flour and salt, for his package of cornflakes. Ollie, round as a roll of pie dough, in her pale cotton wrap and the large soiled apron she wore all the mornings she was at Whitehouse, came over to Lou with the coffeepot, chuckling.

"Irene got up at seven o'clock and made the coffee. It's like gunpowder. It'll blow your teeth down your windpipe."

She poured out some for Oneida, Lou and herself and sat down, repeating the joke about the gunpowder. Lou said crossly, "Any milk? There should be some. I got it myself from the barn at eight o'clock."

"That moron, that dairy boy, got panicked at the sound of the Abbot's voice, and smashed all the milk bottles. He told Dan he wouldn't come here any more. Now we must drink the farmer's milk. Only the farmer is leaving us today. So what shall we do for milk? I'll get it from the Adamses," said Oneida.

"It isn't pasteurized," said Norah.

"I'm not superstitious; it won't kill us," said Oneida.

"Oneida, pasteurization isn't superstition."

"Cows from our own district, that eat our own grass, will hurt us?"

"Don't take my milk, Ollie, that's for the butter," said Norah.

"But what does happen when you churn? Where does all the water come from?" asked Lou.

"Where does all the water come from anyhow? It's going to rain," said Oneida, looking at the floor. The boiler was sweating profusely and had formed a pool on the floor.

"H_2O or K_9P," said Lou. He sipped his coffee and looked inquiringly at a young man who was having breakfast and had been sitting with an expression of pleased reverie amidst the confusion of the busy kitchen. He was about twenty-eight, tall, dark-skinned, long-limbed, dressed in a tailored air corps uniform and, in all things, well cared for. Lou smiled at him good-naturedly and continued, "Well, Bart, how are you going to bomb New York City if it is raining? You'll run into one of the skyscrapers and end in smithereens."

"We'll bomb it in fine weather. Besides, I said we'd bomb Washington rather."

Lou snickered. "What about the underground capital Congress is going to run to?"

"I never heard of anything so disgraceful, senators and congressmen running and hiding their heads in the sand," said Oneida.

"And Bart could put DDT down their burrows," said Lou. He smiled and cut himself a thick slice of bread and ham.

"Dig them up in the year three thousand all pickled," said Ollie.

Bart had returned from the war excited, convinced that the government of his country was controlled by a set of villains who were milking the country to their own profit and would presently plunge the country in another war to get more profits. He believed that they were only a few, about one thousand persons, but that they and their followers were many, say fifteen millions. He believed that they were cowardly because they had not seen the war and had spent their lives in comfort, had seen no misery and could not bear any. Bart had not yet been discharged from the army but was in a camp in the South for nervous cases. He was well treated, allowed much liberty. He had a brilliant, hardy, desperate mind. He and his cronies left camp almost every night to go to town for wild entertainment which did nothing to calm his conscience or mind. It was impossible to prevent the war-weary and sick soldiers from smuggling drink and even dope into the camp. The authorities winked at this as much as possible, had threatened Bart with expulsion but were unwilling to discharge him or others into civil life for which they were not fit.

They had already given Bart several leaves of absence, and he was spending this one with the family of his buddy, Edward. He had arrived with a scheme which he discussed openly and which he said was matured, only waiting for the occasion. He and one hundred other ex-fliers had formed themselves into a squadron which was to take to the air "upon the first appearance of fascism in the United States or upon the next threat of war, or upon the first use of an atom bomb for whatever reason, upon innocent people." They had assistance and knew where to get guns, bombs, whatever was necessary.

They had planned their hideaways, had a starting-off place in the Maine forests; spoke of an island off the coast of South Carolina. They had taken an oath to cripple Washington and New York City at the risk of their lives and would bomb any other place they thought necessary to preserve the democracy of their country. They knew the names, situations and purposes of numerous black-hearted rogues whose only thought was to devastate the entire world and eventually the United States with it. Said Bart, "Their object is to destroy the human race to the last specimen, if they cannot get their way."

He alleged that certain young scientists had taken a similar oath and that nihilism would be the next appearance in this agonized world. Edward's family and Edward himself, listened to this wild and sanguinary scheme in a dreamy way. Brought up in peace, safety and openhandedness of a singular order, these words were for them only sparks flying out of the roaring fire of Bart's embittered, noble, still youthful mind. They heard his projects without awe and expected to tease him. This did not bother him. He saw them as herded, mild, innocent civilians who would dream their lives away in this "aimless endless existence." He said to them suddenly, "Who knows? You might be the last people left alive. You would not be a bad crowd to start the human race with again."

"We are a bit old," said Ollie, throwing up her hands, then clasping her sides with laughter. She grasped her apron, squeezed, cried jovially to her sisters, "We would be white-haired in the Garden of Eden." She could not get over this pleasantry for a long time. Lou made some observations about the appearance of the sisters in a nudist colony.

"There's always Edward," said Oneida thoughtfully. "And the bridal couple!"

"Look at the first batch," said Flora, holding up a tray of round fat breads.

"Do you know what Boris Karloff said when he was at the maternity hospital and they told him it was a son?" asked Lou. "He said, 'Don't wrap it up, I'll eat it here.'" The sisters had to think this over before they made sounds of shocked delight. Lou continued, "The first thing he gave it was a choo-choo."

"Like gunpowder," said Ollie thoughtfully, pouring out some coffee for Bart.

"Fascism could come to the United States and Victor-Alexander would sit up there growing tulips," said Oneida crossly.

Mrs. Walker, dead brother Henry's mother-in-law, now came into the kitchen with Sambo, an old black-and-white spaniel. Sambo was on a lead as Mrs. Walker pointed out with unction. Oneida complained that Sambo was an obstinate quarrelsome dog. A furious towrow at once began between him and Madame X. The lady wore a blue bandanna on her head and Mexican slippers. Although seventy, she was still a coquette, had blue rinses and wore costume jewelry with her Mother Hubbards. Mrs. Walker sat down in front of the prettiest coffee cup she could find, stirred her coffee, and remarked, "Irene is up on Edward's balcony, talking to him. Edward is still in bed."

"This scandal ought to be hushed up," said Lou, getting up.

Ollie laughed mischievously.

"You know Irene has changed her room to the one over mine. I expect she didn't sleep very well. I heard field mice scratching in the wall. And poor Dingy was frightened, I heard him yip."

"Were the mice married or single?" inquired Lou, fixing Ollie with a sharp eye.

Bart said, "If you had a piece of liver you could put it out, then a skunk would come and chase away the field mice."

"It was a lot of scratching, I don't say field mice," said Ollie.

There were faint noises on Edward's balcony, which overhung the kitchen window. The piano-tuner was playing his tune.

"Field mice? I'll take you up on that at noonday. IBCNU," said Lou. His piano began again.

Oneida bounced through the kitchen, followed by two waddling dogs. She ran upstairs talking to her followers, in a language learned long ago from Thekla, an old childhood Polish servant,

"Yes, *babitschke,* yes, *pischinke,* yes, *uglitschke,* you fat pig, waddle fast, little bird: o-oh, *faygele,* move on, do, *lump!*"

From the top of the stairs she saw Irene, fully dressed, sitting on the edge of Edward's bed and bouncing it. Edward rested his head on his bare arms and looked at her. Oneida called, "Irene do you want us round the kitchen till the reverend gets here? There we all are quaffing gunpowder down our noses like pigs, snuffling and routing like pigs."

"Edward intends to stay here till twelve or one, he says."

"Well, get out of here. I've got nothing on," said Edward.

Irene laughed and went downstairs. Oneida went impatiently into her quarters where Mr. Vines, the old piano-tuner, was fingering his manuscript, unable to leave it. Oneida looked over his shoulder, hummed a few bars, placed her hand on the old man's shoulder and urged him to go downstairs. "O-oh, de-ear Mr. Vines," she cooed. When he had gone, Oneida began to change her dress. Between her remarks to the dogs, she carried on a conversation with Edward through the open doors.

"Opsa and Pelayga are coming to the wedding. How stupid! And Old Mary told us only last night. They don't know the young people well. They are coming for Musty's birthday. Did you bring anything for Musty?"

Old Mary was Oneida's oldest sister, over seventy. Opsa and Pe-layga were the nicknames of her two daughters, unmarried and middle-aged. Musty was a pet name for Mrs. Mustbrook, old employee and friend of the family, who ran the paying Little Farm for the Massines, a chicken, egg and vegetable farm. The Massines always celebrated her birthday. The young people coming to be married, Mark and Marian, had become attached to the Massines as children and had often spent the summers at the Big or the Little Farm;

and out of love for the family and Mrs. Mustbrook they had chosen to have their wedding at the Big Farm and on Mrs. Mustbrook's birthday.

"Edward! You brought nothing! You ought to get over that childish feeling about Mrs. Mustbrook."

"Ugh, not if I live to be a hundred."

Oneida chuckled. "You'll have to! Bart is going to put DDT on all the senators!"

"I'm one of the few who never want to be a child again. My memory's too good! What boredom!"

"Oh, I used to wish for a little baby and all kinds of things. And there's Musty ado-ored you when you were a child. You were her li-ife." Oneida was matching ribbons.

"Oh, hell!"

"She's a good, industrious, splendid woman. She's run the farm for us for forty years. And look how good she is to her brother."

"Ugh."

"She keeps him! And he mutters like Ibsen's Ghosts!"

"Ugh! Oneida!"

Oneida chuckled once more. "What have you against her?"

"I hate her. Isn't that enough to have against a person?"

"When you were a little boy you used to hide in the sump plantation when she came."

"So did the dogs."

Oneida shrieked with laughter; then, "Edward."

"Save it! I'm up!"

Edward got out of bed. Two patchwork quilts were hanging on the balcony, weathered and wasted by exposure through many seasons. They were at present partly damp and had a cellar smell. Edward wrapped one of them round him and was about to go inside when he saw a procession going down the barn road. He shouted, "Heh! Ben! Are you really going?"

Van Kill was driving, Aline his wife sitting with a bundle on her lap, the old red crossbred dog, Bones, standing up on a heap of furniture, and the two little boys in overalls were walking behind. Their household goods were piled casually in a big hay-wagon. The old one-eyed horse walked behind, led by one of the little boys: and picked his way timorously down the road. Behind came the herd of nine brown and white cows, two not far from calving. The other little boy, in faded overalls and bare feet, came after them, guiding them with a stick. They were nervously lowing. Ben, just before he reached the bend of the barn road, where the road was gullied between high banks, turned and called, "I'll be back for the other load."

Edward waved and went inside. "The van Kills are leaving. Didn't Leander fix up about the water?"

"The cows have no water this morning and hardly any yesterday. They're not giving any milk. Poor Aline! I ran up to see her and she was making him another pot of black coffee and he was running round looking mad and murderous; and cussing. She said to me, 'I know it's hopeless, Oneida. I'm sunk. I'll never get out of it.' I said, 'Yes, you will, Aline, you're so young, you're only twenty-seven and you've got two lovely boys who'll soon be grown up and help you. It looks black this morning, but you'll find the cloud has a silver lining. Don't despair.' 'No, it's no use, I'm done for, Oneida,' she told me, poor thing: 'I'm old, I look at least ten years older, and my arms and legs are like sticks. I'm sorry I ever married him.' 'There's hope for everyone,' I told her. 'Not for me, I see clear,' she said. I couldn't shake her. She said there's so much work, and he doesn't love her. And she asked me to explain how she could get out of it."

"They are going to take that job on the Morgan farm?"

"She says the accommodation is awful, but there's water down in the valley and he's made some arrangement with Morgan. He'll pay us for the cows when he can. I said, 'Wait till you get settled. Maybe you'll change your mind.' The barn is no good to us without a farmer. I think he'll be back."

"He keeps going away and coming back."

"They don't know where to turn. It isn't farming country. There are only a few patches up here worth scratching for vegetables."

Edward pushed aside some things on a trunk and sat down, looking at the low hill sloping upwards. The windows of this studio were at the back of the house.

He could see the kitchen steps, the old fruit trees, a line of rose-bushes now in flower, that bordered the barn road. He could see the superb double barns painted and in good condition and a tarpaulin stretched over the roof of one against the cloudless blue sky. Behind the barn, higher up, was a derelict farm shed, his old car from which he had sold the engine during the war, a ragged path leading up to the farmer's cottage. A scouting branch of the wild hops vine had crossed all that space and embraced one shaky veranda-post. Beside was Bones's kennel and a rosebush. Beyond, the path wound to a cowpad, lined on each side by a railing fence; and beyond the two gates across the cowpad lay a high field of thick grass in which was a thicket of old elms and pines and laurels, the roof of the house used every summer by his cousins Opsa and Pelayga.

Mary, the eldest daughter, had married fifty-four years ago; and had four children, unmarried through her jealousy, so they all said. The two girls, Laurel and Rose, were called, except to their faces, Opsa and Pelayga, and the two boys, Ralph and Richard, were called Suttinlay and Solo. These names had the mysterious family meanings of the Fat Goose (Opsa = Laurel), the Tall Shrew (Pelayga = Rose). Suttinlay, Ralph, studious and a gold-medallist in youth, had once acted a Southern gentleman in a play and said, "Sutt-in-lay, suh," and Solo, Richard, had once performed, with an orchestra, a drum solo.

Oneida, following her nephew's idle stare, remarked, "Those idiots are coming this morning. They won't even bring Musty a present. They're coming to eat, that's all."

"Didn't Leander speak to the man at the waterworks?"

"Yes. There's all that copper piping lying in the laundry but you can't get anyone to put it in. They want salaries like the President."

"Oh, won't you raise our salaries, salaries," sang Edward, to the tune of Beethoven's Eighth Symphony.

"Edward, what shall I wear?"

"Why don't we sell the damn Little Farm? I thought Leander was going to fix this place up this summer."

"Leander had a good offer from Philadelphia but he thinks we should wait a couple of years. And Dan wants him to sell. Dan wants us to sell everything so he can get a share and buy himself a row of houses on Long Island."

"O-ne-i-da!"

"Oh, you know Big Jenny will do anything he says."

"I think we're near the top: he should sell anyhow."

"Why don't you take down the pergola, Edward? You and Lou could rip out the old veranda flooring too."

"It looks good yet but I think cracks are appearing, in the business situation."

"But Old Dad said that the Little Farm kept the Big Farm afloat."

"You and Lou should have quit long ago and had a life of your own. Ha-ha. Do you know what they call you now: The Comedians on the Hill."

"Your father was an artist: we always protected artists. Where's the comedy? Where would Lou prepare his concerts if not here? Where would we go for the summer?"

Oneida was silent, and stooping down, began looking through her things for something to wear. Presently she said, "The family insisted upon Opsa and Pelayga going off there because none of us could stand them; and now they come snooping after us at every chance. I know human nature. Old Mary brought Opsa and Pelayga up to be too good to work and they never want to open up their house: too much work!"

"*Absolut!* To be sure, Old Mary's going to get a terrible sun tan sitting there in the sun."

Oneida burst out: "Oh, why did we have the wedding on Musty's birthday?"

"Because Mark and Marian stay with her every summer." He laughed.

"But we might have known those Outcasts would come snooping in."

Edward went back to his balcony and dropping the patchwork quilt on the floor looked for his drawers which he found under his own quilt. The last traces of the mist were crawling over the high fore edge of the mountains. The mountains were so high and the slopes at such an angle that the crests filled half the sky. The crests, where pines grew, looked like an old-fashioned city crowded with watchtowers, defense gates, steeples and pitched roofs, tall hats and storm-mantles.

On their own land, a private road to the right ran to the other end of the estate. In this direction he could see the roof of a two-room shack with a veranda the size of a packing case; and two pots of geraniums. This shack, which belonged to the Massines, was rented for a very low rent to two of the Adamses, an old valley family; and here was Charlie the tied Spitz.

Edward looked quietly at everything and had no desire to go upstairs or downstairs. Every tree and every acre had a meaning to him: this was his native soil. For many miles round he was known; or he would be known at once if he said his name, Edward Massine. By saying Edward Massine, he could get food, lodging, friends, get his bus fare paid, his shoes mended, get provisions if he had forgotten his purse. The dogs and cats were descendants of other Massine dogs and cats; and the cows and horses all of the same stock. The families were all van Kills and Adamses and Flannigans and the young families who came up for the summer were like Mark and Marian, people with whom he had played tennis or swum each summer. Through the open kitchen window underneath came voices and the barking of dogs, the smell of what the women were making. Bart was talking through the barking and Lou was at the piano. Madame X began barking in a different way. Edward called to Oneida, "What does she want?"

"She knows something we don't know."

"She knows Darly is here; she's running along the bank," said Edward.

Sambo and the other dogs began to bark.

"Oh, let her go. She can't hurt Darly. But watch out for Sambo," Oneida screamed through the floor to the kitchen which was underneath.

"Ollie, lock up Sambo. Here's Darly."

A moment later, a chain of little dogs appeared gamboling over the bank. The Abbot rushed down from the vacant farmhouse which he had been inspecting.

"Oh, Lord, I forgot the Abbot."

Oneida began shouting through the floor again to tell the sisters in the kitchen to catch the Abbot. Several stout elderly women rushed up the kitchen steps, one armed with a wet dish towel. Oneida shouted from the window. The Abbot lost his head and ran down the barn road. A grocer's delivery wagon driven by one of the Flannigan family shot up the road and came to a stop at the top of the kitchen steps. Sambo was delivering salvos from his window: they heard him hurl himself against the door. A mess of dogs was now roaring round the two shut doors of the delivery wagon. Oneida shouted from the window, "Get out, get out, they won't hurt you."

The grocer's lad was big-boned but timid, about fifteen. He stared from the door, opened the door and put one foot on the running board. The angry sea of dogs leaped and shouted at him. He backed into the car and shut the door. Oneida shouted, "Ollie don't flick the Abbot. It frightens him. They're only dawgs. Aren't you ashamed to be frightened of dogs? They can smell it. It's adrenalin in your blood. Ollie, don't you dare use that towel on them. They'll bite each other. You're scaring them. When they're scared, it's only natural, they fight back. Stop it, you moron. Oh, that Abbot. Get out, you moron."

Edward looked about for a pair of Lou's farm trousers. He had come up overnight with his hands in his pockets, armed only with an old leather purse containing his ticket and the fare for the mountain taxi.

Some of the sisters had gone into the kitchen. Now, there emerged from it Flora, the Abbot's owner, a broad dot of a woman with bright white hair, white teeth, a snow-white starched apron, one of those fine thick white skins that look like pure, crusty snow. She had the finest eyes in all this family of handsome browned women. She smiled maternally, threw out her arms and cried in her thin voice, "Abbot, bad boy! Bad boy! Upstairs with you. Go this minute. Come, Abbot darling. Where's Daddy? Where's Arnold? Arnold's here, Abbot. Come boy, Daddy's here."

The Abbot hesitated and turned to look.

"Bad boy, bad boy, go upstairs this minute."

At this moment, Ollie, tired of waiting for the groceries, rushed out and flicked the Abbot with her apron. Oneida screamed. The other dogs had worked themselves into a frenzy. The Abbot rushed upstairs to hide in his room. Oneida, running, met the other sisters at the head of the stairs and, seeing him hiding under the bed, coaxed and soothed. They all bent down to spy him. The dog rested his revolver head against the skirting. Flora, laughing and calling in a sweet voice, came panting round and peered under the bed, followed by Ollie with the apron which she began showing and explaining to the Abbot. The three fat sisters bent double, looked under the bed, and tried to get the Abbot to forgive. At length he turned his head slowly, looked at them with his sad humid eyes and rested his head on the wooden floor. Flora reached under the bed to pat him. Ollie and Norah went back to the cooking. Oneida went to continue dressing. The dog crawled out and hid his head in

Flora's lap. She too returned to the kitchen and a moment later, the Abbot scampered downstairs and rushed out again to join the scrimmage which continued round the grocer's lad. He had got out of the car and had advanced about a yard, surrounded by the furious dogs. He looked despairingly at the kitchen door, raised a pale face to Oneida and again at the window upstairs. Exhorted by all, he shuffled a foot forward and at this Madame X sprang at his thigh, imitated by old Musty feebly. The Abbot flew through the air with snapping jaws, intentionally missed the boy's outspread arm for the pleasure of floating round him and snapping. The boy, unable to move backward or forward, waved his arms — this caused them to leap. He looked at the people watching him and burst out crying. This threw Oneida into a rage. She shouted through the window.

"Call them off, Oneida," said Edward and shouted at Musty.

"They're innocent, they think they're protecting us."

The boy blubbered and tried to shove a foot forward. At this moment Irene came out of the kitchen with a towel, stormed into the milling dogs. Madame X turned on her with a growl. She flicked Musty who retired in fright. She kicked the Abbot. Oneida, at this unprecedented horror, began to shout at Irene from the window.

"What about the boy," shrieked Irene, looking up at them.

"They'll turn on him, they'll kill him," said Oneida, beside herself with fury and misery. But she meant that the dogs would turn on the Abbot.

"Why don't you call her off?"

The boy stood trembling between all the contenders on the garden path. Irene said impatiently, "Oh, get your basket and come in, for the love of Mike. I'll hold the brutes off."

"I won't let her, I won't let her punish the dogs," cried Oneida. Throwing a large piece of batik silk round her shoulders, she ran downstairs. Irene took advantage of Oneida's disappearance to shove the dogs about and get the boy to the kitchen door. Oneida arrived weeping.

[136]

"She kicked my dawg, she kicked my dawg, you know she's sick."

Edward exhorted them from the window to break it up and forget it. Oneida seized her angry old dog in her arms and stood facing Irene, speaking in a rough voice, ironclad in anger, and to Flora, who appeared speaking gently at the kitchen door, she stormed only, "She kicked my sick dawg, I'll break her neck."

Edward shouted, "She only kicked the Abbot; she flicked Madame X."

Edward whistled, Musty turned tail and ran out of the embarrassing scene. Things quieted down. But Oneida followed the boy relentlessly, saying to him, "Why are you afraid of little dogs? Coward!"

"Everyone says they'll bite me," said the boy, now in the kitchen. The sisters were unpacking the big baskets. Mr. Vines was sitting at one end of the table having a cup of cocoa. Oneida continued her remarks to the boy. Edward leaned out the window and shouted at the kitchen door,

"Come and get dressed, Oneida!"

Ollie, in the kitchen, began to laugh.

"During the whole fight, Old Mary sits in the sunken garden with her skirt over her head and pays no attention."

Oneida telephoned the grocer about the stupidity of his lad and went puffing upstairs with her old dog in her arms. Arrived in the studio, she dumped the dog on the floor, saying, "Now pipe down, you nuisance. It's all the fault of your old dog, Edward. He jumps about and imitates her and it drives her on. She shows off. She thinks she can do what she pleases. And then Sambo barking all the time from the window and that stupid fat Dingy. I wish Big Jenny would keep that little brat Darly at home when she's in heat. They all come up here and excite my dog."

Edward was looking for a shirt. There were piles of all kinds of clothes everywhere in these quarters. He found an old Lacoste shirt in a heap on a box seat under the window. The rain had come in recently and dampened them. The clothes had for long been rolled about by others looking for things. Edward put on the shirt and was going out to get his breakfast, when he saw the light falling in an old mirror stuck against the wall under the gallery. His small head stuck like a dark vegetable in the frame of the mirror like a lily pad at the bottom of a brown lake. He passed his hand over his bony protruding chin to feel the beard and irresolutely moved a few things on the chiffonier looking for a comb. There was a curious bird cry near the house. The dogs burst out of the house below, with the people behind them. Madame X bounded in one movement from her doze and thudded out with a tolling bark. There were shrieks and shouts below.

"Westfourth! Oh, I can't look — oh, oh, Westfourth's caught a rabbit."

The dogs became maddened and people plunged in and out. Bart, returning from a stroll to the bowling green, said, "Oh, my God!"

Ollie, with her head in her apron, ran about blindly following the others. Norah and Flora in their snowy white aprons were running in the sunken garden, wringing their hands and crying out. Ollie kept saying, "Oh, don't look, don't, don't touch."

Westfourth, trembling, was crouching with an ugly look near the latticed porch, an injured baby rabbit on the ground before him. The rabbit was playing dead. The dogs, not daring to approach Westfourth, stood trembling, yelping and leaping. Even Madame X did not dare to approach the old cat and his prey. Bart took the rabbit; the cat hissed and jumped. The dogs leaped at his arms, skirling and howling. Meanwhile Lou had reached the fourth item on his program for the fall concert; Madame Sarine singing Donna Anna was sending husky and angry tones from the bowling green.

"It's Westfourth who caught a baby rabbit in the lettuce patch," said Edward.

"The dogs get too excited," said Oneida, fixing her hair in a crown and looking in the dark-olive mirror. She continued, "Oh, it upsets me. That means Westfourth will die soon. Westfourth is fourteen. Tobacco was fifteen and Tobacco caught a bird for the first time in years just before he died. I heard a thump in the kitchen and thought, what can that be? I couldn't imagine. Tobacco had jumped in the kitchen window with a bird in his mouth. I said at the time, it's a bad sign. What are they doing now?"

Edward went to the other end of the studio and looked down.

"It's all over. My goodness, Westfourth has lost his collar. He looks decayed with that naked ring round his neck."

"It was rotted, that leather. Your father bought it for him."

"Father loved Westfourth."

Oneida said, "But he's only a barn cat, you'd never think it to look at him. That's very strange, his catching the rabbit and losing his collar."

They both leaned out, looking. They eventually spied the broken collar on the center steps leading to the sunken garden.

"That's going to haunt me," said Edward, gloomily.

"What shall I wear, Edward?"

In the studio were three old pianos, a baby grand, an upright, and a soundless practice piano. Oneida stood between them in the middle of the floor by the baby grand, one bare arm holding up an embroidered blouse which she had just unearthed from a pile of things on the piano and one arm holding up a new linen blouse into which old bands of dark blue embroidery had been introduced. All their work in the country was done by a village dressmaker, one of the Adams clan.

Edward said, "Where's that white one with the white silk embroidery?"

"Under a brown pinafore?"

"Are you going to wear a pinafore to the wedding?"

Oneida, bare-footed, was wearing a thickly gathered white lawn petticoat with eyelet embroidery round the hem. She was naked from the waist up. She had bound a blue, red and gold necklace in

[139]

her hair and pinned the broad thick plaits on the crown of her head.

Oneida's face, plump and pert would, if not for its excessive feminine chubbiness and its dimpled fleshed chin, have resembled Edward's. Her nephew now looked at her with admiration. She was dun-skinned, with lips and nipples approaching mulberry and she was dragging out a pile of things on a trunk, some dull, flat, discolored things, a lifeless brick-red cotton, a black and white stuff, a dead violet which had once been some other color, a black satin blouse into which lace strips had been let, an old Indian scarf in yellows. She pulled them about roughly, saying, "I don't know what to wear, I'm sure." She hung a dirty Roman scarf round her neck. Many of the things in the room had once been some other color. Her sense of color was never satisfied, so she dyed and redyed her things, always aiming at some curious bastard shade, bituminous, olive, French blue, rusty bronze, dirty copper, and when she got it, she would be dissatisfied with that too. There it would lie, after her labor, for months, years, just where she had thrown it on the trunk, the piano, the floor.

"You'll do like that," said Edward.

She laughed, put on a black satin bra and pulled over it a white silk smocked nightshirt which Edward himself had just given her, a very short thing in a new fashion which came only to her knees. Over this nightshirt, she pulled a blue serge drill tunic such as schoolgirls wear, and she belted it with a belt of red and black straw. She put on the blue rope sandals of the morning.

"Are those your wedding slippers?" said Edward.

"Edward, you know I have to make a hundred trips round the farm, up to help the farmer clear out and down to Mrs. Mustbrook's to get the chickens for the wedding supper — I have to see to everything — I don't see why you and Lou get away with doing nothing at all — Ollie and Flora spend their whole time in the kitchen amusing themselves with baking and Norah has to go down to the village for the cake, I don't know what else! Yes! I must do some digging in the garden, put in those seedlings and see if those Outcasts have come — Opsa and Pelayga. Fooey, I hope not. I must get the rooms ready for the young people and send someone off for the dogs' food to that camp and I have to go down to the village to get some sauce that Victor-Alexander wants for tomorrow. Why don't you go to Musty's?"

"You know Musty makes me sick in the stomach," said Edward, lying back on the sofa in a profusion of things.

"Why don't you go down and get your breakfast? What are you yawning for?"

"No will power."

"Oh, my soul, and there's Old Mary still sitting in the garden. It's too bad. Why don't they call her in? Oh, I hate martyrs."

Oneida leaned out of the window. "Mary, get your breakfast, what are you doing? Don't be obstinate."

The old woman sat still.

"There she goes, pretending she is deaf now. She can hear me quite well."

She ran downstairs and Edward heard her brawling with the old woman on the path. He looked out the window. Oneida was stiffened, blazing like a wild black kitten. The old woman held up her hands to show the swollen veins.

"With my trouble and my usual insomnia, I didn't sleep a wink last night."

"Why did you drink all that brandy down at Dan's last night?"

"I can take that. Four glasses and not turn a hair. Never fear for me."

"And then you don't sleep and you're in a bad temper when you get up."

"I had to roll out, my legs were like logs. I couldn't bend them to get my stockings on."

"You heard us all rioting here the whole morning."

The old woman's steady iron voice rolled back at her. "Why do

[141]

you breakfast without calling me? That's not the right idea of hospitality. So as not to disturb me. You know I don't sleep. That's not hospitality."

"You crawled out of the house, right through the hall: you could see us all at breakfast."

"My dear child, keep your blood pressure down the doctor said, do you know what that means? I used to climb those mountains opposite. Besides, I thought you had all finished and there was no sense in bothering you with so much to do."

"Isn't that stupid to think we've ever finished breakfast at nine?"

"The clock wasn't striking."

"You heard that all right."

"I hear nothing, I see nothing. And I don't like to be intrusive. It's not my way. If people are hospitable, they are."

"A lot you know about hospitality. You never even gave me a ham sandwich after I was married. And why didn't you let Laurel and Rose get married? You thought you might have to make a spread. Ha-ha!"

"Keep calm, said the doctor and I'm deaf as a stone, deaf. What do you think of that? I know four languages and I can't hear the radio! And I can't hear what people are saying. When Louis was alive he read the newspaper to me every night, he understood my condition. He pitched his voice just right."

"Pitched! He spoiled you! You're spoiled! And so your sons are your sick nurses!"

The old woman was engaged in settling her costume. She smoothed her hair, picked up the stool, bowed her head stiffly to take the unbecoming handkerchief from her neck, asked if she looked tidy.

"You must be starving," said Oneida, stamping her foot.

"The doctor said plenty of sun, the sun is a cure for everything, the doctor said."

"Fine thing. Sun a cure for high blood pressure."

"Plenty of sun, nothing but sun, and my injections."

They entered the house under the old vine-covered porch. Very hungry, starving for coffee of which she was very fond, Old Mary stood in the hall, looking towards the kitchen and perceived her sisters; Flora, reading a recipe from a book while mixing flour for milk rolls, Norah drawing a chicken and chopping parts with a big knife, Ollie chopping onions fine and mixing them with herbs. Westfourth, on the old disused stove, was waiting for the entrails. The Abbot kept effecting an entry through one of the three kitchen doors after being chased out through another. Old Mary came forward stonily, stiffly, searched for a cup and plate, went to the sink and washed them. Oneida dragged a chair forward and Ollie took the cloth from the old woman's hands. Oneida scolding still brought her coffee. The old sister sat down bending her square white head over her plate and reached for a piece of bread. She accidentally put her hand on some peeled onions. She started up, saying, "I can't bear onion smell, you carry it with you."

Ollie laughed and peered into the coffeepot, murmuring, "You should have come before. It was just like you like it, gunpowder. It would blow you sky-high."

"Mary shouldn't have coffee at all."

"I like coffee. I stayed awake all night. My legs were like rocks. And the clock was not striking."

"She stayed awake all night because she drank four brandies at Dan's and he encouraged her," Oneida said.

Ollie tittered. "She never turns a hair. She could drink wood alcohol."

"I did drink wood alcohol during prohibition. Louis always took me to the speak-easies. Louis took me out almost every night of my life. One time the pharmacist who supplied the liquor made a mistake and he gave some bad stuff. It was a wedding party. Everyone was sick but me. They couldn't kill me. Like Rasputin. Like Rasputin."

[143]

"A wedding party!" cried Oneida.

"Like Rasputin, ha-ha-ha," said Ollie, delighted.

"I can drink wine and rye and bathtub gin and those girls of mine can't touch a drop. They didn't get married either. My husband told me the politics every night and here at Whitehouse you haven't even a radio in the house."

"Your husband Louis spoiled you and he sacrificed those four children to you and that's why they never got married," said Oneida bitterly.

"Is my dress clean, Flora? You know I broke my glasses."

"It's fresh from the laundry, you know yourself. You look beautiful, Mary. Everything is all right."

Oneida said kindly, "You look very nice, like a queen. She changes three times a day."

"Four times is not too much if I am to be clean."

"Is Dan coming to the wedding? He promised me a bottle of wine," said Old Mary. Ollie giggled. Oneida, impatient, quarrelled with each one in turn; with Norah because she had given some entrails to Westfourth on the stove, with Flora because she was reading a recipe she had done a hundred times, with Old Mary because she had never drawn a fowl, and with Ollie because she kept repeating the joke about Rasputin. She then tried to quarrel with Norah for being intimidated by her mother-in-law — "A woman your age kowtowing before a mother-in-law," and with Ollie because she wanted to leave Albany and come to live in New York — "What would you do in New York?" and with Old Mary because of the jewels, diamonds and rubies and sapphires, which she kept in a safe-deposit box.

At this moment, Edward appeared. He was greeted by a chorus of loving words. He sat down at the table which was now buried under plates, chopping boards, bowls, tins, loaves of bread, chickens and such, and waited for someone to serve him. Ollie busied herself with the coffeepot and once more made her little jokes about gunpowder and about Rasputin. Meanwhile, Old Mary had washed her plate and cup and had got down on her knees to wash the floor. It was hot and damp. The boiler had formed a large pool on the floor in which they were all paddling. The bowls, pans and plates which the dogs had used lay about on the floor and on the old stove in a corner of the kitchen were huge stew pans and caldrons in which all kinds of foods had been cooked, including a soup for the dogs made from lungs, hearts and bones. Irene was in the pantry rummaging on the shelves, sorting out oranges, potatoes, onions and other vegetables from the bags on the floor, enumerating the twenty kinds of breakfast foods found there. Whenever anyone mentioned a new whim in breakfast foods, it was included in the order and came up from the grocer the next day. Ollie had begun cleaning out the large overworked icebox. Flora laughed fatly. "Arnold telephoned me this morning from Long Beach, to come home. I told him I had to stay and make milk rolls for the wedding."

Oneida cried indignantly, "Whoever saw the like, to come into another person's house and arrange their shelves, wash their floor and pull their icebox to pieces?"

"Ben-son heard that if you put a saucerful of charcoal in the icebox, it doesn't smell," said Ollie looking at them innocently, with her big black eyes, her cheeks rosy with exertion. Her apron had become dirtier than ever.

This galvanized the women. Oneida cried, "Where can you get charcoal?"

They all appealed to Edward who opined that it might be got at the wood and coal store or at the pharmacist's. Oneida went and telephoned both places for some and said she would get it when she went down for Victor-Alexander's sauces. Victor-Alexander was a bachelor who lived on the Massine acres. He had been a friend of the family since Oneida's childhood.

Norah recited, "He was a musical prodigy; but after he gave his first recital, he gave up music because he felt he had not sufficient talent."

"He's a perfectionist," said Oneida.

The fowls had arrived, were stuffed and ready for cooking. Edward kept on eating and drinking. The new loaves were in the oven. The dishes were washed, even the dogs' pans; and Ollie had washed out all the dish towels, oven cloths, and other rags. Old Mary went out and put along the stone coping of the sunken garden in the sun all the pots, pans, tubs and caldrons, while Ollie laid along the grass all her washing. By this time, the cream cheese was taken from the press, the butter was made, the kitchen tables cleared off from the first cooking and again filled with flour jars, boxes of spices, opened cans, big trenchers and chopping boards which for a moment had been set to dry. It was now Oneida's turn. She was making for lunch a meat loaf and a soufflé. Mustbrook, that morning, had sent up six dozen eggs; these were being cracked and used or stowed away.

Oneida, in between times, went to the pantry to look at her oils and sauces for Victor-Alexander. He thought no one could prepare sauces or dressings but himself. More than that, when he came and made them, he allowed no one in the kitchen but Oneida. If everything was not just so, he blamed her also. He himself had telephoned and said he would bring fresh lettuce and tomatoes. He must get garlic. Oneida had brought from their own garden celery, parsley and Lou had found some mint in a wet patch: but Victor-Alexander would not have any of these. Victor-Alexander would be cross at finding a dirty kitchen. They must hurry up and clean up. The morning was getting on and nothing ready. Edward kept on eating and drinking and took this all in in a tranquil frame of mind, saying nothing. This kind of scene had been going on round him all his life.

"Victor-Alexander visited Big Jenny last Saturday for dinner," said Ollie.

Oneida flushed. "And not a word to me, how stupid!"

"Opsa and Pelayga are going to ask him to their place as soon as they come, like last year, I wonder?" said Flora.

Oneida punched her meat loaf gently. "And do they think he'll marry one of them?"

She punched harder. "What will Victor-Alexander think when he sees that old wives' fair?" she inquired angrily, tossing her head towards the exhibits of pots and towels in the back garden. She rushed out and began to take in the things. She scolded them for turning the house upside down without any effect. They laughed. She came back and plunged her hands deep into the meat meal, mixing it with the sauce, soft bread and egg, molding it into the greased tin. She murmured, "This will turn out all right, I feel it. What are you doing now, Mary?"

The old sister had left the kitchen, her strong back slightly bowed, a basket in her hands. Oneida scolded, "When she's in my house, she can scrub and scour; at home she has a woman in to clear her kitchenette."

Putting the meat loaf on the side shelf, she looked through the window at the pergola. On the broad stone table, Old Mary was arranging brass and copper pots and kettles, an immense samovar, a set of candlesticks. Oneida grumbled, "She must have got all that energy polishing her diamonds."

Norah, tallest of the sisters, wide, bony, with a fleshy face and her hair still rather thick and dark, her sleeves rolled up to her broad white shoulder, came and looked over Oneida's shoulder. She chuckled and said firmly, "Leave the poor thing alone. It makes the house look nice to have the old things polished."

Down from the old bowling green came the affirmations of the *Norma* cavatina.

Edward, leaving his cup and plate on the table, got up, stretched, and went out to the veranda to wait for lunch. He sat there for a while, on a rocking chair, gazing at the glorious valley and mountain in full summer leaf under a clear sky. He heard voices, music, saw heads bobbing up through the laurel bushes, and he strolled inside. In the sitting rooms and hall were shining copper pots and plates; the electric brackets were full of rose and olive reflections. There were flowers in some of the vases, the work of Irene. The kitchen was clean, with the towels hung over the pipes and the shining pots heaped on the old stove. The lid of the bread tin hobbled on the heap of new breads stuffed into it. Ollie and Norah sat and stood at the kitchen table, peeling vegetables for a big stew for the next day.

"It is always better the next day," said Norah, who was the family stew and sauce cook. Oneida was chopping onions fine to make chicken stuffing. Bart was now stretching his long legs from a broken seated chair near the back door, massaging Westfourth into a frenzy, and saying, "I hate dogs, but they are too stupid to know it. They love me because I understand their greedy flattering natures. Dogs swear by me. On the other hand, cats love me."

"Dog lovers rarely care for cats, and vice versa," said Oneida.

"Oh, I love my vice versa," said Edward, sauntering in, picking pieces from the plates, looking into a boiling pot on the stove.

Bart said, "People only like pedigreed dogs so they pretend the pups are pedigreed, and that's snobbery. It's folly, for how did the breeds arise? By miscegenation."

"Miss Who?" said Edward automatically, taking a new bread from the tin.

"You get hummingbirds that way: a moth and a bird," said Oneida. Ollie volunteered:

"A Hindu lectured to us at Albany and he told us in India background is everything. You wouldn't marry anyone unless you knew their background. The whole trouble with America, he said, is that we don't know the background of people. A girl of fine family could never marry the son of a butcher and so there is never any disappointment in the children."

Oneida said loudly, "What happened when Mr. Marchant married the tailor's daughter down in the village? Nothing. They're very happy."

Norah meditated. "Yes, but you remember when they took the garage, she chopped off her finger and Dr. Edward had to sew it on again."

Edward said, "So she was a cut below him." He continued, grinning, "Have you set places for Opsa and Pelayga? I saw them toiling up the mountains and I came in to see the fun when Oneida saw them."

"Oh, not already?" said Oneida, planting her hands on the table.

Lou came in gaily saying, "Oh, here are Laurel and Rose! And they've brought the mail! Go and say hello, Oneida! There's a letter for you, Edward. You can't get it until you've guessed who it's from."

"From whom it is," said Ollie, giggling.

"To whom you are speaking?" said Edward, in a vaudeville voice. "A letter you want."

"Mrs. Wharton," said Edward, naming the actress he was fond of. "No."

"Mrs. Barron?" said Edward.

"Your girl!"

Edward put the letter in his pocket and took the old cat off Bart's lap.

"Where's his collar?"

"It's broken. We must get a new one."

"Look at Westfourth's foot. He's had a fight."

"There was a hell of a caterwauling in the night," said Bart.

"The poor girls are sitting on the veranda talking to Old Mary; but I guess they're really waiting to be invited in," said Lou, looking at the women.

"I'm going to invite them in," said Edward, sauntering out with the cat. But Oneida and Ollie bustled out and the three of them got to the front veranda in a parcel, where they began kissing, cooing and fondling Opsa and Pelayga.

Edward with the cat in his arms, strolled round the house. He stopped under the low trees to let the cat scratch at the twigs. West-fourth purred and clung. When they came to a smooth path, Edward put him down carefully, saying, "No more scrapping, you old weather-beaten pug."

Westfourth walked up the stone coping and stretched himself out in all his majesty. Edward picked up a pair of shears and went into the raspberry patch. He started on the dead canes.

The patch, though not more than two yards square, was tossed and tormented where Lou, Oneida and various guests had been plucking and tearing at will, getting rid of the latest offshoots of the great wild hops vine, tearing away at its roots. Here, it crawled over the tool shed, through the grass, to throttle a thin small birch, through the rosebushes, tangling the canes. The vine fell from the roof and the porch and the tool shed and rose from the ground in thin run-ners and pencil-thick stems, and with warp and weft endeavored to trap all the plants and bushes in one coarse moss. Edward, for a few minutes, stripped and tore, ravished, unwound and wound, and then felt stealthily and thoughtfully for the climbing stems which ran down the main stems of other bushes and so followed them under-ground. When, led by these stems underground, he had cut and cleared a little space, Edward began to pull out the runners of the vine. The first were only threads rising from a tough cord; and below this cord was a thicker one from which it arose, deeper down; and the lowest one was the size of a ship's cable, and about a foot below ground. The stringy starved bushes were freed, stood apart with their miserable stems half naked.

He grubbed farther down, pulling out the strong and quick vine from the engaged roots of the bushes but even when these were hor-ribly drawn out from the entrails of the garden, his fingers felt new and greater intricacies of thicker runners, deeper underground, to which these upper stems merely led down; and most of these sys-tems of runners and stems had grown round each other or stones, or things lost in the earth for years. Edward made a hole and plunged his arm into the blood-warm earth to the elbow. Groping, he found old piping in a coil, a hammer, the tapering root of the nearest tree, a shoe sole. The root of the nearest tree was in the grip of the vine and feeling under this embrace, he found another tap of the vine, thick as a man's arm.

The vine aboveground was clambering at a distance of a hundred feet on the farm hand's old shed, now broken in, and farther off on a corner of the barn; and here in the raspberry patch, and towards the bowling green and on the wall of the summer house. The same vine, rising from these great arteries, issued from under the house at the pergola corner, at the corner where Lou's downstairs studio was, at the corner where the newly married couple would sleep tonight; climbed the walls on the other side to his own veranda, and reached out to the suffocated pear trees and through the pear trees to the pergola which it canopied, a heavy stuff which was breaking down its heavy worn beams and spreading beyond that to the first trees of the plantation where the sump water seeped through. Beyond that, it had begun upon the old trees which formed the screen above the sunken farm road, down all the half-acre to the road, the same great system and one vine; and this was more than the foundation of the garden, it was a dark communication of sinew forming the body of a great being. It held, embraced, but did not crush the ground, the house, and all there brought by dogs and men: bones, sheathed copper wire needed for watering the cows, old leather shoes hidden by a predecessor of the Abbot, a sadiron, and all the things lost by this fertile careless family, and all the things loved by this productive, abundant family for seventy years; the deep ineradicable cables plunging into the hill soil and sending up at great distances their wires and threads; and the whole family and house and barns and the home-acres, in the great throttling of the twining vine. It tore away easily, leaving all the growing roots there. In a few days, the injured roots completed their repairs and sent up a new line of roots and leaves and the work of monopoly went on.

Edward said, sitting back half-exhausted and half in anger, "Like what it does to me: the sloth that stretches back into my childhood and had its foot in my cradle."

Edward put his grubby fingers in his pocket and fingered the letter. That too stretched through the years and was suffocating, useless, and was like his life with the sisters, a love of old women. He sat down on the grass among the dry thorns and weeds and opened the letter.

DEAR EDWARD,

Perhaps you will read this letter days after you get it and, knowing you, I will wait two weeks for an answer. Please read my letter carefully. Please do not let it lie around for days and weeks or drop it on the dining-room table and forget it. Do you now, or at any other time, expect to marry me? If you do, please let me know, don't think that because the news is good, it can wait. And say so, write me a letter to say so, and don't be vague. And if not, please say so. There is no need for you to make any excuses. I have made more excuses for you than any man could make for himself. It is another man who is asking me to make some decision myself. I realize the fault is all mine. I have been very weak. I have let you go on and on, whistle our lives away. This man wants to marry me: but I can't make up my mind without giving you a chance. This man knows about you and he asks a very plain question: Are you going to marry him? I told him that it was all very unclear. That is why I write and break into your holiday.

Yours, as ever,
MARGOT

Edward was still alive in the life of the vine in the earth. All was still. The sky did not yet show any sign of the thunderstorm which comes almost every afternoon at this time of the year and pours down the escarpments and valleys with that curious steady hopping boom-boom. One tree in the strip, which stood between the big house and Leander's, began to dance slightly at the top, a few leaves wagging against the delicate sky.

Edward thought, this tree knows a wind is coming and yet nothing else is moving and no other tree is moving, and no leaf, just this branch. They live a life different from ours. They think. How wide the view was! He got up and walked on thoughtfully, but had no particular thought. He passed from the timothy field which was reddening now, across the hidden foot track which led to the front gate and through the laurel and wild rosebushes to the other wild grass patch in front of the house. The great vine had begun to crawl along the trees at the far side of this patch, which overhung the sunken road. This had once been a lawn. It was now a grass patch cut twice a summer by the farmer for the cows. It had not yet been cut and was knee-deep in coarse grasses and large broad-leafed weeds, with numerous potholes made by the dogs and concealed by the tufts, and with old beams, an immense pile of stone crumbling down from the terrace and covered by the vine, old wire, all kinds of building and garden trash, and in a stony half-moon, several stunted pines transplanted when mere green feathers from the pine patch by the weir which had never done well.

The farmer, van Kill, was coming up the road. Edward hopped into the wagon. At the barn, with the usual vociferation, they all got down and went into the barn for harness and implements. Edward followed him to the barn and, after a few friendly remarks, nodded towards the filthy straw, the unwashed flags of the barn, the choked guttering, all fly-infested. A drone of flies rose through the barn. Said Edward, "The girls are complaining about the flies in the kitchen."

The farmer went on collecting things and said at last, "You know there's no water coming down from the dam. I can't water the cows. How can I wash the barn? You want to get in that new piping."

"With what? Who can I get to put it in? Leander will look to it at the end of the summer, when he's finished with the houses in town."

"I can't wait till the end of the summer. That's why I'm going."

"This muck has been laying round for weeks," said Edward. The farmer said nothing, and drove off.

Edward went round the barn to look at the old car. At the prices now given for old bodies or even junk, he could find the money for a down payment on a new car. He decided to walk down to the village in the afternoon before or after the wedding and talk to the garage boys. Edward crossed in front of the farmer's house and came to the white railing fence. He unlocked the gate and crossed the dry cowpad. There were only two fences on all the land, this double cowpad fence and the one round Victor-Alexander's place on the hilltop. The cowpad led directly up to Victor-Alexander's place and was, in fact, blocked by Victor-Alexander's fence. Edward leaned on the fence on the other side and thought about the curious relations of his family. The cowpad was a sort of right-of-way given by the Massines to the Massine cows, and enjoyed therefore by the farmer.

Victor-Alexander, to whose land the cowpad led, had claimed that, as he had no drive or path to his fenced-in land except one way round by the state highway and that passing a broken-down section they called "Tobacco Road," he should be given this right-of-way. The cows must be pastured elsewhere. This was a natural drive to the top of the knoll where he had built his house. The house though built by himself was on Massine land. The same was true of Dan Barnes; he had no land of his own. The "girls" had got very excited about Victor-Alexander's visits to Big Jenny's: they said he was hobnobbing with Dan Barnes about their squatter rights: or so said Oneida, ever wrathful, ever wary.

Victor-Alexander, whose family name was Stepney, had been as a boy and young man a family friend, playmate and schoolfellow of Oneida and the younger members of the family; a talented musician and of all Oneida's friends the one favored by her parents as a husband. Victor-Alexander, then, like many other people, even at that time, had had the free run of the Massine houses and lands, had been considered a member of the family; and the use of the knoll for a house, when he wanted to build, had been gladly offered to him. He had built a pretty house, surrounded it with a garden, planted trees and lived in it with members of his family. When his father died and the others married, he lived there alone and surrounded the garden itself with a high and thick fence intended to keep out strangers and the innumerable dogs of the Massine nation. There he had lived alone for many years, and did not allow any visitors, not even the Massines.

In the youth of the Massines, the family and estate had been conducted as now: it had been hard to distinguish between family and close friends. They had all grown up together, Lou, Victor-Alexander, Oneida and the rest, and many others. Rights had been established without question, duties assumed without roster and times and festivals established without calendar. It had all worked like a charm. But now, Oneida said, Victor-Alexander lived incognito, most of his rooms closed, the furniture sheeted, the concert grand "a dead soul," himself "a living corpse," and what would the great judge of character, her father, have thought? There he lived with a crystal ball. Even the tradesmen could not deliver to the house. They rang a bell lodged in a little shed at the padlocked entrance gate of the white fence. This bell rang a private telephone in the recluse's garden. A barely distinguishable path ran through the thick sweet flowery grass from the padlocked gate over the knoll. From the padlocked gate nothing could be seen of "Solitude," Victor-Alexander's house, but a few thick treetops.

Successive tenant farmers had wanted those acres of fair long grass on the knoll inside the white fence for the cows, but the family in council had left it with their friend. Successive farmers, descendants of old inhabitants of the valley and hillsides, had thrown down that white fence and let in the cows. The fence had been mended, barbed wire put up, the wires cut overnight, the cows strayed in, and so on till Victor-Alexander had thought to settle it by buying garden seats and putting them along the cowpad to turn it into a drive. But in the night the garden seats had hopped over the fence and were found head over heels in the grass. Now the cowpad went up and down, the wire-cutting went on from time to time and nothing was decided.

Then there was the water from the dam. In summer the camps took it all at present as the pipes were too small and old. There was the question of the old house built by the boys Solo and Suttinlay and inhabited by the Four Outcasts. The boys one summer had dug a cellar but never reinforced it and the house squatted dangerously lopsidedly over that hole in the earth as if forever on a midden — yes, and there was no water in that house at all, but from one tap which always ran dry every day. The pergola! The vine! The cutting of the timothy, mowing the lawn round the house, the gardens gone to seed, weeds, the cleaning the barn — there was so much to do that it was quite hopeless.

"I'll never sink myself into this kind of stupid and useless work," thought Edward, nodding his head across the cowpad at the old dark firs and elms which screened the Outcasts' house.

The family was known to all, had many friends, perhaps had wounded some people. Many local families had worked as servants for them, or done odd jobs for them. Some hated the dogs. These poor local families and the Massines called each other by their first names. Who had cut the wires? Who let the cows out of the barn at night and sent them down the road? Who were the saboteurs? Edward said, in the strict privacy of the family, "I know damn well who did it."

Then he would add a family word, culled long ago from some friend who had passed out of their acquaintance, "Victor-Alexander is a dark soul."

Oneida would exclaim, "Oh, I don't believe for a minute that Victor-Alexander had anything to do with it."

"Did I blame him? I said he was a dark soul."

Interminable arguments, anecdotes always followed. Oneida herself became flushed and irritated, would sometimes say, sometimes not, what she believed. Sometimes the farmer would threaten to go, sometimes he would go. In general, these incidents were hushed up, repairs made and, as before, the farmer pastured his cows where the good grass was. The Massines could not bear to quarrel with anyone, farmer or squatter.

In the withering top of an old cypress near the barn, Lou's catbird was singing. The land dipped to a bottom and to old orchard land so long neglected that the crabbed fruit trees were half hidden in grass; and at any time of the day the bird might be practicing his scales and trills on some conspicuous dry branch. He copied Casella and Mozart — but at Mozart, all the birds of the hill and glade would start chirping and then the catbird irritated by competition would sometimes fly away. . . . Birds hung too in this dark stand of trees round the house belonging to Old Mary's exiled children; and along the grass Edward could see the little brown forms of the light-bugs (fireflies).

On the other side of the estate there were other deep low fields but never cultivated, and beyond them a mountain stream that fell there in the Massine woods to a large pool built to form a weir, from which the water fell steeply and once more formed a thin mountain stream. The pool emptied and filled up quickly and was surrounded by groves of trees.

The two old maiden sisters, Opsa and Pelayga, had not yet climbed the steep road to their house. They hated their house, for its dirt and discomfort. They had been exiled there by a decree against which was no appeal. They had fixed up a nursery in the upper story for a niece, and a little run for a goat and chickens at the back, but the child never came and the run had fallen down. At the end of each summer, they threw out all their pans and pots, to be cleaned by the snows and rains of half a year; but when they returned from Long Island, in the late spring, they had no heart to face the opening, the washing of dirt from pans and pots, the airing of old curtains and covers and mats in which moths had probably gathered. The weathering walls were falling down, going crazy, feathering and mossing away. Neither of the sisters was a house-keeper. The musical brother, Solo, did the rough work, but the other brother Suttinlay, who was a traveling salesman in pharmaceuticals, rather short, heavy, liked to sit at a table with nothing on it and talk by the hour.

Edward followed the rarely used cart path, picked up a heavy bit of chain, presently dropped it back in the grass where he could find it on the way home, went on to the little red barn or garage which stood outside Victor-Alexander's gate.

Edward looked again at this field, now wild with heavy grass and pollened heads. He leaned on the locked gate and gazed across the rounding field. To the right, far in the distance, was a high mountain which some of the family held to be Mount Hunter (but after generations neither they nor the Adamses and van Kills had confirmed this), to the left, the trees and bushes of the estate road and in front, beyond the sweet field, the show of another knoll and another, and, beyond that a mountain ridge, blue, and all beyond that, unsettled and mildly wooded. There was a faint track which soon dissolved in the field and over the field to the crests of the trees. Those young trees stood round a fence twelve feet high in which was a locked gate. There was no way of seeing through the gate or over the fence. The limbs of the trees were shorn off up to twelve feet and laurel bushes between them. Behind that barrier Victor-Alexander waged wars with green fly, Colorado beetle, snail and caterpillar; from its mysterious paradise he brought out glorious blossoms for festivals and color compositions in vegetables for Harvest Home. In several rooms of the muffled house, in showcases, and on all available space he had on display only for himself his extensive collection of teacups. They had seen some and had given some, cups in gold, silver, minted metals, wood. The sisters laughed about them when they set out for breakfast their seven or eight ten-cent cups with saucers bought in a pile from the grocer. Oneida was indignant at the hoarding away. Thinking about Victor-Alexander's life and his own Edward came back and sat down on a seat which lay in the grass at the bottom of the Outcasts' hill. It was the remains of one of those bought for the cowpad. It had fallen on its back and the thick grass grew all round. All round Edward now was nothing but grass with thick bushes and trees in front along the cart track. He was out of sight. He heard a cow lowing. His heart was thumping and the caustic calm with which he had first read Margot's letter had passed away. His decision plunged from one extreme to the other: "He can't have her!" and "If she wants to go let her!" He began all sorts of letters in his head, lofty, gay, poignant, rallying, and bitter. "And to think that a month hence it will be all over, I won't be in this torment: it will be settled one way or another. I must keep that in mind and it will help me to do the wise thing." He felt that a door was about to close on him; he didn't want to marry now: it was too late: he was used to his rambling freedom: he was afraid to be free and to pick on the first girl who came his way merely out of loneliness: he would be sure to pick the wrong girl again. "How many fellows came back from the war to a thing like this? Plenty I suppose." He lay looking at the midday sky and tried to think out his future. He fell asleep. When he awoke, it already seemed easier for him. He would forget about it for a day or two till things arranged themselves in their own way and the right things came cleancut to him.

When he reached the front veranda again, they had lunch nearly ready and were waiting for Mark and Marian the bridal pair.

He lounged up across the wild growing lawn towards the veranda. "Here's Edward! Here's the boy!" they cried. "Oh, it's like old times to see Edward coming home!" "Oh, djarling, bless you, djarling!" Edward waved but kept his face which felt pinched small and

[159]

mean directed towards the trees, fields, anywhere but at the brilliantly aproned row of women, with great bosoms, white hair, and sparkling eyes. Oneida, the black-haired one, sat on the weather-eaten veranda floor with Madame X. As he came up the steps onto the half-made terrace, he asked, "Where's Lou? Where's lunch? Where are the kids?"

"Lou's gone down to Mrs. Musty's with Irene," said Little Jenny.

"For eggs and honey," said Ollie.

"Why doesn't she hang out a red light: it'd be more honest," cried Oneida.

There was a partial silence; but Old Mary sat upright in the rocking chair talking to Flora who stood, in her shining white hair, kind smile, white starched apron, before a table over which was spread a faded old rug made of plaited rags, a homemade rug, like the others in the house. The braids had been loosening and tripping people for years, and the dogs had been chewing at it. There were several big needles in it at various parts and the sisters took stitches in it whenever they passed by. Oneida with a pert expression, went on wiping pus from Madame X's corrupting anatomy. She threw the bits of lint over her shoulder into the garden which was now tall with globe thistle, giant lupin, baby's breath, roses, larkspur. She kept on kissing the old dog: her savage and innocent heart believed that her kisses would restore Madame X to health.

"It was that white kitten Mrs. Annichini took down to Big Jenny's, that infected Madame X," said Oneida. Edward squatted down by his old dog Musty and ran his fingers through his clotted coat: Musty turned half-blinded eyes upon him. The tall old brother Jonathan was sitting with his broad shoulders bent, his big hands loose on his knees, listening patiently to all Old Mary had to say. Jonathan had just remodeled a house belonging to Dan Barnes in Long Island. The old woman seemed to be feeling her way through the remodeled house.

"That apartment looks out on the street; and on the back, too."

"No, only on the front," Jonathan said.

"On the front and on the back. That apartment has the big front room, their bedroom, and the room beside it which looks on the street; and the other rooms which look on the back street."

"No; the apartment looks out on the street; it is just two rooms."

There was a slight pause. Jonathan and Old Mary resumed their conversation, which presently included a minute discussion of the front staircase, back staircase, wooden staircase, the front door and other such things.

Bart had come to sit on the top step, with Westfourth in his arms. Bart said, "I'd have his paw looked after if I were you."

The dogs began to bark. "It's Lou," said Edward judging from the barking.

Bart told Oneida about a woodchuck he had known once who had saved himself and his family from the great summer flood of 1938.

Meanwhile, Jonathan and Old Mary went on talking about the house in Long Island. Oneida stopped listening, just said, Yes, yes; got the old dog on her lap, looked at its ears and at a sore spot on its back and hugging its fat body in a tender passion of flattery, lost both stories entirely. Nothing could be seen of her but her black hair, now loosened, falling over the stout dog, and the dog's convulsion of affection as it licked her face through her hair. She raised her face, all merry tenderness, to Bart, and on a heartfelt note, "Oh, Bart, tell me, why do I love dogs so much?"

Edward said, "Lou, you arrived for the sixty-four-dollar question."

"You are Mama's loveliest darling, baby doll," said Oneida, kissing Madame X's head.

"If you keep on telling her that, she'll believe it," said Edward.

"I'd rub her out and start again," said Lou.

Ollie put her hand to her mouth and giggled.

Oneida said, "Madame X, get down, I have to get the lunch. If they had their way, I'd get nothing done. They think all I have to do in the world is to nurse them."

Bart assented. "They have a dog world: now, for instance, they see things in black, white and gray; they don't see us in colors."

Oneida would have liked to deny this but did not know how to.

Unexpectedly, Edward said, in a sugary voice, "Madame X is my Mexicali Rose, aren't you, old girl?"

Bart said, "Who's going for a walk to the gas station? I'll get some ice cream."

"I'm going," Irene said.

Edward looked away.

"I'm not going. I have other things to do," said Oneida.

"Let's go to the village and get a drink," said Bart.

"Sugar plum," said Edward to Madame X.

Bart burst out laughing.

"You nitwit, stop it, you idiot," cried Oneida. The Abbot stood at the netted door waiting to be noticed. One ear was pricked, the other flopped comically. His stupid young brown eyes shone with gaiety and he had in his mouth a shoe he had stolen from some bedroom. Oneida shouted, "Oh, my sandal, you idiot dog, oh! Why doesn't he grow wings and fly away to some far green hills and leave just you and me, Madame X?"

Bart shouted, "Bad dog, bad dog!" The dog, delighted, tossed his head, caracoled and dashed back into the dining room, round and through the sitting room. The women laughed. They heard him slipping on the rug, and running through the rooms again, slipping. In an instant, he was back again, attentive.

Bart said, "Bad dog, bad dog," and he was off again.

"Don't encourage him! He's stupid enough! How can anyone have such a stupid dog?"

"He's a dog off the cover of the *Saturday Evening Post,* don't you see? He's a boy's dog. He barks at strangers, he protects the home, he chases birds, he hides shoes, he growls over bones. He read about the perfect dog and he's it. He's the cardboard dog," said Lou.

Oneida jumped up and threw Madame X to the floor. She cried tri-

[162]

umphantly, "The cardboard dog, moron, cardboard dog, I'm going to shut him up in his room, cardboard dog. No self-control, that's why."

"I'll bet he steals legs of lamb from the kitchen table," said Bart.

Madame X jumped to the alert and running to the edge of the veranda followed by Musty, growled. Musty barked. The Abbot dropped his shoe and flew out through the door to help them. Sambo tore out of the nearby plantation where he had been in the undergrowth.

"We can't see or hear anything but Madame X knows someone is coming," Ollie deduced.

"She's never wrong," said Oneida.

"The remarkable performing dog," said Edward.

"We saw Mr. Mustbrook," said Irene.

"He's a nice old man, but he seems to sneer at his sister," said Bart.

"She turned him into a housewife with a pinny round his waist and taught him to make bread," said Ollie, bursting out into laughter. Oneida was angry and did not know where to turn.

"What do you want to say that for? Well, she spoiled him and now she can't get rid of him."

Edward chirped up, "Mother, give me the sun to play with!"

Oneida called, "Edward, you idiot!" and to the dog, "Ah, my darling: come to its Mummy for a moment!"

Lou remarked, "Don't you really think, Bart, life is for something else than to be spent over dogs? Don't you think there is something better to do?"

"I dare say."

Lou answered mildly, "Well, tell Oneida that. I don't see why a whole life should be devoted to dogs; it's the waste of a life, don't you think so?"

Oneida said, "Every living thing needs love."

Bart looked away.

Lou said, "Well, to be continued in our necks. Farewell children, I make my eggs-it."

He went inside, closed the wire door carefully.

"Darly, Darly," he called softly, opened the door again, came softly back, his face tender, saying, "Look, here's Darly come again to visit us."

The little piebald dog, a toy Boston bull terrier, ran timidly and softly to the door, stared at them brightly with its ears pricked, scurried out around the table legs and their legs. Madame X flung herself from Oneida's lap and Musty, who had been hiding, because it was the hour for his medicine, floated out from beneath the china cabinet like a large fluff. Excitedly barking, the dogs ran after their visitor, while Oneida screamed their names, exhorted Lou to separate them, said the Moron must go upstairs because he might attack. However, Darly was not in a certain state. When Bart asked if Madame X had not had puppies, Oneida said no, because her breed could not give natural birth on account of their large heads; they had to have a Caesarean and she would not allow Madame X to go through that. She called Madame X meanwhile, but the toad-faced dog was indifferent to her and soon they could see four or five of them gamboling along the field. Oneida, without her pet, was ill at ease.

"I wish Darly would go home and not disturb the dogs, they get so excited."

They kept talking, the hands went round the clock. Ollie went in to lay the table and Old Mary said, "I don't know how to explain to the women that I have two sons and two daughters and no grandchildren. I would almost rather say they were my nieces and nephews."

Bart would not let go. "They say dictators love animals and are sponsors of antivivisection leagues. You know, they are the ones who vivisect human beings."

"Dictators couldn't love animals, they are too cruel."

"Yet Hitler and Mussolini were constantly snapped with dogs."

"Then it was their only redeeming trait. There's Madame X dig-

[164]

ging at the root of that old tree. It will come down some day. She knows it's rotten inside."

Edward sat inside in the long cool sitting room that ran along the sunken garden. He sat at Oneida's desk and tried to write. Just near him at his right, Flora and Norah, with cooking going on, were admiring silk cloth and aprons of many colors which Ollie had brought out of her valise and which she had made by hand for them.

Edward had a sheet of paper in front of him and Lou's pen in his hand and he had written on the sheet of paper, "Dear Margot," and then a series of phrases which he had been revolving in his mind all the morning: "Do you want the sort of guy who puts it on paper?" — "After our long friendship, you don't show much faith in me" — "If you love me, how can you consider another man and if not why ask me?" — "I feel myself rebuffed by your question" — "You wait till I am away to tell me you have another attachment; I cannot understand it, how long has it been going on?" He was not satisfied with these remarks, beyond the time it took to write them.

Irene came in with her quiet swift tread and stood behind him.

He heard Irene say, while mussing his hair, "I asked Lou why you are so thoughtful and he says Margot wants to come up here and get married."

"Margot is not coming here. It would put things on a different level; the question of marriage would be unavoidable. I don't want to have to think about that now. I don't know what I want to do with myself the next few years."

Irene went into the kitchen, put on her apron, which Ollie had made for her.

Edward thought, "What a position I'm in now! If I say yes, I can no longer look round for something that suits me. I must upset all my habits and plans without the wish to do it."

He wrote, "How can you even consider me if you love someone else, or consider him if you love me?"

He heard onions frying and the sisters exclaiming over some new recipe. The sisters and Irene now went out on the veranda to show everyone their new aprons. They showed them to him again as they went through. The delightful smell of butter-fried onions came to his nostrils. He was hungry.

Bones, the dog on the hill, gave a yelp of pain. Everyone knew he had been chasing a hedgehog for hours. Now he had caught up with him. "Big sucker," said Edward. He heard some people come into the kitchen from the back. The dog gave a long howl of pain.

"He sure caught up with that hedgehog."

Oneida came fast through the house, front to back, and said to Edward, "What's that howling?"

"That's Bones, I guess. He must have caught up with that hedgehog. His muzzle's full of quills, I suppose."

She became thoughtful. "And where is Ben? Ben must look after him."

The dog gave a long howl.

"It sounds as though Ben is pulling them out one by one."

"I must go up."

Ollie came through, found out what was the matter and went back to the front veranda, to tell the sisters. Edward walked about the cool large house, played a "Largo" on Lou's piano and then went out back to the sunken flagged yard. The dog continued to howl long hopeless cries as if it thought it was dying. Vera Sarine, shrugging and looking nervous, went by.

"Did that hedgehog get Bones?" called Lou from the grass. Lou added that he would go up and join Vera Sarine. He padded out with his wiry hair on end, in his crumpled old denims and discolored rope sandals and looking as if he had just come from sleep. Lou came along the sunken yard to Edward. They walked together to the immense apple tree, up the steps, and then Lou said in the husky voice he had after meditation, "Writing to Margot?"

"She says she had an offer of marriage. I don't know what to answer. Maybe I'd better not answer."

"That would be an ugly thing to do."

"It wouldn't be elegant. Besides, I want to answer. But what?"

"Poor Bones. Listen to that. He's suffering."

"Poor brute. I'll see if there's something to put on his snout."

Up by the veranda, the farmer, his boys, and some of the Massines were squatting round the sick dog. Lou said, "If there's something, I'll go down to the village for it."

He went up. Edward came into the house, determined to write to Margot. The long sitting hall was dark and cool and the airy kitchen had strips of flypaper everywhere. Someone had shut all the wire-netting doors. In the kitchen were the brothers and sisters, Opsa and Pelayga, Suttinlay and Solo. They were collected round the stove sniffing at the slowly frying onions, opening the oven door, looking under the cloth that covered the breads, punching the cottage cheese, studying the recipe that Flora had left open on the table, tasting with their fingers the tomato sauce left in the can. Another pot was on the stove and this contained chicken legs, heads, combs, with onions and spices for chicken soup, while another pot again contained a number of chicken gizzards, legs, necks and hearts, which with vegetables and spices were being stewed for soup and eating. Oneida's meat loaf was in the oven: the pail of milk for a "Chilean" soup and the eggs for it stood on the table.

Opsa and Pelayga, Suttinlay and Solo had not yet been invited to lunch. This was something everyone knew without being told. They had opened the door to their rickety old house up on the hill and the dust, heat, waterlessness, misery, had come out in a great revolting puff. They had sat on the veranda a considerable time, talking discontentedly, and then Pelayga had declared she was going down to the Big House to get some water and they must all come with her. They had at once risen, picked up pails and milk jugs and come quickly down, behind the barn, through the lilac and other bushes, and were already in a procession down the sunken steps when the dog started to howl. At this sound they had stopped and stiffened.

The entrance to the kitchen, although in the sunken flagged yard, was concealed from the rest of the sunken yard by small thick yews, webbed with vines, and by lily plants and berry bushes. There they stood for a moment with their pails and jugs till Oneida had gone up to the farmer. Then they went into the kitchen and stood idly about, slowly filling their receptacles and sniffing, talking delightedly about all that was cooking.

"Plenty to eat," said Opsa.

"Not invited to the wedding!" said Pelayga.

Opsa went into the dining room and saw the table, rather carelessly set by Ollie. She had to count and re-count several times before she knew how many had been set for, and before she could reckon how many were in the house. She went back and in an undertone mentioned to the others that they were not set for at lunch. Down the road they had seen Big Jenny's husband, Dan, who had uproariously greeted them and talked about the wedding. Dan had said everyone was expecting them.

"And he has a great big surprise party! But tell no one. Dan has a good heart," said Opsa.

"I don't trust his word," said Pelayga.

Suttinlay, the drug salesman, frequented concerts and was a passionate music critic. He had a gramophone, many records, had written several as yet unpublished books on his hobby, correcting old histories, and now bought successively all the improvements in radio, frequency modulation, television. He was not friendly with his brother, a violinist, who was a merry earful man, at one time a *wunderkind,* but now lazy and money-making, and who despised the radio programs upon which he regularly played. Solo imitated even without understanding many kinds of foreign languages and accents, Hungarian, Russian, Cockney, Basque, and his long amusing stories were always for the purpose of showing off his accents. The family at large thought of him contemptuously; Oneida hated him for having taken tours through Europe and playing in orchestras outside New York City, and, indeed, because he rarely came to White-house where he was bored by his mother and all the tedious conversations which had been the same for years. Solo smelled the pots and, with a merry sneaky look, went out of the kitchen to look for some company. He had a bottle of sherry on him which he did not want to share with his greedy sisters but with Lou and Edward.

The other three sat down in the kitchen and began to talk. Suttinlay drew up a chair to the table and with his head resting on his hand began to give his views of life. He hated his sisters but he needed an audience. He had no habits such as twitching or kicking his foot, he just sat and talked dully and earnestly. He was talking, as every year, about building a new house. His sisters had money, one being an executive in a large office, and the other a high-school teacher; they had fat salaries and good vocations and he himself was doing fairly well. They had no need to contribute to the support of their mother who had money from the father; but they had no spirit to get married. For years Suttinlay had gone to the same prostitutes twice a week on fixed days. Then the need to explain himself clearly to a woman overcame this habit and he had got the girl friend with whom he was still going. "She's a good cook," said Opsa. "He'll never marry her," said Pelayga. At present, he sat talking with one elbow on the table.

"A man starts out in life without the need of an ambition. Then he must get a job, that stifles the growth of an ambition. Then he feels he should have had an ambition but does not know what it should have been: he feels disappointed and defeated but he can't point to anything. I was the brightest boy in the class, they thought me most likely to succeed. What did they mean by success? Succeed in what, you see? What did they see in me that I couldn't see in myself? You can't succeed without some material to work upon. That is what I mean."

The sisters sat and listened to him. Presently, Opsa said the onions would burn and took a fork to turn and taste them. Pelayga said, "It's a funny thing we can sit here without a soul coming to say a word."

Suttinlay was dry. "It's funny the experiences you run into. I'm known in so many towns and villages, you might say I know the U.S.A. as well as any man. You can tell the kind of place it is from the drugstore. There is a Jewish chap runs a drugstore in Utica. It is one of those drugstores that sells books, magazines and comics, you can hardly tell it is a drugstore."

At this moment, Irene came into the kitchen to turn her onions. Opsa was poised over the stove, tasting the chicken soup with a spoon. She had the onion fork. Irene took the onion fork from her and turned the onions. Suttinlay turned to her and said earnestly, "I was just relating the case of a man who runs a drugstore in Utica. He has a pyramid of bookshelves in the middle of the store with the cheap best-sellers on it and farther down the Sunday newspapers and on one side a counter for socks and rayon ties. He sells liquor too. He is the emporium of the village. The only thing he doesn't sell is gardening implements. But he sells children's pails and shovels."

"What time are they having lunch today?" asked Opsa.

"About one-thirty. The bride will get here any minute. Marian wants to go and visit everyone she used to know up here and they thought that would give them nice time to dress and not too much waiting around before the wedding at four o'clock."

"It would have been better to have the luncheon after the wedding," said Opsa.

Irene said, "There will be something to eat after the wedding: I myself am making chicken liver and eggs. I'll make it after lunch, as it is better the fresher it is."

"How will you get enough chicken livers?" inquired Opsa.

"I bought them down at Mustbrook's."

"This Jewish drugstore-owner turned out to be a boy I had sat on the same bench with for years at school: and he was my only rival for the medal. . . . See how things turn out. I asked him if he didn't regret a career in New York. His parents wished him to be a lawyer;

he was good at argument. He said no, here he sold useful things, he cured people, they came to him when there was no doctor around and he wanted to acquire the farming implements store which was run down, across the street, so that he could sell other useful things. He said, for me, it would not have been a success, as I see it now, to join the hairsplitters' union: I would rather belong to the rail splitters' union. New York, he told me, burns up its own talents and every newcomer's life. And what is the end? It is just the morning after fireworks. That is the end. He said to me, here you are handling something real; not wasting the country's time and money going to the Supreme Court to win a case for a fraudulent client because of a technicality."

"First you cook the chicken livers in chicken soup; and it improves the soup for you too," said Irene.

Opsa said, with whistling speed, "Then you mash them fine?"

"Then you cook so many fresh hard-boiled eggs of the first quality."

"And you mash them fine?"

"You can mash them through a strainer, that makes them finer."

"And then you mix them."

"No, then, you must have little white onions shredded fine and cook them in butter."

"Chicken fat is better?"

"Goose fat is the best."

"Yet I feel there is something lacking in my life and I wonder if I would not have felt the same thing if I had been a successful lawyer too. I might have wanted something more material, with more to it than chicane. For example, suppose I had just become an ordinary hack and not a legal light? Or a lawyer and then discovered I would have done better as a judge? There is a certain truth in what my Jewish friend says. He said, to be successful in success you have to have something in you which makes you satisfied with yourself even without any success. You must not believe in God, or society, or success: you must just believe in yourself and a man is born with that, you can't learn it. That I thought a very cogent remark. It bears examination. You can think it over and it explains a lot of things to you. But I must express myself to someone, that proves a deficiency in me."

"That's a sort of *alioli,* I suppose. You eat it with potato chips and cocktails. You get three tablespoonfuls of the best Roquefort cheese and mash them."

"Blue cheese would do."

"I'm hungry," said Opsa.

"We are not set for at luncheon," complained Pelayga.

Irene fell silent. The man walked up and down the kitchen looking anxiously into the pantry. Opsa waddled over to the icebox and her brother joined her there, peering at everything on the shelves, poking paper parcels.

The kitchen door, which swung open of itself, had been fixed ajar by a doorstop made of wood and representing a Scotch terrier. Edward, writing, heard this without hearing it, he heard the movements and, through long habit, knew all that was going on, without paying attention. He looked abstractedly towards the door. On each side of the glassed-in bookcase, which held Gibbon's *Decline and Fall,* Motley's *Dutch Republic,* and an old edition of the Cambridge *Modern History,* his father's favorites which he had never read, were China ornaments, representing dogs and cats, all ugly, but some quaint.

At this moment, Opsa said bitterly to Pelayga, "You know Mr. Leroy was interested in me but Mother practically shut the door in his face. She had such high ambitions for us. No one was good enough for us."

Suttinlay had resumed, "There are two kinds of men who are defeated: those who admit it and those who don't. It is not a question of a tide in the affairs of men: it is a yielding to habit, a habit in the affairs of men. Who has not thought, if I could only take a drug and wake up tomorrow not knowing my name or situation or family, I

[172]

would make a new life, be a better man. I have talents: I am just dragged at the tail of old habits. *Canst thou not minister to a mind diseased, pluck from the memory a rooted sorrow?*"

"But would you marry a man in whom you are merely interested?" said Pelayga.

"Good God," said Edward aloud. Someone opened the door and looked out. It was Irene.

"Ah, you there?" she said, and smiled maliciously. She returned to the kitchen.

"Edward was trying to write a letter."

Suttinlay remarked, "It is a wonder to think how many people you could put to bed in this house, using all the divans, window seats, lounges and old cots: a whole camp. If there was a war, with refugees from New York, they could certainly quarter people on us here: I mean the family houses. Victor-Alexander has a whole house which no one has ever seen. Look at the broken old boardinghouse on the other side of the valley, that's Massine property and hardly anyone in it. Look at the summer cottage down the road boarded up. The house on the weir is only occupied by summer visitors. The farmer's cottage now is empty, today at least, and our own place is fitted up for a nursery in the attic and we have room there for more than ourselves. . . . How about the log house down the road? It is remarkable what you have here, enough for an army. You had better not let people know. You will be quartered on. Suppose there is an exodus from the cities? So many people know about you. Here, in the town, everyone knows about you and your houses and by some you are not very well liked. It is because of the dogs. They bark at everyone. So people would tell — scores of beds. Suppose there is a war, and they evacuate the people from New York."

"What a crazy idea; that will never happen," said Pelayga.

"It could happen and it will happen," said he. The others remained silent.

Irene said, "I have been here every summer since I was thirteen." She continued, "Did you ever think of all the women we thought Edward was going to marry? If you are interested in Edward, it means you will marry some other man in a few months."

"That's an interesting trait," said Suttinlay.

Irene said, "Well, Laurel, I don't see why you two girls don't sleep here tonight, till you get things fixed up. I'll go and set the places for you at the table. You'd better get the other leaf. You know where it is, behind the woodbin there."

This was followed by great activity on the part of the hungry sisters and their brothers. Irene went out to the veranda and said, "Opsa and Pelayga are hanging round the kitchen. You should see them! They wanted to come to lunch, so they are getting out the extra leaf and I am going in to set their places. There will be enough. Do you think they will be here for the sherry and snacks after the wedding? I just want to know for my platter."

Oneida flushed and said very low, "They would stoop and snoop — rather than open their own house! I don't see how we can stop them, if they want to. We must use the chicken soup."

"Oh, Big Jenny sent up some meat balls, djarling!"

"I'll make a pie!" said Flora.

"We'll come and clear them out of the kitchen!" said Oneida. While the pie was baking, Oneida sat in the kitchen with Madame X. Her anger for the Outcasts had turned into emotion for the dog, and almost made her dizzy. With wet eyes, she bent over its head, seized it by its ears, shook it vigorously, grasped its skull between her strong palms, squeezed it so that she kneaded the thin coverings of skin and hair between her fingers, looked into the inquiring protruding black eyes, dulled with senile blindness; a haggard intensity sharpened Oneida's cheeks and chin. She looked like a woman in a robber forest, she had suggestions of old romantic operas and fairy tales, rabid clan tales from wild woods and highlands where the clan women are vixenish, strong, careless, potent.

She had everything of this, a torn white coat on her shoulder which she had flung on last time she had gone upstairs, the sun-tanned skin, the hazel eyes in which sunspokes wheeled as she looked to the bird-flown plantation, the marked brows, the wiry hair: and she gave the feeling that with the black thing on her lap (dog or toad) she would be a terror to whomever she opposed. However, now she opposed no one.

Bart had followed her to the kitchen, looked at her brooding, knew what she was brooding about and sat down. The black dog looked at him with interest.

Oneida said, "Would you believe that when I came back after six weeks' holiday, I found Madame X and Musty hardly knew me? They circled round me very confused and their instinct was to go to Big Jenny because she had been feeding them?" She repeated this incident thoughtfully and without rancor like a mother who is glad at last to have something against her son that she can rake up on blue days. She went on, "But tell me, Bart, dogs are faithful, that is why we keep them. Is it? Or is it just egotism? Do we love them because they fawn upon us? Some people say that."

Bart declared that most dogs were forgetful, cruel, selfish and cowardly, lazy, dirty, stupid, merely lumps of inedible meat.

She burst out laughing, said eagerly, "Like women! And like men! And I suppose in famine, people eat their dogs and cats just the same."

"No, no," Bart insisted, "dogs are inedible."

Oneida mumbled her old dog's head, exclaiming, "Ah what a good thing for you, you are inedible. If I tell her this," she declared, interspersing this with kissing and stroking, "she must be grateful at any rate for what I give her; she must realize she couldn't get it for herself."

"I think Madame X is too strong-minded to think that."

She burst out laughing, "Like me, like me."

Bart illustrated, "When I was at Santa Fe, a clerk in the Atchison, everyone heard about a murder by a dog in an isolated house some miles from there. The man was rich and was afraid for his cash and he lived alone with a very large dog. One day it was thought necessary to force the doors and look for him — they found him in two rooms, with the door closed between; the head in one, the body in the other, the door locked between. They said he fell over the dog, the door slammed, and he lost his head, just a doggone accident. Other people said the dog killed him."

"And where was the dog?"

"With the head."

"Thaïs's great Dane can unlatch doors, I don't know about locks." Bart mused:

> "Very smooth he looked yet grim:
> Seven bloodhounds followed him:
> All were fat and well they might
> Be in admirable plight
> For one by one and two by two
> He tossed them human hearts to chew
> Which from his wide cloak he drew . . ."

"You can hear a bloodhound baying near here on moonlight nights. It is because it smells or sees an opossum, I think, but people don't like it."

"I heard a beagle baying early this morning."

"It's that old beagle. But there's a rich old woman at the end of the valley here keeps real bloodhounds on her property. You've never seen such lawns, a man goes the rounds with a little electric lawn mower, and the conservatories and rose garden! Victor-Alexander wanted to improve the place. And he, you know, won't do the hard work, he has to have workmen."

Bart became interested.

"What happens to his garden in winter?"

"He covers it all up carefully, puts things in the potting shed. Last fall, he was here after us and did not give a glance to my garden. All the baby's breath died off, it must be covered from the frosts."

"You cannot stay here in winter?"

"I've never been afraid," said Oneida, "I've been here alone. It's very cold here in September and in October, we live only in the kitchen, in my room above the kitchen which is heated by the old oven and in the dining room where the big fireplace is. We huddle round the fires. When it gets too cold for Lou to play, we go home."

"It's not a frightening place; it has no spooks."

"It's quiet this time of year, but in autumn and winter, you should hear how it blows. Then you wouldn't think it so cheerful. I've been here all alone too, when winter was coming on."

"Without the dogs?"

She hesitated, "No: they were here. I have never been without them."

Bart said intolerantly, "Alone, but for a dearly loved cayoodle."

Oneida murmured, "cayoodle," to herself, as if trying it out regretfully, and trying to swallow the insult and accept the word "cayoodle" as just an old slang word for dogs, like "pooch."

"Yes," said Oneida, after a while, forcibly, turning round and pushing back the hair from her ear with her wet hand. She turned to Bart, her cheeks flaming and her eyes bright.

"Yes, I know they probably don't love me much more than the next person. Cayoodles!" she cried, without a laugh. "Well, out of sight, out of mind."

Madame X felt she was being insulted and set up another rough barking. Oneida had begun to make pastry. She continued meditating:

"I got so tired of dogs when I was a child. In the winters here we spoiled them so. They were at home on the stove, on the kitchen shelves, on the beds, anywhere, and they did not trouble to move, not they. They have a right to do what they like, Flora said. She hadn't the heart to scold them for being so ignorant, she said. I was almost turned against them. There was Mutt, he simply broke his heart because he thought I gave him away and he knew I'd done it purposely because I didn't want him. And he never forgot me. He remembered me and rushed out to meet me, barking so excitedly, trembling — but he was too lively, he died: his little heart — " tears were streaming down her face. She touched the flour with her finger tips.

"Just like my little Caprice, my darling, my Chihuahua, who just danced herself to death. You see how dainty they are, how they run on the tips of their toes like little deer, how sensitive they are."

She paused and said mournfully, "When I came to Victor-Alexander Stepney's house after Caprice — wasn't with us — Mr. Stepney Senior, who was ill then, said, 'I hear you had a great tragedy.' He blurted it out from the bed, thinking it was a joke, meaning no harm, and I burst out crying. They couldn't comfort me and the old gentleman said, 'Oneida, I didn't know it was so serious'; but I couldn't stop crying for hours. I just put my head on the table and cried. Victor-Alexander brought me here and Big Jenny put me to bed; here, in this house. It was at Victor-Alexander's house, on the hill, this took place. But I cried all night when everyone was asleep. Even Lou didn't know how badly I felt and I got up and lay on the sofa. I was ashamed to let him see. He said, no more little dogs. And I don't blame him."

At this moment, the Abbot, barking, flew round the side of the house with two other dogs in pursuit, and turned towards the gateway. Musty, slow in his old age, flirting his tail and long fringes, danced through the grass a long time afterwards.

"Ah, they are coming, they know, they know," said Oneida, rushing out of the kitchen, "but who is it that is coming?" She ran through the house. She ran down the steps, stood on the grass, by the stone balustrade, calling them. She stood up, clasped her floured hands together and tried to peer through the bushes. She had a stout confidence and self-conscious movement, all the freedom of her ungirdled unembraced body, which was almost rich grace. She was full of movement, unrestrained, and it was perhaps the plenitude of this one love, her dogs, which had given this life to her small thick-set frame, which had no noticeable dwindling and spindling like other women. Wherever she was, with a glance, a tone, she could call her soft-bodied anxious scolding toadies to her. She called them now. Grudging, they came back. She clapped, called again, angrily. They came to her, circled her. She sat down, and they climbed over her thighs, rested on her breast. She kissed them and said, "Who is it, who is it?" and looked over their heads to the slope behind the laurel bushes. She cried, "Oh, gracious, look at Big Jenny! What is she doing here? Jenny!" She threw the dogs away, jumped up and walked towards her sister. "How do you feel? How is your hip?" Big Jenny had Perry's disease.

"All right, all right, fine, fine," said the old woman, "how do I feel, I feel splendid, fine, fine; and how do you feel?"

"But you said you couldn't get up here this summer," protested Oneida. "My dogs told me you were coming. I sat on the grass, I thought they had gone crazy."

"What is it? Why all the surprise? I only live a hundred yards down the road."

"A mountain road? Why did you come? You said you wouldn't even come for the wedding."

"Ah, the dear children, where are they? I saw them, Mark and Marian. They stopped at my place on the way up. I said I would do my best. See the new silk dress Dan brought me!"

She was a tender, melting woman, very much too large, but with the broad forehead, dark hair and immense dark eyes of the family, the white teeth and charming smile and so much generous love in her as is rarely seen. She had never refused anything to her family nor to anyone. Everyone was welcome to her house. She cooked for anyone, received anyone, loved all, stranger, family, friends, with a great love; though, no doubt, her sisters, family, her dogs and cats came first. But no stranger could have been offended, so great was the love she showed for himself. Her face, beautiful, now overflowed with this genial tenderness. Her voice clouded, her face became troubled, she bent nearer to her young sister and said, "I came to see if you had seen my little Darly."

She smiled delightfully, though her face was strained, her lips darkening. She waved to the relatives sitting on the veranda. She struggled up the steps.

"I'll just sit a moment. My little Darly, that naughty little monkey, poor pet, has been away since this morning, early. She didn't even have her breakfast with me. Have you seen my little Darly?"

She smiled eagerly and affectionately at the dogs and at Ollie, Flora and Mary, and Little Jenny who were seated discussing interminable affairs. "How many children has she? And boys or girls?"

"Hallo-o, girls, Darly ran away! Think of that!" She laughed at herself, chirruped all round, called, but no little dog appeared. "She would never run away from me, oh, she is such a sweet little monkey."

"Yes, she's a nice little dog, I think she came to visit my dogs," said Oneida.

"Oh, that she would do, yes, that she would do."

Now five of the sisters, all fat, squatted on the veranda, looking over the green valley and at the mountains. Would it rain at four in the afternoon as usual?

"Every Sunday morning, I go past the church, on my way to the baker's."

"It was just ten past midnight, and I heard a sound."

"The woman who lives next to me said, with such a big house on your hands . . ."

"Isn't it funny, Ben-son has a bag store and he never brought me a bag from his store. In thirty years, and I said to Mrs. West, Ben-son has a bag store but . . ."

Edward, coming from the kitchen, unshaved, in his dirtiest clothes, stood inside the screen door, listening to the aunts.

"Edward," called Oneida joyfully. She came inside, kissed him

[180]

and said at once, "I'm in a foul temper. I feel I'll be sick, but really sick. I can't stand it a minute more. They're telling stories I've heard a thousand times and they've heard a thousand times and I thought if I'd sit there another minute, I would really be sick. I sit there nodding and agreeing and my thoughts are a thousand miles away. But they don't suspect anything. How can they tell the same stories they've told for forty years — fifty years — before Mark and Marian or you were born. Even I was not here when they were first told," and she began to laugh into Edward's arms, while he said drily one thing after another. The tears came, tears of pleasure and anger. She said stubbornly, "I can't listen any more. I just sit there and think about my dogs."

She went into the back garden where she saw Lou, Bart and Vera, tidying up the garden round the well. They had three pails of windfalls, a rake, the old pole-shears. Lou had clipped the branches so that a photograph could be taken. Edward followed her.

"I wonder if Victor-Alexander will come over the hill or by the road?"

"On special occasions he always comes by the road," said Oneida.

"They are talking about Victor-Alexander on the veranda."

Oneida frowned. "Oh, I know why! Big Jenny invited him to dinner last night. She invited Ollie too and Ollie let it out. I think it's stupid for us to have secrets from each other."

"Victor-Alexander will not keep the secret; he's too candid," said Edward.

"Oh, besides, he thinks everything is ordained; that lies are of no use." Oneida turned round and marched into the house. "Just the same I will find out what they are saying about Victor-Alexander."

Big Jenny said, "You know when we lost that purse? You remember Victor-Alexander consulted Dr. Asthur, his astrologer, and Dr. Asthur had a dream in which the purse was under something animal and we found the purse the next day in the wool-basket under some balls of wool? That was strange, wasn't it?"

[181]

"Do you remember, djarlings, that little booklet Mrs. Mustbrook sent us where it said that if you prayed to the Higher Will you got everything? You remember the man who had to telephone for a job, he was out of work. He went to the pay telephone and found he hadn't even a nickel. He went out sadly with his eyes down, and he found a nickel on the trolley track?"

"Oh, do you remember when Victor-Alexander used to have séances up at his house?" cried Flora.

"Oh, that was twenty years ago; before he met Dr. Asthur, I know."

"No, it was more. Oneida was a young girl then, we thought she was going to marry Victor-Alexander."

"How can they talk over all that trash all the time," said Oneida to Edward. She went out on the porch. The big-eyed, aproned sisters looked fondly at her and said, "We were just saying — just saying that you were once in love with Victor-Alexander Stepney. Everyone thought — down in the village they thought — it was a sure thing: especially, when Father gave him land to build his house on."

"I was only seventeen, and Father did all that without consulting me."

"Victor-Alexander was always a Galahad," said Little Jenny.

"You make me sick, you talk about people for forty years and you don't know anything about them. Must I explain everything to you? Victor-Alexander loved his father and mother, and then he loved Greek poetry, the violin, and now he loves his flowers and 'Solitude,' his garden. He never loved man or woman; I am supposed not to know anything. How can you sit there for forty years, tell the old stories and not understand a man you all look at once a week at least for forty years? He would never have married. He told me afterwards."

Ollie, who had brought up Oneida, chuckled. "You remember, Oneida had three beaux and we didn't know till the last minute who would marry her?"

"I didn't know myself until the last minute. Victor-Alexander had gone away to California with his father and he made me promise not to make a move without telling him." She said furiously, after a slight pause, "Well, I made a move and then I told him! He telegraphed back, *You have betrayed the letter and the spirit: do nothing till I come.* When he came home, I was married. He had to swallow it."

Everyone was silent at this moment. Suddenly Oneida burst out: "Oh, I remember the time I kicked him: because he detested my dogs. The dogs spoiled the del-ight-ful silence of his re-treat from life. The only thing he ever loved was — dead — silence!" She laughed.

Oneida ran off the porch down the steps and started to work in the gardens in the midst of roses, globe thistles, as tall as herself. As she stopped and straightened, she went on recalling incidents of thirty years ago. He was then holding séances in the house on the hill, which was not then called "Solitude." He begged Oneida over and over again to attend them. Once she went "for fun" and she had told him, mirthfully, maliciously, brimming with music, loving opera, painting, life, full of ardor and talent, without any seriousness, despising the spiritual life, that the spiritual life was one and the same with a rich physical life. Her mother had just died but it had not affected her at all. He was very much attracted to her then, himself only twenty-one; and he was considered the best match, on account of his wealth. She had gone up there one afternoon without her dogs, because Victor-Alexander had always insisted upon that. He had insisted that she substituted dogs for a moral and spiritual life, even a life of sensuality, talent: dogs were a deep-rooted and a dangerous vice, he had said then. She had gone nicely dressed, with her cloud of hair round her face in the style of the early twenties, and in a white dress. Just to show him what she thought of this hocus-pocus, she had said in the doorway, "I only came for fun, I don't believe in it at all, Victor-Alexander." When the circle had been formed, the

[183]

shades drawn, the lights turned low, she found herself with her hand in Victor-Alexander's. He did this only to control her. She had begun to tremble, she jangled like a wire; and when asked solemnly by Victor-Alexander if she wished to speak with anyone, the earnest response broke from her lips, "Oh, I do want to talk to my darling little Picky!" and her darling little Picky was only a dog, Picayune, that she had lost three years before, just a crossbred, mongrel fox terrier she had got out of the street somewhere, that had died after being with her only four months.

Victor-Alexander, then as now, a serious, ivory-faced man, had withdrawn his hand and said, "You're being decidedly unfunny, you're being decidedly unfunny," saying it twice rapidly, as he said everything.

She had cried then, "But Victor, I do believe in it, I've got such a queer feeling. I'm not joking, at all: oh, do try to get me Picky." She had then placed her little square hands firmly on the table and had called, "Picky! Picky! Honeybunch!"

What a scene! Victor-Alexander said she must leave the room. She said she would leave the house forever. He said she was coarsely materialist, grossly sensual and that no spirit could or would manifest itself when she was there, thinking only of dogs; and she had said, he wallowed in superstition. She had told him that he thought himself superior to everything and had never loved anything, for anyone who could love, loved some kind of animals and did not feel that human beings were a super-race. "You are a man of shadows," she had told him, "you're the man in the moon." What he said and what she said was scandalous; but it happened that at that moment, with a mad patter, and a loud hysterical barking, there ran into the house her three dogs, their leashes trailing. They rushed to her, jumped up on her, nearly tore her to pieces with love, and then stood defiantly barking at the others. "The fact was I didn't tie them up properly; I wanted them to come up. If there were spooks, they would see them. Dogs always see what we can't see."

Victor-Alexander commanded her to take the pups home and she, with a kick at his shins, and a face at the others, turning only at the door to poke out her tongue, ran home, laughing out loud, loud, all the way, stopping halfway on the path, when she reached the smooth top of the hill and could see all the mountains standing up before her and the spillway of valleys, to breathe and shout with laughter. When she reached the Big Farm, she threw herself on the grass, while tears ran out of her eyes with mirth at the whole scene. "No dogs could appear" . . . Was that so? And in fact nothing but dogs had appeared; that was all she could call up.

She had collected the exciting, prancing, loyal little dogs round her, hugged them, kissed them, all over from head to foot, Donder, Blitzen and Prancer, while they threw themselves upon her, giving her fierce embraces, madly joyful because of her, "more than that man of shadows," and giving her caresses that no one had ever given her. While they were frolicking there, the afternoon storm had arisen in the west and rushed upon them. The thunder bowled and hopped in the Catskills, and the rainfalls, like ghosts, real ghosts, on stilts stalked over the hill and she had run home in that supernatural pink light that precedes the storms in summer.

"Victor-Alexander did not forgive me for months: I don't think he ever really forgave. And I never forgave him!" she said frowning.

"Victor-Alexander and I went to dinner at Big Jenny's last night," said Ollie again, grinning.

"You see the sly things he does. All he does is only to pay us out. He brought the sow-thistles over in a basket in summer one evening two years ago and planted them here; that was to pay us out," said Oneida.

"Good Lord, don't say a thing like that," said Edward, startled.

She bit her lip, "But it's true."

Ollie, taking no notice, kept poking round pridefully at the rag rug, her eyes shining like plums. Little Jenny smiled coyly, her pink little cheeks, her neat curls turning younger every minute. The fact was that she had given a secret invitation to Victor-Alexander for the next night, none of the sisters knew, nor would know.

All the dogs started to bark and rushed down the slope.

"It's Musty-Brook."

The dogs, satisfied, were coming back, escorting Mrs. Mustbrook, a tall powerful, brown-haired woman of about fifty. Mrs. Mustbrook's face was freckled, flushed: she had made a long climb from the Little Farm in the bottom of the valley, she laughed and called out, "Hello, hello, hello! I'm coming, I'm coming, I'm coming."

"Musty! Many happy returns!"

The swarm of ample sisters in their gay aprons rose from their seats, their eyes sparkling. They kissed the woman, complimented her. Several of them had been sitting with parcels in their hands and now handed presents to Mrs. Mustbrook. One had made an apron, one a doily, one gave her a length of material for a dress, and Oneida gave her a carved bracelet. Mrs. Mustbrook kissed and pranced, she gave harsh cries, she spoke very loud. She now called out, "And where is dear Victor-Alexander; and the dear chicks?"

The sisters were a little nervous. If anyone detested Mrs. Mustbrook more than Edward, it was Victor-Alexander. Her face lit up, she cried out, "Oh, where is dear Edward?"

Mrs. Mustbrook hugged Big Jenny again. "Oh, it was so good of you to toil up the hill for my birthday — and the wedding! But the wedding is for my birthday too — eh? He-he. Did you ever hear of anyone having a wedding for their birthday? Oh, what a good birthday present, I told the dear chicks. And they brought me this blouse. Do you see it?"

"Oh, I saw you were wearing a wonderful blouse, Musty!"

"Oh, there's Madame X. Hello, darling. Come here to old Musty. Give Musty a big kiss for her birthday. Oh, Oneida loves you so, Oneida loves you so."

"She knows it better than you do," said Oneida.

Meanwhile, as they sat there, the dogs, sensing the fête, kept mak-

[186]

ing sallies at strangers or members of the family or visitors who passed on the private road. The Abbot was pretty to see, skimming over the grass, his uncut ears flopping at all angles, barking eagerly but missing rabbits and birds that moved not too fast before him. He was fast but not accurate. The old broken-backed horse was being led back to the farm by one of the little van Kill boys, who came just to his nose. The Abbot assailed them for a quarter of a mile as they turned round the slope. The farmer, his wife and the other boy, with the other horse, as well as a redheaded woman asking for milk, two people taking a walk who had missed their way, a bridge-player looking for Dan, Opsa and Pelayga who had gone down to the village for provisions, and a Rabbi of a Chassidic summer home all received salutes of this kind as they wandered up and down, round the farm. The Abbot had plenty of work on his hands. The Rabbi was looking for a lost cow. Behind him, he trailed four little children in a homemade wagon. The children, frightened by the Abbot, cried, "*Chaver* * Bear! *Chaver* Bear!"

Dan came up from his house at the noise and took the children in the trailer away from *Chaver* Bear and said he would mind them while the Rabbi looked for his cow. He came up, in his strange hat and long frock, to the veranda, and asked the old sisters if they had seen his cow. "No, no," they murmured; they smiled and nodded and stooped amply over the edge of the porch.

"And yet there were cows around here this morning," he said. He went sadly away.

"Oh, does he think we stole his cow?" cried Oneida.

"No, no," said the sisters, "he doesn't think that, but the children must be fed."

Down on the lawn, the children, four little boys in their little skull caps, were afraid of the faces Dan was making and had begun an uproar, "*Chaver* Bear! *Chaver* Bear!" The young Rabbi met Dan coming to meet him with the little trailer and together they went

* Hebrew for "comrade."

[187]

down the dangerously rutted farm road. The Rabbi didn't stop asking where his cow could be.

"I saw a herd of cows go by here this morning; perhaps it went with them."

Two old ladies from the city, in black dresses and fashionable black hats, started to climb the farm road and were turned back by the Abbot. They stood near the stone gateway, screeching, trembling with fright and endeavoring to bend low enough to pick up a stone. They struggled away. The Abbot rushed back, satisfied.

One of the reasons for all these stray visitors was that they had heard there was a lovely mountain stream, with a swimming pool which had medicinal qualities, not far away and they all wanted to see it, perhaps to bathe in it. There were no landmarks on the Massine land, no road marks, no signs of property, no painted boards saying *No trespassing, No thoroughfare,* or *Private Property,* no hints about laws and infringements.

The owner of the Abbot, Flora, was silent, patting her dog with a calm tender face. The Abbot laid his revolver head on her knee. His mindless pathetic brown eyes looked into her face. All at once, he flew from her like a bird and down the steps, the path, following the path of a bird in the air. They all craned their necks. Oneida did not even look up; said, "It is Victor-Alexander, coming by the road."

The lovers, having visited all the village, were just coming through the wood, to the left of the garden. The wood had once been a garden. Berries, rosebushes, some other flowering plants were still to be found returned to their native state under immense trees. Although it was only July, one tuft of leaves on a high bough in the last tree of the plantation had turned yellow and red: but it seemed to be a firebird sitting between the leaves. Under this tree, looking from the porch, stood some birches and laurels grouped round a flat boulder. The lovers, who had gathered some wild strawberries in the patch and some small flowers, were now sitting on the rock playing with Westfourth who had gone over to them mewing painfully as

[188]

he took each step through the field of timothy; shadows fluttered. The dogs rushed up the slope, the lovers waved their hands.

The sisters saw Victor-Alexander stooping, with his long stride, up the slope. Leisurely the young couple came to meet him. He was carrying a plant rolled in tissue paper and on the other arm a long shallow basket covered with a cloth. He drew back the cloth and took out of the basket a bouquet composed of five blue clematis, several pinks and some small white flowers. This he handed to the bride. The composition of the bouquet was unusual, delicately beautiful, and the effect of it wonderfully startling, like the sight of bluebirds perching on a bush of reddened twigs against a burnt field, something incomparable in fact. From those simple elements he had composed a masterpiece. He waited courteously till they had finished their compliments, let them climb the steps in front of him, reach the porch. He then drew another bouquet, the same, composed with fewer flowers, from his basket and came alone up the steps. He was a slender, active man with a small well-formed head, tall, in gray with a slight affectation in his dress, a faint, acceptable dandyism. They greeted him in their rich affectionate way. He smiled, nodded a little, and presented the other bouquet to Old Mary, dean of the women. Her ringed hands clasped the bouquet. Nobly sitting bolt upright, as always, gracefully dressed in a thin silky material and lace, she became confused in a womanly way, thanked him in a firm voice. Oneida went up to him. He offered her his basket. It contained about forty small lettuces. The women began to exclaim about them and Oneida to thank him, when he took the basket from her hands, put it on the rag rug on the table and, unrolling the tissue paper, politely offered her what it contained, five Iceland poppies, each about the size of a pint bowl.

Oneida cried, "Oh, how beautifully they're made!" And as she took them she said, "But they're real!"

These flowers appeared miraculous; their size, color, voluptuous fragility set them apart from other flowers. Victor-Alexander was pleased with their exclamations and concurred faintly. He murmured, "I-rooted-it-out-three-times-I-thought-it-had-quite-gone, I-thought-it-had-quite-gone. It began to grow again, it began to grow again and, at last, I left it, you see, I thought I would see what it grew to. I thought I would see what it grew to. It insisted upon life, it insisted upon life."

Though they were accustomed to Victor-Alexander's miracles, they were curiously stimulated, filled with chaotic emotions, at the sight of these. In the many years they had not seen his jailed garden, they had had to imagine it: it had become, in their imagination, an Eden. Yet, each time, they were surprised by the splendor of his blooms.

The women scattered to put the flowers in water. Oneida trotted back and sat down with Madame X on her lap, and listened to Victor-Alexander who, with a slight smile, was talking to Big Jenny. The women were perfectly quiet, because to understand Victor-Alexander, one had to pay attention. Although born and bred in New York, he not only had an old Knickerbocker family accent, but had acquired a slight British accent from one of his tutors and spoke very fast and soft, being slightly deaf, as well. Through his years of solitude he had acquired an incomprehensible fragility of speech. As it seemed to him, also, that no one understood him, he took pains to say everything twice, trusting that the vocables lost the first time would be brought to light the second; and for this reason Dan had baptized him Victor-Victor Stepney-Stepney. Secretly it amused him to lead people a dance. In the family, he was perfectly well understood. If a stranger came, it amused him to see the puzzlement in their replies at random, their anxious politeness, their glances aside. If anyone came who understood him, he spoke faster and faster. But if one listened without hearing, this speech resembled the speech of birds. It was not monotonous as ours is, but full of semitones, inimitable ventriloquial whispers, and it hurried out of his mouth like their trilling. For many years, the only voices around him had been those of birds: and perhaps those of his fancy. He was persuaded of the unseen world and did not fear it. Victor-Alexander had believed last summer that a stone urn would improve a landscaping in Dan Barnes's place and had installed it. Once installed he did not like its position and wished to employ workmen to move it. Dan Barnes had refused. He could not see what difference it made, but said gaily, "Let's shift it ourselves." Victor-Alexander had refused so indelicate a task. The stone urn remained, an eyesore to Victor-Alexander.

"A stone urn, a stone urn," said Victor-Alexander, in derision, "two feet to the left."

He became angry. Oneida, smiling slightly, bent her head and caressed Madame X. Sidelong she watched the man with her bold black eyes, from time to time, her face musing: her eyes could never muse. The flock of birds, that was his voice, were chirping, nestling, fluttering, shrilling: it was a whole tree full of birds, rather near now. The women concentrated their attention on his slender, bright, flushed face. He gestured with his long hands. His face turned from side to side, like a bird drinking and listening. As she passed her hand lightly over the fat sighing body of her old dog, Oneida's hand stopped and her smudgy finger worked away at something. Now, she wore her everyday expression. She said, "Madame X has a sore on her back," and she continued with piercing tenderness, "What is it, Madame X? Oh, my darling, what have you got? Oh, why didn't you tell Mummy?"

She bounced from her seat and carried the dog round to show the spot. They all looked and sympathized; only the man turned slightly away.

"It is not kindness to let her suffer in her age, it is not kindness to let her suffer in her age, your love is cruel, your love is cruel."

"Oh, and we thought her naughty! When she barks she is saying something, you see."

And then a secret deep smile sprang into her face, she looked handsome, and she said, "Ah, if we put her to sleep, where would your astrology be? You don't mean us to get ahead of the stars, do you?"

Victor-Alexander looked pained and bored, but he decided to speak.

"This joke is *mal à propos:* this joke is *mal à propos.* The aspects require an effort in order that their meaning and intention may be realized . . . it does not abolish free will . . . or action, it does not paralyse the will . . . the stars refer to everyone . . . the wilful and active man . . . the slothful lethargic and lazy . . . your land lies here uncultivated, it could have been cultivated . . . you could have turned these acres of sloth into a garden as I did . . . the entire place would yield vegetables . . . why don't you put it into my hands to cultivate, if that is your attitude? Do I dream away my life because there are stars above me? Do I dream away my life because there are stars above me? In heaven there is no desire nor destiny. Not here, not here. You live in a false thought which is that you think the revolutions of the hours will bring you happiness: you think the revolutions of the hours will bring you happiness."

Down the road they heard the voice of the young Rabbi returning, calling, "Koo! Koo! Koo!" Lou and Dan came out from the back and sat down on the porch, saying, "We are all ready."

"There is a car coming: it must be the Reverend Doctor Barkis."

"Oh, where is Edward?"

"I'll run and get the girls and the boys," said Oneida, rising hurriedly and starting out for the little house in the grove. They could hear her a minute later calling, "Laurel! Rose! Ralph! Richard!"

There was a bustle on the veranda. Everyone smiled with delight and the young couple were in a solemn excitement. Victor-Alexander, rose to do them honor, yet stood slightly apart because he was a guest, not a member of the family. Norah said she would go and see if all was right near the well, and Lou went to get his camera. The sisters took off their silk aprons and arranged the seats they had occupied. Ollie laughing took down the rag rug and threw it on the floor. The farmer's family was seen driving down the road again with a tarpaulin over the cart. Oneida came running down the barn road. The Abbot leaped across the lawn and to the horses' legs, darted like an insect from the whip, skipped back again. Oneida called repeatedly to the farmer, "Ben! Stop! Ben!" She yelled at the black dog and explained to the farmer, "He's so gay now, because he's showing us he's forgiven us. Someone hit him this morning." She then begged the farmer and his wife to back the wagon up to the barn as the minister was coming and besides she wanted them to attend the wedding.

"You've known Mark and Marian since they were children."

There was some excitement while the wagon was backed up and while Oneida took the farmer's wife upstairs to fix her up a little, lend her a dress. The minister's car came slowly up the drive.

They then heard laughter and cries, a song and rabble coming fast behind the car. Said someone, "Picnic going to the pool." But the picnic ran in through the stone gateway. They saw colors flashing through the trees and up the slope. Weaving over the thick grass came Edward, leading a serpentine of youths, girls and boys, hand to shoulder, joined, singing breathless snatches of songs, in their ringing voices. They wound over the grass and up the steps. Cries of delight broke from the porch, "oh-oh-oh!" and they named the people coming, Anne, Doris, Jack, Boy, Thaïs. Dan smiled. He and Edward had organized this surprise. Edward carried a bouquet, the boys had paper streamers and bands of paper flowers and all the girls had fresh flowers. They poured onto the veranda, and standing there in a tumble, flushed and smiling, their hair blown about their shoulders, they held their flowers and sang first to the bride and then to Mrs. Mustbrook. Edward placed his bouquet in the bride's lap and kissed her while one of the girls brought a wreath of garden flowers to Mrs. Mustbrook and placed it on her dark-brown head. She moved swiftly from her seat, the wreath on her red face, and clumsily but accurately she danced a few steps of a folk-dance. The wreath fell awry; and indeed it turned her face queer, she looked debauched, old. The flowers looked fairer still on her old forehead.

"You must wear it at the party," said Edward.

"No, no, no, I must wear it now, all the time," she cried, starting away: and once more she danced her strange steps, in an innocent abandon and confidence. She kissed all the girls and boys, whom she called, "My chicks, my children," and went round the sisters showing them her happiness, her wreath. The young people now gave her small gifts which she piled up on the table.

In the excitement, the minister had been forgotten but Lou in his best suit had met him and saved him from the dogs and now brought him in. They stopped romping, and a gay, timid joy took hold of them all. They stood about breathless and naïve, and looked startled, envious, benevolent at the young pair. There was a slight pause. Then Oneida came down with the farmer's wife, lacing a new ribbon in a velvet peasant bodice which she had substituted as being prettier for the photographs. Dan took his beautiful grandson by the hand and his beautiful daughter, Thaïs, the boy's mother, a slender, bronzed amazon, leaned passionately on the arm of her husband.

Old Mr. Vines, who had been tuning the upstairs grand all day, now began to play the Wedding March and they assembled at the well, above the sunken garden. The sky was still, but a faint breeze stirred the withered tops of the two Lombardy poplars. Ben, the farmer, had put the tarpaulin back on the ventilator of the greater barn.

While he had been standing behind the couple and the minister had married them, tears of suffocating joy and tenderness had come to Edward. He had a sudden perception that two persons could give themselves entirely to each other and promise away an entire life with pleasure. He did not wipe away his tears. His shortsighted eyes felt large, beautiful, and an adolescent passion made him feel unlike himself. Presently, he recovered from this feeling and was inclined to laugh at himself. He went walking about with the guests, looking at the color of the flowers and the dresses, laughing at the torn-up raspberry patch and explaining to the bride how the vine ran all over the acres and perhaps even under the house. Half an hour later, when the bride and bridegroom had gone to sit on a flat boulder in an open stand of trees, in full view of them all, but distant, and the others had settled themselves to various things, he went into the hall and, after hesitating there, he sat down at the writing desk. He wished to reflect for a moment and then answer Margot. Most of the company had assembled in the downstairs music room where Lou was giving one of his rare private concerts. Edward listened in ecstasy.

He heard Mrs. Mustbrook cry out, "Where's Edward, where's dear Edward?"

Edward glided from the desk and out into the grounds.

Apparently, Oneida and Victor-Alexander had not been in the house for the music. Oneida, still in the velvet dress and ballet slippers she had worn for the wedding, was digging in the garden, weeding out. Her friend, Victor-Alexander, stood in the tumult of tussocks alongside. They were disputing about what Victor-Alexander called the sloth of the land. Oneida disputed with her head in the earth, her black eyes glaring at Victor-Alexander in the intervals upside-down.

"That was no reason to cover the place with sow-thistles. I suppose you thought we'd have to dig them up. But you have to blast them out and the whole ground is poisoned. Scorched earth."

Victor gobbled something.

"I know you better than the others, Victor. It makes me sick to think here they have been fifty years and they don't know anyone's character. They don't even know mine."

Victor emitted something. Edward sauntered up. Oneida saw him, still bent among the weeds and she said, "Victor admits he brought the sow-thistles."

"That's an outrageous statement, that's an outrageous statement. Why all the lies? Why all the lies?"

Edward was silent for a while, thinking it over, then, "But why on earth would he do it, Oneida?"

"Because he hates all this land under grass. He wants to make it either agricultural land or a pleasaunce — a pleasaunce, ha! I ask him why poppies and roses are better than grass. As soon as I smell earth I feel better. The dogs are years younger the first day they come here from town. But for him, it's a crime. So he ruined it for us. He says the land is kept for the dogs. He says the stars insist upon our not sitting around in idleness. What harm do we do? Satan finds work for busy hands to do is what I see. People who can't keep still are soon at work poisoning or throttling — or slaughtering — each other. . . ."

"In a year you'll be overspread·with thistle, in a year you'll . . ."

"Last year Lou had to break his back weeding out only a few square yards of thistle. This year he won't. What will keep it off your land?"

Victor looked strangely at her.

She laughed, "Your land produces so much you will have sow-thistle ten feet high. You will be sorry for what you have done."

Edward said, "Oneida, Oneida!"

To his surprise, Victor remarked, "Not one of you ever did anything for society. Here you were during all the trouble, in perfect peace."

"We all voted for Roosevelt: you never even voted in your whole life. What use is your garden? No one ever sees it so it doesn't exist. You never had a wife or a child or even a dog. Besides, Edward was in the war."

"Edward was in paper-shifting, paper-shifting."

"I did some leg-shifting," Edward flushed.

"Don't criticize me, Victor. You're only a squatter here. All you do is accept secret dinner invitations from Big Jenny and Pelayga and Lady. That's your entire usefulness. You make salad dressing and look in a crystal ball and you think that's useful to society?"

"Are dogs useful to society?"

"You hate my dogs because you hate me."

"Kindly credit me when I say that I hate no one, kindly credit me when I say that I hate no one."

Edward had been idling farther and farther away and he now lost the sound of their dispute; but turning back from the fringe of the wood to look at Whitehouse Big Farm which was dearest to him from this aspect, couched in a fold of the hill, the valley hidden, the mountains near, he saw Victor-Alexander start for the house, picking his way carefully over hidden mounds of earth, huge tussocks and potholes made by dogs. Looking to the west, Edward saw thunderheads of glassy vapor and smoke pouring into the sky and bellying towards them. The trees were now all murmuring, each one inside itself like a swarm of talking leaves. The first towers of rain, still light, stood on the most distant western spur of the mountains. Edward moved towards the house. Oneida was still bent down in the earth. Edward came back quietly to her.

"Why did you say those things to Victor-Victor?"

"I don't want him ever to set foot in this place again."

"Oneida! He's a dark soul; you don't know what you do to him."

"I know him better than any of you; he's capable of anything."

"Victor is just an artist."

"He wishes harm to all of us and it isn't obscure."

"But why should he?" Edward asked in an irritating reasonable tone.

"Don't argue with me. I'm furious."

"I'm going in to help him make the salad."

"He won't let anyone near him in the kitchen but me, he won't let anyone —" she broke off and bit her lip.

[197]

Edward laughed and started for the house. Madame X and Musty, who had been digging in the garden with Oneida, began to bark and hurled themselves down the slope. Oneida was so angry she did not even notice this. A moment later, they were leaping round a running figure, halfway up the path. Was it man or woman? Edward now saw that it was one of the family friends, a husky-voiced strong, shy girl in a blue land-girl suit. Her round cheeks were flaming, she was shouting, "Big Jenny says to come down if you can!"

"What has happened? What has happened?"

"Two carloads of morons have arrived and they are asking for food. And Dan has got the kitchen stacked to the ceiling with meat and beer. Oh, do come and help."

"Oh get everyone! Quick, get everyone, Edward's in the kitchen."

At this news, everyone left his occupation and chattered furiously. Mrs. Mustbrook seized her new apron and started off at once. She was followed by all the relatives laughing, serious, meditative, ex-postulating. Oneida cried, "I refuse to go and see his capers."

The people began to pour down the slope among the dogs. Oneida, intransigent, but anxious about her old friend whom she had ter-ribly insulted, could not make up her mind to go and she cried to Edward, "Don't you go, Edward; Lou will find out what it is about. There's an army there already. Oh, Dan will kill Big Jenny. That is his object. Then he can get hold of the house, he thinks."

"Oh, Oneida, have a heart."

"And a storm coming up too," she said.

The wind had been blowing harder for some time and the woods moved. Even on the distant mountains, the trees, massed like crys-tals in a reef, moved slightly in their crusts, a pack of winds run-ning lightly up a flank and the trees struck turning gray or pale in one broad trace. The clouds, mushrooming up above the banks of vapor, advanced from the west and the light changed. The last guest had gone down the road to Dan's. Only Musty and Madame X

[198]

remained of the dogs. The air became tender, moist and the famous thunderballs of the Catskills bounced along the ridges and away to the east. The old cat, Westfourth, went slowly down the steps, sprang to the ledge and stretched himself out at length, in full display of his beauty. His blazing eyes watched the trees, the valley. Old Sister Mary, however, still sat like a stone figure on the veranda and murmured to Victor-Alexander who stood there, in his impeccable gray with a spoon in his hand, "The mountains are still clear. I have only failing vision but I can see them in this light."

But at once they dulled. The rain smudged the western spur, flared towards the valley and began climbing the hill rapidly in sheeted hordes, with great strides on stilts that stepped through the trees, crowded in the necks and funnels of the mountain and drove up the crests not hesitating a moment and poured over them and down the facing valley bowl with immense vaulting, a kind of drifting gallop, as of a life, but not ours. This is the way the storms come at this point in the Catskills.

The storms of rain passed on the other side, escalading the farther bluff. Scarcely had they passed but vapors rising in the heat, from hollows and clefts, tall, slowly forming and moving, spirits, savage men, with weapons, daggers, things habited like the Rabbi, question marks especially, and puffs of smoke, rose out of the new wet earth and shaggy heads of trees and clots of water, rags of steam, began to tear themselves out of the woods and vacillating, tried to get up again in the moving air. Meanwhile, the nearer air became purple, the garden flowers took on the flat brilliancy of silks, the lawns changed and precipitated yellow and the trees blew with the strength of the storm: they moved as if frightened, birds were hurled from their boughs, the boughs waved as if being torn away. The dogs were uneasy. On the porch, Old Mary remained with Victor-Alexander and Edward. Lou, in a blue shirt, was seen coming up the path. Victor-Alexander, for the last few minutes, had been staking up some flowers.

"Your larkspurs need staking; and look, someone has broken one of the giant phlox."

"Dogs," said Edward.

The first drops of rain had reached them; and, a moment later, a blow of rain came, the high canvas sky reeling with wide-placed sheet lightning and jags, the thunder going great guns. Westfourth sat in his place till the last moment, watching leaves that flew, grasses that bent, unable till the last to drag himself away from the sorcery.

When the rain reached them and the guttering began to spout, he leaped down, scampered up the steps, and, finding a place on the porch just inside of where the rain blew, he curled himself up once more and watched the weather.

In the kitchen Oneida, who was making coffee, saw the storm on the mountains and the dashing about of the near boughs; and worried about Big Jenny; yet exulted. She was unusually moved. It was true that she spent too much time with the dogs, so that nothing ever got finished and yet everything was finished, everything was in order. The wedding had come off to perfection and the day was not yet evening. She was not unhappy, as other women, such as Irene and Ollie, and she had no ambitions, she was not dissatisfied. Why? It was merely candor to say that it was because of her dear doggies. She was still a lonely child, hordes of friends had evaporated, from those that remained, like Victor-Alexander, this love had gone, the dogs had been her only friends. She did not care for furniture or clothes as such, only for affections: and what alone was faithful? But she hardly thought these things: she only thought them out in dogs as mothers think them out in children. She had her family, the farm, her town house, Victor-Alexander, Lou, Big Jenny, Edward of course, Thaïs and all such people; and the sweet close honeying ones who were her intimate life, her perpetual joys — her dogs. But she thought these things with her flesh because she was excited and upset with the tingling of her dispute with her old friend-enemy Victor-Alexander. He had said plainly today that she had wasted her life, since the day her own wedding had taken place at the well. She loved storms: her brain lived in them. Now she was obsessed with ideas of her life, the eating, drinking, wassailing, the barking, feeling and lingering love in thousands of images that tumbled through her brain — dogs leaping on and off her, racing down the garden, jumping at people who were not her, giving them cruelty while they gave her love, even the Abbot, going out of his senses when bells rang and cars came, but leaping round her. She was so united to them that when they tumbled down the stairway and surrounded some timorous visitor, it was herself tumbling down, greeting the visitor with a malicious gaiety, shaking hands; and when they jumped, pretended to bite and tear, it was their way of doing what she felt, a sort of hot, exasperated, unsatisfiable greeting.

"No one ever loved dogs as I do," she said to herself, "that's it and that's what they don't understand. And with such a great love . . ."

But a certain lost feeling came to her. It was a fact that the dogs did not understand her love, for a human being has so much more passion and devotion than they. Here she broke off and thought, "Lou is right; I must work."

The dogs would be frightened by this storm. But no doubt everyone was seeing to them. "I don't see how anyone can say that I have a bad nature. I don't like wild animals. A woodchuck clawed up my poor Picky — " tears came. "Victor-Alexander is against the dogs because they jump on his flowers — I know it's a substitute for children and, as I told him, his flowers are a substitute for every human responsibility. And at this he takes umbrage." She smiled and repeated maliciously exactly like Victor-Alexander, "I am obliged to take umbrage."

Edward sauntered into the kitchen. As he approached, thinking how she had quarreled with their old friend, a curious idea came that she had never loved any man but Lou and could not: that she lived sheltered from crude and bestial life, from passions, in short that she was very much like Victor-Alexander and that she owed this, after all, to Lou, himself, the family, Edward and most of all the dogs. When he came close to her, with a gentle expression, but without smiling, she turned to him, with a cup in her hand (she was trying to match cups and saucers, but none fitted).

"Don't you agree that persons who hate dogs are afraid, dogs are so clever, they know at once if there's something wrong under the surface."

Edward said, "Well, we all have something savage in our nature."

"Just what I think! Anyone is capable of anything: but especially when you know them. Dogs sense things we don't."

Edward laughed. "You are the only person I know that really has a cult of dogs but dogs don't understand adoration. They're always just greedy and blood-shedding."

"How true that is, Edward, how true that is! And you see we have idolized Victor-Alexander, made a lap-dog out of him."

Edward looked far away.

"It's midsummer but the leaves have changed already; whole patches are coppered. Lou just brought in some fall leaves from the road; at the bottom of the tall beech, they're red and yellow. You should hear what Lou is telling them about the party down at Dan's."

She said, "Edward, if I went away and left the dogs to Lou, he wouldn't even feed them." He laughed. She added, after a while, "I can live without them, never fear. But, Edward, without them at all in the world, the world would seem empty. You have to have something to take care of and love; and to have something love you unquestioningly."

"All people don't need that."

"I think it shows selfishness not to want love unquestioningly — like our star-gazer friend, like our star-gazer friend. Ho-ho!"

"Don't talk to me about love, Oneida. I can't bear the subject."

The storm swept the porch and flapped at the doors. Oneida, Old Mary, and the three men sat inside in the near darkness listening to the sound. Lou described the scene now in progress down at Dan's. During the previous night, Dan had secretly fixed up the basement with tables, checked cloths and streamers and put up a sign: "Big Jenny's — ask for free beer and planked steaks and fries." The slow-witted young fellows he employed in his factory from time to time, with their friends and the girls from a home for feeble-minded girls, upon Dan's recommendation, had hired two trucks and come all the way to Whitehouse expecting dinner and to be put up for the night. Dan's house was on a steep slope and they had all entered the basement at the front where Dan, with the aid of his friends, the bridge-players, that he had met at six o'clock in the morning, had put up another notice saying: "Big Jenny's Free Fry House," and they had gone into the basement, turned on the three radios, danced, drunk beer, eaten pretzels and then had begun clamoring for the planked steaks and French fries.

There was a wooden staircase leading from the basement to the kitchen and the door had been locked by Dan. Big Jenny, hearing the rude knocking in her kitchen went in, opened the door and was almost knocked down by the storm of "morons" asking for planked steaks and French fries. Guests from the wedding who were in the dining room came in, and Big Jenny, who had not been in the kitchen all day, suddenly observed, turned on the light and saw the meat, the sacks of potatoes, the fat. She had sent the young people there up to the Big Farm for their stew-pans and caldrons. The wedding guests all helping, they had begun to make the French fries and the steaks. The morons had all returned to the cellar led by Dan and an immense celebration was now in progress. Meanwhile, Dan had invited, it seemed, all on the state highways between Hunter Village and Wyndham and even Tobacco Road. Those sounds they now heard, horns, braking and shouts, were the sounds of new guests. They would be there till next daylight, for sure; and

Oneida had better go down and help the sisters at slicing potatoes and wiping and drying dishes. He invited Victor-Alexander to do so too, but Victor-Alexander, after finishing his coffee, thanked them and said, "I was invited for the wedding and that is done, that is done. The storm is over now, the storm is over now, and so I may go."

He arose and thanked each of them politely and when they were all standing on the porch, he turned to Oneida, with a slight bow, and said, "Since you don't wish to see me here any more, of course I cannot come here any more. Good-by. Good-by."

"Oh, Victor-Alexander, how can you be so sensitive?"

"Good-by," he said, and graciously turning away went down the steps.

Oneida looked after him for a moment and then turned to the others, Lou, Edward, Old Mary, "Do you know? He will never come again. I know him."

"Oneida, what could you have said to him?" cried Lou.

"Don't think he likes you any more than any of us," said Oneida, dispiritedly. She went into the dining room, then threw down her apron, and said she was going straight to Big Jenny's.

"I shall get them all out of there as fast as possible. I don't intend to be there till two in the morning, cooking for morons."

The storm had passed. The cold shadows were coming across the lawn and the garden to touch the house, but these had not yet come. The lovely old farmhouse with its balconies, shingled roofs on various levels, its numerous gardens, overgrown places, lay against the sunset, the woodland and the mild slope towards the west. The lawns and meadows sloped above and below it, from the crest of their own hills covered with trees, towards the valley while the town was hidden. The air was clear but soft, and already a heavy vapor was rising from the valley and crawling up towards them again.

"Let us all go. You know you are invited for a bottle of wine," said Lou offering his arm to Old Mary. She smoothed her dress, and begged Lou to get her blue scarf.

"Oh what a vain little girl," said Lou, kindly.

Oneida and her dogs came pattering downstairs ready to go; but Oneida and Madame X no longer looked like some strange kind of sisters. Oneida had put a diamond comb in her hair and was wearing a magnificent embroidered coat which had once been used by Nijinsky in one of his ballets and had come to her somehow. She went ahead of them down the path, the splendid fantastic raiment of a Slave of the Lamp flashing between the laurels. Presently, they heard her voice way down between the trees, then it was lost in the din coming from Dan's house.

Old Mary was ready. The last two, Edward and Lou, went down with her, one on each side, guiding her. They left the house as it was, doors, windows open; and as if all ready for a hundred more guests, for anyone who might drop in.

Late in the night, they began to come back again; and as the young couple had gone to the village for the movies and the others were still at Dan's "moron" party, the few who returned went back to their usual tasks in the house. Until late, Flora was in the kitchen, cleaning, settling things in their places and keeping Ollie with her. Ollie had put on the big soiled apron she wore in the mornings. The old sister sat in her clean dress on the French settee beside a lighted lamp and talked in gay, dry, phrases. She had drunk a whole bottle of wine given to her by Dan and he had sat by her till she had drunk it. Lou stretched out, with his glasses on, read a book in the basket lounge and Oneida, with her sick dog beside her, stitched at the neckband of a silk peasant blouse. Once the Abbot came smelling round the old sister's knees and she put out her hand with fingers widespread to touch him. A laugh appeared on her bright stony face. "Good Abbot, dear boy."

Edward, who had come up "to get a bite to eat, and get away from the charivari" reclined on a window seat out of reach of the lamp; his hands behind his head, while Bart, under the floor-lamp, read Gibbon's *Decline and Fall of the Roman Empire,* volume II. This missing volume he had found in one of the box-seats open, where it had been open for years since Dr. Edward had left it there; and he had begun to read it at page sixty-six, the page at which it had laid open all that time. Nothing was said. Presently, Ollie came in, taking off her apron and sat in her faded morning dress beside Old Mary.

"Have you finished?" "Just cleaning up a bit," was all that was said. The two sisters sat side by side looking at the group by the lamp, at the room, the dogs, and beyond them, at Irene who sat in a chair knitting fast, a dissatisfied expression on her pretty pointed face. From time to time, Irene looked at Edward stretched out along the window seat. She sighed. Madame X broke wind. Oneida said, "Those morons," and Lou turned a page. From time to time, Lou raised his head, looked shamefacedly at the sisters, and once said, "It's dull for you, Mary?"

Old Mary answered, "Yes, to think I know four languages and cannot read anything. What good was it all?"

Another time, he asked Ollie, who sat straining, half smiling, with her round black eyes, "What do you do at home?"

She said with a burst of laughter, "Nothing, oh, nothing, we go to bed early. Ben-son must get up early." She sighed and said she wished she could come to New York.

Oneida cried, "Why, what could you do in New York? You don't know anyone there?"

Irene said, "Oneida, why do you always take offense at that re-mark?"

Bart said, "This is a college education."

The evening wore on. At last Flora came in from the kitchen, white from head to foot, snowy hair, clear fine skin, white teeth, starched apron. She sat down, third on the old settee, between her sisters.

"Have you finished the dough for tomorrow?"

"Yes, I'll bake first thing in the morning before breakfast. The children can have fresh rolls the first morning of their married life and ha-ha, the morons will be here for breakfast!"

Oneida said dreamily, "You do too much. We can't eat it all. Oh, who would believe it! And Father always thought the world of Dan! Just like him!"

"I can't sit still," said Flora. She chuckled. "What harm does Dan do?"

"And where are those morons going to sleep?" said Oneida suddenly.

And at this moment, a slow movement had begun towards the Big Farm, and youthful creatures full of inexplicable gravity, clever grimaces, snatches of song, silly catchwords, uncommonly bashful, uncommonly pert and gay, began to invade the house, through its open doors, and ask for lodging. It was late. They could no longer go back to town. Oneida cried, "Just as I foresaw," and bustled about in a moment, thinking what beds she had to dispose of. She had the farmhouse just empty, the upholstered window seats, spare rooms, verandas with beds, some camp cots, and so could perhaps take the overflow from Big Jenny's; and Leander and Lady might help. She thrust on her glorious coat again and ran downhill again to Dan's, and so up and down; but the strange guests that had now fallen in on them hardly took any notice of this unusual sight. They made themselves at home and did just what they were told without embarrassing questions.

Afterwards, Oneida and Edward sat long on the stone wall in the sunken garden. The stars were out over the house, the mountains and the trees and the grass were full of fireflies. The sky lightened. It was coming on to moonrise. At last, they went to bed, and were soon lying on their sleeping balconies in the western corner, separated only by a rattan blind.

The moon rose. "There is nothing to stop it," thought Edward involuntarily, in the New York style. The dogs began to bark. All over the valleys, a hundred degenerated and misshapen wolves, some with bulging eyes and snuffly flat noses, some with flap ears and some clipped, patched, blotched, streaked and flecked, some shaggy brown and some rusty black, some yellow-white, these twisted, dwarfed wolves' children like old dwarfs in courts, brought to light under irons and brought up in casks, so that no feature of theirs would resemble the human and yet they would be human, brought up to be vicious, foolish, coarse, snarling and flattering, richly fed and well combed, for the pleasure of kings, but at all times dressed in their master's insolence, and insolence their sole profession, a hundred court fools, hangmen and watchmen and killers; so these hundred dogs, whether chained like poor Charlie or free like Madame X, furiously, unhappily in the dark gardens, stirred by an ancient passion, fear and awe beyond their feeble souls, barked at the moon, at the furtive shadows come alive, at the strangeness of a world born again at night, in which their poor minds, seduced and debauched, were stirred and so rankled. The wolf came back. Thus they barked, Edward and Oneida listening with beating hearts, to that great arrival in the world, the moon, the cold sun of night; and presently with their rattling and yelping, their leaping and racing, they got the moon in all their bewildered eyes while birds woke and fireflies swarmed and in waters things rose to the surface. The dogs let out a roar, and howled in unison and singly in the hills. Their masters heard them, were pleased, and slept.

Edward, dozing, woke when the moon fell on him. The fireflies kept dancing in the blue light till late. The moonlight, slightly misted, was all invisible feathers. One firefly clung to each branch of the pear tree, one was at first as high as a star, and then went down from tip to tip and up and down, then over the grass. After a doze, Edward opened his eyes and saw a firefly taking a slow bobbing line following the line of the winding and ascending farm road; and then he heard a faint cry. He was heavy with sleep. He looked and listened. It was perhaps Dan — or the farmer? Or a moron? He heard the scratching and stirring of the vine on the pergola and then the Abbot snorting in Flora's bed on the next balcony. He raised himself to look. There, under the fresh pale night sky someone was stirring. There was a light moving through the trees. He heard Big Jenny's voice. He got up and went downstairs in his bare feet, and old cotton pyjamas, that he had put on because there were strangers in the house. The under night was cool, white, with mountain vapor. He went down through the dew feeling his way, looking up at the dim forms of bushes and trees. He let out a cry as he stepped on something in the grass that pierced his foot. He raised his foot. Halfway up, the thing fell off. It was the sheep's skull which the Abbot had brought up the morning before and hidden in the grass. Edward laughed ironically and began softly hallooing as he came towards the great gateway.

"It's Edward. Who is it?"

When Big Jenny saw him she exclaimed, and threw her Chinese shawl over his shoulders. It was one of the ones they said she never used, embroidered with roses and butterflies, red, green, on yellow silk. She had a chest full given to her at various times by Dan.

"I am only looking for my little monkey, dear boy," she said. He walked her down to her cottage and made her go to bed, promising to scour the entire countryside tomorrow looking for her little dog. People were sleeping everywhere at Big Jenny's house, on the porch swings, on the floor, even in a broken-down shed near the road where there was a quantity of soft red sawdust. The moonlight fell on a wonderful web hanging and glittering over the railings of the veranda and trailing on the wet grass. It was Oneida's Nijinsky cloak, forgotten there. Edward whispered, "Isn't it too much for you, Jenny?"

"Ah, but it gave Dan so much pleasure, bless his heart," she said.

[209]

He sat down with her for a while by the table covered with glasses and broken bits. They whispered and he took her hand and patted it.

Coming back he picked up the Nijinsky cloak and threw it over his shoulders. The dogs heard him on all the balconies and rose up barking with jealous anger. But his voice quelled them and satisfied the family. The doors as usual were not shut. On the stone steps leading round by the rose pillar to the cellar, under the pear tree, he found Lou, sitting and looking across the lawn to the wood. "I saw a beautiful thing in the wood, a midsummer's night's dream: and it was you," said Lou laughing softly. He followed Edward between the sleeping groups and up the stairs.

In the morning, it was Oneida, running out with the dogs, running down the slope, jolly, round in her near-nakedness, her rosy plump feet bounding over the thick dewy grass, tumbling over the rolling stones, who heard Darly's little bark first, and saw the neighbor's boy bringing her and saw Jenny in her nightdress, open the screen door and rush out, great and shapeless and joyful, her short white hair shining, crying:

"Oh Darly, oh my sweetheart, oh, darling, where were you?"

So Oneida heard the whole story and was able to bring it back to breakfast. The entire house on the hill, the great house, the comedians on the hill, with their wedding guests, their bride and bridegroom, and Irene, Edward and Lou and the "morons" became joyful, began to laugh, and Lou went in to play and one after the other, in twos and threes, in the morning, they went down the hill to see Big Jenny and to ask where Darly could have been to.

Part Three

A NIGHT IN TOWN

PEOPLE who came up from New York looked pale, the men had thinner hair. The town was sweating out its life desperately, living from hour to hour. "They don't sleep at all: in the morning you can wring out your pillow!" Lou went to town every fourteen days for pupils, stayed overnight in a friend's penthouse, all Sunday by a swimming pool, and came back lively with tales of the heat-struck city.

Said Edward, "No sane man would go there unless he had to."

At Whitehouse the nights continued their sweet sterile cold. Edward would go down to the village and talk to the shoemaker, the grocer, men in the poolroom, pick up some briefly dressed fat young people from the camps, eat here and there, play baseball with a scratch team, pick up a hand of cards in a bridge game as he passed Dan Barnes's house on the way home. When he got back he sat on the veranda and droned away flatly with the old women, or strolled into the kitchen to tease Oneida by "poking in the pots."

In mid-August came an announcement of Margot's marriage, addressed to Edward; and one for the Solways. Edward put his down on the kitchen table. "I'll stop her," said Edward. "I'm going to call the taxi."

"Well, as they say, he who laughs, laughs, laughs laughs," remarked Lou.

"Oh, how cruel," said Oneida.

He telephoned Margot at her home, hummed at her, cajoled.

"Hold everything," said he. "I'm on my way now."

"Imagine when he is up here and nothing farther from his thoughts," said Oneida. "Oh, we must go too."

When Edward set off for town, dressed in the best outfit he could find about the place, he was accompanied by Lou and Oneida, and farewelled by the sisters lined up along the veranda, wearing their best aprons, weeping and calling out.

"When next you see me I'll be Edward the married man," said he, turning back and laughing ironically. All the way down to the bus in the village people farewelled him and wished him luck: the news had already spread three quarters of a mile. They went along the broad valley between the hills, and dropped down by wooded ravines and curving hillside roads to the distant station. Edward said to the taxi driver, "You can tell the boys at the garage to go up and take my Willys-Knight, tell them to take it and pay you the money."

"O.K. Major."

"He madejer Major," Lou murmured.

"Oh, my pie's still in the oven," cried Oneida. "I'll telephone the house! No, I won't! They are never out of the kitchen. You'll be looked after, pie! We'll all be looked after." She burst out laughing. "It's just what you two always think!"

"What?"

"That dinner makes itself! That weddings make themselves! Oh, what a toad! He waited here naïvely thinking everything was running smoothly, thinking everything would suit his book, my angel! She knows here we doze our lives away: the mail takes days to get to Whitehouse! It was a plot, a plan. Clever, clever! Too clever by half! Too-oo clever by ha-half, hey, hey, my sweetiepie, and she has not got Edward after all, my darling! And we have got Edward to ourselves."

"Not if I know it," said Edward.

Lou chuckled but watched him.

Edward had a couple of whiskies with Lou at Grand Central: Oneida asked crossly, "What are we drinking for?"

"My wedding," said Edward.

Oneida poured hers into Lou's. Edward looked grave and solemnly drank Lou's. He left them and took a taxi downtown to Chatham Square in old Chinatown, at the end of the Bowery. Here he had another whiskey and went round the corner to Margot's place. The place was in disorder: it never had been, not once; and Margot was dressed in a long white negligee he had never seen before.

"Edward! — oh, why did you? Why did you? Everything is settled!"

"Feel how my heart is beating!"

She would not let him touch the packing. When he left late in the evening he was exalted and said to himself, "This is my wedding eve!" The people passing him in the streets had a new significance: it seemed to himself that he had joined society. When he got home, he went up to his new room on the third floor. Irene had taken over Miss Allison's flat on the same floor. Irene heard him opening his door and came out.

"Oneida has been ringing here all the evening!"

He shrugged.

"Oneida was very mysterious! What goes on?"

"I'm getting married, Irene."

She laughed lightly, he heard her moving about in her room and unexpectedly the door shut with a bang. His own room was just about uninhabitable: Nate the Croat had just moved his ladders, pails and planks in. Edward crawled through them and into bed, without removing the covers. He heard the phone ring again in the flat opposite.

"Poor Oneida! She'll feel time is passing now." He tossed for a long time and went to sleep so late that he woke very late. When he rang Margot from Irene's phone, she was ready to start for

[215]

church and said only, "Good-by and good luck, Edward! I've sent you a parcel and a letter!"

He was stupefied, and hung up. With his torso bare, he drooped on Miss Allison's old rose satin couch. He thrust his bare feet under the couch and looked sadly at Irene with wide open eyes.

"I don't understand it!"

"Don't you?"

"But I offered to marry her!"

The phone rang and while he was talking drearily to Oneida Irene went into his room and fetched his dressing-gown which she draped round his shoulders. She put a fresh cigarette into his yellowed fingers and brought him some tomato juice.

"What's in it? Tabasco?" he snarled.

"Too much smoking?"

"I was smoking nearly all night," he admitted, and continued into the phone, "I'm only being nagged by Irene!"

He dressed and went over to the Solways', where Oneida, in high spirits, waited on him and pretended to solace him.

Lou said nothing to him at all, but the whole time he was there sat by the high windows and played the piano. He played for a time Beethoven's Sonata Opus III and with what passion! Oneida, all of whose days were filled with such music, took no notice but with her dogs trooped about the back rooms. She said to Edward, laughing, "Don't hang yourself at any rate like Les Chubin! The night his girl was married to that West Virginia fellow — you remember — "

Edward said he was going back to the house to get his mail. There was nothing there from Margot. He heard Irene in the house playing her piano. He went out again. Where to? He started out to walk towards the church where Margot had been married that morning, came down Third Avenue under the screaming and pounding L, turned off at Cooper Union east by little Stuyvesant Street slanting towards Second Avenue. There are ruinous two-story and three-story buildings, lofts, a home for the aged lower down. On a doorway leading to stairs beside a coffeepot a sign read: *Dorothea and Waldemar Block, Toys, Dolls, Puppets.* On the second floor was a laundry for barbers and restaurants: on the third hung a yellow clown outlined in neon tubes. The windows were half open. Edward climbed the stair past the smell of strong soaps and detergents to another landing where there was a smell of new shavings and faint coffee and cat. The stair continued half a turn to the attic door where the Blocks' tenant, a very poor young sculptor lived. Edward knocked several times at the Blocks' door, one long, two short, one long. Then steps came, the door was unbolted and Waldemar's large fleshy pale face looked out, smiled at him.

"What time is it?"

"About two-thirty," said Edward.

"Dorothy is still out and I'm waiting for lunch!" The puppeteer smiled strangely, quietly. He led Edward in round an electric saw, into the front part of the workshop: there was a stage on one hand, windows in front in which hung a sign and a hussar puppet, and shelving and rough solid benches everywhere, with a few books and ranges of tools on the walls.

On a steel arm projecting from the wall hung a girl puppet in Dresden shepherdess costume, beside her on the bench under a flock of sheep with two separate sheep.

"Do you mind if I look?"

Waldemar smiled as vaguely as ocean glimmer and sank into an office armchair where he sat unstrung, lost in his feelings. He was a blond stub, large, energetic, flaccid. He wore a pale loose shirt and neat though uncreased belted trousers of a remarkable soft dull stuff, black socks, black suède shoes. His large muscular and fat hands hung at rest, not loosely over the arms of the chair. Presently he moved one hand and placed it on his thigh: his large pale blue eyes stared a little away ahead as if at something real but invisible: his mouth was rather large, pale. His lower lip jutted out.

When spoken to he smiled faintly, moved, looked, but he seemed sunk in himself. After a while he said, "It must be twenty to three!"

"Later than three," said Edward.

"She has been out since before one," he complained.

Edward picked up the hip-joint of a dancing girl, cut beautifully and polished like a six-sided chestnut you might say. "Beautiful," said Edward. Waldemar Block watched intently but without moving or answering and gradually he became morose, his eyes turned almost white. He grumbled, "I don't understand it."

The roomy unpapered and unpainted loft stretched away to the fire escape and the back alley: there was a small closet fitted out in an old-fashioned way for a kitchen. The afternoon light slanted along the walls, the street bloomed with ash carnation colors: men in shirt-sleeves, sorting woolen goods moved slowly along the shining tables of a loft opposite.

Suddenly an immense striped gray cat leaped down from somewhere on the wall.

"Gee! a warlock! What's his name?"

The congealed figure from the armchair replied, dispiritedly, "He has no name: he's a gutter cat."

The cat, with an air of cold supernatural authority, walked up and down much displeased and then went towards the kitchen.

"Dorothy is coming," said Waldemar brightening. He stirred, but still sat in the same attitude in the chair.

The door opened and Mrs. Block came in with parcels. She greeted Edward and asked, "Are you hungry, my pet?"

There was a sound like wheels whirring and the man replied, "It must be nearly four: I haven't eaten yet."

The wife said she would not be long, begged Edward to stay: and at once accompanied by the cat disappeared into the kitchen. A smell of frying onions began. The man retired into himself and it seemed as if his belly expanded inside the loose shirt and the tight belt: but his eyes had brightened and his face was now delicately flushed. The wife began to lay a table in the middle of the long room against the wall between a curtained cabinet containing puppets in bags, looking very strange indeed, like people hanging without their bodies, like Bluebeard's cabinet and between a back scene painted in strange colors, for night lighting. On a blue strip of cloth stood a singular tower which reached to within fifteen inches of the ceiling of the loft. . . . While Edward brought a few things in from the kitchen, some rolls in a basket, some pickles, fruit and cheese, the wife explained that this was a Christmas decoration, characteristic of old families in Thuringia, and that they used it also in summer on their anniversary.

"The first Christmas after you are married you receive or buy the first platter or roundabout: and each Christmas you add one. Generally, of course, there was a new baby at each Christmas with each new tier."

Their first tier gaily painted represented the Crusades: there were many little figures on horseback and on foot. It had been made by Waldemar's grandfather, a toymaker. The second tier, a little smaller, represented the Kings of Israel and had been made by Waldemar's father, also a toymaker: above this, came the Ride to Bethlehem, then the Twelve Apostles and so on. This immense little tower, colored and gilt, was balanced on a pin on a crystal ball in the base and was moved by the heat coming from twelve candles. The candles sent their light up through the perforated ceilings of the platters. The top platter was pierced with the twelve signs of the zodiac and as the tower rotated, the ram, the bull, the twins, the scorpion, the lion moved round the ceiling. As Waldemar's sign was the lion, it was cut very large.

"We shall begin eating soon now," said the wife, aside, after having glanced at the husband slumped in the chair.

"Are you very hungry, Waldemar?"

"Yes, I am faint," he said irritably.

She went with Edward to the kitchen. "On birthdays we eat for hours," she said softly. She was a tall severe gentle woman of about fifty, with unwaved gray hair plainly but softly drawn back, and a plain gray dress, brown shoes. She said shyly, "You see, I have lipstick on today? I went to get an engagement for Westchester County: if you don't wear lipstick here they don't think you're properly dressed."

"I like you in it."

"Oh, I don't feel myself." She brushed her lips.

"Leave it on, Dorot."

She smiled in a sweet way at the young man. "Just stay with us, you'll eat something, I have cinnamon cakes and butter, birthday cake, look I have smoked salmon, veal cutlets and tomato pudding — he loves that, do you like that? There's fried rice, with chicken — there's so much."

"I'll stay for the salad," said Edward, "and I'll go and get some champagne."

She laughed, "No, no!" She said shyly, "I have white wine, he likes white wine. He doesn't like champagne!"

"I'll get a liqueur. Do you know it's my birthday too?"

"Oh, no, no — " She laughed. "Is it really though? Once he met three people in a restaurant and it turned out to be the birthday of all."

Edward went out unobserved by the half somnolent man in the chair. The sloping afternoon light had left him: behind him across the street, the cloth inspectors were beginning to slouch about, look out the windows, crack jokes. The rich smell of different foods filled the loft, the cat went out on the fire escape eating. When Edward returned, the man was sitting on the end of a bench turning about and twisting his hands, shoulders and legs, with a twenty-inch puppet, a sailor, in his hands.

"Come to dinner, Birthday Child," said his wife coming out of the space near the electric saw and smiling. He looked over his shoulder, got up in one movement with the puppet held out and came forward dandling it along the floor, making it walk, jig and smiling at Edward.

"See the hornpipe? It took me three months to get that right."

In an eager dazed way, he smiled and held the puppet delicately over the floor making it dance, very deftly: at the same time he whistled.

"Waldemar, dinner is ready!" called his wife, looking anxiously at Edward.

Laughing, eagerly he hung up the puppet on its hook and trundled rapidly to the table where an immense meal was spread, but only three places set. The wife served three plates of salmon, pickles and such things and Waldemar began to eat, hastily, with both hands, without raising his eyes and without a sound. Soon his plate was empty and with his mouth full, raising his eyes smiling excitedly, rapidly but as if with hesitancy, he passed his plate and as she heaped it up again, he breathed excitedly, watched the plate, and gave Edward a glistening look.

"We don't often eat so well," said he.

With a maternal glance, Dorothy passed his plate and he at once fell to. She now helped Edward and the two ate, but without glancing at the eater, making conversation quietly. When they came to the chicken and rice, he flushed with pleasure, slumped further down in his chair, loosened his belt and as it were voluntarily expanded his whole belly. He seemed to become of a more healthy pallor and all, his shirt, his hair and himself of this same gilded health. Edward also loosened his belt. "Well, the difference between a European family and an American family diet," said Edward gaily, referring to a newspaper inquiry.

Mrs. Block shook her head at him and indicated Mr. Block with her eyes. "Don't start him," she said faintly. Waldemar now paused however and his largish blue eyes had moved for a moment in Edward's direction.

He hastily finished his plate and after looking for permission in

[221]

his wife's gentle attitude, he passed his plate again and she heaped it up for the third time.

"It's very good," he said to her. Edward put both elbows on the table and leaning forward carried on a quiet conversation with the lady who was meanwhile putting titbits on Edward's plate. Edward gulped them down.

"I need this," said Edward: "it's like getting drunk."

At this Waldemar raised his merry eyes and laughed in satiric agreement. "Better," said he.

"Do you know that Waldemar is a terribly hungry man: he can never get enough to eat," said his wife. "As soon as he has finished a meal he is hungry; any meal whatever is just hors d'oeuvres to him: and of course we couldn't afford it if he ate all the time. So we decided to eat on certain days."

Waldemar laughed and looked at his wife. She passed him the big dish containing still a goodly proportion of the chicken, rice and sauce.

His wife continued, "His birthday, mine that's next week — "

The man lifted his big head, looked at Edward and laughed cheerfully.

The wife smiled. "Christmas, New Year's and St. Valentine's Day."

"Why St. Valentine's Day?" said Edward languidly, taking an olive.

"Our wedding anniversary."

When Waldemar had finished the big dish, he sat with his hands in his lap and looked shyly at them both.

His wife said, "There's some more in the oven: could you eat it, Waldemar?"

"Yes," he said shyly, looking at them both.

She crossed the loft and came back with the blue and cream oven dish.

"You, Edward? There's enough."

"I don't mind," said Edward languidly. She gave him a plateful and put the big glazed dish in front of her husband, saying, "There's Bolo work ahead."

"Yes?" said the man.

"In the kitchen, when you've finished."

He laughed and his eyes shone. He looked quaintly at Edward.

"Bolo," said the woman to Edward, "is an imaginary puppet we have: wherever we go we are harassed by Bolo's appetite. If we can't pay the rent, it's because Bolo is always dieting."

"Yeah?"

"Bolo costs so much when dieting that our expenses rise," she laughed, sitting straight and severe in her gray gown and smiling at both men. When the men had finished their plates, she said to Waldemar, "Light the candles!"

He got up happily, his eyes now sky blue, dancing greedily from one figure and one tier to the other. He touched one figure and another delicately and began telling Edward about them, "My grandfather Fritz made this, a toymaker in the Harz, and my uncle Christian made this, a toymaker too, in Dresden and I made this—"

He lighted the candles and the gilt halters of the palfreys, gilt spears, red cheeks and gold and silver crowns were picked out. Though they were in the center of the loft it was scarcely dark enough for anything but a faint blurring to appear on the ceiling: the air grew hotter, slowly the gold red and blue tower began to glide round. Dorothy clapped and laughed, kissed them both, they all clapped and laughed and cried and drank in their tall wine glasses!

"White wine!" said Waldemar.

"Let's drink to the happiest day of my life," said the wife.

"Nothing could be better when one partner says a thing like that," said Edward.

Both remarks were unheard by the husband who with both hands on his tall stemmed glass was drinking to the last drop. Neither took any notice.

"Pour more wine," said Waldemar. Edward poured. He took the glass in both hands and drained it, with a deep breath. "Ah, white wine!"

He looked round at Edward and said, "We only drink on my birthday and on Christmas Day! Otherwise my hands — " he held them out — "would shake! Puppeteers must not have shaking hands!" With this great joke he began to laugh, shaking and snorting "Ha-ha-ha! or all our puppets would dance! Ha-ha-ha! Shiver and shake! Ha-ha-ha."

The wife looked at him with a sly smile which gradually grew and broadened into an immense laugh. "Oh, Waldemar," she said. "Oh, Waldemar, you funny thing! Oh, Waldemar, ha-ha-ha."

"What, no salad!" said he roguishly. "We want salad! Don't we, Edward?"

"I'll get the salad," she cried and bustled out to the kitchen.

"Next time I'll come and make the salad for you," called Edward, on his way to the kitchen. The big cat was asleep on their bed in a dark corner of the loft. "I hope you have a big salad!"

"Yes, I have." He took from her hands a big mixing bowl full of salad and she followed behind with three lettuce-leaf plates, one large and two small. The large one she put in front of Waldemar. He took it up in both hands and laughed, "The biggest is for me!"

"Yes, why not?" She heaped it with salad and then served Edward and herself. Waldemar allowed her to mix it for him and put on it anything she pleased, himself taking nothing from the table and when it was arranged to her liking he began to eat automatically, and was finished before they had begun. She put the bowl in front of him and he ate all that was left. She put a piece of bread on his plate and he broke off a small piece at first, saying, "Just a little for the dressing, to clean the bowl," but in cleaning the bowl of dressing and olive oil he used up all the bread and even without

[224]

thinking took another piece from the silver bread-basket. Thus they went through the cheese, the several desserts, jellies with fruit and cream, cake-puddings, several tarts and sweets and when he had finished, a few slices of almond and date cake were left and he said, "I had better finish these or the flies will get them."

Edward laughed and pushed all the plates towards him. The man quite rosy now, laughed good-naturedly.

"Oh, I can eat my weight at any sitting, I think: but I mustn't do that or I should be simply a pork-barrel, a big vat! I should like one day to eat all I could but I mustn't! I don't feel well, but I have the capacity for infinite eating!

"Ha-ha! Oh, I'm that kind of lad! If I have a toothache, I don't know it's a toothache, I think, I must be hungry! I'm tired with work, but I go on working, because I think I'm hungry, but it'll soon be dinner! Dorothy's a good cook; too good, it's her fault, I'm so fat. Then the heavy damp weather doesn't suit me, I get sinusitis: but it never occurs to me it is sinusitis, I think I'm hungry! When I'm finished eating, I'm too heavy, I fall into the armchair and I fancy I'm hungry! I'm a boy that's always hungry! I went through the hungry years in Germany quite easily — I'm always hungry anyway!"

His wife who had returned to the table with coffee, looked anxiously at them both and said to Edward softly, "Don't encourage him on that!" Edward could not tell whether Waldemar had heard her or not. He turned a shade more serious and began to argue with Edward, as it were.

"Once Dorothy was ill for over a month and the whole time I was so miserable I didn't know what to do, but it wasn't till she was better that I realized I wasn't hungry, I was afraid she would die and if she died, what would I have to live for? But I thought I was hungry."

"Ah, poor hungry man!" said Dorothy.

Meanwhile the tower was gliding round at a regular speed with

[225]

the heat from the eight candles and the light from the eight candles in the darkening evening was sending the little golden signs of the zodiac, with the Leo largest in a circle over the ceiling: the white black and piebald horses were galloping to the Crusades, the little ass and Joseph, the golden star and the three holy Kings and the manger, the cows and pigs and sheep were going round and round and above them in the greater haze of red and gold darkness above, the other ancient holy figures, tiny and spirited, went on living their life on the turning tower. They went on eating, candies that Dorothy had made and bought, Turkish Delight, fruits, nuts, and Waldemar was changing; he was getting stronger and it seemed more muscular and serious. He got up to show them a remarkable thirty-inch clown, with red and yellow patches and tufts and extensible arms which had taken him three months to fix, he got up on the stage, Mrs. Block brought a large clownish lady and showed how the puppet with extensible arms could embrace her and dance and then hung up the lady again. Edward had not moved from his chair, but had merely swung it round on the leg and sat watching, while they both eagerly explained to him: and Block began to explain how he had got into Switzerland through Grenzach, a pretty little border village near Basle on the banks of the Rhine, the hills above them bristling with gun-nests, the shells flying back and forth over a Swiss pleasure park, and even the awful roaring of some stags in the forest strip that borders Switzerland there.

"I laughed and looked like a baby and told them we were twenty-two: and I showed them my puppets! They lifted the striped barrier. I walked from one cottage to another on the other side of the road and I was in Switzerland."

"Ah, don't," said Dorothy, "this is forgotten, Waldemar."

"To me it is not forgotten," said the great eater, rising to his feet to hang the clown on a hook provided for him: and solidly planted on his feet thus, he swung round to Edward and made an amazing speech.

He had been a candidate for the Reichstag, he had foreseen the Brown Terror. When the Reichstag had been burned he, like many others, had known what it meant, people had known in Germany if not in America: and he had then been on tour with his twenty-two puppets.

"How did you get to the border?"

Dorothy became anxious and intervened; but Waldemar not hearing her, made another twenty-minute speech. Dorothy retired to an Austrian chair near the window and looking desolate, afraid, religious, seemed to fade out of sight. In the darkness now, lit only by the candles and shadows of the turning tower, the pale immense figure, flowing and golden and pale like wax spoke faster and faster, without periods, building up a political speech in a wonderful way, fascinating Edward who was drawn to him and even despised the gentle and timid woman now completely lost in the darkness. There was a click: outside and between their two loft windows a red blue and green neon sign began to walk on air, it was a puppet grenadier advertising the Blocks' toy business. Inside the tower kept on turning and the warlock, the immense gray cat came up to them and began turning round the toymaker.

Edward and the woman heard the strokes of a clock. Edward lit a cigarette, got up and when he could get a word in, said that he must go: he was picking up Dr. Sam Innings.

"Perhaps if I were married I'd run for congress."

It was about six when he got to Sam Innings's office in Madison Avenue. He waited in his reception room until the last patient had gone. Then he went to Sam's apartment to have a drink. When he had last seen the place in spring it had been properly furnished, with a theatrically cosy pair of rooms to lure Madame Sarine. Now the corridor was bare, the immense living room contained only a settee and two upholstered armchairs near a small table. The pictures stood against the wall and the carpets had been rolled up and stood in the corners. The corridor continued past two rooms to an angle where

[227]

there were other rooms, a bathroom. Edward was able to see how bare it was.

"That's where Rudolf sleeps; I sleep at the end of the corridor."

Dr. Sam half-opened a door. Edward went in. Rudolf was a famous journalist of American citizenship but foreign birth who had worked in Moscow, Budapest and towns of the Eastern "People's Democracies." He passed at present for a friend of the Soviet Union. The switch at the door turned on a little reading lamp on an upturned packing-case. The bed was unmade, the clothes thrown as Rudolf had thrown them in the morning, a ski-boot in the sheets. The other ski-boot was inside a gaping paper valise in which Edward saw Rudolf's underwear, both clean and worn. Newspapers, cigarette butts, an empty cup trailed over the floor. The Venetian blinds had never been raised. Neither said anything. Edward went down the corridor where Dr. Sam showed him his room, small, with only a high skylight on a court, but neat and clean. "I made it up myself," said Dr. Sam.

"Don't you have a woman in?"

"Evidently not," said Dr. Sam, stiffly.

"Why?"

"Rudolf doesn't care, and since Vera won't come here, I don't care what happens. I don't speak to anyone but my patients. I am very polite with them, and sometimes I bawl them out."

"How long has Rudolf been staying here?" Edward said impressively.

"About a month, ever since Vera left me," said Dr. Sam in his queer careless china voice, which he used to cover or to introduce the story of his sufferings. He led the way back to the sitting room.

"You see what a clean sweep I have made. I got myself nicely installed for her and now she won't come, I just took and rolled everything up. I will get you a drink."

His movements were nervous. He brought out some Scotch whiskey, and some soda, and put down two glasses, bought in the ten-cent store. His eyes were blue and white, with an enamel shine. His blond skin was faintly flushed on the cheeks and his rare golden hair shone over his head. He stuck out his beard, said, "Chin-chin." When they had drunk one glass, Dr. Sam said, "Where will you eat, Edward? At home? With your girl?"

"No."

"Then let's eat here, I can fix up something. Rudolf will be here soon and we can eat. We both put on aprons and do the cooking."

Dr. Sam began to tell him the latest episode of his unfortunate relations with Madame Sarine. Neither wished to marry, at least not on the terms proposed by the other. Madame Sarine had many admirers, said Dr. Sam. Madame Sarine had said Dr. Sam had too many beautiful women coming to him to have their beautiful eyes examined. "I have always loved beautiful eyes and that is why I love Vera," said the doctor, of Madame Sarine, a small polished dark beauty of Hungarian origin, a social success but preferring the company of artists. She was petted by the White Russian community and other foreign communities of anti-Soviet tendencies. She said she was "not against the Eastern democracies" but no one saw it in her behavior or associations, said Dr. Sam. "Artists have no conscience: they will play to anyone," said Dr. Sam, caustically. "She says, I won't have a Commissar telling me how to vocalize Ravel." But what did she do? Arranged her programs to have the big pieces in before ten-thirty when the critics left for their roundup. Since she had become more and more popular with them, Dr. Sam found himself "more and more of a misanthrope — and a misogynist too," said he.

"Concert artists are mere charlatans, the receipts, the public are everything to them: they are cold-hearted! And then she is perverse. She won't make the little arrangements necessary to get into certain blackmailing sheets! And she will take nothing from me! What do you think concert artists make? They're in the red at the end of the year! I have enough for us both! I want to see her in furs and silk robes, in Paris dresses! She has two: it's enough, she says, I paid for them myself."

Edward shrugged and looked bored.

Dr. Sam was querulous now, "You asked me to tell you why we fight!"

"You'll lose her if you fight," said Edward, wearily.

"What is money? When she can have all my love?" cried Dr. Sam in a high voice. Edward looked round the bare dusty floor, the dusty edges of the tables and chairs pushed against the wall.

"She prefers success and applause to love!"

"Why can't you let her have all three?"

"Vera and I have had this discussion a thousand times and now we have reached a satisfactory solution: she has left me," said Dr. Sam in a cold mincing tone.

There was a latchkey in the door at the end of the long unlighted corridor. An unprepossessing dark hunk of a man walked along the passage, raised his hand. "*Salud,*" he shouted. "Pour me one!" He trundled on: the light at the other end shone on his thick spectacles.

"Why did he come in with you?" inquired Edward with respect.

"Why not with me please?" said Dr. Sam.

"This is something you can't know because your girl is a decent woman and besides she's not in public. Now she leaves me without even a calling-card with her address on it. One day, when I come home from a little ride in the country to a girl's place and I call for her she is gone, taken everything, bag and baggage. I found out her address by asking round. I sent her a white fur cape. She sent it back by the messenger, without a note. One day, I scolded her for talking about a cape and I thought it might have been that that annoyed her."

Dr. Sam got himself another drink. He was drunk now and tears were pouring down his cheeks.

"I have been living a month with Rudolf. Fortunately for me and for him he came to town the next night and could get no place to sleep. I said to him, Come home with me. You could help me too."

They drank the wine and, leaving the table as it was, went in to have another whiskey and soda. Tears were streaming out of Dr. Sam's eyes. He said, "Let's go down the east side, to the Rumanian restaurant and listen to the gypsy band!"

"There's someone waiting for me at home," Edward said.

"Come with me, spend the evening with me, I don't want to go to bed," begged the oculist.

Edward listened to the two bachelors commiserating with themselves with strategic smugness. He even laughed at them sourly and told them about Chubin, the man who went round town on his fiancée's wedding night with a pair of suspenders round his neck, going into one bar after another, saying this was his last drink and they'd find him on the bedpost in the morning. "He didn't have no bedpost, just a divan," said Edward in his Chimmy Fadden tone.

The men were standing up now getting ready to go. Dr. Sam was pouring more whiskey into a glass and begging Edward to drink with him: tears gushed from his fresh round blue eyes. He was pink and very neatly and gaily dressed: he looked like a playing-card king. He implored, "Eddie, Eddie! Women are so cruel, they are taught to be cruel!"

"Yes, they are." But Edward began to want to smile as he looked at the two middle-aged men.

"Women are such liars; their given word means nothing to them," said Dr. Sam.

"I can take 'em or leave 'em," said Rudolf, "come on, let's get out of here."

Dr. Sam put his hat on and walked to the door, then came back to put down his empty glass. At the coffee-table he refilled his glass instead. "Don't leave me, Rudolf! Don't go, Edward! Take another drink! You've never seen me like this before, have you? I've been like this for a whole week, Eddie! If she weren't so beautiful, she wouldn't be so cruel to men!"

[231]

"Don't put your money on that," growled Rudolf.

Dr. Sam wept in the elevator and argued with the people in the elevator.

"Why is it wrong for a man to cry? I feel like crying."

Every night the two bachelors went to the newsreels. They accompanied Edward on his way and he left them at the door of the newsreel theater in Madison Avenue. Then he trekked back across the park and worked his way up Central Park West in the direction of Al Burrows's. He thought, "I, a month from now, I won't feel anything like this." He referred to Margot's husband, in his thoughts, as "my stand-in" and became more cheerful. "Why did you have to do it that way, Margot?" he reasoned, "I would have understood that you couldn't go on in the same old jogtrot." As he began to get uptown his spirits improved and he heaved an immense breath. "I'm free, altogether free of that old incubus," the idea whipped across his mind. He let himself go: there was a mounting feeling of liberation. "I'm free." At the same time there grew in him a strong yearning, he wished he had a girl to go to that he loved passionately, they could laugh — what a night! He could go to her without any reserve, "I'm a free and happy man now. What do I care! What she sent me? She let me down."

Edward walked about Riverside Drive, had a conversation with a redheaded young man who was studying at the University; met a couple of girls he knew. He called them Hunchback and Cross-eye. Hunchback and Cross-eye were women in their thirties, lived together, were employed in some social work and were of an execrable character. They spied, informed, gossiped, drawing their views from their inexperience and profiting by their ugliness and frailty: people were afraid to attack them. Hunchback had a somber contralto: Cross-eye chattered in a lighter tone. Hunchback at once began deploring the mental attitude of Edward's cousin, Solo. Solo did nothing for politics in his Assembly District. He sat at home playing the violin instead of going round ringing doorbells and distributing leaflets in favor of their local candidate for Congress. Here was a man with great influence: on the radio, Richard Massine and his Serenade Band, from New Jersey.

Edward stood a considerable time on the street-corner talking to these girls in indulgent tones. Their appearance under the lamplight, their dead seriousness, devotion, even their trouble-making, touched him. They were miserable creatures; but they were trying to do something for society; he felt his inferiority. He walked with the girls a block or two away from the corner of Cathedral Parkway and Broadway where they held him and went upstairs with them. They lived poorly in one room and kitchenette, toilet downstairs; they earned well and spent most of their money on their political causes. "Massine has big influence now he is on the radio," said they. Edward laughed, "My Uncle Lou used to be considered the *schlemihl* of the family by my Old Aunt Mary because your candidate Richard Massine was a *wunderkind:* really made money in Europe! Now, he's going to make tours in the Banana Republics and the Sandwich Islands. He can't get back to playing Beethoven. He's no good for classic orchestra even in Punxsutawney, Pa., all the result of getting popular," said he. The girls wanted him to join their group. He said he would, some time. "You want to get active," said they. "What about Little Stage?" said he. They talked a bit about Little Stage and they wanted him to produce the race-drama of a friend of theirs, a young blond chap of twenty-three they were protecting. Edward presently saw it was past eleven and he made his way on to Al Burrows's pharmacy, downtown a few blocks.

When he went in, he got a cup of coffee and a liverwurst sandwich at the soda concession and waited for the pharmacist. Al saw him from a distance, gave him the high sign, shouted faintly, "How's the dog?"

At the counter, at this time of night, were sitting three or four prostitutes from the side streets. It was a "high-class" district and the girls had one-room flats or sometimes collectively took a seven or eight-room apartment in a building waiting to be renovated, near the older parts of the Drive. They had blonde crops or pompadours, short-sleeved dresses and in general looked like rather overdone campus girls; blowzier, had less assurance. Al Burrows knew them all; they both talked to them fatherly. Presently the man with the cigar stand closed his counter and the counter man began wiping up. Al Burrows came out with his street coat on; the girls went slowly out, the lights went out one by one and Edward picked up the package of Madame X's medicine. He said cheerily, "Well, whatever happens, Madame X will get her medicine."

"Is your girl up at Whitehouse?" said Al, arranging the counter.

"My girl's in a bed of roses."

"You don't say?"

"I got an ex-wife now, Al. Thank God, I still have Madame X."

"That's a comfort," said Al, saying good night to the assistant druggists and leading the way out. When he had got the little old Ford started, he folded himself into place behind the wheel and asked Edward what he wanted to do.

"Anythin' — nothin' — suit yourself."

Al started the car and began to laugh. "Two nights ago I was pickled. A friend of ours has a new apartment, he's a black marketeer, and he bought a new apartment bar. He don't know liquor, never drank anything but celery tonic and Coca-Cola before, but now he's in the money, he has to have liquor. So he bought the bar, then invited everyone and then went to the liquor store on his corner for liquor. He didn't know what to order so he ordered everything they suggested, like rye, Scotch, gin, and rum, and then he started asking the prices of things: he wanted to give his friends a good time. So the man sold him the most expensive stuff, benedictine, akvavit, imported champagne, amontillado, anything. He asked for the stuff that cost most; he wanted to show them he knew the right stuff. They sent home some booklets on cocktails. Well, he had started with bad rye and cheap Scotch and he also had white mule, and good rye, and good Scotch; he didn't know the difference — it was liquor. He stacks his cabinet. It looks wonderful. He starts to read the directions in the cocktail book, but he can't make them out, neither can his wife. Previous to this she has only drunk coffee and ice-cream soda.

"I had the day off. I had a sleep in the afternoon and we didn't eat anything because Maidie, that's Sid's wife, Sid's the fellow, Maidie told us not to overload our stomachs, she wanted us to eat at her place. We got there early and Sid had just started to serve drinks. He didn't know how to mix, but he didn't want to let on, so he had just gone round, and taken a measure of four or five things, thrown it into the cocktail shaker with ice and shaken it up as he had seen in the movies. I nearly passed out at the first mouthful. I said, 'What have you got in there, Sid?' I saw people drink rot-gut in prohibition: it was nothing to this. I took charge: I was afraid we'd end up in Bellevue. I said, 'Hey, Sid, what's the idea?' He said, 'It's liquor and it's mixed, isn't it?' My wife Edie passed out. We didn't get home till six-thirty and I had to open the store at eight.

"One time, Edie drank a cupful of a paregoric cough remedy you used to be able to buy by the half-pint for twenty-five cents. Edie never learned any pharmacy; though she was all right for giving out aspirins. She thought it was safe because it was cheap and she had a feverish cold coming on. I had to walk her up and down all night outside the house. We covered miles that night. I had to drag her. She wanted to lie down on every bench and even on the sidewalk. Every time we passed a cop, I had to pretend she was sick and we lived around the corner. A pharmacist's wife who's poisoned; it's like a doctor. You wouldn't stand a chance with any set of twelve good men and true. I had to open the store at eight; so I took her along with me and gave her to one of the chaps, the guy who has the cigar stand, and told him to give her an airing and take her home."

He laughed tolerantly. "That guy didn't come back till two in the afternoon."

Edward sighed. They were toddling gravely, as was the style of Al's old car, and had reached 72nd Street.

"Where to?"

"Thirty-third. Do you care?"

"No. I got nowhere to go."

"Hold on. With these substitute clerks we get, I don't dare go to the movies. All the way through the film, I'm thinking, did that new fellow put in one-eighth of a gram or eight grams. Once I had left a prescription which contained atropine, I was so sure this new fellow'd put in the wrong quantity that I left Edie in the movies and came back to the store. The bottle was tied up. I looked in the prescription book casually to see what had been entered and there I see I'm right: he has written in sixty-four times the quantity. I sent him out on an errand and I analyzed. He had done it. I'm responsible you know. So I made it up over again and scratched out the entry. When he came back, I told him I'd relieve him. So there I was without a clerk again. When we were going through college, there was a nut going through who believed anything because he was always wanting to know the short-cuts. We used to tell him, use the spoon-hollow between the two sinews of your thumb — see, it makes a good measure, it's just one gram; and this fellow had a big hand like me; the hollow in his hand was the size of a teaspoon.

"Years later, I read in the paper one day the trial of a pharmacist who is supposed to have assisted in an arsenic poisoning case. The name struck me and gradually I remembered who it was! He had put into the medicine about a teaspoonful of arsenic; enough to kill a horse. So I went home and measured with my thumb — it was just right. I went to see him in jail and said to him, 'Hey, Eddie, what did you use to measure with?'

"Because this fellow kept on saying he was innocent. He did not mind answering: he told me, 'I used the hollow in my thumb.' He was quite surprised when I told him what a boner he'd pulled. He was going to tell the court about it. We warned him, and he was let off. The jury was impressed with his innocence and there was a chance someone else might have put it in."

"Good God! How many people did he knock off, do you suppose?"

"Oh, I don't suppose any. You'd be surprised at what happens and people don't die. We had a bromide fiend one day . . ." ·

It was just on midnight when they reached Seventh Avenue and 33rd Street.

They stood on the sidewalk. Al looked west and pointed to a white-fronted house with a basement and railing, one of a row. He said, "Louise lives there, but she's not showing a light."

He gave a troubled but proud laugh.

"Louise told my wife that there was no sense in taking hormones: all a woman needs is the right man. Eh? Ha-ha-ha. She ought to know. Louise has had four or five children: four. She didn't reckon on marrying any of the men. Of course, most of them were married. Ha-ha-ha."

"Why do you suppose women want to get married?" said Edward.

Al said good-humoredly, "As the fellow says, if a woman came along and told you she'd keep you all your life just for the pleasure of looking at you, what would you do? When you get a good horse in the shafts, you don't take off the harness and shoo him off. The horse gets all set to bolt, but where can he bolt to? Where can you bolt to even if you're not married? Still, I used to think I'd get out of it. Just before I married Edie, we both went to Los Angeles on a truck just to get out of it. Maybe I'll meet a woman to get me out of it. Do you think I can get out of it?"

"I don't know, Al."

"Someday when I'm drunk I'll tell you something. I won't be drunk enough tonight. Where to now, Edward?"

"Do you want to sleep?"

"Do you want a drink?" said Al, caressingly. They set out for Greenwich Village, continuing down Sixth Avenue.

Al pulled up and pointing, said, "You see that house with the cistern on the roof?"

They were in the Village on Carmine Street, near Bleecker Street. Al laughed. "My mother ran a still there. She'd throw potato peelings, plum stones, anythin' in it — and it would come out liquor. When prohibition came she wanted to go into it with us five boys, so we bought two stills and we had to hoist them up the fire escape one Sunday morning and the super pretended to be at church. We had it all arranged with him. But it was a terrible hoist, and we had to work quick, so that the other tenants wouldn't see it and make it tough for the super. One Sunday it blew up, went through the roof. Everyone ran out in the street. Ma had no idea how to run it. We used to beg and pray her, Ma, don't make it too hard on the still. When we heard the noise we knew what it was and we five ran out in the street and down a whole block, pretending the explosion was a block away. Then we had to sneak back the back way and look for the damage. There was a hole in the roof, the boiling mash everywhere and a stench you could smell ten blocks off. We had to clean up everything before they made an inquiry. We paid off the super and had to work all night. Then we had to get guys in to patch the roof. Well, you know the story. The old bootlegger is dying and he calls his sons round him and says, Let all the women get out. Then he tells them he has a great secret to tell them, it will make their fortune. And he says, You can also make wine out of grapes, boys and he dies. Ha-ha-ha-ha!"

"Let's have a drink," said Edward.

After some discussion, they agreed to go to the Café Royal, on Second Avenue, where Al had been going since his boyhood. He had met his wife there. His friend, Ben Simpson, was always there. He was a sick man who had little to live on and lived meagerly with his mother, in Stuyvesant Street. His mother had not once left this district since she had come over from Riga as a young girl. Ben had an uncle who lived with a horse on Avenue A not far away.

"With a horse?" Edward said and later, "An icebox?"

About three-thirty, Al said he had to open the store at eight and the couple left.

"Where to? Do you want to go to the Turkish bath?" said Al.

"Who's there? Men with no home and damn little hope?"

"You give the man a dollar and he'll get you a bed at the back of the room. There's one room for the men, with about fifty beds; no window though."

"Isn't it better to be at the front?"

"No; everyone tries to get to the back. The men pass you all night going out to the dump. You don't have to go to bed if you're not sleepy. You don't have to stay; we can just look in. The beds are a dollar a night and you can always get in there, when the rest of the town's full, if you pay the guy another dollar. You don't have to take any towels or baths or anything like that."

Al parked the car in a dark side street. In a white brick building, a light burned and illuminated two flights of steps. At the top was a landing from which rose another flight of steps that led to the entrance.

Al stalked ahead of him into a large floor which was divided into dormitories, one for men, one for women, with an assembly room beside. Al winked at the attendant and said, "Are there two beds?"

The man nodded. They looked in and saw a long dormitory with men sleeping on cots. Some of the men had brought their pyjamas, some wore towels, and some were in Adam's costume, sleeping heavily, snoring away, turning and nightmaring in the heat.

"Jesus, a lot of dead men," said Edward, turning away. He walked into one of the assembly rooms which was brilliantly lighted.

Deck-chairs and lounges stood around the walls and in the center were several large tables at which sat enormously fat women playing cards. The women wore light wrappers open in front, or slipping from their shoulders, or bras and drawers both pushed down as far as possible on account of the heat. Some heads were wrapped up in

[239]

bandannas, some were unwrapped with wild black and reddish and dyed blond hair, naturally curled or freshly permanented, writhing in fresh tendrils in the damp hot air. Alongside the women on chairs or on the tables were huge shopping bags gaping, collapsed, with loaves of bread, packages of cooked meats, pickles, Kraft-paper cones of mustard, dried fish and other delicacies pouring from them, each bag a cornucopia. On the tables beside the women, on bits of cloth brought for the purpose or sheets of paper, were hunks of bread, mostly rye and black; but some machine-cut white bread pouring from waxed paper, and beside this slabs of fresh butter, pots of sour and fresh cream, with Italian, Hungarian and German kinds of sausage-meats, galantines and sausage-links beside them, with bits of lettuce and little cardboard boats of potato salad, Russian salad and mixed sour pickles, slices of smoked salmon and "whitefish," little curls of anchovies, sweet-and-sour herrings, their handsome blue and silver-white showing through the milky white of the cream sauce, with onion rings, peppers and capers. The women chewed and laughed and fought holding up their cards in their fat ringed hands, chuckling, roaring with laughter, shaking their huge fallen bellies and breasts, circling on their immense bottoms, wet and pink through the damp wrappers or drawers; and telling, in a language partly American and partly a composite of many foreign languages, the most horribly indecent and ordurous tales that Edward had ever heard. He laughed, blushed, his hair prickled, and sweat ran down his back.

"How do you like these Minnies?" said Al, standing behind him and laughing softly.

"Let's get out of here; we'll go to my place," said Edward.

"Why: can't you stand the Minnies?"

"Sure; but I couldn't sleep on a cot back there at the end of the dormitory; it reminds me of the army when we were in Texas in summer."

Al stood listening to a tale told by a glistening jolly ogress, sitting

[240]

opposite to them and shamelessly exposing her monstrous fat parts, with chuckles. As she told, she dealt with a dashing, cunning air, her strong fat face with its straight clear eyes was the kind of face that is called masculine, but she was an immense projection of the feminine, in all. She was winning. The tale was about her husband and his partner and some woman they had both thought they would win: and all told with a huge carnal application to the bestial joys of body union and to every part of the body as it wound and writhed in those acts; and all with a gay slobbering smacking power that was almost grace, like the youthful sports of a giant. The woman spotted Al and waved her fat hand briefly.

"Come in and have a sandwich; bring your friend," she said with eagle looks, trying to penetrate the nature and business of the friend and then returning to her cards with the contempt of a matron for any youth of Edward's appearance and nature.

"No thanks, Goitie; my friend's got to get home."

"What for? Is he married? And if he is, what the hell does it matter?"

"No, no, we've got to get home. I just looked in to see if Mrs. Franklin was here; I've got a message for her."

"Rose has gone home," said the fat matron shortly, looking at her cards and dismissing them both. A woman at the head of the table, a good-natured, neighborly sort was giggling and telling a story she thought very dirty. The "Big Minnie" frowned, clacked and stared at her cards impatiently. She shouted to the neighborly one, "Idiot, idiot; shut your trap."

The men went away, paid the attendant half a dollar each, took their valuables again and got into the car. Outside, for the moment, it seemed cool. They heaved big breaths of air.

"What is that smell?" said Edward.

"Don't expect me to say the fresh air," said Al politely.

At Edward's home, they took a beer and then Al went upstairs to sleep. Edward looked round in the icebox for something that Al could have for breakfast. This icebox, which was his, was used by Mrs. Annichini and some of the girls upstairs who had none. They did not mind him taking some little things; in the end it worked out. He found some of those glossy hard jaw-breakers, called bagels, some ham belonging to Miss Holland, took one of a large plate of cold meat balls, coated with white grease, and covered these with a piece of paper on a plate, then put them back in the icebox. One of the quarts of milk belonged to him. He wrote a note in a big blank bound book which he had got from some publisher friend, and which he kept for messages to Al. He wrote, "The ham and hamburger and bagels are for you, Al," and left the book open, and was so engaged with other thoughts while doing this that he did not hear the door open. He heard Mrs. Annichini say, "Why didn't you say you were coming home, Edward?"

He turned round and saw her in her pink trimmed nightdress, with open flowered wrapper.

"My boy, you look tired! I can't sleep in this hot weather. And poor Blanche cried all night. When the light is out, she cannot see us and she thinks everyone is dead. What shall I do with her?"

"I don't know, Annitchke. Give her back."

"And the fleas worry her. I cut ten dog-fleas out of knots in her fur."

"For God's sake, don't tell them that."

"Her fur is all ragged looking now. They will think I did something to her. Every morning, when I get up, I wring out my pillow, it is sopping wet with perspiration. It was so hot today you could have fried eggs in the bathroom bowl," she said, repeating one of Edward's own jokes.

"It was a blisterer. The rain did nothing," said Edward.

"A ball of blue light as big as a cabbage came over the church and fell in the street," said Mrs. Annichini.

"It was a wonderful day. And lions roared in the streets."

"It was like lions. What is the matter, my poor boy, what is the matter, Edward?"

"My girl got married today, tonight, the night that is passing, that is, my wife, Margot, I mean. And Al took me out to heal my so-called mind."

"Oh, my poor boy, my poor boy, my poor boy. I am so sorry, so sorry."

"Don't keep it up Annitchke; or I'll burst out crying."

"I'm sorry my boy, so sorry. Why did she do it?"

"I never thought she'd leave me."

"Oh, Edward, why did she do it?"

"I asked her to marry me yesterday but she turned me down."

"You see, you came too late," said Mrs. Annichini, going to the stove and looking at the coffee. She took the coffee off the stove and threw it down the sink. She put on a kettle to make more. She turned round to Edward. "Sit down, Edward; I'll make you some fresh coffee."

"Yes, all right, I am going to take a walk. The coffeepots are closed now and I want to walk until it's light, and then I'll come back and then go up to Whitehouse. The trouble with me has been, Annitchke, that I'm selfish, I live too much alone. She wanted me to marry her before I went away and I wouldn't. I don't like her funny brother. I didn't want him up at Whitehouse."

Edward realized that he was hurting the feelings of Mrs. Annichini who was very rarely invited to Whitehouse. Mrs. Annichini said, "Go back to Whitehouse tomorrow, dear boy; it is such a lovely place. You will rest there."

"Yes."

They drank their coffee. It was well after five. He looked in on Al and found him pulling on his big greased shoes.

"Aren't you going to get some sleep before you open the store?" asked Edward.

Said Al with his ringing laugh, "You must have been in the clouds!

Didn't you hear me arranging Al's Ride with Bennie? The man who wants to put me into business, the one who likes carpentry, you know? My pal Truex found me an apartment on Third Avenue near 86th: there's a store near there that I could get for three thousand dollars: there's a concession and that's the only part of the store does any business, and all night girls and young housewives running down, flirt with the drug clerk. I could get rid of that concession, patch up the floor, you can put your leg through it now, and start out with premiums — Truex will put up the money and put up the shelves. There's an apartment, the store — no furniture. I'm moving in tuhmorruh. The old lady's jibbing a bit, but she don't mind sleeping on the floor, we've done it before — when we were married! Be good for the old lady: she'll settle down a bit perhaps."

He laughed.

"And Uncle Bennie?"

"I'm borrowing the horse and cart. Uncle Bennie's giving me an old chest of drawers someone left on account and a bust of Mozart! Bennie's giving me some drapes his sister doesn't like and a big white dressing gown with a tail from a play, that's for Edie. Some pals in 8th Street are giving me a picture a yard square, reproduction of Renoir and someone else don't want his Burliuk no more."

"There's all that junk in the basement, two ironing boards, two old bikes, a rubber bath curtain, you can have that iron bed of West-fourth's," said Edward.

"I'm taking all offers: I'll call at your place on the way up," said Al.

"I'll meet you there."

Then they parted. In the morning Edward and Al drove the cart uptown. "Louise" gave Al the remnants of a dozen glasses he once gave her and Al got some new electric goods from his brother, while two actors Al played pinochle with gave a blue tomcat, a large stew-pan and some books, and Edie's sister, the one who was going to camp, was waiting at home with a chair and a milking stool: so they went to Oneida's where Edward (after telephoning) gave them a cut-glass fruit bowl too heavy to use and a set of dishes Lou won (he always won) in a bingo at a cheap movie. The cart moved uptown, with Al stopping at all kinds of addresses to get things: the stop at Hunchback and Cross-eye's — "they're good girls," said Al: "they're good for Al the Fixer" — and from them he got a Mexican palmleaf horse and a Mexican fireproof dish. "I just blew in and I blowin' out and on."

Zestful, jestful they arrived at the new home — the store — Edward bought a bunch of flowers. Truex came with planks. Edward was left alone once more. But he was not depressed. He remembered a friend of his in the army who had been in the jailhouse for a couple of days. When he came out he had thrown everything, identification, papers, money, everything in the river. Edward had a sturdier attachment to the earth: he could not bring himself to throw things away — what difference would it make? The house is mine, the family is mine, Whitehouse is mine — I have too many things that cannot be thrown away. That other fellow had owned nothing, had been in debt, had been unhappy with his wife, and later had got killed.

The earlier part of the night he had forgotten. He began to walk back and as he approached 42nd Street he realized he would be in time for the first bus to Whitehouse. He felt in his pocket; he had Madame X's medicine. He just made the bus and squatted in it when it rolled out. It was raining in the country, but fresh and inviting. As they entered the Pocono hills, and stopped at the halfway house there, he realized that he was going home. After this, he fell asleep and only awoke at the next stop. Presently the clouds were higher and parted. Then the bus began to ascend towards Whitehouse, with the long wall of mountains, and their strange cloves rolling alongside at the left, and the lower country mountains rolling towards them. As the road kept rising, he began to feel happy. As they entered the true uplands where Whitehouse is, he smiled to himself and felt a boyish happiness at the sight of heavy grass-heads outside a church, and old thick trees and the mountains still rising, new-cropped grass, long thigh-like rises spattered with old fruit trees, the half-neglected rich-earthed farms which have been turned to pleasuring and summer homes, interspersed with a few real farms; the land ever rising, and the trees surging over home-stands of grass and vegetables, well-fed cows in tan and white, brown earth, rainy blues and grays, the sullen still aspect of heavy-yielding fields and more and more the wooden houses surrounded by crook-limbed apple trees and sculptured pears. As they entered the country of upland valleys and high mountains in which Whitehouse lies he had forgotten the dark blood and smoke and sorrow of New York. All this during the war had lain and was then as now, and his family's life had been the same. The years flew past, they did not know they were getting older, neither did he. He left the bus in the village to get a loaf of bread and some butter and bacon and a few other things he thought they might like. Plodding up the rising road which led to the Massine home farm, he felt his life flow back into him, strong, heavy, with an assurance of long life. He had never once thought of committing suicide, every thought of death was repugnant to him. "It is only conscience makes me want to work; what is wrong with Whitehouse? What is wrong with a quiet life and hurting no one?" he thought as he began to puff up the last rise. The Massine road had now branched off from the main road which was solid and asphalted and ran between half-cleared stands of trees and the family houses.

He hoped to walk in on them while they were having breakfast, Lou pouring the milk on his cornflakes, Old Mary thanking every one robustly, blindly, looking with her hand for the sugar, the spoon, the sisters sipping their coffee while they moved between bread-oven and cream-cheese filter: while they let the dogs and the cats out, or the other way about, Oneida feeding Musty in one part of the kitchen while the Abbot cheeped at the wire door and Madame X ate else-where. While he was smiling rather grimly at this vision he heard a sharp voice, and looking up perceived Oneida stoutly toddling down the rutted and grass-grown road, with Madame X waddling in front and Musty panting behind her. The Abbot, to whom she was calling, could be seen flying like a swallow in cloud and his movement, like a swallow, over the tall grasses of the near field. Edward smiled. Oneida had pulled on her faded much-washed overalls, which were, with much wear, soft as satin, but were muddy round the ankles from her gardening. Underneath she wore the beautiful silk night-smock Edward had bought her: it was hand-worked in pink round the neck and had short puffed sleeves. She had hastily pulled up into a crown her two fat black pigtails, tied with flowered cotton. Her black eyes were alive with her present squall, and her freckled cheeks rosy with exertion.

"Edward!"

She rushed to him, he to her, and panting both, they hugged and kissed. She asked him nothing about his trip to town, but started about Dan. Dan was causing Big Jenny to be ill, and how had Edward gotten there so early — oh, they would all be so glad to see him; it had been dull with him away.

They had stopped, in the long shadows, in the warm dewy air, opposite the stone pillars, built for the gates which were never hung.

"Grandfather is buried in one of the gates," said Edward: "and I shall be buried in the other."

"Ha-ha-ha," she said laughing and weeping, "oh, you will never die!"

"Won't I?"

"Oh, the day after I do, the day after I do."

He turned away from her, with a set face and thoughtfully, without answering her, climbed the slope: but she, clever and kind, came quietly after, whispering to the dogs. From the windows of White-house, Sambo and other dogs who had just come, sent out their salvoes: and there was Lou, in old blue cotton dungarees, with his iron-gray thicket of hair tousled, waving both hands in welcome.

Part Four

WHITEHOUSE IN
AUTUMN

THIS year, they stayed till mid-October and missed the first of the concert season. It had turned bitterly cold by that time. The Solways, Lou and Oneida, had at last moved from the sleeping balcony to their room with the pianos; and Edward had moved to Little Jenny's room at the head of the stairs cold from exposure on both sides. But under the blankets he had brought from the army and patchwork quilts and covers faded in the use of dogs and man, he was very warm. His army coat reposed on top of him. He slept between blankets now without linen. He slept long and comfortably, hid from the cold and every night, now, since mid-August, he had slid quickly into sleep in the voluptuous long embraces of his rich delicate and rosy thoughts, fragments of the many night hours he had spent with the woman he now called "my ex-wife." Westfourth, wounded in a midnight battle with some wild animal, could not get well: he was dying with a gangrened foot. The others had to go home but the three of them had decided to wait up in the mountains until it was time to "put him to sleep." They would then bury him in the old overgrown apple orchard where Tobacco and Axy and Picky and many another old family friend reposed. The beautiful old cat moved from chair to chair and cushion to cushion through all the benches, window seats, armchairs, mattresses of the house making plaintive sounds and trying to ease the ache. Although nothing could be done to cleanse the rotting wound properly, they nursed him as before, Lou went for walks with the animal in his arms and they were delighted when he purred. Meanwhile, Oneida was humming with indignation, flashing with life: and the entire family talk heaved and bubbled with several sensational bits of news. They throve on it: how happy and concerned they all were! Richard (Solo) engaged himself for a professional tour in outlying parts of the world, South Africa, Australia, and was trying to visit Russia, too. Ollie giggled, Oneida had never heard anything so ridiculous and ungrateful: "He doesn't know how to live; what is the idea of leaving us? Besides, he never invited the family once in his life!" Big Jenny said, "The dear boy: that's great news!" Old Mary said, "What does he want with blocked rubles? He can earn good money on the radio." Solo himself came up to Whitehouse for several week ends to practice with Lou, and was pursued all over the house with Oneida's taunts. "Why must you leave the United States? Isn't it big enough for you here?" But her real lament came back every day, "He's going away to enjoy himself and his idea is never to let us see him again! He's sick of us! Old Mary tied him hand and foot and now he's taking his revenge." Suttinlay laughed a lot and Solo, imitating Russian, Hungarian and Viennese musicians, was called by Lou, "Maestro!"

Victor-Alexander flung his bombshell suddenly in a dinner hour at Dan Barnes's house in Long Island. He was going to pull down the high walls of Solitude. They had not been high enough to keep out the sow-thistle and though he had nearly pulled his arms out of the sockets, and worked from 4 A.M. to midnight, and mined and blasted his land, nothing could be done. He had spent the last remnant of his money following the astrological stock-exchange advice of a Dr. Asthur and had now to go to work. He proposed that the family should buy in his house (the land was theirs) and let him as tenant overlord run the whole of Whitehouse as a farm: in the winters he would live with various members of the family, organizing their social events, as receptions after Lou's concerts, weddings, dinners and the rest of it. He proposed to begin with Dan Barnes whose wife, Big Jenny, was now almost entirely incapacitated though as good, big-hearted, loving as ever.

They asked Edward's advice. He laughed. He felt only a pleasant boredom, the ability to stretch each day out endlessly, and enjoy its fat and empty hours, like an invalid in hospital; and he luxuriated in the thought that this life could go on like this for a long, long time "centuries of Massine time." He often lay in the grass and felt only an ecstasy, no thought, no form, no sound: a wave of night, a sea of living sleep. Now, night after night, and when he was alone in the daytime, wandering in the thick grass, hidden in the plantations, old grass-grown orchards, or behind the windbreak where his father had slung his hammock, he, when alone, heard the birds that called, the catbird or some other bird, perched on the withered top of the Lombardy poplar, saw the oriole flash through the sump-planting, the American canary through the weeds, and lay down, his head pillowed on an arm and watched the grasses, the insect clouds, a tree tremble slightly as it was told mysteriously of a wind many miles distant, but that would come this afternoon.

There was plenty to do. The vegetable garden and the flower garden should have been got ready. The roof of the huge double barn needed repairs; the chicken farm had to be fixed for winter, holes filled, fences repaired, seeds taken in, plants cut down.

It was getting colder. Lou's hand, hard, supple, large, now began to get blue and stiff as he practiced. His programs for his tour were ready. They spent much of the long evenings in the warm kitchen playing family games of cards, and a good part of the mornings sitting by the fire in the sitting room. When they had to build a fire in Lou's music-room it was time to move to town. The heating would be turned on in three days in their town homes.

The hills had turned red and yellow, wiping out the streaks of pale and dark green. There were ground frosts. But Westfourth could not travel.

One day when Oneida, depressed, was with Madame X on the

bench outside the music-room, Madame X began to bark furiously at her mistress. The intolerable barking rose in intensity, went on and on. At last, Lou came to the door and looked at them both, "Music hath charms to soothe the savage breast."

Then he went inside and began to build up the walls of music again with which he surrounded himself. But later, he said to Edward, "Poor Madame X; I should not have let her see I was angry: I thought she would leave us this summer." His large eyes clouded and he continued, "Why shouldn't we be buried with them, with the others? I should like them and all of us to be buried in Whitehouse. I am an outsider like them, but they shared my life."

At night, he kept the poor old cat near him in spite of his ill-smelling wound and as he loved, before closing up, to go and look at the heavens if the night was clear or at the storm if it moved the grass he would take the cat with him, to see that darkness that made his splendid eyes gleam.

"He is beautiful but he is ill; why must he suffer any more?" asked Leander, in the beginning of November, when he came to shut up all the cottages for winter.

Oneida said nothing. She was beating eggs in a basin; the basin rang.

Even Oneida at last relented. She carried on a fierce courageous resistance to death, but in the end, Leander, Edward and Lou and Oneida weeping, and Dan Barnes who had come up for the occasion with Big Jenny who had got out of bed, and Victor-Alexander, went down to the Whitehouse vet, and brought back the dead cat and buried old Westfourth in the gnarled orchard, half buried now in withered grasses and sow thistles.

"There is Axy," said Oneida. "There is Carrots, there is Tobacco, here is Westfourth, he was only a barn cat, everyone made so much of him, he was only a barn cat: when they were all kittens the three others stayed up in the barn but Westfourth always found his way in through the door. He was so clever with doors! I never knew a cat like that. He would stand up against one with a defective latch and bounce himself against one with an automatic close and scratch hard when he knew a door was bolted." She turned round to Lou with sparking eyes. "Lou, we have no cat now!"

"The day he ran out on the road on July the Fourth," said Lou, "when he was a kitten and we knew, the drunken drivers, we knew, and he kept stealing across to that field of grass, in his cute sly way looking back at us — the cars came hallooing down the road — and you remember he would follow us down the road, flying after us when we weren't looking, before we had him altered — "

"That same summer the boys stole him, but he came back," said Oneida. There was now a silence for no one, Edward, not Leander, no one was fit to speak. They turned the sod over old Westfourth and all went to the house. "I'll make you a soufflé for lunch," said Oneida. "There's just enough." She had a hoarse voice, she could hardly speak at all: and on the way to the kitchen she gathered up all the dogs, and shut herself into the kitchen, ringing on the basins and whistling and talking to the dogs.

"Everything goes on the same and yet something is dead and we will never see it again," said Lou. "This is stupid and Lou so fastidious!" thought Edward but he felt out at elbow with himself. "Perhaps Lou is right." Lou had large globular eyes sunk deep in his straight slits: these eyes between dark fringes shone. He had high long cheekbones, a squat yet open face. "What can things matter if some one thing is dead, after all?" said Lou. The high light in the sky rainy, gray, blue, but as if filtered through a rainbow made all spectacularly clear. They sat looking at the change of scene as the rain approached from up the valley. Said Edward, "*Imperious Caesar, dead and turned to clay, might stop a hole to keep the wind away.*"

They were all weeping.

"We were here one whole winter, alone with the two great Danes," said Big Jenny. "Oh, it was cold! And every night they rattled their chains and at last they burst them and rushed at the kitchen door and

[255]

burst it in with so much thumping and roaring!" She laughed and laughed but weeping: "They rushed upstairs to where they knew Oneida and I were sleeping, only we weren't sleeping! We thought it was burglars."

Thus Victor-Alexander came back to Whitehouse to lunch.

They were now free to move and they moved two days later. It was decided that Musty was to live now with Oneida so that both old dogs could get their injections on the same day. Edward was so absent-minded, they said, he would neglect the old dog: and the "principal thing was to keep Musty alive till spring when Whitehouse would rejuvenate him." One of the great subjects of discussion was now the new Russian "cure for old age" as they termed it. They heard, after many inquiries, that a Park Avenue doctor had sent to Russia for it and would soon have it. But the price of the injections was so high that with all their good-natured scraping and pinching they could not buy it for their old dog friends. They had always been in favor of socialized medicine but moved into an active family propaganda for it now. How angry Oneida was that the dogs of the rich could have this treatment, perhaps, and her poor dogs not. "And then there are poor old men and women," said Oneida.

Edward, in all this, was living with the Solways, waiting for Nate the Croat to finish his room. Materials were hard to get and painters were scarce at that moment. He walked over every day to chat with Nate and the repairman and when Irene came home at five-thirty he went in to chat with her. They often went out to eat and drink in some nearby Third Avenue place. "And to think that I might have been married now instead of at a loose end." And he would snicker at the grotesqueness of that remark.

The same long, naked nights went on and Edward, going out for his walks, "no wife, no dog, no hall bedroom," would come back to find them still discussing the problem of Victor-Alexander. In the meantime Victor-Alexander was nursing Big Jenny and he proved an excellent nurse, strong, gentle, an. excellent cook but given to bursts of creative fury when no one could restrain him from giving dinner parties to the family all in the best French style and all a source of ridicule, of course, to the family. "Well, he knows how to live" said Oneida.

Another problem arose. Nate the Croat had mixed the wrong paint and got a violent blue on Edward's new walls. He had to repaint it. The family became intensely interested in blues mixed with black, red, gray and so on. Victor-Alexander came to see them about it. He disdainfully said that Edward could not put in (as he had proposed) those wax candles in the candlesticks from his mother: he must put in gray or pale yellow. Victor-Alexander made a special trip to Whitehouse and brought back from Solitude two very fine and dainty Sèvres china groups of young lovers. At the same time he would envisage the room as holding also a picture of blue shadows from Whitehouse woods done twenty years and more ago by Edward's father. "We must have Doctor Edward's picture in Edward's room." Then came the question of Dr. Edward's sign plate. "It would be simpler for me to study medicine," said Edward.

Oneida said, "I have a feeling that he is not going back. I think he is discouraged."

Lou spoke gently.

"There, Oneida, where is your theory now that he put thistles in your land?"

She said, "He told me himself it all came from some cheap manure he got from the farmer in the next valley. I said to him at the time, You will regret, Victor-Alexander, departing from your custom; it never pays. He said he could not afford tested manures at that time."

Lou scratched his head and swung round on the piano stool, began his exercises on the dumb-piano. He said in his soft sorry voice, "It just proves you cannot see tomorrow's stock market quotations in a crystal ball, as Walt says."

"Then he will give up Solitude."

It was necessary, of course, for them to find a home for Victor-Alexander.

"He can live in my bachelor's boudoir" said Edward dryly.

This earned him a sharp look from Oneida who thought he might be about to marry Irene.

Edward spoke to Nate the Croat the next day and found that he could refinish the apartment in its new color, a dull blue with ivory black mixed in it, by the week end. He thought, too, "I would give my right arm not to see any of us again. It would be a good idea to leave it to Victor-Alexander and get the hell out. I hope I never spend another evening chewing the rag and telling the old snapper-end stories."

Where could he go? He knew two hundred people at least who could put him up for that is the way in New York, people become friends overnight and are at once and forever ready to offer bed and board. New York is one of those villages. But all of these friends would mean the old life. At one time, the family had meant everything to him, he had been sulkily, greedily happy in it. Now he had lost Margot — and even Musty — Since he had been left alone without Musty, a perpetual daily ache in his heart had come to reinforce the irregular pain of Margot's indifference. The little foolish dog that he hated to see now, for his aged imbecility, still recalled to him his old-time days. Since the departure of this little foolish dog, coming after Margot's marriage, he had felt a hunger in his heart and when he got up in the morning, he wanted to sleep again, for fear of facing the empty day.

"I have too little to do, but nothing attracts me."

Part Five

SCRATCH PARK

EDWARD began to arrange things in his room which had not been touched since his father's and mother's time; for in a day or two they had to be either boxed and carted down to the basement or to Oneida's, or be taken upstairs. He had little room upstairs. Among them he found a life-size mask in plaster, painted green-bronze. It was a mask of his friend, Philip Christy, Dr. Innings's optician who had a fashionable store on Madison Avenue near 57th Street and who lived with his old sister in a poor rooming house near 125th Street. Philip Christy made glasses for various Massines and charged them various prices according to their bank balances. He admired people in the measure that they were failures in life and had lost all ambitions. Those who succeeded or still struggled for position in the big town he regarded as comical sorts, unreasonable, mere jots of souls, something like animals or children. His grandly indifferent soul was gifted with the kind of penetration which is called cynical, satirical; in fact he was unscrupulously sharp and instant in his judgments. He saw what men and women did for a small, dreary, mediocre position in life and he mocked their miserable crimes, their petty venality, their inconspicuous success, the dreadful failure of the heart, which they tried to compensate by lechery (he was indifferent to lechery though a lecher): and out of indifference and a passionate attachment to all the wonderful early ways of the century, the Tammany Hall days, the dirty days when anyone could find his way out of anything, and the anarchist days, when anyone could

[261]

hope his way out of anything, he liked large misdemeanor, generous crime. He showed this divine humor only to the nonchalant like Edward, or socialist theorists like Walt or (his beloved) the disabused, kind fixers like Al Burrows, or disgraced people and poor, the Third Avenue element, or unfortunate criminals.

Christy had no patience at all with the climbing and made-over suburban women spending black-market money and full of clumsy coquetry; to these he was rude and he overcharged them. Philip Christy, with a wealthy client, was a formidable creature; no one would have dared familiarity with him. The next moment, the client gone, he would go to the back room which was separated from the studio only by a little passage and a handsome heavy silk curtain, and he would call out some friend of his, Walt, Edward, who was keeping him company, or, more often than that, some dead-beat actor out of a job, defrocked priest, itinerant worker, wretch who had drunk himself out of a job, gangster in hiding — the naturally guilty scapegoats of the population, the hungry and the rats.

Some such humble friend would sit with Philip on the leather divan, a piece of furniture so well and deeply upholstered that it felt like satin. They would lounge against the fashionable cushions, and spread their broken shoes on the beautiful dun carpet. His own shoes were run down. When the shop downstairs warned him that a client was coming, he dismissed his friend, placed himself behind the desk and assumed the air of a society consultant. The glasses were always ready in time and, if they were still in the workshop behind, he had only to press a button, and his assistant would bring them to him. He rarely left his desk and if his courteous act of the moment asked for it, then he maneuvered skillfully so that his shoes never came into view.

He was not too poor to buy shoes: he did not care about them. Besides, he needed his money for other things; his friends, his pleasure and a little for the upkeep of the store and to take food home to be cooked by his sister. His pleasure was only one and it was simple. He drank enormous quantities of one brand of bonded rye whiskey and mostly lived upon it. He was fifty-seven and so robust had he been originally that in spite of his vice only in the last few years had he given up polishing the lenses himself. Even now he would go into the workshop and show some assistant how to polish: he had at one time an incredible precision.

He was short, with a singularly deep and broad chest, strong limbs, large face and large hands of beautiful cut and mobility. Edward's plaster mask, although carefully done, was by no great artist and, in any case, could not show the luminousness, proportion and expression of the face. Under a steep and broad forehead, were two large blue eyes, the flesh about them cut like gems. He had a large, fleshy, sensual nose, a long, well-opened but finely cut mouth which disappeared into light folds at the corners. His striking beauty was not only in the refinement of sensuality expressed in the lines but in the expression. His flesh could shine from within as a lantern; he was often masked by an expression of noble contempt, rage or indifference.

His remarks were not all humane. He was moved by no usual considerations. He did not say the polite thing and coaxing old age, pretty youth, simpering childhood, the benevolent, the public altruist did not move him: he would say, "This is a dishonest back-biting old woman; he's flabby, he'll sell out for professor's pay; he's just a two-by-four fraud, a chameleon; how did you get ten thousand a year, George, if you're a socialist? They know you're not."

At the same time, he started, snarled, and would battle in his confident way with anyone who described an unfortunate as "poor, vulgar, mean, a self-made man, an auto-didact" in short, for any expression which indicated to him pertness in the speaker. He was large about vice and fraud. Strength, skill and low vice are levelers. Lifelong soaks and drifters and ne'er-do-wells are likely to have a great humanity, wisdom; they are sages of a sort, on condition that they never reform. The reformed drunkard and wastrel is usually undependable and will corrupt for two cents.

In Edward's boredom, loneliness, aimlessness, when his family and old habits were repugnant to him, the mysterious pleasures of Philip's life, these pleasures, affections and lives which cost nothing, were worth nothing, and took place in an even stranger setting than that at Whitehouse, appealed to him. Here he was acceptable, as acceptable as in his family, but an unknown. He was not "that man Edward we have heard about all our lives." In that circle they spoke about no one. He did not know from what came his horror of his present condition. Oneida took it lightly. She had been startled to know that he had actually offered marriage to Margot and said she was indignant that Margot had turned him down. He was surprised to see that he did not care to take walks. He had lost his dog and he had no interest in the people he used to meet with their dogs. He no longer recognized them and they, since he was without his dog, and they had never looked into his face, did not recognize him. Once he had to explain, "I am the man who used to have the Scotty." He had all the appearance of the homeless bachelor who is looked at with patronizing good-will or concealed irritation by families.

He put the plaster mask of Christy on the table in the mess of things and sat down to look at it; though it was not it that he was looking at. He remembered how once his father and mother had rebuked him for being without ambition. To escape reproach, he had at that moment gone for a week to the rooming house kept by the Christys, relatives of Mrs. Annichini, in Harlem. They had not been surprised at his arrival; they gave him a room; and they had not been surprised when he left. It all seemed to them natural; and to Edward himself. And he had the joy of thinking that for once he did not know what his family was saying about him, nor did they know anything about him.

"I will do it," said Edward. For the first time in weeks, he had a sparkle of activity. He began boxing his things in heaps, went upstairs to tell Nate that he left the painting and finishing to him, and he gave Lola, the Negro girl, instructions about the furniture upstairs. Nate would get someone in to move the stuff. He then invited Victor-Alexander to dinner and, after dinner, took him to look over the flat.

"While I am away, you can use it," he said, "and when I come back, we will see what other arrangements we can make. In the meantime, it is your home; arrange the furniture as you like, do whatever you like."

Victor-Alexander then spoke solemnly about what he would owe, on what terms he could arrange to pay; and afterwards showed a grave eagerness to move in.

"If you will leave everything to my taste, you will never regret it."

In the morning he threw some things into a grip, took the L at 18th Street and got out at 125th Street, about twenty minutes later. The rooming house which Christy called the "Flop," was a few minutes' walk from the station. It was about ten in the morning. Housewives were sweeping doorsteps, buying food in fish or meat stores, the sidewalks were dirty, busy. He felt very happy as he turned into the street which ended almost at the Triborough bridge. Garbage was thrown about on the sidewalks, coal was going down the chutes and children were hopping in the gutters. He felt a long way from his own home. It was a long time since he had been there and he hardly recognized the "Flop" at first. But his feet had a good memory: they led him to it. He saw that there were clean curtains in the first and second floors and that they had washed the windows of a second-floor room, his, he supposed. Christy's whippet, Lady, curled like a pool of molasses on a worn bit of coconut matting, at the door, getting the thin sun. She looked sick. Some bedroom mats lay across the entry with a carpet-beater beside them, and a mop stood against the banisters. He heard Nell Christy talking on the phone: so he put down his bag by the mop and went across the street to a small

[265]

grocery store where he had bought things on other occasions when he had visited the Christys.

"Hello, Mrs. Narks."

The fresh-faced middle-aged woman looked at him curiously. He grinned. "I remember you from seven years ago. I'm going to stay with the Christys across the street."

"Plenty of people from downtown stay with her. They're old Harlemites."

"She used to live over near Mount Morris Park."

"It's all colored there now," said the woman.

"Sure," he said in his grudging, meditative tone. He went out slowly, lifting his finger to his hat. He deposited his goods in the entry and went to the A & P to get a duck. He did not like the A & P grocer to see that he had been elsewhere; he fancied he would be hurt. The clerks in the A & P were new: he was disappointed. He liked to astonish people pleasurably by remembering their names. At any rate, he listened and learned the names of the new clerks. After careful inspection, he bought the best of three ducks and went back to the Christys'. It was a short slum street ending in a patch of grass with a bench, which Christy called "Scratch Park." Homeless unemployed men sat there in the daytime, slept there at night until the nights began to freeze. A lame boy, in braces, laughed and shouted with a crowd of children who treated him without consideration. He was a bright lad with red cheeks and brown curls, the son of the man who sold coals in the cellar. When Edward crossed the street, two small boys, with a homemade truck, were standing in front of Nell Christy's door, knocking and shouting feebly, "Miss Christy!" In the truck were splinters of wood. Edward went in, saying he would call her.

"What's it for?"

"Miss Christy always buys our wood, mister."

"O.K. I'll tell her."

He went in along the passage and Miss Christy came out, with a broom, a duster tied round her neck and her old apron around her waist.

"Hello, Edward: I thought you'd come later: I thought you got up at noon."

"Shame, shame! What a greeting! You have callers."

She went out to the little boys and came back with her apron full of wood. The little boys went away seriously, talking, pulling their truck by a string. She said, "They bring me wood whenever they pick it up on the lot round here and I give them ten cents. They help their mother."

So saying, she led the way into the kitchen. This was a big room stretching the width of the house and taking up one half the depth. It looked out on a small back yard partly paved and partly earth in which were some rags of plants. Several chickens appeared behind wire netting at the back. The large-paned windows looked out there. There were four doors, one to the yard, one to the coal cellar, one to the corridor, and one, blocked up, led into the front room. A couch stood across this one, but the panes of glass of the door, masked by a curtain, looked into the front room. In a white-washed alcove stood a wood and coal stove, no longer used, and a large gas stove stood beside it. An old horsehair couch stood under the back windows. In the middle of the room was a battered wooden table, covered with an oil cloth, and flanked by several wooden chairs. There was a radio and a few old books. Edward put his provisions on the table.

"Oh, Edward, I bought a duck for lunch. I got it at the A & P. There were only four and this was the best. I'll wash my hands and put it on." He showed his duck and they joked about the two ducks. Nell said, "Sit on the couch while I get the duck ready. I sleep there usually. I like to sleep in the kitchen, I have a room upstairs but usually someone comes along to sleep in my room."

"Will I finish the stairs for you?"

"No — a girl comes tomorrow. You know, Flossie?"

"Is Flossie still around?"

She put the food away in the icebox, prepared the duck. He sat idly on the older couch under the inside window, not her bed. She put on the radio. The plastered walls of the kitchen were dingy. There were half curtains on both sets of windows. It was an icy day. He could see the street children down the passage, running round in ski-suits. When she had put the duck in the oven and told him he need not watch it, she went out, shutting the passage door. It was very quiet, much quieter than Edward's own house, which, though supported by stupendous oak beams, trembled with every truck and roared with the passage of the elevated. Nell was cleaning in the corridor. It was reasonably warm in the kitchen and there was nothing to distract the eye. Edward sighed, took off his coat, and rolled up his sleeves. He leaned back on the couch and listened to the radio. Presently, Nell came in, washed her hands and took out the vegetables. She was a bright-faced woman about sixty, with short white hair. She went on talking rather nervously about friends, lodgers, and made him feel as if he had been there already six months.

"Is that all there is to ducks?"

"Yes. What else do you want me to do?" she said anxiously.

He laughed, "I don't know. Will it be all right?"

"Yes. It's not a good duck, but they generally turn out all right."

"It's nice here. It's a real home."

"It's very ordinary here."

"I'm happy here anyway."

"There was a woman we knew a long time ago, a French woman. She came here once or twice when she was tired of being at home with her husband and mother-in-law. When she felt they were going to quarrel, she came away for a few days."

"Why did she go home again?"

Nell laughed, but went on, "There was an English woman used to come and stay here too. I understand why you come. She said she

[268]

wanted to feel she was with people. She was an artist. She stayed three months once. I have her photograph somewhere."

Nell got out an old cardboard box and sat down on the couch but in the dumpy alert way of a woman who may have to answer the door at any moment. She held out the photographs in her swollen hands, sorting them out: she was now neither tense nor nervous. She showed Edward several photographs, some of which were faded and yellow. She said, "That's the English woman — no, that's a model my brother Norman used to have; she stayed with us, too." She showed a picture of her brother with his wife and child and said, "I love that little girl." Then she found another photograph and showed it to Edward, but she said, "I don't know if that's a picture of Betty, the English woman, the model, or myself. It is so faded."

It showed a handsome woman of thirty, with a broad forehead, strong, well-modeled face, and body, dressed in a blouse and long skirt.

"It looks like you."

She considered it, then found another photograph.

"No, that's Elsie, the model; she stayed with us for months; I loved that girl."

This was a woman in her late twenties, with a fine figure and strange eyes, like split unshelled almonds.

"This one's blonde."

"Yes, that's Elsie. I was dark."

She gave him the old cardboard box, and said, "I understand what you want; I understand it. Many people have come to us." She got up, smoothing down her faded housedress.

"I must give Lady her lunch."

"She smells like distemper, Nell."

"I know, but Philip says she has a touch of the grippe. I don't think she's well. He gave her a dose of whiskey. He says it cures anything. It was all he had in the house last night. He didn't keep any for himself. It shows how kind Philip is."

"Distemper with grippe is serious. Put her to bed."

"Would you send for the vet?"

"Yes."

"I'll ring him up. But I'll try to feed her first. She just turns her head away."

He went with her to put the dog to bed in the warm cellar, near the boiler; and meanwhile the roasting duck could be smelled all over the house. She took Edward to see his room. It was a large, very high room, on the second floor and looking on the street. There was a cot-bed pushed against the wall, tall windows, and a big wooden partition with a door in it. In the smaller room behind the partition was a cot and a wash-basin.

"You can wash in there. If any of Philip's friends comes, we put him in there. It's not a real room."

She was a small woman. She looked up at him with kind gravity.

"Since you said I must charge you, I am charging you a dollar a day while there's no one in the backroom. Can you pay that?"

At that end of the corridor was a tiny room, with one window, into which the cot-bed could scarcely fit. It was painted white, very clean. This was her brother's room. At the other end of the corridor was a larger, stuffy room with heavy furniture, tapestry curtains and a carpet. This was used several times a week, by Philip's lifelong friend, "Nan-Mann," now a woman of forty-five. Nell slept in various rooms in the house as they were unoccupied; at other times, in the kitchen.

They had their lunch together when the duck was cooked. Edward sat about while Nell cleaned up the kitchen and they then had coffee and listened to the radio. Nell had been up at six or five-thirty, was tired now. She sat in a corner of the cot, against a pillow, and they talked idly. Edward liked her and she had a generous nature, not simple, but dispassionate and fatigued. The brother and sister had been anarchists in their youth and had grown up in that moment when New York anarchists, as also the followers of Henry George, were founding their communities round New York. The hope and belief in American destiny felt by all people and especially immigrants and their children, in the beginning of the century, and just before it, had resulted, among other things, in the establishment of these idealists' communities where, it was hoped, purity of principle, absolute equality, freedom and free land, would abolish, reduce or sterilize human weakness and state iniquity. The ease with which Nell spoke of the most intimate things and of faraway things, her confidence in Edward, was part of the attitude of Philip towards the strange people in his back room, in his Madison Avenue shop.

Afterwards, he went round the house with her while she finished up. He did not help her but idled in each room while she amused him with accounts of the tenants in the single rooms. In the room above Edward was an engineer of German extraction who was now trying to get permission to visit a surviving relative in Germany. Otherwise, he had no friends but his brother, a mining engineer, who sometimes came in from Pennsylvania. No one ever visited his room. A few technical books, a bottle of ink and a scarf were alone visible of the engineer's belongings in this chill poor room.

"Lives of obscure men," said Edward, looking thoughtfully at the scarf, and the black-painted old dressing table on which a mirror stood.

"Yes, and would you like to see the other rooms, Edward?"

This room had once communicated with the back room. The large double doors were fastened and a bed stood against them. In the back room lived a middle-aged Jewish clerk who had parted from his wife over a religious question.

"He doesn't like to be disturbed. He reads the *New York Times* steadily and finishes it at night. He goes to sleep early. Of course, he must keep them, so he has not much money. He never goes out. He seems fond of his wife and boy and he's quite gentle. She comes every Friday, says he must go to religious services and he just says, Oh, no, no. Then he laughs, he asks after the boy, and sometimes he

[271]

takes them to dinner. And then she asks him to think of the child's morals and go to Temple, but he laughs and says, Oh, no, no, I will not. It is surprising to hear such a mild man so firm."

The room was high, dark, and furnished with heavy curtains, a gold-framed landscape, an upholstered armchair. It had a Victorian look. At the head of the third flight of stairs was a small room over Philip's which was used by an old woman who came for a few weeks every few months "when she got tired of her family" and who paid for this very cheap room out of a pension. She had sons, daughters-in-law, and seven grandchildren. Said she, "Instead of quarreling like other mothers-in-law and grandmas, I come away when I am sick of them and the children get too much for me."

She took walks, read magazines, and sat in the kitchen with Nell; but Nell found her tiresome as she had got all her ideas out of magazines. But Nell called her "a strong old shoe."

There was a tin of cocoa, a rosary, a lavender silk hair net and a satchel with the old woman's change of clothes. The top floor front was occupied by a married couple with a child and at the back lived another couple, two Italians, father and son. At present, they were in trouble at work, having gone on a beer party and overslept for half a day. At the side was a small room occupied by Eugene, whom she also called "the Straw Boss." Eugene worked in the navy yard, and, in consideration of a reduction in rent, did the furnace for her.

About five, they came downstairs, for Nell had to do the shopping for dinner. She had Nan-Mann and Philip, as well as themselves. He went out with her. She showed him where she got the meat for the dog: it was the only butcher in the entire district, said she, who sold good chopped meat and not block scrapings. The people of the district naturally bought anywhere for themselves but the dog lovers came to this butcher. Edward suggested going to a pharmacy and getting some medicine for the dog. He believed she had a cold; she panted deplorably.

When they came back, the young wife who lived upstairs was just coming in with her baby. She was a thin girl, only nineteen, with an eighteen-months-old baby boy. With her was her friend with whom she passed most of the day, a twenty-year-old mother, with a queer black satin hat, a pale face and long black hair. They swayed the baby carriages and continued their daylong confidences. When they got into the kitchen, Nell told Edward about the wife as she got the vegetables ready. Her husband was twenty-two. He had been rejected for the army and could have got all sorts of jobs. But he knew nothing, could read and write very poorly and preferred doing odd jobs. He, at present, had a night watchman's job near Central Park. The night before there had been an attack on a night watchman in the district and today he had given up his job. He had stayed at home, gone and sat in "Scratch Park," taken a walk, to see what was over the bridge, drunk some beer, and now declared that he would wait a few weeks to find something that "really suited him." The young wife had another baby coming. At the end, Nell said that they had not paid their rent for a few weeks. They were Catholics and they were getting relief from their own church and from the Salvation Army. The young mother simply explained, "It is for the babies. What does it matter who they give it to? We have a right to milk for our babies." She saw no harm in having babies when so young and in her misery. "You're still young when they're grown up and they are soon able to earn and help you; we're all like a gang of kids together in the house."

Nell could not see where they would get the rent. At the same time, she would not put a pregnant girl on the street; and she must wait till they found another place. The young mother knew nothing about food, preserved the childish superstitions of slum children; her views about children were those held by her priest.

About six-thirty, Nan-Mann got home from work. She was chief accountant in a new and successful cheap bazaar in the Bronx. She was a short sturdy swart creature, in a black satin dress, a Robin

Hood hat, a red sweater and an old sealskin coat. She had wiry hair and red cheeks.

She remembered Edward. She had the tough slangy local manner, the local obscenities, the curious American relative pronouns: *what-the-hell, why-the-hell, where-the-hell, who-the-hell, how-the-hell* were the only ones she used. She had a rich strong voice.

"Well, look who's here! What the hell are you doing here? I know you're Edward, but what the hell's your other name? How is the world treating you? Old Sanderson kept me late. I told the son of a bitch I had to get the hell out of there. It's the Christmas rush. What the hell do I care? I told him not to start slicing off my bonus. He said, Have a heart, I'm here till seven-thirty; I'll take you to dinner. The hell with it. I told him I was goin' fishin' tomorrow. I beat it. What the hell . . ."

She worked hard, was a competent, reliable worker for weeks or months at a time; then would stop work, would play poker, pinochle, bridge, go fishing, spend the days in bars, in male company. She was a boon companion for men. She had affairs with them, slept with them as casually as the brutal expeditive male. She was sentimental as he is. Her name was Nan Pockett. Philip called her "Mann-law Nan," Nan-Mann, therefore. She went upstairs to take off her coat and Nell set the table. She said in a quaint, affectionate way, "But in the morning, I always find her in Philip's room."

Philip was late. The two women, with Edward, sat down to eat some chops. Though they all thought Philip must be drinking, only Edward was anxious. Nell said tranquilly, "He despises chops! I suppose he knew." Nell washed the dishes and they sat round the oilcloth-covered table under the single electric light. They turned to a political discussion on the radio and then played cards, idly, timelessly.

The young man in the front room had come in long ago and had cooked for himself, on his "one-lung burner." He was now practicing the flute, doing physical exercises and writing on a typewriter.

He had not drawn the curtain on his side of the window and they could see him walking about, writing, bending, through their thin curtains. From time to time, Nan-Mann called out something to him and he replied, or not, as he pleased. Once he came to the window, pushed it open, and asked Nell in a begging style if she had any coffee going. He came in for some and retired to his room. He left the window open and carried on a conversation with them all. He told them that his girl was trying to help him reform and he had just typed out the list of twenty-five recommendations which she had given him in a penciled list at lunch hour. He worked in the Natural History Museum, making sets in which the stuffed animals appeared in their natural habitats and settings. There were a number of them at it. All his friends were from the Museum and his girl friend, Edith, worked upstairs in the library; she was a folklore expert. He showed them the list and they saw him pin it up on the door of his clothes closet. The recommendations were of a simple sort such as "Get up early," "Study some French for half an hour every evening," "Keep my clothes in good order," "Don't leave things lying about," "Don't grouse," "Save money each payday."

Nell said, "There are too many. You won't be able to do it all. Why don't you stick to three or four?"

He thought it a good idea but preferred to reform entirely and at once.

"I know it will be a slow job," he said, through the window. The heat of the kitchen entered his room which was large, faced the freezing street and was poorly heated. Presently, the front door was opened violently, held open, and something large bumped down the two steps which led into the passage. "It's Phil," said Nell, getting up slowly. Something large, a tire perhaps, rolled down the corridor, ran into the door, circled, fell. The old floor shook. Nan-Mann opened the door and at once there rolled past her a large circular object brown in color. It wobbled, fell. It was an immense round loaf of black bread.

[275]

"Oh, Philip, you're drunk," said Nell. He stood in the doorway, looking gigantic in spite of his lack of height, his large pale face sparkling, his eyes bloodshot. His fair and white hair fell over his forehead and his hat was on one side. He waved his hand but was unable to speak. He looked at the three of them with a flashing satirical grin. His face changed, but with his mouth still twisted, slightly open, he fell face forward on the floor, with his arms flung out. Nan-Mann went over and, putting her shoulder under his shoulder, started to heave him along. He was heavy. With difficulty, they got him to the couch where he lay.

"Will you put on some coffee?" said Edward.

"Coffee! He won't touch coffee for days now," said Nell.

The three of them sat round the table. Nell laughed sadly, "Poor Phil! We teased him. I was telling him the other day that he was so hungry as a growing boy that he stole the bread from all of us. When it came fresh to the kitchen he'd smell it no matter where he was and he'd come in and start to peel off the crust. He went on peeling until there was nothing left. Phil resented it, you see. The idea that he took the bread out of our mouths."

The loaf of bread lay on the floor. Nell looked at it for a while and then got up and picked it up in both arms, putting it on the table where Phil could see it when he got up.

"He'll lie there till morning; and then he'll want whiskey. And he gave it all to Lady. I never keep any. Perhaps the Straw Boss has some."

Later on, the Straw Boss came in to say the furnace was fixed for the night and to say good night. He himself brought down half a bottle of whiskey when he saw Philip asleep; but Nell rejected it. She took one glass for Philip in the morning and a spoonful for Lady. Edward declared that it was not good for the dog, but Nell shrugged amiably.

"You know he wants to give her whatever is most precious to him."

After sitting round four hours, they all went to bed. The fire was out, but they covered Philip with a blanket. Nell went up and slept in his room.

A new life began for Edward. He got up late, after the others had all gone to work. He went to bed at eleven or twelve, which was early for him. They had shut off the other room, partitioned from his, because "Billy the Priest" had come to sleep there. In the daytime, Billy went downtown with Philip and lived in the room behind the store. He was a defrocked priest against whom, declared Philip, "the Powerhouse" (the hierarchy and its officialdom) had committed every injustice. He could not get work because a priest does not know how to do anything.

Edward would hear the ex-priest breathing and moving behind the partition. A street lamp stood outside the window and lighted his room all night. Edward stayed for long intervals alone, at different times, and in the bare cold high room, night after night, he thought about himself. Sometimes in weariness he would think of the way Margot harassed him, nagging, seeming to hate; he thought of her need to spoil everything. It seemed to him that her black moods came out of nothing, especially when things were sailing along smoothly. She would become furious at their peace, say she did not intend to live like a Lotus-eater. These scenes made him unhappy so that he soon went back to thinking of the love they had had. Each night, without any other desire, he passed calmly into sleep in the midst of some vision or other of his former happiness with Margot. He was astonished at his lack of desire. This intense delicious life in visions gave him deep quiet sleep and his body was asleep all day. Nan-Mann, in her rough, ready and generous way, would have thought nothing of having him in her bed long ago, as he knew. He did not want to wake out of the repose in which he was sunk. His downtown life seemed months away and as if in another city.

Once or twice, he walked downtown with Nell. Every few weeks, her only pleasure would take hold of her, and she would go downtown, on foot, to look at various "opportunity shops," "white elephant stores." She would spend hours picking over the things in these repulsive bazaars, in which the clothes of the dead, old-fashioned styles, stuff from boxrooms is brought together; she would spend a few dollars and come home pleased with a blouse, a mirror for the bedroom, a picture. At home, she had a chest full of beautiful hand-embroidered linen and elegant collars, fichus, jabots, in lace, such as are not worn any more. She had done hand embroidery as a girl.

One day, they went on foot as far as 56th Street, and at the end of the trip back, they were both very tired. Edward invited Nell into a bar in 125th Street. They sat up at the bar, she tangled her small feet in their old cloth shoes round the legs of the stool, and she became confiding, girlish. Perhaps she was a little embarrassed. She began to tell him about her life, how Philip had gone to work at fourteen, how he had brought home money on the very first day and being suspicious she had followed him and found that he took money out of the cups of all the blind beggars on the streets. In those days, there were more than now. It had turned out that they were organized and that a collector came round twice a day to pick up their takings. Phil had preceded the collector, that was all. The same day he had his first drink of whiskey and it was the brand of whiskey he still drank.

Their father had come to America from Eastern Europe, but not because of oppression or persecution, or even out of the love of liberty. The grandfather had had a big business, town house, seven sons; and in the houses several young maid-servants, all got in with the object of keeping the boys at home. As each maid-servant became pregnant, she was given a passage to the United States, so that there would be no claims upon the family. No resentment was felt against the girls: on the contrary. One of the sons had fallen in love with

[278]

such a servant and had followed her — or had eventually been won over by the idea of this country. Now, all the members of the family were in the country. She told Edward about her youth and many times spoke about Philip, whom she loved. She told him about all the people she had known as a girl, people who had long ago become famous, Emma Goldman and Alexander Berkman, many others. She did not see that type now. She knew people in other camps: artists, actors. They had all been youths together. Then, without transition, she said to him, lifting her head so that he looked straight into her large eyes, beautiful as Philip's:

"What is the use of it, Edward? What did I gain by having lived all that? I am an old woman. I never had a child. I never had time to have anyone. You can hardly say I lived, can you?"

When they reached home, the life of all these evenings began. Philip very often came home early, sat round, with the setting sun on his face, in the artist-naturalist's room. The youth's name was Bill. Bill liked Philip, at first, and then became tired of him as Philip maundered about his peculiar friends or made political remarks that dated from the anarchists, and from the days of Tammany. Philip was never tired of regretting the old city. It was not the same since the voting-machine came in, he said, and Tammany had lost out. The good lively old city of his boyhood, the real gay New York was Tammany. He would snarl, yellow with unexpected violence, "Now there's no life in the city. They're all too good."

But he sat in the young man's room because he felt he wasn't wanted. At last he would come out, saying to Nell he wasn't wanted; and with a glare of contempt, a handsome fierce look, he would sit crouched on the old sofa. His face would light up from inside and he would sit with a noble look thinking perhaps of lost days, of insults that had been exchanged at some time, or perhaps of whiskey. He now despised the official anarchists; and the anarchists disliked him because of his drink. He thought them Philistines.

The day of Madame Sarine's concert, Edward went downtown as arranged, although they had not seen each other since Whitehouse and no other word had been given. She was at the piano, in her room, in a white house-gown, with her hair in a rose veil. She let him in quietly, had a reserved demeanor, and at once went back to going over her program. Presently she came and sat next to him, telling him in a gentle voice about some concert experiences, how kind her husband had been (he had never known before that she had been married) and how she had disliked holding a salon in Berlin, where her husband had wished for a brilliant social life.

"No man can understand that I am not merely a lively woman, I am an artist. It is impossible for men to understand that a woman is an artist. But I am an artist. All the little things I do that Sam dislikes is because I must, because artists must, not because I am like that. But men do not try to get any idea of the life. They wish you to be a pretty little woman, a trophy; that is all. An artist's mind can have a pretty face too. I don't care for my pretty face, to tell you the truth. They look at it too much. On my last tour, sometimes more than half, at least half, of every critique was about my clothes, my face."

She smiled and got up gracefully to attend to her wardrobe. She had not yet decided which of her two dresses she would wear.

"You see, I am poor. They will be sick of seeing me in these dresses. They can't write about them every season."

She told him the price of the gowns. "You see, I can't . . ." Then she showed him her jewels, not many, but pretty ones, some rings, a ruby necklace, and earrings, given to her by a woman, a blazing flower, set with brilliants. She smiled delightedly, covetously, and spread them all out before him asking him which he liked best and avidly telling him the story of each one, who had given the things to her. Presently, they ate sparingly and a long time before the concert she went to the hall escorted by Edward. They sat in one

[280]

of the rooms behind the stage and Vera explained her songs to him, tried them over quietly once more.

"If I come early and go through my program in my mind, I am not so nervous. Remember you must stay here until I have finished the first three numbers."

When the concert began, he stayed there, listening to other artists speaking gruffly and coarsely. He listened to a society woman, herself a singer, who had arrived too late to encourage Vera, her protégée for the season. At present this woman was scandalized at something she had seen — a famous musician dancing round with his violin in one hand and a ten-thousand-dollar check in the other. It seemed gross. "Artists should not love money," she said.

The woman, black-eyed, black-haired, all in black, too black, murmured, exclaimed and insisted. She could hear Vera singing and the applause. After the third song, Edward went out and up the side aisle finding a seat at the end of a row. Vera's voice was better, had ripened: she was showing the fruit of her long, intelligent, unremitting work. She had chosen the gown in changeable silk. It seemed to have several shades between lilac and green and the blue of pale air, as lake-water in the evening. This pool of silk fell and spread out on the stage. Her hair, freshly done, stood out in an aura and she wore in it a flight of small diamonds, like water drops, from the side to the back of the neck. The hair curled deliciously at the neck. She was fortunate enough to have a real stage presence: she gave life to the stage and stood out from it, wonderfully visible and passionately sensible. Her brilliant and dry voice, trained by several masters, the songs she chose and the intelligent phrasing, her own contribution, carried him and the others to a point of excitement. It seemed perfect. He was almost under the balcony, which deadened the sounds. He could see a part of the balcony audience, and, in a box, a famous male singer. This personage sat back in his box with his sister, with an indifferent expression. Edward immediately had a low opinion of the singer's character. "To be jealous, with such a talent!"

Edward, during the concert, was in love. At certain moments, it was as if he was giving himself without question to her. It was as if the long nights of silence, interrupted visions, in the rooming house, had prepared him for a passion. At the same time, he thought that it would be no use: he could not travel with her, live entirely according to her plan as he would have to, if the husband or lover of an artist of her sort. There was no question of her giving up her career for him. He felt embarrassed at the idea. At the end of the concert, the audience rose with a great acclamation: it was again a success.

Edward, standing and clapping, let his eyes fall on Dr. Sam, standing in the row in front of him. He had risen the first and was clapping in a marked manner. Edward stared. He suddenly hated and despised Dr. Sam and thought, "If I wanted to, I could cut you out in a day." Edward dropped his hands. "You lost her, but I can win her," thought Edward with a faint smile.

He began to move towards the stage door but already a crowd of people, mostly women, were there. He came almost at the end. There were fashionable excited women, friends of hers, many personalities from New York artistic circles, a sculptress, painters, musicians, many people Edward recognized. He thought to himself, "I know half the people here and the rest are her girl friends, her court." He thought with pride that here he was at home. "New York is my village. Yes, it is true, it *is* better to die in New York than live elsewhere, as Sam says."

Vera stood at the end of a narrow room and the line of complimenters went in a loop around the room which was lined with a shelf. Each one was effusive, tried to thank her for the enthusiasm she had roused in them: and a few had questions, even favors to ask. When Edward reached her, he shook both her hands, "Oh, Vera, you were lovely: and a great artist. We are all madly in love with you."

[282]

She said, "Wait for me, Edward; take me to the Russian Tea Room. Sam is waiting for me and I will not go with him."

Edward waited outside till she appeared with a knot of women, some Russian. These white-skinned, black-haired, richly dressed chatterers, full of fervent caresses and mad words who give an intense movement and life to audiences, powerful, vivid creatures whose parents came or who themselves came from the Baltic states, eaters of herring, drinkers of tea, people who live in a perpetual turmoil, have "hearts of gold" and are intolerable as companions for those who want a quiet life, had taken up Vera. When she got into a cab with Edward, they followed her in cars and taxis to the tearoom. They passed Sam standing uncertainly in the lobby.

"Oh, let us pick him up," said Edward, leaning forward to speak to the taxi driver.

"Oh no, I will not have him. It will give him another chance to criticize and torture me. He cannot love."

"It's going to make it awkward for me," said Edward.

"You don't really care," said Vera.

They established themselves in one of the semicircular seats at the entrance to the tearoom. It was nearly midnight and now the air was clear, sparkling. The town was at its best. The audience poured into the tearoom. All who went past stopped at Vera's table, the Russian women again, billowing, found her, kissing her on both cheeks. Frenchmen and Poles came past and kissed her hand. She sat there dazzling, with furs thrown back, in her lake-water dress, the lights shining on her hair which had the brilliance of metal; and to each one she gave a gracious smile and affectionate words, she bent up her neck gracefully to kiss them back, she looked charmingly at the men. Edward, standing up at the entrance to the booth or opening, felt both embarrassed and happy. Presently, he saw Dr. Sam at the door. Dr. Sam approached and shaking her hand, said to her, "Vera, don't you want to see me too? You are seeing so many people."

"Very well, you can sit here," said Vera, with a society smile. At the same time, she signaled to a dark brusquely graceful woman dressed in black, red and white. "Lydia! One of my best friends, she is very sad, she is just divorced," said Vera hastily to Edward. "The actress, you know of course." Lydia had a dark serious bony face with rather loose dark hair. She struck Edward at first as a pleasant, sober, plain woman with some rough corners but easy to get along with. With the addition of this fourth, things became easier. Dr. Sam from being distressed had turned to pique and was elaborately graceful to Lydia. Edward had seen her play several times. She had had a company of her own and was building another but she was not the usual all-swallowing leading lady: she was in the middle thirties, modern, workmanlike. She talked quite freely and pleasantly, making them laugh and Vera, now that the admirers were all seated in the back of the restaurant, relaxed and talked eagerly with less formality with Lydia. "I have got a passage on a cargo boat and I am going to Brussels just before Christmas," said she. Dr. Sam's face became still as chinaware. He looked at her and said, between his teeth, "Ah, you did not think to tell me, Vera!"

"I only got my passage today: so dear! Not worth it! What sharks! But I shall have the petty officer's cabin and that is better than you can get on any liner in these days."

"I hope I may have the privilege of seeing you off," said Dr. Sam. "There will be one or two others," said Vera. "Then I will come too," said Edward gaily. They took Vera and Lydia to their hotels, 54th Street and 35th Street, and went back to Dr. Sam's place for a drink. Dr. Sam began to cry again.

"What am I going to do? She gutted seven years of my life! Why are women so cruel? Why do they lie to us? We both wasted our lives in this hopeless affair. I always knew it was wrong. She doesn't love me: she just kept me because she needed someone."

"Hunh!" said Edward.

"Yes! But I made her love me! She couldn't let me go!"

Edward sighed.

"She was wild with love for me, she couldn't let go," said Dr. Sam.

Tears came into Edward's eyes. Dr. Sam did not notice because he was crying bitterly. "I mustn't let you see me like this, I am always doing this," said Dr. Sam. Edward dried his eyes without being seen.

The apartment still looked as if a wild wind had blown all the things against the walls. The journalist was at home, lying on his unmade bed, reading, and came out to have a drink with them. Dr. Sam became tipsy, overcome by his misery and a very little drink, and began to weep again. With tears pouring down his face, he confessed in alternating sentences that he loved her and she was a demon; an angel, and he despised her. He wanted them to go to a restaurant downtown with him. Still weeping, he got them a taxi. He said, "I am going to buy a superb car. You will see, perhaps that will interest her."

"Why would a car interest her if you don't?" said the journalist.

"Rudy is cruel to me: he thinks it is the best way out," said Sam.

They went to the restaurant, an overcrowded, noisy place, where a musician like a prize-fighter was playing boogie-woogie and people were shouting to each other at every table. Almost everyone was drunk. Dr. Sam became very drunk. It was three o'clock in the morning when Edward left them. He started automatically towards his own home, then remembering that he had nowhere decent to sleep and it was very cold, took a taxi and went up to the dreary slum wastes of 125th Street.

There he wondered what he should do. What was the use of staying here? He was getting nowhere. He had shaken off the family, but nothing had replaced it. He was not strong enough to take up with a woman like Vera. Besides, would she do it? It was true that she was too many things to too many people — a professional deformity.

"I should become like Sam, a man standing to attention, Mr. Vera.

[285]

Who ever cried for Petrarch's Mr. Laura? — elbowed by Russian birds of paradise, and American hen turkeys. Why do I need that? A man who lives in New York needs just that and nothing more. Edward lives and that is life. Isn't that enough? I must get somewhere or I am dead? But I'd like to do something for someone. I have all the time in the world. I have all day to devote to a woman. There must be a woman. I sometimes see women on the street I feel like going up to and saying, 'You're the woman: come with me now before I lose you!' Why not? Nobody'd give a damn. But why must it be a little woman? That's vanity in Sam. Why doesn't a woman come into my life? I have always been fond of women. Well, some — "

He thought over all the women for whom his affections could have turned into love. Even Irene now, across his hall, he understood her. She was lonely, gone astray a bit, but able to settle down with any one man: but just now, when she was beginning to close round him and he was beginning to feel in her the mother, the sister, the old Whitehouse style of love, he was dissatisfied. She had better get someone else: she would.

Nan-Mann stayed away. Philip was absent. Edward lived in this silent house with the old sister for two days. Philip came home in two days having found money for some of his debts. He came home drunk, at about four in the afternoon, when Nell was preparing hashed meat for hamburgers and creamed onions as the vegetable. He came into the kitchen without hat or coat, his hair astray and his marvelously sculptured face lively, malicious. He tacked and veered. He seized his sister's hands.

"Come along, come with me, Nell the Belle: we'll call on everyone."

He was in that state of extreme excitement when he remembered telephone numbers, addresses, names long forgotten. He enumerated these, told what sort of receptions he would get, laughed at the bourgeois, the "Cozy-Murphys," the strait-laced. He came back to the word, the strait-laced. He insisted, pulled his sister away from the stove, peered into the dish of pearl onions and said, "You eat that and you think you are swallowing your tonsils."

He put his arms round her and waltzed round the kitchen with her.

"Ah, Nell the Belle, Nell the Belle, wait till my friends, the Cozy-Murphys, the strait-laced, see my sister Nell the Belle. They think I'm a souse. They can't say that about Nell the Belle! And then we'll take our dish of creamed onions with us. We'll tell them we eat our tonsils for dinner at the home of Nell the Belle. Nan-Mann and Nell the Belle. I'll tell them you're two gun molls. We're going to see Arnold Brown, that's it. He's got a gun moll; I'll take him my gun molls, Nell the Belle and Nan-Mann. Nell cooks tonsils and Nan gets the boys under the Mann Act."

Eventually, Nell, at first embarrassed, became irritated and shook him off but only with difficulty for he was mischievous and very strong. He found himself insulted by her coldness and to insult her, he seized Edward's arm and cried, with glints of merry fury, "Then you come, Edward. Ned the Fed you come, you're paunchy, you sleep too much, you think about that girl of yours that left you in the creamed onions. Come out with me: I'll take you to see some people you never saw. You need shaking up, Ned the Fed. Let's go and have a drink first, I'm dry. I'm dry. Ha-ha. Aren't you dry?"

Edward let himself be pulled out by Philip. They went to a bar near the L at 125th Street, a red-lighted, red-curtained, red-plush corner bar, and had a few drinks, and Philip, irresistible, dangerous, took him to other bars, all the places where he was known in the district. He got him into a taxi and gave an address away out in Brooklyn. When they got there, in the upstairs apartment of a frame house, they met a very serious young man, Arnold Brown. "His business is in his hat," said Philip. He was a specialist in rare and foreign books. During the war, when everyone prospered, his business had almost failed. He had sold his store to a large enterprise in the Village and himself carried on a little business by correspondence.

Helping him and living with him was a youthful-looking brunette, muscular, all black and white, and in deep mourning. Her lipstick was of the darkest red. Arnold Brown saw, with a dignified and displeased air, that Philip was drunk, but he invited the pair in and the dark young woman got him a drink. She argued about this, in an energetic manner, with her friend, Arnold. Then she sat down and began at once to tell them the story of her situation. She was a real gun moll, and her gangster friends were in jail. She had met Arnold Brown accidentally. He had convinced her that all crime came from society and that she was no more a criminal than anyone else; he had given her an elevated idea of herself and wanted her to write the story of her life. She had started to go to night courses, to learn to write in a literary style, and she and Arnold often discussed whether the memoirs would be better in her own slang or in the accepted medium. In the end they had both decided that it would be better to write her story in the most accredited language so as not to disgrace herself and her companions, all victims of society. "Without society, there is no crime," said she. Philip, having drunk three glasses of whiskey, now impetuously tipped up the bottle to his lips and drained it.

"My friend here," said Philip, "my friend here is a writer who has nothing to do. Nothing to say, no idea of what he wants and so he is a writer. Let him write your memoirs."

This idea appealed at once to the gun moll. She had not smiled once. She turned her face to Edward and her large deep brown eyes fastened on him. He looked at her with equal seriousness, interested in her solid striking beauty, a square white face surrounded by heavy black hair which seemed like a weight on her shoulders.

"Will you do it for me? The story is very interesting. I was really a gun moll. Everyone should be interested in my story."

Arnold Brown himself thought this a very good idea. He was a short solid dark young man, pleasant, even taking; unusually fresh, neat, sober in his appearance. He explained that in Myra, the gun moll, was a remarkable soul, in a way the soul of woman; and that if her sorrows and experiences were revealed, society itself would be revealed. He gave Edward, when they were going, two or three books to read. In these books, neglected, eloquent stories of women, strange views about the relation of women to society were expressed. These books were not on sexual subjects. Edward was so much impressed by this interview that he made an appointment with the anarchist bookseller and his friend, or wife, to visit them the next day. The gun moll was very anxious to begin her purification and justification. "She has lived to the full, taking what was handed out by society and made the best she could of it: that's magnificent: that's virtue," said Arnold Brown.

After this, Philip, more extraordinarily drunk than before, led Edward through a series of visits the chief purpose of which was to annoy strangers, upset meetings and alienate acquaintances. They burst in upon the meeting of a cell of socialist youth on Lower Third Avenue, not far from Edward's own home. They visited a meeting in a private home of communist free-thinkers (that is, they were free-thinkers in communist theory), in the Village. They blew in on a strange couple, a man and wife who were sitting moodily before an empty grate, eating *tortillas* and drinking beer. This man usually made seventy-five thousand dollars a year in Hollywood, and spent one hundred thousand dollars. At present he was "in the doghouse" for having supported a scene-shifters' strike. "Romantic red rash, you should have got over that when green," slobbered Philip. "There's nothing you can do about it," said the man downheartedly to his wife. "Pipe down, Phil, and have a drink," said his wife. "Suckers!" said Philip, but drank. At another time they called at a city club looking for and finding an old inventor in his late seventies who had supported the Haymarket martyrs many years before with all his money. "I called on you, Mac," stated Philip, "to tell you you're a god-damned sellout, I never saw you stumping the country for Sacco and Vanzetti: what are you, a socialist now? There aren't enough socialists to pass the buck. You always were too canny, too ca' canny!"

The old man frowned. "I'll show you to the door, Philip, since you can't find the way yourself." Philip laughed all over the writing room, dining room, staircase and front hall. "Don't commit yourself, Sandy, eh, don't commit yourself: I think I see a sail, eh?" shouted he yelling with laughter.

"I commit myself when I see the lifeboat," said "Sandy" gravely. Philip, now on the sidewalk, turned round, shook his great white fist at the man and the building. "Lousebitten creamskimmers! Malefactors of little gains! My price is higher than a million berries!" The old Scot turned inside with a calm expression. Philip chuckled. "Hard as nails! He's already got options in heaven and hell."

They visited a Trotskyist and Philip standing in the door shouted, "You're a self-seeker, a stoolie"; and to a writer who jogged along and had no opinions at all, "Grubstakes! Bread-and-butterfly! Potboiler! Sellout!"

"I haven't sold out," said the middle-aged, half-bald, agate-eyed grinning writer.

"Have you got whiskey? Because you've nothing to sell! He's a writer too: no idea, nothing to sell!" he said kindly, pointing to Edward. He grabbed the bottle of whiskey and said, "And no one has my price, no one has my price! Every man has his price but no one has got the price of Me!"

And so on and on. Philip, always drunker and drunker with his libations on the way, a bright demon in the doorway, a loathsome oaf on the couch, even rolling with fanciful leers upon the matting, the bare boards, repeated his jokes of earlier in the evening about Nell the Belle, Nan-Mann "that whore" as he now called her because she had been for days on a party, the creamed tonsils, the gun moll, the price of Man, and so on with memories of his mixed Tammany and anarchist youth, the characters he had hobnobbed with, school-teachers, editors, judges, congressmen; and other personages now known to all New York, political figures, socialist, communist, Henry George adepts, anarchists of long ago.

They ended in a hall on the East Side, where anarchists, mostly poor Italian barbers, waiters, bootblacks, a few Spaniards and Hungarians, were listening to a play in Italian. Philip crashed to the floor in the corner of the hall. This enabled Edward to see the play, a gaseous *Commedia dell' Arte* jest with improvisations twenty minutes long. When the lights went up, Philip, who recognized many people there, was so badly considered and rebuked for the scandal of his condition and presence that he grew angry and pulling Edward by the sleeve, said, "Let's get out of this band of Pharisees, white supple-curs, downtrodden Philistines, revolutionists of the absolute, worth two cents, let's get out of here and get some clean air in a barroom." They got to another barroom; and shortly after this Edward was able to get Philip lifted into a taxi and take him home.

The kitchen was warm. Philip threw himself upon the couch and at once went to sleep. Nell's heavy figure as if crumbling, boneless, from fatigue, slumped in a chair at the table. She helped Edward with Philip and then had a cup of coffee with Edward. She told some stories of Philip's youth and Edward could see how she loved him.

He ventured, "You have sacrificed your life to him. He is almost your husband."

"He is not my husband. He is my dear, dear brother." She turned to Edward with a calmer face. "Do you think a life can be sacrificed if you give it to someone? I don't."

He told her about his gun moll, Myra. Brown's love for her gave him a force and purity he had never seen equaled in a love affair. Nell smiled. "You are rather happy here with us, I think."

"Am I turning my back on life or looking at life?"

"That question has no sense, really."

"No. Brown said, To live is virtue, or something like that. A sort of coincidence with what I was thinking."

It was December. He walked through the freezing muddy streets near the rooming house, and saw the households cramped in the rat holes they called apartments. He had no desire to know them and could not feel that he would find what to do with himself in those quarters. He did not suppose he would come back to this part of town any more. In the meantime, the old woman had got used to his company, though she did not cling to him any more than to anyone. The whippet had seemed to get better but was ill once more and they were sure would not survive the winter.

Nan-Mann never came to the house, because she had become engaged to the man she worked for. This man had a grown daughter of eighteen, and Nan-Mann came only once or twice to the rooming house to talk to Nell in an important way about her "daughter's future," her future home. She was cutting out all low company, going to become a proper wife and mother. She bored Nell and Philip would not see her but to tease her, "the reformed rake, the methody whore."

Twice a week, Edward went out to the back parts of Brooklyn, where he took down what the gun moll had to say about her life. What she had to say was scarcely interesting. She had started to think about herself for the first time; she had no idea how to tackle it. She would say, "I left my father's home in 1935 when he married my stepmother. She beat me up. I just went to town thinking I'd get a man to look after me. I was romantic. I wanted to have just one man. I found a man the next week and we were together for a year." Edward would laugh and type out the sentences, bring back the notes next time. In between the lines he had left six spaces. They had to fill up these spaces with details. From the details, he would pick out a story. "We must have a story." Myra had no idea what were details and they did not interest her. She declared, "Oh, no one will care about that."

"That's the real Mexican Jumping Bean for you," thought Edward: "and me, Episode 21: or Life in the Eye of a Flea."

In the meantime, faster than himself, she had been to see an editor, and had got herself a contract but since she admitted she could not write the story, the editor wanted to have Edward's signature too. This took some time and Edward began to warm towards this business. He began to look upon her with the same tender admiration as Arnold. She had lived; she had dared to live; she did not even know she was living. He, for example, had been to Egypt, Italy, Germany, France — and it had meant nothing to him. On a road outside Cairo a man had been killed before his eyes. That man had been walking along the road with a New York boy, telling a "shaggy dog" story. In Italy, they had been in an unpleasant affair, several of them had been killed by bombing; they had spent the whole time telling stories. In Georgetown, he had sat in class with a number of New York boys and they had spent time out of class telling "Little Audrey" and "Pentagon" stories. In Texas, in the brutal heat, with some young fellows dying on the route marches, the only strength he had had left had been to talk about air-conditioning in New York in the hot days, ice-cream sodas, the pleasant barrooms, and what was new in New York now? They felt suckers, young green corn, in exile out there under that sun, with New York whizzing far ahead of them on its comet track. He had flown the oceans in big planes. On one of them, he had met Bart. On each occasion, he had sat in the front with the pilot, or back with the relief pilot, swapping "zany" stories. It nagged him to hear of some joke of the war or rear he did not know.

And though he wondered now at how his life had passed without incident in this strange way, he could not regret the hours he had passed, entire nights, days, weeks, a European war, in hearing New York stories and living the New York life. He was such a

Gothamite, in fact, that he could not live for himself, he could only live through, and thus for, others. Through the stories the American city view of life, its cool, salty, insolent, indecent, fanciful humor, crazy turns of phrase, its gruesome debonair, penetrated him, seemed to him to sum up exquisitely what he knew of life and people. He had never formulated a view of life or himself. It had all come out of these stories.

His gun moll had no idea of humor. Her reflections were sometimes sensible, usually flat and all bathos. Still, his job grew on him and he thought he could turn out a good book. The illusions grew. It might take on, become a best-seller, reach the stage, Hollywood. Many a career, in letters or otherwise, had been founded on just one book or even one collaboration. If he had a project well-delimited, he always found in himself a great capacity for work. He worked mostly in the warm kitchen. Nell passed in and out. He shared his meals with her. She respected his work, though scarcely impressed with his ambitions.

Philip, after his one outburst, was staid, bored. He came home every evening about seven and the family played mild games of cards. Philip dealt and played at dazzling speed. The cards whizzed round and out faster than sight and all the time he wore his satisfied clever smile. He cheated consistently as a pastime but he could wipe the floor with them in any case, as he said. The cards flashed out like the spokes of a wheel. He scooped up the points, threw down the cards. Bored with his partners, suddenly a pattern of insulting courtesy, he rose courtly and went down to the basement where his dog Lady wheezed on Philip's own blankets, near the stove. Philip covered himself with his overcoat, up in his icy little room. His penetrating voice, with its sweetest accent reached them.

One evening he came up with the dog in his arms. "Lady's sick; my Lady's sick."

He brought her to the sofa and placed her there on her blanket, keeping one hand near her to warm her. She whimpered and presently tried to move; she licked his hand and stood up arching her thin flank. The smell of distemper was strong. Philip said, "Lady's elegant, isn't she? She's a maiden, a young maiden, she's very young yet. She's delicate yet. How graceful! You're my lady love, Lady, Lady." He put her back in her bed, with his smile. The others were playing cards. He looked at them with a wicked twist of the lips, watching them as if both fools: he followed the cards automatically with sharp glances. He called ironically to them, telling each play.

Nell laughed. "Philip can't bear anyone else to handle cards."

"You don't know how to play."

He lingered by the dog. The dog whimpered and licked his hand. He said, "Lady loves me, you see."

"Why not? I love you," said Nell.

"And it's just the same love. Love is all one; there is no difference," said Philip.

"A goldfish loves me," said Edward.

"Fish." Philip sat, with his eyes resting insolently some feet above them, curiously twisting his lips.

"I read isinglass comes from a fish; I never knew it before," said Nell.

"Now Nell knows that isinglass comes from a fish."

Presently, Philip got up and came to the table to deal the cards. He kept the sharp glance and twisted smile all the time; but as he dealt in legerdemain, a demoniac look of astuteness and pleasure came into his face. He won three games then threw down the cards, and got up without laughing, intensely, coldly, restlessly.

"Do you play much?" asked Edward.

"With Billy the Priest," he said with lazy insolence. He told the story all over again although he knew they knew it.

He sat about by the dog, with a lofty insolent stare. It happened that that evening, Nan-Mann came by to say hello. She had on a new fur coat and a new hat and wore her engagement ring. Philip

[295]

saluted her with impudent commentaries but plunged at her, seized her by the strong wrist and took up the cards.

"Come on, play, Nan-Mann!"

"I can stand up to you," said Nan.

"Both cardsharps and sharks; it's a question of who can cheat the other oftener," said Nell.

"That's half our game. Look at him, look at that Buddha look!" said Nan. "Now he's at it."

He kept his Buddha look. She tossed the cards down and kept up her tough patter, laughing, crowing, bantering. He answered never a word, though sometimes he smiled faintly. The game went on till long after midnight. The others went up to bed, Nell saying, "See the lights, the gas and the stove are out!"

In his dark, cold room, on the spare mattress, Edward began to think about his book, to break ground for the next day when he was to see Myra. Each time he saw her, he took her a list of questions, the answers to which would break out the details in the thin account she was giving of herself.

The street lamp outside shone through the Venetian blind, on the ceiling; and he looked at the shadows for a while, thought again how Margot had offended him by saying, during a trial black out during the war (the people opposite had been slow in putting out the lights), "See the lights on the ceiling? I don't suppose you ever sit by yourself and study effects, or think. You are just imaginative."

By imaginative, she meant "without imagination." She meant plots of suddenness, crime, adventure.

"I like analysis only and that's something you don't like," she had told him. Edward had never been able to get this grain of sand out of his hide. She despised his brains and soul. Really, they were not suited for each other. A man does not avoid a woman for twelve years for nothing. Habit speaks one way, instinct another.

Edward heard the front door open. It stayed open. He knew Nan-Mann was staying there that night in her old room. Therefore it was

Philip going out for something. He liked to get the bulldog editions and take them to bed with him. Perhaps Edward dozed. Some time later, he heard Nell going down, to see if all was tight and safe. It was nearly morning. She closed the house door. She did not go upstairs again, and must have been resting on the kitchen sofa. He felt the morning, when the air and sounds have changed and the lights begin to penetrate the flesh. He slept again uneasily and was awakened by someone knocking at the house door, Nell's steps, exclamations, and Nell's cry, "Nan! Nan! Eugene!"

People went into the kitchen and Edward, putting on his winter coat, went downstairs. It was very cold. The Straw Boss, who had been sleeping near the furnace, because his room was cold, had just come up in his pyjamas. He was a tall rotund red-faced man. Nell was dressed in some nondescript grayish clothes and with her were two men, one a policeman. Lady, the whippet, in a very bad way, lay on her side on the blanket on the couch, gasping, her eyes turned up and her limbs stiffening.

Nell was very pale, as if breathless, trembling all over and when the policeman asked her something, only shook her head and looked at Lady. The Straw Boss said that about four o'clock in the morning, a man had been knocked down and injured by the trolley in 125th Street. The conductor saw it all and it wasn't his fault. The man had crossed the street when he turned, whistled, called and walked back across the road. At the last moment, he ran stooping in front of the trolley car. The stranger was a taxi driver. He had been parked there and half asleep. He saw a whippet just creeping along and only saw the man later. The whippet started to cross the road, then stood still trembling. The man whistled and called and the whippet got in front of the trolley car and dropped on its haunches. The man ran in front of the car and pushed the whippet off the tracks but was himself knocked down. The man had been taken to one of the nearby hospitals and the dog, apparently dying, taken to the sidewalk and left there. But someone had come along who had recognized the

[297]

whippet as Lady; they supposed the man was Philip. He had no identification marks on him. He was unconscious, was being given oxygen and probably would not survive.

Nell stood up and said she would go in the taxi to the hospital. Edward waked Nan-Mann, who came down in her nightdress, a skirt and her fur coat and hat, ready to go.

The two women were away the whole day, and until late in the night. About two o'clock, they came home. Philip had just died. He had never regained consciousness. Nell said, "If it had not been for his great strength, the doctor said he would have died at once." After a moment she added in a firmer voice, "He had not been drinking. He had not taken any liquor all that evening and it was certain he had not drunk anything. He had gone out for the papers and the dog followed him."

When she asked they told her the molasses-colored whippet had died of pneumonia and was lying in the cellar in a box. She said, "If I could, I would bury Lady with him; he died for her, didn't he? And he said I loved him only as much as Lady; or she loved him as much as I did. It is the same. I would not mind if they buried me with Philip, would I? But they won't allow it. We will bury Lady in the back yard tomorrow."

This they did.

After Philip's funeral, Nell was resigned and did not seem to weep. She told people that the whippet followed him across the trolley tracks under the L and made him turn back and that he threw her free. She told them what the doctor had said, and the nurses too. He never recovered consciousness, but he was fighting in the dark for eighteen hours: he would never have lasted so long but for his great strength; they had rarely seen such a strong man for his age. She went with Nan-Mann, the Straw Boss and Edward to the local movie, a very poor one where they had Bingo every night; and Nan won a set of teacups which she gave to Nell. The Straw Boss took them to a Chinese place afterwards, and coming back, Edward bought frankfurters to eat at home. They talked a little, Nan told them what was going on in her boss's business, how she had gone fishing last summer with Big Boy Al Burrows and spoke of her "daughter and son" still meaning the grown daughter of the man she was to marry and the girl's fiancé. Nell was interested, laughed; but she did not move about very much. After three days Nan left; and the Straw Boss, of course, went to work every day. But one morning, when Edward came down to the kitchen for his breakfast, which he took with Nell about nine-thirty, he found Nell stretched on the couch, with a rug over her.

"There's coffee there, Edward."

"Anything wrong, Nell?"

"I'm going to die," she said composedly.

"For crying out loud!" He was frightened and went to her. "What's wrong?"

"I'm going to lie here until I die. . . . I don't want to live any more."

"Don't talk like that, Nell. Get up and have some breakfast with me. Come on, dear."

"I made up my mind, Edward."

He got down on his knees beside the couch and took her hands which were crossed over the blanket in a restful position. He began pleading. "Come on, Nell. Get up. It's the effect of the terrible shock. You don't feel like that. That's not for you. You're not that kind of person."

"You don't know me. We don't know each other."

"That's true."

"You'll excuse my saying that. It's cruel."

He made his coffee, hoping she would have some; and drank it sitting beside her. He laughed, held her hands, creased, with old stiff skin, as if both were blistered, ruined by strong cleaning fluids, and dirty water, he unfolded them. He kissed them, rubbed her feet, brushed her hair.

[299]

"I did this for my mother."

"I never had a son."

Her disinterested frank eyes looked at him continuously, she had no bitterness or melancholy. He said, "You don't think you can die by just lying down on the sofa, do you?"

He kept it up in the same commiserating strain, never smiling or wounding. She said several times, "I'm not going to eat or drink. You must die that way."

He did some shopping for the house; and did his work. When he came downstairs, in the afternoon, she was weeping and turned her back to him. He telephoned Nan. When he saw Nan from his window, he came down and told her about Nell. Nan went out with him to a bar. They had drinks and telephoned several people, Nell's sister, and some very old friends, comrades of Nell's and Philip's youth. The sister however refused to come to the house, saying, "It's Nell's fault that Philip died. She let him drink and he died drunk. I told her so. I told her she'd never see my child again. I won't have a child visit such a house."

Nan wished her the worst of fates and destinations through the telephone and came out raging, "It's that so-and-so's fault that Nell's in this condition." They brought home some things for dinner and ate in front of her. Then they piled the things in the sink and sat at the table playing cards just as before Philip's death. Nell lay quietly on her back but did not speak.

At about eight, two old friends arrived, Mr. Atkins, who had been Philip's best friend, though separated from him later by differences of political opinion; and another old friend, Mrs. Morrisey, a strong squat woman of fifty, with graying hair but fine brown eyes. Mr. Atkins was a printer and Mrs. Morrisey a pharmacist, who was district leader in Borough Park. They had been anarchists in their early youth, had long ago changed politics, but remained quarreling friends with Philip. He usually called them turncoats, rats, political mongrels and so forth; and exalted the golden age in the beginning

[300]

of the century. Nevertheless they were like a good many ex-anar-chists, humane; at any rate they would be able to talk to Nell in her own terms, thought Nan. But after greeting her and hearing what she had to say, the two friends merely sat down and played cards with Nan and Edward as if everything were in order. Edward be-came angry. His heart thumped away and at last he asked the two visitors if they were not going to reason with Nell. This was at a moment when they were not playing but were sitting, scarcely saying a word. Mrs. Morrisey's eyes were softly and lustfully shining; her thoughts were far away. Mr. Atkins had been having a discussion with Nan about the Third Party question. Edward spoke to the woman pharmacist twice before she heard him. She was dressed all in dingy black with a string of white beads and a new hat. She was fat, her figure crumbling, but she had a certain beauty in her present mood. She roused herself and spoke slowly, detaching her thoughts with some difficulty from the other object.

"Don't you think that Nell's right — to do what she likes? Is there someone in the house who cares for her? Life and death is the same. We do not owe anything to society; it depends, eh? We can do what suits us best; it is the best thing for all. Even if not, what use is it to the individual? Have you a right over Nell? If she wants to die, she has good reasons for it. You have to live with a reason for living, or what's the sense?"

"The living and the dead are just the same," said Nell.

Nan turned her chair round.

"Oh, have a heart, Nell. You're giving us all the heeby-jeebies. Think of us. We lost Philip and now we must lose you? Get up now. Once you get off that couch, you know you won't lie down again. What the hell, baby, according to your own argument, if the living are the same as the dead, then you're the same now as you would be, so get up and live. If it's the same. We love you, we care for you. You'll break our hearts if you die before our eyes. Are we to sit here all that time until you pass away? You'll make us murderers. People would call us murderers. They'd say we should have sent you to a hospital, forcible feeding, that horrible stuff. You can bet we won't, lovey Nell dear, but for Pete's sake, take up your bed and walk. What do you want to make it so tough on us for?"

"You loved Philip, you said. The same as me, all love is the same. And you don't want to die. But I do. There isn't anything to talk about."

"Ah sweetheart, ah god damn it, Nell, you don't know what you're saying; would Philip have lain down to die for you?"

"He died for Lady. Why not for me?"

There was a pause. Nell said more nervously, even feverishly, "Philip believed, well, when we were youngsters, we knew, all of us, all things and people were equal, dogs, girls, gangsters, bums, republicans, reds — friends and enemies. He only couldn't stand sneaks and climbers. They were a bit lower than the rest. My brother Philip once had a man implicated in that Murder Incorporated gang behind his curtain for three weeks. He fed him himself and played cards with him half the night. He had a leper there, a man with a huge face; it made you sick to look at him. He wasn't afraid of the gangsters and then they called him Doc. I asked him about the leper, because it's contagious, and he was angry at me. Doesn't it give you goose flesh? I asked Phil. They're just the same as you or me, what's the matter with you? Do you give me goose flesh, he said? He looked at me with contempt. He's still looking at me with contempt. No one is better than anyone. Only Philip could feel that."

They had some beer and icebox cookies brought by Mrs. Morrisey, chiefly for herself, it seemed; and they went about eleven o'clock. Edward was left alone with Nell. He sat quietly near her reading a book until she said she wanted to sleep and then he put out the light and went upstairs. He believed she would get up in the night and eat. In the morning he found on the table the dishes used by the Straw Boss. He said "Good morning" to Nell but she did not answer though he knew she was awake. He ate his breakfast and piled the dishes with the Straw Boss's in the sink. Nothing had been done in the kitchen for two or three days. She turned again and asked how his work was going.

"Slower and slower."

"You'll make something of it. You found something to do, while with us," she said. She was flushed now, her hair untidy and her eyes bright. Her lips were cracked, she gasped occasionally and drew heavy breaths. She said, "Bring your work to the kitchen; it helps to pass the time. What day is it, Edward?"

He brought his work and began to type out the notes he had made before. He left the kitchen door open and the house door, so that fresh air from the snowy street would come in and purify the air. The sink was filled with dirty water and there was garbage on the floor. Nell asked him once suddenly whether they had buried Lady. This startled him, since she had been there at the burial in the back yard. Later she said, "Whenever Philip came in, he came into the kitchen to see if everything was out. I seem to hear him often, you know. I hear his footsteps, and his voice when the door opens. I suppose it will go away soon. I am listening for his voice all the time and at times I am sure I hear it."

"Yes, those hallucinations are very strong."

"Yes, you can hardly believe it is a hallucination. It is like some sort of reality. I suppose there are other ones than the one we know. It seems to me so strange that we think we know the reality, the only one there is."

"Yes, it's questionable, isn't it?"

"Supposing what they say is true: that looked at one way, Philip and all the others are still alive. I don't mean the afterlife, I mean the present life, the fourth dimension. I read that there are other dimensions. We only know three, but there are others, about eight. So there can be another reality."

"Yes, yes, there can, there is."

"So it is true that we are alive and dead at the same time: the living

[303]

and the dead are the same. And Philip and I are both living and dead at the same time."

"Yes, yes, Nell dear."

He had turned to her very attentively. She sighed and said she was very thirsty, that was the chief thing.

"I'm afraid I'm getting funny, I don't want to be funny in my mind. I feel different now. I feel happy in a way. Before to me the dead were dead; now I just feel as if the same earth covered with small plants, as I see it, is stretching far, very far away; and quite near me there is a grave. But all round it and as far as you can see is the same earth we tread."

"That's very beautiful, Nell. That's so touching; that's very true, dear Nell."

He went and sat beside her again taking her hands as before and kissing her forehead. "You see, you are feverish; you are very thirsty. Let me get you some cool water, just a drop. It would make you clearer in your mind."

"No, no; I am going to die."

She turned her back and tried to go to sleep. He went back to his work. When the Straw Boss came in the evening, the young naturalist came in and asked if he could eat with them. It was lonely for him in there. The three young men sat round their meal, cooked by the Straw Boss, and talked of anything, at first quietly, and then louder. They presently got out the cards and played for some time. Then they all went out for a drink. At the bar, they discussed the possibility of Nell's really starving herself to death; but all concluded nothing could be done about it, it would not be right to do anything against her will, and her provocation was real. The Straw Boss and the naturalist, opposing Edward, said she had a right to her life, she had earned it and she could cast it away. Edward was indignant, sulky; he simply said, "I can't say why, but I know this death is wrong."

They argued about life and death, responsibility and society, for a while and returned to the rooming house for their beds. In the morning, all went on as before and once more Edward brought down his work. Nell was now very ill, feverish, murmuring, tossing. Edward was relieved. He felt that now she had left her senses, he would be excused for calling a doctor. However, he telephoned Nan-Mann at her work and begged her to come to the house. If she thought it right, they would get a doctor. Nan-Mann said, "She would never forgive you; and what you are doing is wrong according to her view of life."

"But I shall be held criminally responsible!"

"Oh, if that's what's worrying you, go back home to your neat little roost, my lad."

Edward went back to his work on the kitchen table. At a certain moment, finding her very feverish, he took a glass of sugared water and, holding her head up, put it to her lips. She drank it. He gave her a little more and later a little more. She smiled slightly, slept and woke about five, seeming more sensible. He said, "Nell, you have drunk water, you know. You didn't know, did you? You can't starve any more, can you? Get up, darling. Come get up? You'll feel better soon. Your back must be aching lying there."

She said she was very weak and he must help her. He brought her to an old armchair and sat looking at her with a satisfied air. Then he went to her, took both her hands, looked into her face, knelt beside her and pressed her to him, looking up at her. All his grace moved him. She looked far away, abstracted. He put his arms round her and pressed her to him again, full of love and grace. "Nell the Belle!" He went back to his chair and looked at her, pleased with himself and her. Her eyes were large, her face pale. She said hesitatingly, doubtfully, "Do you think my life was wasted, Edward?"

He came and embraced her as before. "Nell, don't think along those lines: that leads nowhere. We mustn't ask too many questions."

"Have you anything to live for, Ned?" she said, looking his face over carefully, when he went back to his chair.

"No." He laughed.

"Then it doesn't matter, does it?"

"No."

"My sister, the one who's in the Third Party movement, told me I'd wasted my life. She said if I'd got into politics I'd like them. She said, if Phil had got into something he wouldn't have died like that. She said it was my fault."

"If she had been there — !" said Edward ironically.

"Then you don't think there's anything in it?"

"The things people say in families!" He laughed. He took both her hands and pulled her up, "Come on, do a little bit and then I'll give you lunch."

She reflected a moment. At last she said, "All right, boy."

"Oh, how calm and pleasant it is here! I suppose that's a sweet truth: to know there is nothing to live for? To have the sense just to live? But when I'm older? How is it that I feel old already?"

"It's a long way to go, from thirty-three to seventy or eighty," she said anxiously, still looking at him.

"I know: I must get married," said Edward, very seriously.

"I never felt old till you came here; you did that for me. A person should live in reality."

They looked at each other, calmly, in a pondering way before each turned to work.

Part Six

NEW CONFIGURATIONS

EDWARD had nearly finished the first draft of his book by the middle of December; a good thing, since Myra had got tired of it, had got engaged to a publisher and had her picture already in several magazines. Edward, like Arnold Brown, believed in her sincerely; and like him, rarely saw her. Vera Sarine was packing to go to Europe and had cases and valises strewn about her two-room apartment in 54th Street. Once when Edward called, there were two other men there; Al Burrows with a steel-strapping machine, a hammer, doing up wooden cases for her and looking rebellious and full of compunction; and a soft middle-aged dark man, a writer it turned out, who was packing Vera's things into an immense brassbound steamer trunk. He brought out a few handfuls of delicate things in black, rose, white, and a few ribbons. They took up not more than six square inches of space. Vera still had a few things but, "No, no, there's no more, Simon," said she.

"You don't have many feminine things," said he reproachfully. Presently, he went, after pressing her hands between his soft hands and saying enthusiastically, "I'll see you again, I'll see you in Europe, my wonderful artist!" When he had gone, Al Burrows turned gayer, began to laugh, turned over one of the heavy strapped cases with his foot, rolled down his shirt sleeves, picked up his hammer and sat down, with his collar and tie loose, grandly brawny, in a thin stick of an armchair. "I'll come and pick you up at seven-thirty," said he to Vera: "you'll have to get a taxi though with all this stuff."

[309]

"I'm coming with my chauffeur, Al," said Edward.

"Is that fellow coming too?" inquired Al.

"Simon! Certainly not."

She started to make coffee and sandwiches for them. She said after a moment, interrupting their desultory talk, "But Sam is coming!"

"And who else?" cried Al sharply.

"Joe Ryman," she said apologetically. "I wouldn't let anyone else come; otherwise — I'd be ridiculous."

"Is Lou coming?" asked Edward.

"No, no, no," she said darting an angry glance at him. When Al went reluctantly, she called the giant as he stood under the entry, his head almost touching the arch, "Al, would you go round to Simon's one day this week? Take him this photograph? I promised him and I forgot."

"All right," said Al looking and pocketing. "You didn't give me one."

"You're — but you said you were coming to Paris to do business!" She twitched her head round and laughed. "You can get a better one there."

"I'm to come to Paris to get your photograph!" Al exploded. She said nothing, looked at him, came to him, shook hands. "I'll be here about seven-thirty," he said briefly. In the passage he turned, touched his pocket, "I'll see he gets this."

When the door closed, Vera and Edward looked at each other and laughed. "Those cargo boats," said Vera, "never sail on time. I've been warned to be there at ten; and I'm sure it will go next morning about three A.M."

"I'll be there to the last," said Edward.

"I know you will."

He asked her nothing about the men and she told him nothing. Presently he took her out to the Plaza cafeteria where they had coffee and drinks; and about midnight he took her home. They sat quietly talking for a long time, when Vera said she was tired and Edward said he'd go home. At the door he turned. "I like your friend Lydia!"

"Oh, did you see her? We're not speaking at present."

Edward laughed.

In the festive season, it was he who took her out. Everyone imagined she had hundreds of friends — she had. The men were occupied with their businesses, year-end parties, families: Simon telephoned her daily, "If you go out, wear a fur coat, it's very cold." Edward would say to her, on leaving, "If you're lonely tell me to come and I'll come." She said she would and she did. She told him all the things the other men had told her: whether they loved her or not. Once Edward and Lou and Oneida, Leander and Lady all called upon her laughing. They went out in the cold jolly snow, by the Christmas lighting, to call on Mrs. Annichini, Nate the Croat, all the family friends.

"Won't it be funny to spend Christmas on the high seas?" said Lady.

"No," she laughed. "Why I've spent Christmas everywhere."

"Don't you feel strange, not having a home?" said Leander.

"Where my cello is, there's my home," she laughed, quaint and delightful.

"How can you leave the United States?" said Oneida, irritably. "It seems to me not like living."

"The United States?" Madame Sarine was puzzled. "Must I stay here forever, then?"

"It's a very great privilege," said Oneida, looking round dubiously at her family. She said it in a louder tone.

"Why are you smiling?" she cried at them.

"Now you've seen it!" she said to Madame Sarine. Edward burst out laughing. "Solo going to South Africa and you going to France, what's the sense to it?" burst out Oneida.

"Must I give up where I was born?" said Vera Sarine, in surprise.

"But now you've seen it?" said Oneida. Suddenly they all laughed. It was so delightful tramping through the snow, rousing, bright.

Union Square was clean with snow and the buildings rose higher in the dark.

"Oh, I'll come back in the summer," said Vera Sarine.

The next day, Oneida, Lou and Edward went to buy a farewell gift for Vera and went to a cousin of Mrs. Annichini's who lived in a basement where she had her own workshop and little forge. She was a jeweler. After long inspection and thought they clubbed together to buy a beautiful necklace, a "river" or aquamarine and silver which would go with her stage costume: and Edward called upon her with it, in its velvet and satin-lined case. How beautiful it was! With her was Lydia, and another very charming little woman with snowy chest and shoulders exposed in a low round muslin blouse tied with black velvet ribbon. They all tried it on and it suited Vera only. "I shall wear it to the Paris opera for you, Edward!" said she. "How clever you are! You should have been a Frenchman."

"It is too late now," said Edward regretfully. "I suppose the Paris opera is full of Continentals, just like New York."

"It is nothing but Continentals," said Vera.

"Just as I thought."

"I must get a necklace and I'd like you to come with me, you are so good at it," said Lydia. Edward sat down on the plush-covered divan, crossed his legs and looked at her thoughtfully. In his mind, he rummaged through the jeweler's store, and a few other places he knew well, kept by friends of his, another jeweler who worked mostly in beaten silver and copper, several who kept stores on 8th Street and elsewhere in the Village.

"Yes, all right."

"Let's go now," she said to him, when they were leaving. He went with the actress round the stores, found nothing for her and ended in a drink place in the Village, where they spent many hours, Lydia telling him about the company she had almost organized; and about the plays they were planning. Said she, "Have you got a play, Edward?"

"Yes: but it's no good."

"Why not?" she asked him sharply.

The manager of the place, a man with broad soft feminine hips was walking up and down near them, thumping with his feet and swaggering his loins in what he supposed was a feminine way. He eyed them with resentment. Their coats hung on the chairs next to them.

"Kindly remove your coats to make room for customers," said he venomously. They laughed. He went away and hung in the back round behind the two long files of paintings along on the walls.

"He won't last," said Edward.

"He hates seeing me with a younger man," said Lydia.

"I feel old, I'm getting old," said Edward running his fingers through his hair. "I wish I looked older." He told her about his play; and they sat there for an hour or two. Once the manager came close with one of the waiters and said loudly, "I've never seen anything like it: this is the first time —" Lydia turned and gave him a look. Two black cats, thought Edward. When she turned back, they grinned at each other, a long grin. Lydia was rather tall, and angular, superbly bony; in no matter what lights she sat, she was handsome, sometimes like a polished wood carving seen through smoke and sometimes smoky reds and blues over a dark background, like an Impressionist painting. "I guess all you have to do is to stand on the stage against plain curtains and drama takes place," said Edward looking at her through their cigarette smoke.

He kept telephoning her and would call upon her unexpectedly, expecting her to be alone, and would sit round her apartment for hours waiting for her visitors to go. At last he would drift away, not always able to make an appointment to see her. To be sure of seeing her he began to work with her, doing odd jobs for the company.

On December twenty-fourth when he called, she had Christmas candles lighted but no one there. Packing cases stood around the floor. She looked haggard and once more different, this time like an

African beauty, dark, pale, remote, of a different race entirely. She was cold in her manner. He felt heartsick. He knew nothing of her life. She wore a black wool sweater and black jersey skirt which did not flatter her coloring but brought out her muscular long waist, knobby breasts, broad shoulders. The desire he had felt for her from the first time increased and he did not know what to say: everything he did was wrong. He fell over the lamp wiring, his voice grated, he felt angry with her and she seemed very ungrateful towards him.

"Let's go to dinner," she said.

"All right, if you want to."

She looked at him in rude surprise, about to say something. He had telephoned her for a dinner date.

"Well, I will go and change, I've nothing on but this." He put his hand on the light switch, it hung there: this would never do. "Go as you are." He came close to her. She turned towards him and looked at him somberly, sourly. That was how they came together. She suddenly laughed, showing her magnificent white teeth, and her eyeballs rolled, she kissed him with her long, mobile, soft, open mouth. "Oh, this is so natural," said Edward, spreading out his left hand and sighing. "Let's go out to dinner," said Lydia: "I've been working all day."

After dinner, he left her on the sidewalk outside her house. He felt raving, drunk.

"I'm pie-eyed with love: I'm caught, I'm caught." Streets were brilliant with Christmas light, there were flakes of snow: he walked across all the streets, without noticing the traffic lights or so it seemed. He changed his route when near home, went back to the Village and bought a ring for Lydia for Christmas: a large shiny red stone of some sort in a fanciful setting; "It will just go with the black; and I'll ask her for a ring for myself." Getting near home, he saw Al Burrows walking along with Irene, fingertips touching. He hurried up to them and invited them to come for a drink. They were pleased and he saw as a stranger Irene's sharply soft, pretty, dry face. She had one of her frequent expressions, of rather vapid sensual dazzle. Edward could not help showing them the ring and he noticed Irene's expression of dislike. Al was showing him a seal ring he wore on his little finger. Edward tried it on. It slipped easily over his middle finger. "I'll get you a ring for Christmas," said Irene, to Al Burrows sharply. The man's big chest heaved: he laughed, ha-ha-ha. Then he thought he had offended, "Yes, do, I'd like one," he said.

"Where did you get that one, Edward?" Edward told him.

"H'm: I can't go there, know the woman who runs it," said Al.

Irene looked at him. He lowered his head. "Had this ring enlarged there," said Al, showing the seal ring again. He rapped with this ring on the metal side of the table to make the waiter come. Then he laughed, ho-ho-ho-ho. A funny man for her to pick, thought Edward, but he's big as a prairie breeze. His big white shirt, open at the neck, seemed to boil round him, like a sail full of wind: his soft muscular chest, without a hair, flowed in the opening, polished and broad as an ocean: his big face, with little eyes and little mouth, with its spectacles and big nose, expressed goodness — and his great strong neck and his arms gently, almost limply operating, now, for instance, he took a gentle peck at Irene's nose with his fist, something she had sharply said — it all expressed smoothly working strength, goodness. "She is not very good: I suppose such goodness is a gold mine to the poor"; thought Edward. He remembered the time Lou had been on his back six weeks in a darkened room, with no complaint, no disease — love, Edward had been quite sure. But for whom? He looked at Irene's pretty little dry face, like a biscuit, her jeweled amethyst eyes, her dark-gold hair, shining like wires. She was a splendid musician, had a little ear but with a large straight opening like a man's, broad short fingers. Irene, for all his knowledge of her, was in her soul a mystery to him. "You're all hair-springs," Al was saying to her. Al did not understand her either. Edward felt safe from them all, really happy, even smugly happy.

[315]

"She isn't married to anyone, why shouldn't she marry me," thought Edward about Lydia. "I'll see how she takes the ring."

Because Dr. Sam had a bad attack of ulcers the week before Christmas, Vera put off her sailing till just before New Year's Eve. For a Christmas festivity, Dan Barnes had got up a Christmas tree for the morons (which Victor-Alexander had refused to attend — "Please don't take it amiss, but I could not participate!") attended by all the family and in the night following Big Jenny had quietly left them all. She merely went from frying a steak for Dan who was hungry after his exertions, to the big soft bed, and sat there, and lay there and sat up a moment to call Dan, and held his hand smiling and so died. The sisters and brothers stood and sat round Oneida in the big living room overlooking the paved Italian court and the fire escape and muttered or sat silent and brooding like a flock of turkeys uneasily perching. The old dog, Madame X, was breathing very heavily, gasping out her oldest age on the ancient leather sofa. Horse hair was escaping from it but it was covered with old rugs, silk scarves, a fine soft Shetland blanket. Oneida and the sisters and Lou faced with all these things did not know what to say or do: all were uneasy and could think of nothing appropriate. There is nothing appropriate but old saws in so large a family where even such sad things have happened many times. There was no one so loved in the family as Big Jenny, no one so lovable. Of all the great unquestioning hearts, lavish unacquisitive natures, big dark eyes, and broad smiles hers had always been the greatest, the sweetest. If they all helped each other and anyone, she was most disposed that way: if they all had old boxes and trunks and drawers overflowing with the possessions, goods, gifts that all had always showered on each other, she had the most. This was partly because of Dan. Dan had loved her and never been tired of giving her the old-fashioned things she liked, big pieces of silk, brocades, exotic rugs, things that were in the order of Massine family life. Big Jenny's children were modern, did not care for such things, they liked the utilitarian, called "streamlined" and "functional."

They liked to change their style of goods every few months: they had no use for the "horse-and-buggy approach" of the older family. Now Dan Barnes had just brought whole trunkfuls of Big Jenny's stuffs, bracelets, rugs, all kinds of possessions to Oneida's and told her to get rid of them — "Distribute them, she would have wanted every living soul to have something if she could have managed it," and Dan had gone away. "He killed her with his parties," said Oneida, staring angrily into the dark front of the apartment and not knowing what to say or do in this mess of trouble. "Oneida! She was glad to die that way," said Lou: "she loved Dan." "Hmph!" said Oneida, hunched forward, frowsy-looking, tumbled into her clothes, weeping, resentful of her sisters, an active nature in a situation where no energy could mend anything.

They were all sitting like this, fluffed out, plump, disturbed and irritated, huddled together and fearful, when Edward paid one of his daily visits, leaving the front door open and after murmuring to some one, who stood at the door, coming straight to Oneida and saying,

"Oneida, would you like to see my girl?"

"Oh, yes, Edward," cried Oneida, clasping her hands and getting up from where she was snuffling over Madame X's painful snuffling.

"Well, here she is," said Edward going to the door and bringing in Lydia.

"Oh, oh," cried Oneida bustling about — the sisters too got up, rearranged themselves, with habitual friendly ease, like the Court of the Empress Eugènie. "Oh, how do you do," said Oneida, "oh, what will you have? Oh, Edward, how *like* you, Lydia is."

"Oh, my aunt," said Edward, looking towards Lydia with a boyish smile. "I like Lydia's looks."

"Oh, how lovely she is, yes," said Oneida. "Oh, Lydia, you have just come in time. Come into the other room and choose something from my sister's things — there is so much, oh, anything you like!"

[317]

In they went and when Oneida heard that Lydia was in the theater, in fact was the frequently named Lydia Black, she unfolded, spread about, here a twelve-yard length of Madeira flounce, five inches deep and for some reason dyed orange, there a hand-painted white silk scarf in the style of the 1900's, elsewhere a modern silk square from Lyons, blouses never used, a bolt of silk, pieces of pink silk, cards of Calais lace (from Dan's place), an old black velvet evening coat with black silk tassels.

"You," cried Oneida enthusiastically, "you can make use of anything, on the stage — oh, how fortunate!" Lydia, not staying long, went away with Edward and a packet of things mostly black, a long scarf, a pair of high-heeled strapped kid shoes!

A few days later, Madame X breathed her last and Edward, alone, came back to the little apartment. This time it was like the Island of the Dead. The poor sisters were there again, with Mrs. Annichini, who had just run down from her new house, and sat weeping and holding Oneida's hands. (Oneida was very unwilling and tried to pull her little hands out of Mrs. Annichini's big ones.) Edward sat down against the wall, the impure light of the court lighting up his reddish hair, thick dark skin and the startling whites of his eyes. Lou, unnerved, impatient, stood against the dumb practice piano and eventually put on some records made of Edward playing a dialect part in a play he himself had written at Yale.

"Oi-oi," wailed Edward's voice, "vonss a Yenkeh, olvays a Yenkeh."

"Tch! Tch!" said Edward.

"Oh, Edward was born for the stage," cried Oneida and suddenly began to weep again burying her head between her black satin knees.

"Oh, Edward, thank heavens I have you! We've always been together. Oh, Edward, how nice of Lydia to take an interest in your play! How good of her to take an interest in you."

Edward leaned his head against the wall and turned a shade sterner.

"Edward's women friends are never possessive, never jealous, they

[318]

know he's not the kind to go off into a hole and live for himself — that was the mistake Margot made and Irene made — Edward doesn't want that kind of life, that isn't the way to live! To live in a community is the way to live. Oh, how well I know it now, now that my darling is dead: I lived for her, I lived for dogs and dogs can die! We must live for others, mustn't we, Annie? Oh, we mustn't live for ourselves. Why do we live for dogs? Because we know we mustn't live for ourselves."

"No more dogs," said Lou. "You'll have to live for me!"

"But I've never lived for only one person," cried Oneida frantically, "I couldn't! Oh, I must live for all my darlings. To live for one person only is death, the end, oh, so black and dreadful."

"To live for dogs is not ideal is it?" said Lou to Edward.

"Waldmeyer wrote to me at Scratch Park," said Edward abruptly, to Lou, "telling me I must look into living conditions in my place. Miss Nebworth from the Church Community House in the next street has got two and two half Formosans, a couple and two children, installed in my front basement room, their brother-in-law is sleeping on a cot in the hall, that used to be Westfourth's cot, and the Hornsbys have got some hitchhikers from Calif sleeping in the backroom. Meanwhile Holland has a living room downstairs and two studios upstairs all unoccupied, that is by beds and there is my apartment without anyone in it. Does it constitute overcrowding or not: and what am I to do about it? I'm going back into my apartment tonight to begin with. Miss Nebworth's Formosans are on their way back to Formosa full of Community and Church hop and Miss Nebworth is following them with Bibles, so that situation will clear itself up; and the hitchhikers will take themselves off. But I've got to do something about the basement: I'm really ashamed in this scarcity. *A roof for all!*"

Oneida cried out, "Oh, Edward, I think a love of dogs makes you understand human beings. You learn how to take care of everybody. You *realize* people have their weaknesses and faults but they have their wants too, isn't that what you feel?" You always loved dogs, Edward. I don't believe that monsters like Hitler and torturers really loved animals."

"Oh, djarling," said Little Jenny, "but if you have children, then you feel you are part of the community and you have duties and you sacrifice self."

"That's just boloney," cried Oneida her eyes flashing: "why everyone has children — judges and executioners, too: but dogs — they're no use, they don't understand us, they don't love us, they only want to be coaxed and flattered and fed and when there's a war on you've got to get them the food because you can't explain to them, as you could to children. If children take your food it's because they know they have an equal right with you and they take more than their share, they're monsters, they know they must grow up and live longer than you — but dogs don't know all that! If you sacrifice for your children, what a torture it is! Children are Frankenstein's monsters! They grow up and leave you: but dogs never leave you: and yet we know what they are! Oh, how cruel the world is, how terrible! Children or dogs! Or women, Edward, isn't that so? Edward, oh, Edward! Are you going to leave me?"

"Jesus!" said Edward getting up and strolling to the window. Beyond the fire escape, down in the paved, asphalted courtyard with trees in boxes and rows of privet hedge between the pavements, was Anthony, the Italian doorman, with his grandson in his arms. In the Italian style he was kissing this child rapturously and noisily, "Smsh! Smsh! Smsh! Ah-h!" cried Anthony. Mrs. Annichini came to the window, looked down and put her large arm round Edward's back, "Pretty! Eh? Nice! He has three grandchildren."

"Victor-Alexander's selling off all my old Chinese junk," said Edward turning from the window: "he says it's shocking, all that ebony and lacquer in a French-style house."

"Victor-Alexander never approved of Father's purchases: it is the whirligig of revenge," said Oneida. "He has been waiting all these

[320]

years to get his hands on that stuff. But it was beautiful when I was a child, a houseful of that furniture. In those days it was just the thing. He ought to go into the antique business! Then he'd be satisfied. He could sell off everything," she said vengefully.

"Oh, djarling," said Little Jenny, "but djont you know that djear Victor-Alexander is going to live with Djan now; and arrange his house and cook for him and run everything for him and show him how to live!" Her laughter chimed out. "And djear Victor-Alexander is so very clever: he has decided to reform us all: we must have French dinners and French streamlining everywhere! And poor djear Djan! He has no idjea how to cope with Victor-Alexander! He has just simply given in!"

Lou took on a bright interested look. "Well, that's something new in the Massine hemisphere."

"Oh, he is a tcherrible martinet! I went there with Jonathan; and we were not allowed in the kitchen: and we couldn't have cocktails, we had to have sherry, and we had a different wine, all horrid, djarling, dry and sour, for each course! Oh, you should have seen Djan's face: he was so miserable!"

Little Jenny kept on laughing: they all began to laugh, a regular family clatter started up. Oneida took up onto her lap, Musty, Edward's old dog, his coat weighted with dirt, his old eyes turned blue as marble. He snuffled and nestled and barked pettishly at Edward. Edward patted his head. "Dirty little traitor! poor old man, you're too far gone to recognize the boss."

"This is my last dawg," said Oneida in a deep voice. "Lou says no more; so I must give him all my love. Oh, Edward, you don't know the longing here — " and she touched her deep bosom and rich firm arms.

She murmured, "I just haven't the heart for it, Edward. But, oh, Edward darling, Musty has been such a comfort. I think he knows. He loved Madame X. They were like dogs out of one litter. He misses her too. He runs into the corners, he sniffs everywhere. He is so puzzled. Of course, the doggies cannot understand death, but he misses her. You know he followed her everywhere, he just loved the ground she walked on and he wouldn't eat unless she had eaten out of the dish. You know how rough and strong she was; but she could bark at him for half an hour, she could growl, run at him and he never touched her. He would only bark to be forgiven. For Edward, male dogs never touch female dogs, no matter what they do. That is a law of nature. Dear little Musty. Oh, Musty has been such a comfort for me. He is such a good little man!"

Lou changed the subject abruptly. "How's your work getting on?"

Edward had every hope for it. The publisher was sending Myra and him burning telegrams about it: "Our sales conference aflame!" Edward entertained them for twenty minutes with stories of Myra and showed several photographs of her, at the beach, in a garden in a bathing suit, several full-length pictures in various costumes. She had a good figure. They had got a good advance and she was spending most of hers on photographs and clothes: there were pictures of her in *Life*. Oneida murmured, "What a publicity hound!"

"She deserves it," said Edward hotly.

Edward, who had been at Lydia's after the theater, arrived early at Madame Sarine's apartment the morning of her departure. The doorman was absent for a moment, so Edward slipped by without notice and found Dr. Sam banging away at the inner door which opened electrically when Madame Sarine pushed a button in her flat. But Dr. Sam had no idea how to manage it and had got very angry, rattling away. "I thought I should be first," said he. His fine new car, in apple green, stood outside the building. Presently, Al Burrows with his little old jalopy arrived and then one or two other friends, all men. They hired a taxi and led by Al Burrows who knew every turning of the downtown streets, along Sixth Avenue, Seventh and Eighth and where the early morning traffic was, the little procession with Madame Sarine in Sam's car with her cello and some boxes and

Edward and the others behind with the rest of the luggage, maneuvered its way towards the Christopher Street Ferry which within a few days would close its gates for the last time. The little notice which was up on the ferry gave them all a heart squeeze. "We might have missed it for the last time," they all thought. Madame Sarine and Dr. Sam got onto one ferry leaving all the others behind. "Tell the Captain to hold the ship," shouted Al: but it was not quite a joke: there was the anxiety of departure on all faces. It was a bitter morning, with a fresh breeze sharpening the waves in the river. The ferry slid along by the moored ships and presently they saw the Victory ship she was to sail on, the Blue Peter flying, faint smoke from the smokestacks. It was a sad gripping sight: for though each had made a promise to see Vera in Europe, part in joke, part in seriousness, and though Vera had promised to return to them next summer and give "a big banquet" and go to Whitehouse, with the way things were shaping up, as they put it, both in Europe and at home, all felt they might never meet again. Madame Sarine was at home in Europe; and their home was here. In the freezing morning, over the stiff snow, they shot around the quayside streets of Hoboken missing the right gate, past the untidy paved courts and lofty sheds of commercial wharves. It was in the early days just after the war. There were still rusting idle ships sleeping in the white sunlight alongside notices in Polish and German and grass-grown yards. It was all sleepy and old. They met Dr. Sam looking flushed and desperate, Vera looking quickly this way and that: they had gone too far right over to the Polish wharf. Presently they all turned in to an immense courtyard and gingerly, big men and little men and one slight woman, stepped out into the cutting cold and began moving her packages and trunks back and forth. They went down the length of the immense shed dodging packaged automobiles and crated oranges and eggs, machinery and cotton goods for Europe and South America and marked with the names of ports long out of communication. It had a fresh, rough and pioneer air. Dr. Sam was disgruntled because

[323]

his little woman, in her silks and furs should have been leaving in the gala hour of a passenger sailing. But she was happy! "They are crossing eight and twelve in a cabin, all women, all sick — I shall have a cabin to myself and be able to practice all the way over! And — " she said smiling at the men — "the only woman aboard: I have found out!"

"The ship that never reached port," said Edward.

"I am surprised they take you on board with that," said Dr. Sam sourly pointing to her huge funereal-looking trunk. One by one the men, even Dr. Sam, left to go uptown: the town's morning was beginning — it was mid-week. Dr. Sam had patients, Al had to be at the store at eight. "Are you staying with me, Edward?" inquired Vera. Yes, he was: he had the day before him. He had not slept and was in a dreamy mood, "just ripe for tranquil farewells" said he. All the men had gone visiting Vera's cabin, tripping up and down the rope ladder which was the only access to the ship and now Edward and Vera went back and sat in the only sitting place, the officers' dining room. With them were the other two passengers, two Europeans in America during the war, now returning to their families. The ship was still loading: they would not sail, they found, till ten that night or four A.M. or even midday next day. Vera and Edward, off and on, saw these two figures, the little blond Dutchman and the dark Belgian townsman, all through the day, as they went back and forth from Hoboken to New York, strolled through the back streets, dazzling in the sun, stamping firmly over the frozen snow hard and slippery as marble. Along the streets everywhere were notices of Kilroy: "Kilroy was here," "Kilroy was not here," "Kilroy for President," "Vote for Kilroy," "Saint Kilroy," on every second doorpost of the crumbling Chinatown houses, on walls and fences everywhere. They amused themselves with Kilroy. When Madame Sarine began to tremble with the cold, they went into one wharfside bar after another, here was a debauched bobby-soxer, probably not sixteen, a wartime prostitute, with wild blonde hair piled on the top of her

pretty little head, her voice raucous, her manners raw, cheap: a
sailor, casuals, two rouged dames who looked like — a fat man who
was drinking too much, proprietors of other bars, a man smelling
of fish, some small businessmen, members of Local 65 and so on.
When they were tired of sitting, they went back to New York and
at lunchtime, after walking up and down the frozen streets round
Union Square, gilded by the intense winter sun, Edward said, "Come
and see my gentleman's boudoir: You'll carry a different impression
of me to Europe": so they walked that way. Madame Sarine bought
a few odds and ends on the way, all her money, fresh drawn from
the bank. She was carrying it in her handbag, several thousand dollars; and Edward kept twitting her about it, "Don't spend it all before you get on board!" She wanted to take him to lunch. "You'll
have nothing left!" He stopped several times before drugstore windows and pointed out several things, "My ex-wife gave me one just
like that one birthday: my ex-wife gave me a Rolls razor for Christmas." "Let me give you something," said Vera. He laughed, took her
elbow in his arm and led her towards his house. "Wait till you see
Edward Massine in his transfiguration. I have a strong drink, too."
They went homewards down Third Avenue, Vera with her snakeskin handbag in her right hand, Edward with her snakeskin dressbag
in his left hand. The snow crunched underfoot: the sun threw a
strong mesh of light and shadow through the "L": the train crashed
overhead. Edward bought some ham and a cold roast chicken at a
delicatessen above 20th Street. "Suppose we called on Oneida?"

"Oh, no, when people are gone they are gone."

But their morning and their walk was anything but an anticlimax,
it was the most delightful perhaps either had ever spent in the daytime in New York. The night New York — which they both knew
so well — that was romantic, sensuous: but this fresh morning one,
when they were freed of all responsibilities, when Vera had no
more home to go to, no rent to pay, when Dr. Sam had gone forever
out of her life, when the Russian ladies had given their last bouquets

[325]

and trinkets and Vera babbled the last fragrant and dishonest compliment over the telephone, this pure, new young New York made them laugh like children. They were both delightfully happy and Vera said, "Oh, Edward no one knows how to say good-by better than you."

"But you never cry, Vera," said Edward: "I never saw a happier leave-taking than yours."

"Why should I cry? It isn't right! It isn't honest to yearn and cry! One ought to get ready to be fond of other people. There are so many people over there and I am sure to love some of them!" Edward laughed as hard as he could. "Oh, I'm sure you won't write to us!" "No, I won't," she said solemnly.

The front door was still freshly green. "The rest of the place needs doing up: I'll do it in spring," said Edward. The doorhandle and the notice "Dr. Massine" were freshly polished. Edward's mail, months old, yellowed on the little table with the bead plant. "You see what happens when someone writes to me," said Edward, rather sadly, pushing the letters aside, but not taking them up. The whole stairway wall had been done and Nate the Croat had even painted round the *œil-de-bœuf* in the top of the house, a job requiring scaffolding and young limbs to risk. The door to Edward's old room, on the second floor was open. The yellow curtains had been taken down and smoky net curtains were up instead. Light streamed into the room showing a white ceiling, French gray walls, paneled, white silk curtains at the outside windows, a calico cat on the gray carpet which stretched from wall to wall. The white marble mantelpiece had been cleaned up and a Marie Laurencin hung over it. There was hardly any furniture in the room. It was sweet, strange, sterile. "Do you remember when I had socks hanging on the chandelier?" The French chandelier, its hanging crystals opalescent and glittering still hung there, but cleaned up. The heavy carved furniture, the bronze slaves holding up lamps, the mother-of-pearl and ebony throne had been taken from the landing.

[326]

"The reign of taste," said Edward, pointing to the pale niches and the newly cleaned oriental carpet. They went upstairs to what had been the missionary's apartment and which Victor-Alexander had newly prepared for him. It had always been very pleasant. It overlooked several back yards and old houses in the next street, with iron balconies and fire escapes. Several Chinese plantains escaping from the municipal order against them, still lived and grew fast in these back yards: and one stood right against Edward's shutters, rustling and shading in the hot days. The "L" rattled not too loudly a few yards away and the dazzling winter light shone all round the Consolidated Edison tower, lifting its red blue and gold lantern in the sky, to the right. Several cats, very like Westfourth, were to be seen, trapping spikelets of sun, so it seemed, for spikelets of sun like icicles stood in their fur.

Victor-Alexander had had the chesterfield and an armchair recovered in French silks, and made a lamp from an old Persian vase. He had put up hand-painted satin curtains, in delicate mushroom and magnolia shades, of a heavy satin with a sensually exciting flesh grain. Over the mantelpiece was a long lost portrait in oils once done by Dr. Edward, his best perhaps, of Edward's grandmother, a powerful brunette with solid cheekbones, a George Sand hairstyle, eyes of a dark eel color, a smoky and a tiger cat one on each arm of her chair, a dark dress and black-metal shawl. Where had it come from? Had he secreted it all these long years? In any case, the very dark background and dull gilded frame slightly touched with red, fitted well on the dark blue wall. The end wall was of a lighter blue like afternoon shadow. On the mantelpiece were Edward's candlesticks holding yellow candles of pure wax. With them were two porcelain figure-groups of a remarkable charm and sensuality. One was a youth with a girl, the other, two girls, the forms and desires of the adolescents, boldly, impudently suggested and yet with so great an art that longing was beauty and beauty longing. Edward's writing desk was there. On the walls hung the picture of Edward as a child, lent or given by Mrs. Annichini, and on the far light wall, a scene from Whitehouse, the pool held in the hollow of the hills. As these two last were not very well painted, it was a pleasant attention of Victor-Alexander's; he had made this room for Edward, not for himself. Edward and Vera stood looking round the room, met each other's eyes and laughed. Where were Edward's clothes? They looked at the bookcases, corners, chairs. Then Edward opened a large closet in the entry and found suits in dust-covers, coats pressed and cleaned, shoes on shoe-trees, a patent shoe-rack, a trousers press; and all these things were Edward's. In the drawers of a commode the household linen had been arranged with scented bags; in a blanket chest were winter clothes and blankets. Vera and Edward ran, looked and shouted with laughter.

"Oh, you are a gentleman at last," cried Vera. She sat down on the satin seat and began arranging her richly coiffed head.

"And my papers in files in a long drawer with patent preventives against silver fish: and come to the kitchen — "

He made some strong sidecar cocktails and they sat down and drank. The telephone tinkled — it was Oneida. In the middle of her long vocalization at the other end Vera came to the open piano and played some Mozart.

"Who is that?" she heard Oneida say.

"Just my girl, Oneida."

But they explained it all. How doleful Oneida sounded. "And I thought you were already on the high seas!"

"I am gone, Oneida!"

"But I am going to Paris in the spring to meet her, Oneida!"

"Oh, Edward, you are not," she heard faintly.

They went to Vera's apartment for a last look round: someone else's valises already stood in the room. In a closet Vera found a pair of gloves, a Picasso original in black and white she had forgotten! "These are for Lydia — this is for you!" All the way back to the boat Edward talked about the Picasso, "I've never had anything I liked so much; and it might have stayed in the closet!"

"Oh, I'm so happy you have it of all my friends!"

"Are you sure there are no more up there?"

"Oh, there might be — but I don't think so."

"What a way to live!"

"Can you think of a better way?"

They laughed and laughed all the day. At four they were back at the ship, and again at six and again at eight and at ten, she sailed. Just before Edward came down the rope gangplank now lighted by immense floodlights, for the last time, a steward brought him a couple of telegrams, "For your wife," said he. One was from Simon, the writer, one from Dr. Sam. The hatches were closed: they were beginning to fix the loading booms into place and pull the immense tarpaulins over the hatches. They switched off the flood lights.

Edward went down and stood there on the precarious wharf edge till she was out in the river, black and smoking slightly against the wonderful brocade, the skyscrapers of the city. Edward picked his way down the wharf among the piles of goods: the little trucks swung down the railway in the middle of the shed: another ship of the same line had just begun to load. He passed through the courtyard and through the black unlighted streets and so back to the warmth of his city. She was gone — what a pleasant thing! And if he really saw her in Europe next year, she would be different, already changed, already taking on the distant glamour and salon manners of over there. He turned towards Lydia's home and was surprised to find himself unsteady and his heart beating heavily. "Can she really have this effect on me? Is it Lydia makes my heart beat like this?"

Edward could not see the windows of Lydia's apartment from the street and had to climb four stories, on a wide old marble stair and walk along a tiled corridor, through some doors with frosted glass before he came to the big old-fashioned door of her apartment. One of her traveling trunks with a domed lid stood permanently outside in the corridor. He rang and rang: no answer. He had telephoned her that afternoon: why had she not said she was going out? He was angry, injured, troubled, turned away after pressing against the door and thumping at it — she might be resting? — thinking. She's had many a young dog at her door. But how could he have let Vera Sarine go off like that alone? He knew only too well what could happen in New York: people became your blood brothers — Cains and Abels — overnight: people forgot you casually; it would never have done. Resentful and rebellious, he went downstairs again, left a message with the clerk — it was a hotel with apartments also — and turned downtown towards 14th Street and the Solway apartment. It was very cold, dull, with puffs of rain: he had on only his leather jacket and army cap. It was New Year's Eve, places were lighted and people were getting drunk. An Irishman with a good voice was wavering along Fifth Avenue, declaiming polysyllabically, about Man's Estate. "What gave Hemingway the idea that drunks grunt?" thought Edward. "Why couldn't she have asked me out on her party? It's muckerism, saying we all grunt in monosyllables! Everyone's going to a party but me: it's crazy: and I know half New York." He saluted Anthony grudgingly, remembered, turned on his heel, smiled and gave him a dollar, "Happy New Year!" and went on up. There was no one with the Solways and they fell on his neck, but Musty, having completely forgotten him, tried to prevent him getting in the door, made a horrible noise and tried to tear his pants. "That's a welcome for you!" Oneida said they never saw him now! Was he Myra's gallant to all the parties she was billed as attending? Yes, she almost wished Edward was still paying visits to Margot. "Margot would have been here with us as on all other New Year's."

Edward said, "Oh, it would have been different this year any way, Oneida. I asked Margot to marry me and she turned me down."

"Oh, stop clowning, Edward."

"On my word of honor, I did so."

Oneida was overcome when he at last made her believe it.

"She would not have lived among my totem poles you know. I should have had to get rid of those old Chinese hulks anyway."

"Well, I'm glad she didn't marry you."

"So is she."

"How could she have done better than you, Edward?"

"I ask myself that every time I look in the mirror," said Edward in a sulky fury, looking in the mirror. "Perhaps no one will have me now! Look at the intellectual forehead I'm getting. Why don't you sell all this old stuff and get lighter furniture! Give it to Victor-Alexander and tell him to make it disappear. You ought to get forty dollars for that cut glass set."

"Oh, but we lend it every time there's a wedding or a party: people love it so."

"Lend it to me. I might get married. Why not?"

"Oh-oh: let's get Victor-Alexander to go into the antiques business."

Lou laughed, "He wouldn't sell what he didn't like; and he wouldn't sell what he did."

Edward said gloomily, "New Year's — and I'm thirty-three and a bit. The age of reason or vision or getting religion or whatever you have in you. And I'm living like eighty-three. Fifty years in the desert before me. Am I going to end up like Victor-Alexander? I'm not an aesthete — or Suttinlay."

Oneida bridled, "I don't see what's wrong with Suttinlay. He makes a good living, adores his mother and sisters, they're a very united family: he doesn't go scouring in to South Africa: he has a girl friend and they have been going together for eleven years: it's a very regular life."

"That's what Edward said," said Lou.

At this moment Leander and Lady came in, with greetings, a bottle of wine, some biscuits and everyone cheered up. They asked

[331]

where Madame X had been buried, if Madame Sarine had sailed, and Lady said, "And how's Myra?"

"She's at a party out in New Canaan," said Edward unkindly.

"Edward's been all over town, trying to sell off his beautiful old furniture," crooned Oneida, keeping a sharp eye on Edward.

"Little Elvie heard Edward's joining Lydia Black's new theater company," said Leander.

"Oh, it isn't true — " said Oneida turning round; but at that moment Edward's face flashed into life, it became rosy and his eyes shone with youth. Oneida said with envious affection, "What has happened to you Edward? You don't often look like that."

"He's happy, Oneida," said Lou.

Oneida, almost with a cry, "Is that it, Edward?"

Edward stood in the center of the carpet, looked at them all and maintained it. "I'm happy. I think I am. I know I've been acting strange. I can't help it. I've led such a scattered life and I suppose I've lived for us all. But I'd like to live for myself. News from nowhere! I'm talking crazy: let me be. And I'm not sure but I think I'm happy. I don't suppose I thought happiness existed: it was like Kilroy. Kilroy has been here. It felt a lot like it. Ha-ha-ha."

Oneida looked at him sorrowfully: after a moment, she said, "If it really is so, Edward, I'd be happy for you too."

"No wonder you've all got the impression I'm a sort of eunuch, I mean in the affections."

"What's a eunuch?" said Oneida.

"It's a bald man: not me, look at my thatch: I'm too bald," said Edward. "I must be off. I have a date. I'll be back before morning: keep the champagne for me."

And he went, leaving a silence and then a quick murmur behind him. He heard Lady say, "It's strange tonight without Madame X."

"Oh," cried Oneida, "let's forget that dead dog: let's come down to earth. What does Edward mean?"

"Cheer up," said Lou. "The worst is yet to come."

It was nearly midnight. Edward sped back to Lydia's apartment and this time she was in, alone, fixing things for a party, neatly dressed in black and red, wearing his ring, her hair piled up, lacquered, her face elegantly tanned, and newly made up. While he sat down with his glass in his hand he looked at her coming and going and wondered how he would put it. For example, "Lydia, we might get married. What do you think? I don't think we'd be taking too long a chance." Or, "The worst thing about knocking around is this callousing, this unworthy mean fear about other people. It's maybe just as well to go into it with your eyes closed. You restore your faith in human nature, at least, mine has been restored this winter." "Sloth and incapacity and a roof over one's head makes mean: perhaps, but I just haven't been trying. I feel a different man since I joined the company. I know I have capacity, talent: I've always believed in myself basically. I was first in English at college." Or, "I don't know how to put it, Lydia; I didn't think it would come suddenly like that: but perhaps I was ready for it — " Terrible. Every one was worse. He looked at her, very much the fashionable New York woman tonight, quite the leading lady. He was very nervous. He put down the glass half full because his hands were trembling so and he sat quietly pressing a cushion into his ribs to make himself relax. It was a fact that his blood pressure was going up. The way he lost his temper on the street corner the other day; and he couldn't bear Musty any more. He looked at Lydia's photographs on the wall opposite and became absorbed in selecting the one he liked best. It was the cheesecake one with the muslin across the lens he liked best. He looked at it for a while and next time she came into the room he rose resolutely.

"No, sit there," she said, rather disgusted with him, "I'll freshen your drink."

He advanced towards her, so that she pushed another chair aside and said, "Oh, all right, sit there, or help me."

He had now come right up to her. He said in his most matter-of-

[333]

fact style, "Lydia, I've come to talk about something different. I'm not satisfied with our relations. I think we had better close this episode. I don't mean that, darling. What a darn fool I am, clowning around. I want you to make an honest man of me, marry me. I wish you would. My darling, I've thought it all over, and I realize the danger of my position. If I go through the Holland Tunnel with you, I may get picked up in New Jersey on the Mann Act; and then there's the profit I can get out of you. Under the G.I. Bill of Rights, I can get a hundred and five dollars monthly, just by being a married man. Then you can take the place of Victor-Alexander in my life. You see, he's going to be too busy with his cuisine to arrange my shoe-trees. Then they say married men live longer, though not as long as married women; so that's an argument for you to think over. Then of course, an argument on your side, too: I can give you all my money and I won't become a pinchpenny. You see, I've been darn lonely since Musty went out of my life and there's been nothing to fill the . . . I'm an idiot. My darling Lydia! They say the Massines make good husbands. Will you take a chance?"

He had caught hold of her; she had automatically entwined him in her arms and they were looking into the whites of each other's eyes, nose to nose; at this moment both recognized that their eyes and noses were just alike. But Lydia said under her breath, "Edward! Oh — " and she continued aloud, "you're serious, aren't you?"

"Yes, yes," said Edward nervously, "never more so — "

The doorbell rang. They stood for a moment close, unused to each other, awkward, as if that other embrace had been only a dream, a moment in a nightmare: they broke away with difficulty. Two young actors, boy and girl, entered, stared at them, turned their backs and went to sit on the couch.

"Come and help me in the kitchen," said Lydia tartly. When they had gone they heard the young actors laughing. "It shows," said Edward. "You didn't answer!"

She said under her breath, "Yes; of course."

After a while, Edward resumed, "Ah, one condition. I'm bashful. At present, I'm supposed to be courting Myra, the newest sensation of New York. Let's get it over with before we tell the glad tidings to the family. You don't mind? We'll get some friend for witness and I'll take you to the Valentine Anniversary — that's an idea. We'll get married on that day and we'll go straight to the party. Then they'll always be able to remember that that dear boy Edward is now a married man too."

Edward saw little of his family during the next six weeks; the theater and its all-night shop sessions knew him a great deal. And here Lydia's new play was of more concern than Lydia's new stage manager.

They picked on Al Burrows and Mrs. Burrows for their witnesses. Al was delighted and flattered. "Haven't I always helped you out? Ain't I always there to fix?" said he. However, when Edward telephoned Al's home the night before, Mrs. Burrows answered and said she did not know where Al was. He had left home two days before. Said she, "He's in the doghouse."

"Eh, Edie, what did you do that for? What about my wedding? What do you want to do that to a nice man like Al for?"

"Yes, everyone thinks Al is a nice man; but he shows a different face to his family. He's a Jekyll and Hyde."

Edward burst out laughing, "What did Mr. Hyde do?"

"Hm? What do you mean?"

"Mr. Hyde was the bad guy in the association."

"Al broke a window with his fist because I didn't sew a button on his shirt."

Edward laughed, "Say, not such a bad idea. I'll think it over. The way to tame wives. You see, Edie, you're talking to a trades-union member now. I'll be a husband myself in a few hours. But I'm not joking, where is Mr. Hyde?"

"He's hiding. I don't know where. Some Turkish bath he always goes to. Maybe he needs analysis."

"Maybe he needs Turkish delight."

"He said he was going to hop a freighter."

Edward scratched his head. "Well, anyway I know the dump: I'll go there. Look, Edie dear, I want you at the wedding. Get dressed in your best and come down to Lydia's at one tomorrow afternoon and I'll meet you there with the missing link."

She became very cheerful. "Maybe I should have married you, Edward. You're more my type."

"I'm the first man who ever was attractive on his wedding day, in that case," said Edward and rang off.

He hurried out and took a taxi to the Turkish bath to which he had been with Al Burrows the night of Margot's marriage. He went straight up to the dormitory man and, slipping him a half dollar, asked him if he could look for his friend who was in a bed at the end of the dormitory. There he found the big man lying on his side, dishevelled, his blue eyes wide open and miserable. He fixed his eyes on Edward and waited for him to speak. Edward said, "Hey, Al, what about my wedding?"

Al looked at him silently.

"Come and sleep at my place. We'll have a drink on the way. It's the usual thing to have a bachelor dinner the night before and Mr. Fixer, you didn't fix that up for me."

Al stretched out his long legs, got up and began dressing. He did not say a word but followed Edward out. His car was downstairs. On the way uptown he pointed to a street to their left, murmured, "Louise lives there."

When they got to a bar they had Al's favorite drink, rye with ginger ale. Al said, "How did you find me? Did Edie tell you I was there?"

"She doesn't know where you are."

"I'm in the doghouse," said Al.

[336]

"Sure."

Presently, Al cheered up and said they'd better get home and get some sleep because he had to open the store at eight in the morning. He was getting the afternoon off for the wedding. He said roughly, "I was going to show up for the wedding. Did you think Al the Fixer would let you down?"

Edward laughed. They sauntered out together and when they got home, Al, instead of going to bed, sat up till two in the morning telling Edward how he had got married, an episodic account full of Rabelaisian and folk details. At last, he rolled into his bed and was asleep in an instant. He was gone to his store when Edward rose. Edward spent some time going round to his tenants and receiving compliments, for they were all in the secret which so far none of the family knew. Then he sat in his "gentleman's boudoir" thinking that these were his last hours as a bachelor, and very happy that this arid stretch of his life was over; and excited, curious to know what the next would be like. And at last he found himself running late.

He was dressing hastily when Dr. Sam Innings telephoned him. He was crying and he said, "Edward, don't let me down. I want you to take me out. Is there some party you can take me to? I don't care if it's one of those cocktail parties you've been going to; I don't care what it is. I don't want to be alone. I can't face myself. You know what it's like here. It looks as if a cold blast swept through it and it looks like I feel. I've had a few drinks but I'm not drunk. I only took them because I've been crying all morning. I just got a telegram from Paris, from Vera. She's married. Marriage is a terrible thing. You can't love without loving over the broken bones of someone else. I don't feel like a marriage, I feel like a funeral bell. I can't stop crying. Edward, won't you do something for me? It's awful to be alone. Rudolf isn't here; and I don't want to go out and get drunk with a wise-guy journalist who's been through it all."

Edward said at once, "It happens I do know a party, Sam; but it's

[337]

a family party, though a big one. You'd be welcome, only I have to ask them. Will you wait for my call?"

Dr. Sam breathed his gratitude and relief. Edward telephoned. Oneida became most interested in the sad condition of Dr. Sam. Oneida telephoned Lady and Lady telephoned Edward who telephoned Dr. Sam. Dr. Sam had cheered up. He replied quickly, "I'll pick you up in my car at your place at what time?"

"Four o'clock."

Edward's wedding was for two o'clock at the Municipal Building and he wanted to have a drink with the Burrowses before he dropped them so unceremoniously.

At the wedding they all wept out of sentiment. When they were toasting themselves and the Burrows family in champagne cocktails afterwards, Edward said, "I want you two to come and stay with us at my place in Whitehouse next summer. Say a month."

Edie laughed. She was all rose and blonde; reconciled to Al and gay in her easily moved, tipsy style. She said, "My old man can't take a month off: he's got to work."

"I'm going to take a month off my feet next summer," said Al doggedly.

"Have we got a house then?" asked the bride smiling.

"Yes. This morning I made up my mind to take Solitude off their hands. We won't call it Solitude. You can write plays there all summer; and we'll have people up."

When they were alone, Lydia said, "But in summer we'll be in Cape Cod, or on the road. I'll have no time for Whitehouse."

"Yeah — we'll have to cut that scene. That's out of an old play I used to be in."

"Imagine being born into your own company. I have to recruit mine," said Lydia pondering. "Handy, in a way."

"Yes, it's a pity about Solitude. I thought I'd give you a country estate."

"*A Month in the Country!* No-o," said Lydia, walking up and down smoking. "How could you make a life out of just a backdrop?"

"But Al's got to get off his feet some time. Well, they'll take him in for me at the Big Farm. And I'll tell Edie there are two summer camps around there, she won't be too lonely."

At four o'clock sharp, Dr. Sam's new green roadster, that he had bought, he said, in the hope of bringing Madame Sarine back to him, stopped outside Edward's house and Edward and his wife came out, attended by Victor-Alexander, followed by all the women in the house. All were wearing white flowers. The bride had a bouquet of colored flowers given to her by Victor-Alexander. He had spent the time between hearing the news at twelve o'clock and greeting them at three forty-five, in selecting and arranging this bouquet at his florist's.

Victor-Alexander himself never went to parties except family ones at Whitehouse. In town he said, "A little conversation between friends, an intimate dinner, yes; but please absolve me from cocktail parties and crushes. I should find myself most uneasy." Sam was miserable, but better than before. He noted the curious appearance of Edward, his girl, and the tenants. He said sharply, "Edward, it looks like a wedding, that cruel, selfish, egotistic event."

"Yes it is. One of the people living in my place got married. It was beyond my control. You can't trust women when it comes to marriage. This woman just went ahead and married the man."

"Don't let's talk about it, do you mind," said Dr. Sam painfully.

"This may be the last roundup, Lydia," said Edward. "Sam like all mechanical geniuses is a rotten driver."

"I will show you I can drive," said Dr. Sam between his teeth. "But I thought you would be more sympathetic, Edward. Your girl married someone else."

They were silent and Edward, seeking Lydia's hand, found it, held it. Ahead he saw for a moment his eyes in the mirror, was surprised to see them crowned by thick dark hair, and then saw that they were handsomer eyes and not his, but Lydia's. He turned and looked closely at her face and saw what he had not seen consciously, that she was not exactly like him, but of the same sort of mankind, the same breed; lovely, resolute, but in a way quite like him. This was why he had been so haunted by the gauzy photograph perhaps. For himself, this was a delightful revelation, and seemed to mean that they were meant for each other; but he did not say anything to Lydia about it. It is the sort of compliment that only works in love and then is dubious.

They stopped before Leander's new home, a pretty brick-faced house in a quiet street planted with Gingko trees. The sky was blue with high small clouds racing. There was a slight wind in the streets. It was the earliest, faintest intimation of spring; two months too early; and not an intimation but a laughing. The house, with broad windows, was on the street level. The Venetian blinds were down and the apartment was lighted from windows on the other side. But the sunlight fell through the blinds. They saw this from the little entry which was carpeted and had a trailing pot plant in a niche. The whole Massine tribe was there, it seemed; people from the ends of three counties with their uncles and their little children. Oneida, in a handsome, simple dress of dark blue wool, ran forward and greeted them affectionately. She kissed Lydia, "I am so glad to see you. Edward, you did right to bring Lydia. What a lovely surprise."

Edward said, "But you don't know this lady, Oneida."

She laughed, "What? Of course I do."

"No. Allow me to introduce you to Mrs. Edward Massine."

It took her some time to realize that he was not simply engaged to her; but Dr. Sam realized it at once, and congratulated them, flushing attractively, smiling, apologizing; and almost recovered himself. "This is a delightful surprise, I am so glad you had me," said he. Oneida turned round and cried to her family, "Leander, Lady, oh, people, Edward is married. Edward is married, Edward is married. Oh, oh, Lou, Edward is married. Edward, Lou gave me a new

[340]

dog, isn't that lovely. Oh, Lou, Edward is married, Lydia, it's Lydia. Look, Lydia is Edward's wife."

"Ah, Oneida," said Edward, going to her and putting his arms round her and kissing her several times on both cheeks, "dear, dear Oneida."

"Oh, Edward, Lydia, come and see my darling new doggie," she said, her eyes full of tears. The people parted and she found on a chair, a weak, spotted pup. "Oh, Edward, isn't Lou kind, isn't he kind to me? But I assure you, Musty doesn't mind at all. He understands. He knows he is loved just the same as before. Musty has been in the family all his life and he knows that everyone is the same, everyone is loved the same, yes, Musty." She ran about holding her new puppy and talking excitedly to people.

Edward and Lydia, after receiving the warm-hearted general congratulations of the family, stood aside by the bookcases that covered one entire wall, beside a pot plant on a glass and wrought-iron table. Edward talked to his new wife.

Presently, Leander came up and said, "Are you planning to take over Solitude, Edward? It will make a lovely home for you two in summer. It makes Lady and me happy to think of you there."

"I don't think we will be there, Leander. We have talked it over and Solitude isn't in our plans."

"But Edward, there is so much to be done. I am going up earlier this year and I have sent for the Government pamphlets about that sow thistle; something must be done I suppose. It is a fearful pest. If you don't want to take on Solitude, we could see about building an extension beyond Lou's studio for you and Lydia, if you would rather live in the main house. You know we will make any kind of arrangement you like to keep the family together and things on the right footing."

"Yes, but the summer's far off and Whitehouse isn't in the picture for Lydia and me at present. I'll lend you an ax to cut down the great vine, that'll be my contribution."

"The vine? You want it rooted up? It is true, it is crushing the beams in the arbor. I thought you might help me with that. It's true, the vine serves no purpose."

"No, Leander, Lydia and I are going away for a long time — to get away from the vine. Only don't tell Oneida yet. It would be too much for her to see Victor-Alexander and myself both gone at once. We'll tell her it's a honeymoon trip to begin with."

"But where away?"

Edward mused. "There's an Arabian Nights sort of place with crumbling old magnolia palaces and huge trees bearded with Spanish moss and dead estates full of birds and a dream world gone forever. It has a camel's-back bridge that opens to let the shrimp boats pass through; and then you see the boats, or their masts and sails, apparently gliding across a rich South Sea island; that is the watercourse which leads them to the St. John's River. Wonderful fishing, swimming, an artist's colony, absolute quiet. Lydia wants to work with me there; and we'll come back for the new season with a new play that they're already crying for. Or, there's a place seven thousand feet in air above the New Mexico plains and from the top ridge you can see the volcanic cones of the range that storms towards Mexico. And then in the late spring there's the Cape. You see we're planning to live in the Never-Never. There's summer stock in the summer and in the fall, I'm rehearsing with Roselli on the Little Stage his new free verse play for the 1948 battle. Is there balm in Gilead? I guess so. Call me escapist? Or politically conscious? Or both, like Roselli's shadow play?"

Leander smiled, turned to Lady and then back, to say, "Victor-Alexander wrote a letter to Dan in which he said that he had been the Prisoner of Whitehouse. In a way it's been at once a blessing and a mistake. I think I'll sell the Little Farm and bring Mrs. Mustbrook up to turn the Big Farm into a self-supporting institution."

"Ah, no," said Edward swiftly, with pain. "Let us have the Comedians on the Hill. What harm do we do? We're creative sloth: what life ought to give but it doesn't. The right to be lazy."

"What," said Lou, "but aren't you coming back to us: or are you going to change us? Maybe you're going to turn us into a socialist colony, a summer camp?"

"I can't bear to see the Massine Republic change," said Edward with tears in his eyes. "The mere idea is a real agony to me. Besides, Victor-Alexander must come up there in summer: he could not manage without the old Whitehouse. We must find some place for him. He's always one of us; he's our fine flower. But will you change the Republic of Arts and Letters and Humane Sloth? Why there with a little good will and mutual aid and sensible mild nonchalance, with live and let live, we take vacations from the epoch of wars and revolutions! Oh, keep Musty away. My soul! Must we be efficient too? I would rather have the vine."

"What's that about a vine?" asked Lydia.

"It's a symbol. I'll tell you later."

"What vine?" said Ollie curiously. "I didn't notice any vine. Did you notice a vine, Norah?"

"Do you mean the wild grape or the wild hops?" said Norah.

"There's a climbing rose on the veranda post," said Oneida.

"And which we mean you must divine," said Lou.

"I love your family: they're all crazy," said Lydia.

"Yeah: I ought to go to work and keep the old place together."

And now Dr. Sam came up to the couple to say, "They are going to toast you two. You must be ready with a speech, Edward. You will come first; then Mr. and Mrs. Leander Massine."

Edward turned from Lydia and distantly said to a little boy in black velvet pants and a blue silk shirt, "Hi there, Ronald!"

"That's not Ronald, that's Freddie," said Dr. Sam hastily.

"Oh, how old is Freddie?" asked Lydia.

"Three or four," said Edward, abstractedly.

"No, Freddie is two and a half, Ronald over there is four, Lilian,

[343]

that's the cute little blonde with the straight legs, is four and a quarter; she's a terrible gold-digger, already she led me up to all the meat pies and said, I want that one, get it for me. She's adorable. What a shame I'll be too old for her when she grows up. Don't think I'll be a chicken-thief. And that's Edward, he's eighteen months."

He went down on his knees to a charming little girl with thick fair braids, and in a plaid skirt, who was standing on thick legs in the middle of the carpet. "This is Alda, and she is drunk," said he, looking up. Over his shoulder, they saw his troubadour's face, high-colored, nervous, volatile, like a frontispiece Shakespeare. He grinned. "Alda had one spoonful of port wine administered by Dr. Sam, didn't she?" He offered his hand to the little girl who was flushed; she tittered. "You see, I know their names, ages and characters much better than you do, Edward." He took Alda by the hand and began to walk towards the center of the room. At this moment, the family, not especially arranged, but in a natural order, stood about, at the door, in the lobby, and on the two flights of stairs, as well as in the room, and round the long table, waiting for the toasts. There was no silence or constraint, no impatience and no flurry. In this moment, as in all others, their long habit and innocent, unquestioning and strong, binding, family love, the rule of their family, made all things natural and sociable with them.

Dr. Sam looked at the flight of people standing on the inner staircase, a broad pretty wooden one leading up through a cast bronze ceiling to the upper floor. This ceiling was cast in the shape of a sunburst through clouds with cherubs and female figures. It was gilded, with cream walls round it. The family, lightly, naturally, moving like birds, seemed to roll up through this ceiling. Others pressed against the faintly colored pebbled panes of the windows which shone in the kitchen. Others stood against the garden in the back yard; an affair with plants, a tree in a tub and a stone coping, all of which did not measure more than ten feet by five. Others stood against the bookcases and under the handsome portrait of Lady done by Dr. Edward. Some had come up the blue carpeted staircase leading into a cellar. Others stood round the long table with glasses in their hands, and Oneida stood with Lou, who was in a blue shirt, near the grand piano which was open. Dr. Sam looked for a long time and then turned to Edward. He smiled childishly. "Edward, I did not think there was anything like this left in New York." He looked down at the little girl and added, "And see Alda. She is going to be a beautiful woman."

Jonathan clinked the fruit dish with a knife and began, "Brothers and sisters! We love each other and today is St. Valentine's Day."

Virago

If you would like to know more about Virago books, write to us at Ely House, 37 Dover Street, London W1X 4HS for a full catalogue.

Please send a stamped addressed envelope